There were a dozen ships out there ~~~~~~~~~~~~ larger, but none of them actually looked like military ships. However, they still resembled an armada. They weren't shooting at us, which was good. They were maneuvering to net us, which wasn't.

"We're in trouble." I hit the thrusters and started Evasive Maneuver #206. I had a lot of evasive maneuvers. Normally I saved #206 for when I needed to impress someone. Right now, I used it because I didn't want to be captured.

"Radio communications are jammed," Slinkie said. "I can't raise Herion Mission Control, and I can't communicate with any of the ships out there."

"Military?" Randolph asked as I spun the Sixty-Nine like she was a prima ballerina while also weaving through the air erratically.

"Nope. Well, not official military."

"Pirate armada." I knew the Governor wasn't looking at any of this. He sounded very sure.

"Right. At least, pretty sure you're right." I spun us past three different attach cables. If they hooked onto us, the magnetism would hold us in place—only a few pilots had ever gotten free from an attach cable and had a ship left to talk about. I was one of them.

However, it wasn't good for the ship or the nerves to let an attach cable hook you, so I was focused on avoiding them. The capture nets held between several of the ships made this a little more difficult, but not impossible.

The laser cannons, now, ~~~~~~~~~~~~~~~~~~~~~~~ into the realm of impossib~~~~~~

Most of them were

they were starting to head things

Praise for *Alexander Outland: Space Pirate*

"In the grand tradition of Harry Harrison's *Stainless Steel Rat*, G.J. Koch introduces us to Captain Alexander Napoleon Outland and his ribald and vibrant crew taking the universe by storm. . . . A humorous romp with twists and turns aplenty."

> —Michael A. Stackpole, author of *At the Queen's Command* and *Of Limited Loyalty*

"A delightful read, packed with insanely funny lines, wonderfully weird characters, and twisty thrills. A total blast of a book!"

> —Carolyn Crane, author of the Disillusionists trilogy

"Like some twisted, exhilarating combination of a theme park and an orgy . . . rocket-paced, sexy, thrilling, and fun. . . . You might need a cold shower by the end, but you won't regret the ride."

> —Jeffrey J. Mariotte, author of *Cold Black Hearts* and *The Slab*

"A fun read and an amusing vision. . . . G. J. Koch has a good ear for dialogue, a mind attuned to devious plots, and a nice argument for why this space pirate would love the beaches and bars of Marseille."

> —T. Jackson King, author of *Retread Shop* and *Little Brother's World*

"A stew of science fiction, comedy, action and adventure that nourishes the eyes, brain and funny bone."

> —Kevin L. Donihe, author of *House of Houses* and *Space Walrus*

"The most engaging rogue to hit the spaceways since *The Stainless Steel Rat*!"

> —Sandy Mitchell, author of the Ciaphas Cain series

ALEXANDER OUTLAND: SPACE PIRATE

ALSO BY GINI KOCH

ALEXANDER OUTLAND: SPACE PIRATE

Gini Koch writing as

G. J. KOCH

NIGHT SHADE BOOKS
NEW YORK

Night Shade books may be purchased in bulk at special dis-
counts for sales promotion, corporate gifts, fund-raising, or
educational purposes. Special editions can also be created to
specifications. For details, contact the Special Sales Department, Night Shade Books, 307 West 36th Street, 11th Floor,
New York, NY 10018 or info@skyhorsepublishing.com.

Night Shade Books™ is a trademark of Skyhorse Publishing,
Inc.®, a Delaware corporation.

Visit our website at www.nightshadebooks.com.

10 9 8 7 6 5 4 3 2 1

Library of Congress Cataloging-in-Publication Data is available
on file.

Mass market paperback ISBN: 978-1-59780-901-6
Trade paperback ISBN: 978-1-59780-423-3

Cover illustration by John Stanko
Cover design by Martha Wade

Previous interior layout and design by Amy Popovich

Edited by Ross E. Lockhart

Printed in Canada

*Mark Twain said that whoever you dedicate
a book to will be sure to buy a copy. In that light…*

*To John and Mary (you know who you are),
this one's for you!*

S pace. I've heard it called the final frontier, the last
hope for mankind, where all dreams can still come
true, and a variety of other noble-sounding phrases.

Know what space really is?

It's the dull stuff in between planets.

Planets, now planets are where it's at. People. Women.
A wide variety of women. Anything worthwhile's on a
planet. Unless, of course, it's on a supply or transport
ship, going from one planet to another.

The one good thing about space? It's a great place to
hide if you've relieved someone on a planet or a transport
of what matters to them.

Not that I do that all the time. Well, not often. Well, not
every day, okay?

You know, I left home because of this kind of pressure.

Never a day I haven't been glad of that choice. Great-
Aunt Clara, wherever you are: Thanks. I like life a lot better now that I'm nowhere near you.

CHAPTER 1

"**V**essel Three-three-six-nine you are cleared to land."

"Thanks, doll. You free later?"

"Captain Outland?"

"Yep."

"Captain Alexander Napoleon Outland?"

"That's me. But you can call me Nap, babe. That's what all my friends, and satisfied ladies throughout the galaxy, call me."

"From me and all the rest of Thurge Mission Control—don't flatter yourself."

"Normally, it's the ladies offering the flattering remarks, doll."

"Captain Outland?"

"Yes?"

"Shut up or I'll direct you to land in an active volcano."

Touchy. Of course, it could have been due to my activities the last time I was here. "You're not Zahara, are you?"

"No. And you should thank your world's god that I'm not."

Well, one potential nightmare avoided. "Why so, doll?"

"Put it this way: When she finds you, you'll wish I'd had you land in that volcano."

"But, I'll bet she thinks it was worth it." I followed the coordinates. Nice, smooth landing strip. No volcano in sight.

"Not sure. I imagine you can find out yourself. We let her know you were here." She had that tone, the one women get when they've really shoved it to you and are happy about it.

"You related to Zahara?"

"No. Not at all."

I pondered. It'd been a while since I'd been on Thurge. It wasn't exactly the garden spot of the Delta Quadrant, and there wasn't a big call for black market magma. We were only back here because our current job required us to pick up a supply of the only thing Thurge had to offer. "Uh, Carolita?"

"Wow, you remember me. Enjoy catching up with Zahara."

Not so good. I remembered Carolita. Amazing in the sack. Nasty, nasty temper out of it. Probably why she was so great in the sack. "Carolita, how you been, babe?"

"Captain Outland?"

"Yeah?"

"I'm going to enjoy watching what Zahara does to you."

I pondered. I could stay, get the magma I had a legitimate order for, and risk the wrath of Zahara, Carolita and, as memories came back, a whole lot of other girls who might not be inclined positively towards me. Or I could leave and find another way to make money.

"Carolita?"

"Yes?"

"To you, Zahara, and all the other Thurge girls I've loved before—goodbye and good luck."

"Vessel three-three-six-nine you are cleared for takeoff. Don't let our planet's atmosphere hit your tail on the way out."

What can I say? My Great-Aunt Clara always said discretion was the better part of valor. Never too late to listen to her sage advice, right?

CHAPTER 2

"**N**ap, why aren't we stopping?" Randolph fell into the copilot's seat. Would have been better if he knew how to fly, but the *Sixty-Nine* ran a mean auto-helper program.

"Busy, busy, busy. Places to go, cargo to steal, new girls to meet."

"Oh. Zahara was around?"

Lift-off. Nice. Smooth. Easy. I ignored the cursing I could hear from Mission Control. Zahara had arrived, thankfully, a moment too late. "And Carolita. Remember Carolita?"

"Yeah, I do. I'm surprised you do—she hit your head pretty hard. You had some trouble with short-term memory for a bit there." Randolph managed to look almost conciliatory. Having a face like a basset hound helped somewhat.

"Yeah, and you had trouble with long term. Why did you let me take an order for magma and then let me come to Thurge to try to fill it?"

"I was working on the reactors and hyper-drives when you took the order. Like always. You know, why do you always try to make things my fault?"

"Uh, because you're here?" Why did I get crewmen who asked the obvious questions?

"Nap, why the hell are we going back up?" Slinkie slithered in. The cockpit was getting crowded. Not that Slinkie was a bad addition. No woman from Aviatus was. The men, on the other hand, made Randolph look like the hottest male on two legs. Slinkie had a real name, not that I knew it. It didn't matter. She was still the most gorgeous woman I'd ever seen, on any and all planets. However, we had a professional relationship.

"I figured if I turned down the legitimate job, you'd realize you loved me."

"Oh, Dear Feathered Lord. Nap, we have been through this. You're not my type." She tossed her hair. Long, thick, brown hair, naturally streaked with a variety of red, gold and copper hues. She lived to toss her hair. Because it shimmered, even in the dark. I dragged my attention back to flying.

"Because I'm human?"

"I'm human, too, moron. We all are. Our ancestors bred like Libsunos. Earth rabbits, that's what my great-great-grandfather called them." Pure-blood Aviatians lived a long damned time.

"See? We're compatible. So, why won't you admit you love the Outland?"

"Aside from the fact that you actually call yourself 'the Outland'? Because you're a dog, and not in the looks department. Let me think, why aren't we landing and doing the one legit job we've had in months... oh, feathers—Zahara, and Carolita. Oh, and I'll bet Zithra, Lucia, and Amber were around, too, right?"

How did she remember them all? *I* couldn't remember them all. "Uh, yeah. Right."

"You don't remember them, do you?" Slinkie's voice could have cut diamonds. I risked a look. Yep. She had the eagle-glare going. Which was better than the vulture-glare. But not the dove-look, which I'd seen three times in my life. I'd been near death for all of them. Not a good trend, really.

"I remembered Zahara. And Carolita! All on my own. Nasty temper. On both of them. All of them. Thurge grows nasty chicks." That came out wrong. I winced in anticipation.

"They grow lavaettes. *My* planet grows chicks." Now her voice could cut space ice.

"Earth term Nap's adopted," Randolph said quickly.

"You know, you've been using that lame-duck excuse ever since I hooked up with this crew. Nap's been to Earth all of once. And he was a baby."

"I was five."

"I rest my case. Anyway, it's still insulting to me."

"Okay, Slink. You're the only one I'll call a chick from now on." I looked at her over my shoulder and gave her my patented killer smile. "Promise."

She took a deep breath. It was a risk to continue to look at her chest, but always worth it. She had the best rack in at least twelve star systems. She opened her mouth.

"Screaming or hitting will cause an immediate crash. We have not yet reached escape velocity."

She closed her mouth and I got the eagle-glare again. "Why do I fly with you?"

"Because you're secretly in love with me, but you don't want to admit it, because you fear that you, somehow, are not woman enough to keep me from straying. You're wrong, of course. I stray because I can't have you. Vicious cycle."

Slinkie snorted. "Please. You were a dog before I met you and you'll be a dog well after I'm gone."

"You know, this is you being planetist. Just because Zyzzx is a canial planet does not make me a dog. Any more than Randolph coming from Weshria makes him a cat."

"True. Randolph looks like a basset hound and you're more cat-like. I'll give you that. But, you're still a dog, Nap. Or, to make you happy, you're a tomcat. And you know what they say about tomcats."

"It's better to neuter them young." Randolph sounded like he was displeased with the basset hound comparison, which was always a shock since you'd think he'd be used to it by now. Of course, he was taking it out on me, not Slinkie, but then again, he was male and shared my appreciation of Slinkie's assets.

"Et tu, Randy? Et tu?"

"Stop with the pseudo-intellect, Nap. It hurts us all. You gonna jump our favorite pile of junk out of Thurge airspace or just wait for the next eruption to do it for us?"

"Everyone's touchy. Besides, there's nothing pseudo about my intellect." I finished logging in the coordinates,

hit the thrusters, grabbed Slinkie, and hit the hyper-drive
button.

Due to the way I'd grabbed her and the force hyper-drive exerted when you made the jump, Slinkie was on my lap, arms around my neck, my face buried in her chest. I was forced to wrap my arms around her, to keep her from flying back and getting hurt. One hand needed to be on her behind and one on the back of her head, keeping it snuggled against the back of my neck—for her safety, of course.

When jumping, standard procedures were to remain strapped in until you were cleared through, which was normally three to five long minutes, depending. I'd jumped us to the Gamma Quadrant, a seven minute hold from Thurge.

Argue if you want, but that's what I call intellect.

CHAPTER 3

Our jump cleared and the pressure against our bodies let up.

"You can let go of me any time," Slinkie snarled. Her mouth was against my skin.

"Mmmmm." I wondered if I could hit the reverse coordinates with my foot. Another seven minutes like this and I could die a happy man.

"Nap. No joke. Let me go or I'll bite you."

"I knew you'd finally come around."

"I'll bite you at the point where it'll kill you."

"Your words say 'let me go' but your body says 'Nap, you da tomcat'. My Great-Aunt Clara always said that the words themselves were only about seven percent of the communication. So, I'm going to listen to your body. It wants me, and it has the other ninety-three percent going for it."

Slinkie put her teeth against a spot I knew actually could kill if she bit hard enough. "I mean it." It's hard to say that sentence with your mouth open and your teeth against someone's neck. I certainly was after feeling her do it.

"Just bounce a little bit while you bite me. I think I'll die happy that way."

Sadly, before Slinkie could either bounce or bite, the alarms went off, big time. You don't survive in space by being slow to react to an alarm. Slinkie was out of my arms and off my lap in a second, I was monitoring shields and navigation, Randolph was checking hull, engine and drive integrity.

"Sensors show nothing, Nap," Randolph said.

"I have nothing, too. Everything looks right, we're where we're supposed to be according to computers."

We all looked out the windshield. Three hundred years of space travel, and somehow, we still called them windshields. Or maybe it was only me. Anyway, nothing. Of course, I'd made sure we weren't landing in any planet's airspace, so we should've been seeing nothing. But we were seeing nothing that would cause alarms to go off. Which was a lot more unsettling than seeing something.

"I'm going to Weapons," Slinkie said. She dashed out. Her voice was on the com in less than a minute. "Scanning for hostiles."

I waited, counting down. Sure enough, in less than twenty seconds, a different voice came on the com. "Alexander, what in the galaxy is going on?" A quavering, peevish, authoritative voice. The Governor never missed his cues, even if I wanted him to. "And why aren't we on Thurge? I was looking forward to the baths. You know how I love the mineral baths there."

"Yes, sorry, Governor. Had a little problem, had to leave. We'll find you a mineral bath somewhere else."

"Why do you let him stay?" Randolph muttered.

"Because it was my fault he got deposed." It wasn't wholly my fault, but it had been enough of my fault that I'd felt guilty. And the old guy wasn't so bad.

"Alexander Napoleon Outland, why are you lying to me?" Most of the time he wasn't so bad. Some of the time he reminded me of my Great-Aunt Clara. This was one of those times.

"Governor, later, okay? Alarms, potential hostiles, all alone in the big bad ether, you know the drill."

The Governor sighed dramatically. "Oh yes, I know the drill. I learned it all too well, back when I ruled Knaboor—"

"Speaking of boors, we have a problem," Slinkie snapped. "I can't see anything on the system."

"So? Maybe that means it's just a glitch."

"Nap, where are we, exactly?" Slinkie sounded nervous. Not good. She didn't really do nervous as a rule.

"Gamma Quadrant. In the vicinity of Herion."

"Oh, Dear Feathered Lord." Now she sounded well beyond nervous.

"What? What is it? We've been to Herion before, no issues."

"Nap, you remember that spacer I was talking to at our last pit stop?"

I remembered him. Herion Military, if his uniform had been any clue. Tall, rippling muscles, built like a battle cruiser and, if Slinkie's reactions to him were any indication, extremely handsome. I wasn't short, puny or ugly, but that guy had outbid my ante before I could get close to the game. "Yeah. I think he was hot for Randolph."

"Hardly. He was from Herion."

"Time to go."

"Yes, but not for that reason. There've been some weird accidents around here. He told me that the last things anyone got from the ships was that their alarms went off, but they couldn't find anything wrong. Usually they were talking to Herion Mission Control and then... nothing. The rescue ships only found traces of ships. Like... like they'd been vaporized."

"Or hijacked by someone who knows what he's doing," the Governor said, and he didn't sound peevish. "Alexander, this sounds familiar, from many years ago, before you were born."

"Great. Plotting coordinates now."

"Nap, don't plot, just fly." Slinkie's voice was tense.

"Why?"

"I have something on my scanners now. A lot of somethings. It's time to remind us all why we fly with you."

I flipped to full manual. "Because I'm the best pilot alive."

"Please do your best to be able to still say that tomorrow."

"Will you sit in my lap again if I get us out of this?"

"I might even have sex with you."

"Wow. It's that bad, huh?"

"Yeah, Nap. I think it's worse."

CHAPTER 4

S linkie wasn't kidding, I could hear it in her voice.
"Slink? Can't see what I'm supposed to be flying
away from."

"Attack shields engaged!" She seemed focused.

Randolph hit the auto-helper. "Captain, would you like
Ultrasight assistance?" The auto-helper had a pleasant,
soothing female voice. It drove me crazy.

"Ya think?"

"That's a yes!" Randolph didn't mind the auto-helper.
Sometimes I got the impression they were dating. I mean,
he'd even named it. "Audrey, we have invisible attackers."

"Going to Ultrasight now, Chief." The auto-helper
called Randolph Chief because he was our head mechanic.
He was our only mechanic, but there were times not to
argue semantics.

A film went over the windshield and suddenly space
was crawling with scaries. Because of how it worked with
and against the hyper-drives, Ultrasight—which allowed
you to see literally everything, including sound and anything cloaked—used up a lot of power, which was why
we normally didn't have it on when we were flying. Most
spaceships didn't even have it installed. Only huge battle cruisers and their ilk could manage hyper-drives and
Ultrasight at the same time.

There were a dozen ships out there. Most of them
were larger, but none of them actually looked like military ships. However, they still resembled an armada.
They weren't shooting at us, which was good. They were
maneuvering to net us, which wasn't.

"We're in trouble." I hit the thrusters and started Evasive Maneuver #206. I had a lot of evasive maneuvers.
Normally I saved #206 for when I needed to impress

someone. Right now, I used it because I didn't want to be captured.

"Radio communications are jammed," Slinkie said. "I can't raise Herion Mission Control, and I can't communicate with any of the ships out there."

"Military?" Randolph asked as I spun the *Sixty-Nine* like she was a prima ballerina while also weaving through the air erratically.

"Nope. Well, not official military."

"Pirate armada." I knew the Governor wasn't looking at any of this. He sounded very sure.

"Right. At least, pretty sure you're right." I spun us past three different attach cables. If they hooked onto us, the magnetism would hold us in place—only a few pilots had ever gotten free from an attach cable and had a ship left to talk about. I was one of them.

However, it wasn't good for the ship or the nerves to let an attach cable hook you, so I was focused on avoiding them. The capture nets held between several of the ships made this a little more difficult, but not impossible.

The laser cannons, now, they were starting to head things into the realm of impossibility.

CHAPTER 5

"Laser cannon warming up," Slinkie shouted. "It's going to take longer because of the Ultrasight."

"Have to make the tradeoffs. Take your time, I'm fine here." I flipped the *Sixty-Nine* end-over-end, which meant most of the laser shots missed us. The couple that hit glanced off. "Structural?"

"Looks fine so far. Think we can make Herion?" Randolph asked.

"Doubt it. Can't jump, either." The *Sixty-Nine* was outdoing herself—a couple of times I wondered if she was going to split apart, but she held on and we did the dance together no one did as well as the two of us. Of course, I was glad we all had anti-motion sickness meds pumped into our systems on a daily basis, because flying while puking is harder than it sounds.

"So, pretty much, we're screwed."

"C'mon. It's us."

"Oh, right. We're completed and utterly screwed."

I managed to dodge another set of laser shots. They had us surrounded, like we were inside a big spaceship ball. The only positive was that they had to be a lot more careful about where their shots went than we did. They were closing the gaps though, and soon we wouldn't have any maneuverability at all.

"Any time, Slink. Really. Any damn time."

"Firing laser cannon in five… four… three…." Slinkie's voice was back to calm. Shooting things always made her feel better. "Two…one."

The blast shook the ship, but I was ready for it and allowed the shock to spiral the *Sixty-Nine* even more erratically. Another attach cable just missed us. Unfortunately, the laser shot didn't hit any of the ships. Which was odd, since Slinkie was a damned good shot.

"So very screwed," Randolph muttered under his breath.

"Maybe." I could see where the laser shot had hit. "Slink, really, when are you going to marry me?"

"Never. Do I need to spell it out for you?"

"No, I got it." I hit the thrusters and raced for the two biggest ships. The ones holding the biggest net. "Let's just cohabitate. Who needs legality? Not me. I'm the poster boy for anti-legality."

"Nap? Why are you heading for the net? Are we trying to make it easy for them?" Randolph shoved back in his seat, braced for impact.

"I'm not heading for the net." Flip, dodge, reverse flip, triple axel, end-over-end, and through the hole in the big net Slinkie's blast had created we went. "I'm heading for freedom." We spun past the ships, righted, and then I hit the boosters and the thrusters at the same time.

We shot away like a Libsuno after, well, another Libsuno. They were an active race, and they liked to play chase almost as much as they liked to get caught.

I, however, did not like getting caught. I was determined to put significant space between us and the armada.

"Ships are following, Captain," the auto-helper said.

"No kidding. You want to offer anything helpful or you just chatting?"

"Don't talk to Audrey that way."

"Randolph, it's a computer program."

"Audrey has feelings."

"We need to get you planetside, and fast."

"I programmed her to have feelings." Randolph sounded hurt. "And she does."

"How about her voice? Did you program that to be consistently calm and cheerful, just so it would drive me crazy?"

"No. I think it helps keep everyone relaxed if Audrey sounds like she's relaxed."

"She's a computer program!"

"Nap, stop shouting at Randolph," Slinkie said urgently. "They're really coming after us. At top speed."

"Think we can make Herion now?" Randolph asked, still sounding upset.

"No idea. How far?"

"Suggest evasive actions, Captain," the auto-helper said calmly. "Would you like rear-view?"

"Ya THINK?"

"Stop yelling at Audrey!"

Rear visual superimposed over front. It was freaky and caused migraines until you got used to it. "All the ships are following us. Why? We have nothing, and we look like we have less."

"They want the ship," the Governor said. It didn't sound like he was suggesting so—he was stating it.

"So, while we run, dodge and, please Lord Avian's Handmaiden, we shoot the damned cannon, why don't you tell us what you think we're up against, Governor?"

"Laser cannon firing in five...."

"I really don't want you yelling at Audrey," Randolph said truculently. "And I think you should call her Audrey, too."

"It's a long story, Alexander."

"Estimate time to destruction in fifteen seconds, Captain."

"Three...."

"Everyone shut up! What was that again?" Silence. "Sorry, what was that again... Audrey?"

"Estimate time to destruction in, now, ten seconds, Captain."

"Why? In one second."

"Engines are overstrained."

"Don't fire the cannon! Ultrasight off! Rearview off!" I counted. "Audrey, we're past ten seconds. Do we get to live?"

"Yes, Captain. Until we are shot by the ships in pursuit, who are both gaining and firing."

"So, if I've got this straight, we can't see them, shoot at them, or run away from them?"

"We can continue to run, Captain. Estimate pursuing ships will overtake us in one minute and closing."

"Herion's at least ten minutes away, going balls to the wall." Randolph sounded resigned. "You know, Ziggy still owes me fifty creds."

"For what?" When you're about to die, sometimes the inane and innocuous seems like a good thing to focus on.

"That shipment of chickens from Aviatus. He bet me that the roosters would kill each other. They didn't. Instead, they ran at each other and then ran away."

"Because you'd drugged them."

"Whatever works, Nap. Isn't that what you always say?"

I thought about this. "Chickens." I felt an idea hit so strong it was like an electric shock. "Slinkie, get ready with the cannon."

"Why?" She sounded like she was just this side of crying.

"Because we're going to attack."

CHAPTER 6

I spun the *Sixty-Nine* around and headed right back, towards whatever we were headed back towards. I couldn't see them now. Just looked like empty space.

"Audrey, are you able to help Slinkie to target the main ships?"

"Yes, Captain. Thank you for acknowledging me as a separate but equal part of the ship."

Great, I had the Emancipated Program on my hands. "Yes, fine, good. Trying to stay alive here, Audrey. Think you can help accommodate that desire?"

"Yes, Captain."

"Slink, calibrate the cannon for short, spraying shots. I want a machine gun, if you can do it."

"If it's a gun, I can do it, Nap."

"Great. Fire when ready. Oh, and Audrey? Please feel free to let us know when we're overstraining the engines again. Preferably before we're less than a minute away from exploding."

"Noted, Captain." Well, at least the auto-helper still called me Captain. It hadn't always been this uppity or demanding. Or capricious. At least, I considered sharing imminent destruction as late as possible to be capricious. Maybe Randolph found it sexy.

"Firing now, Nap." The ship shook, but I could tell Slinkie had gotten the gun set up like I'd wanted. There was a steady stream of white bursts flying out towards nothing. The same nothing we were heading for at top speed.

"Nap, are you just planning on us going out in a blaze of glory?" Randolph sounded against the blaze of glory idea.

The laser shots hit. Explosions lit up in front of us. "Nope. I'm planning on playing chicken."

"Isn't that a sort of archaic choice?" Slinkie sounded just this side of freaked, even while firing. She must have estimated our chances at less than nil.

"Yep. Old and yet still effective. Right, Governor?"

"I don't care for your insinuation, Alexander."

"I'll worry about it if we're still alive in five minutes." It's hard to fly evasively while programming the hyper-drive at the same time, but the desire to survive and potentially have sex with Slinkie was a strong motivator.

Our laser shots were hitting and where they weren't they were identifying escape options. There seemed to be a narrow space between two of the ships—if there was a net there, Slinkie had ripped it to shreds. But from the way the laser shots were sailing, it looked like empty space. And our only option.

I kept the *Sixty-Nine* at full speed, heading towards what I was hoping was one of the main ships. They weren't firing at us much, more warning shots than shots intended to destroy. The Governor appeared to be right— they wanted the ship. My ship. No one was going to take my ship until they pried my cold, dead body out of the captain's chair. Which was probably the idea, only the attackers might have been open to a warm, dead body. I was open to neither.

"Nap, what are you doing?" Randolph's voice was moving up into the register where it seemed like he was trying to hit the high notes to cover the female singer's part of the opera.

"Nap, I'm with Randolph. We're going to hit the ship in a second." Slinkie sounded stressed again.

"Slink, keep shooting. Randolph, shut up."

"Ships are veering off to avoid head-on collision, Captain." The auto-helper sounded calm. As always. Sadly, it didn't make me relax. Then again, I was better under pressure.

At what I took to be the last possible second, based on laser hits, I jerked the *Sixty-Nine* to the left, spun sideways, and headed into what I was now actively praying was really a path through.

"Audrey, as soon as we're through these other ships, I want you to let me know."

"Yes, Captain."

"Nap, what are you doing?" Randolph's voice was back to semi-masculine.

"A little trick I like to call 'staying alive'."

"We're through the ships, Captain."

"Hang on, gang." I hit the hyper-drive button and we jumped.

CHAPTER 7

The jump lasted less than a minute. I hoped it was going to be all we needed. And that I'd coordinated right, because if I hadn't, we were going to go splat in a really spectacular way.

We came out in Herion's atmosphere. "Oh, I'm good." Time to talk to the folks on the ground. "Herion Mission Control, this is vessel Three-three-six-nine, requesting immediate landing. Have been attacked by pirate armada and wish to get the hell out of the air."

"Roger that, Three-three-six-niner." Male voice. Very official. "Coordinates uploaded to your ship's computer. Welcome to Herion."

Landed smoothly. I didn't like Herion much, but there were advantages to a planet under martial rule—things tended to run on extra-crispy.

"Audrey, please search for any outstanding warrants for any crew personnel, past or present, for Herion or their surrounding planets."

"Running, Captain. All crew cleared of last several warrants. Only outstanding warrant is for Jack Rock."

"Ah. Audrey, please advise the Herion Master Computer that Jack is serving time on Omnimus. Herion can add onto his sentence with them."

"Done, Captain. The Master Computer asked me to share Herion's appreciation of your adherence to their laws."

"I live to stay within Herion's laws." I did. Because living outside of them was dangerous, especially while in their vicinity. Their military tended to run to the same type as had warned Slinkie about our invisible attackers—big, strong and mean.

Slinkie and the Governor met me and Randolph at the hatch. The Governor looked none the worse for our little escapade. Not that he looked good. I'd known him for what seemed like forever but was really only about five years, and even five years earlier he'd looked like he wasn't dead only because someone had forgotten to bury him. But for a frail old man, he still had it. I wasn't sure what it was, exactly, but he had it.

He also knew how to play up being ancient. Slinkie normally found the Governor annoying, but she was the one who always helped him in and out of the *Sixty-Nine*. The Governor used these opportunities to cop the cheap feels. I envied him like no other man alive.

"Ready to be the best-behaved crew in the galaxy?" The three of them nodded. "Then let's go, make our report, recharge the *Sixty-Nine* and ourselves, and figure out how to get back into space, pronto."

I hit the hatch release and the door lowered to the ground. As captain, I went first. This was always fun, since those on the ground could see me well before I could ever see them. I'd never had someone shoot my legs out from under me yet, but in a couple of cases, it wasn't from their lack of trying.

Got down without lasers firing. So far, so good. Complement of Herion Military waiting there for us, standard procedure, especially since I'd radioed about an attack. The others joined me.

"Nap, I think I recognize the major," Slink whispered to me. I knew without looking she wasn't moving her lips. We'd all learned that trick ages ago.

I took a closer gander. "Oh, it's your boyfriend," I whispered back in kind. "You know, the one who's probably married. Or likes men. Or even animals. Maybe all three. You never can tell with that type."

Sure enough, he recognized Slinkie. Sadly, he beamed a smile at her, said something to the others with him, and strode over. He strode impressively. I really hated him. I watched Slinkie out of the corner of my eye—she was standing up very straight, chest out, casually flipping her hair around. I decided to loathe him.

He reached us, clicked his heels together, and gave us—well, Slinkie—a short bow. "How good to see you again."

Slinkie extracted herself from the Governor and stepped a bit closer to the military stuffed shirt. "Bryant, how wonderful to see you here." Her voice was a purr. I wondered how many years I'd get for killing Bryant right here. Probably so many that sex with Slinkie would never again enter the realm of possibility. Better to let him live and just catch him in some compromising position, preferably with a holocam on hand.

"Did we hear right? You were attacked?" He sounded concerned and ready to go off and slay space dragons for her.

"Yes. Captain Outland was able to get us to safety." Slinkie turned to me and gave me a smile I knew meant play along or die. "Captain, I'd like to introduce you to Major Bryant Lionside. Bryant, Captain Alexander Napoleon Outland."

Lionside offered his hand. I took it. His grip was painful, to the point where I wanted to cry like a little girl. I didn't, but I sure as hell wanted to. "Interesting middle name, Captain."

"It's traditional in my family. For some reason." I happened to love my middle name, though Great-Aunt Clara had never shared why every Outland had to be named either Napoleon or Alexander, or both, even the girls. Alexandria's a great name. I felt for whoever got stuck being named Napoliana, though. Not that I actually knew any of my family other than Great-Aunt Clara. She was more than enough. "Lionside. That's an interesting name."

"Name of kings. In Herion's older times. I wouldn't expect an off-worlder to understand." I managed not to share that I was named for not one but two kings, though it took serious effort on my part. He looked at Slinkie. "I thought he was the ship's cabin boy." He sounded serious.

Slinkie didn't miss a beat. "Oh, Bryant, you're so funny." She trilled a laugh. I considered barfing. "Captain Outland is quite experienced."

"He looks like he's maybe sixteen." Bryant clearly didn't like young boys. Dammit. One potential compromising position out.

"I'm thirty. Almost thirty-one." I got this out through gritted teeth. He still had my hand in his rock-crushing grip.

"Captain Outland, why is that man holding your hand?" The Governor's voice was both quavering and very, very loud. It carried to the other men in Lionside's unit. They all looked a tad concerned. Lionside dropped my hand. I remembered why I kept the Governor around.

"Just saying hello the Herion Military way, Governor." I put both hands behind my back so I could massage feeling into my right without looking pathetically obvious.

"Huh. Interesting ways they have here." The Governor sounded unimpressed and a little grossed out. Extra brew for the Governor, that was today's motto as far as I was concerned.

Lionside did his best to recover. "We'd like to get a debrief from all of you. You're the only ones who have survived the attacks, at least as far as we know."

"Happy to help. We want to be able to leave and live longer than five minutes."

"You don't need all of us for the debrief, do you, Captain Outland?" Randolph knew how to sound official when he needed to. And on Herion, you always needed to.

"I don't see why, Mister Billur. He's our Chief Mechanic, Major. Not involved in any of the, ah, excitement. Same with former Governor Murgat here." I wanted to suggest that Slinkie wasn't necessary either, but since she was Security Chief and Weapons Controller, I knew that idea wouldn't fly.

Lionside nodded. "Agreed. Gentlemen, please be sure to follow Herion's visitor's policies. To the letter."

"Yes, sir, Major." Randolph pulled off a decent salute. I was almost impressed. He took the Governor and they moved off, slowly, because the Governor didn't move quickly as a rule. I wondered if they'd get to a bar before we were done and ready to leave. Decided that was a no bet, could go either way.

Lionside and the rest of his unit surrounded me and Slinkie and escorted us to a briefing room. I was relieved to note it was a real briefing room, not a cell. I never took the "not a cell" idea for granted.

We were seated around a large oval table, beverages were provided, as well as a fruit plate. They did it up nice here when you'd survived the invisible pirate attacks, I had to give them that.

Of course, I also had to make sure none of this stuff was drugged. Conveniently, Randolph was good with any and all things mechanical, including tiny things. Every one of our crew had a sensor in a ring. Each ring was different, so they didn't look obvious, just like jewelry. My sensor showed everything as clean. I could tell Slinkie's was the same, since she took a drink. I decided to follow suit.

"Herion Bitterroot. Excellent. And my favorite. I haven't had this since, well, the last time I was on Herion." This was a lie, but Herion Bitterroot was smuggler's gold. I knew, I'd smuggled a lot of it all over the galaxy. I figured they weren't drugging us, just testing us.

"You're sure?" Lionside asked me pleasantly. "Because we understand there's a lot of Herion Bitterroot out on the black market."

I shrugged. "Sure there is. I don't drink it illegally. I figure it would be an insult to your planet." The Governor tended to prove his worth when it came to what we should and shouldn't say on certain planets. He'd spent a lot of time discussing Herion's little quirks with us. Herion was a scary planet, run by scary people. And I'd had to run here for help. The thought that we'd leaped out of the firing range and right in front of the firing squad leapt to mind.

"Bryant, I thought you wanted to get our information." Slinkie sounded sweet and confused. I had to control myself from making the gagging sound—she clearly had the hots for this guy.

"True." He gave her a beaming smile. "Such a relief you're safe."

"Yes." Slinkie looked at me. "Captain, I counted a dozen ships. You as well?"

"That's right."

"You saw them?" There was something about the way Lionside asked this. All the warning bells went off in my head.

"Yes, of course. A dozen ships. We couldn't recognize their markings, though."

"How did you know they were unfriendlies?" Lionside was giving me a stare worthy of a robot—intense and unblinking.

"They tried to attach us and fired on us. They jammed our communications and didn't respond to our requests to cease and desist." I hoped Slinkie was picking up how I was answering and would follow suit.

"They also tried to net us," she added.

"How did you escape?" one of the other military gang asked.

"Captain Outland was able to hyper-jump us to Herion." Slinkie gave them all a relieved, girlish smile. "I was never so scared. Or so happy to see a planet."

Good, she'd picked it up. "So, we understand you've had problems in your vicinity recently. We'd hoped to avoid it, we didn't. Any suggestions for how we avoid it when we leave?"

Lionside shrugged. "You could just stay on Herion."

CHAPTER 8

I let that one sit for a moment and used said moment to take a quick look at the expressions in the room. They didn't seem overly threatening, but then again, this was Herion, where the military tended to assume their way was the only way to go.

"As great an idea as that sounds, we do have a job we were hired for."

"Just what would that be?" Lionside sounded curious in the way of all law enforcement through recorded history.

"We have an order for magma," Slinkie answered. "For the Ipsita Company."

"What do they need magma for?" Lionside didn't sound like he believed us.

"New production. They're doing something called the 'Fall of Pompeii'. No idea what it's about, but the Props Master said it was historical. You know Ipsita—they try to be authentic."

The only other one from this unit chatting it up spoke again. "Then why not film on Thurge or another volcanic planet?" I took a closer look. He wasn't quite as big as Lionside, all the way around. He was fairer, too, though I got the impression Slinkie thought Lionside was better looking. No matter, all women loved a man in uniform—I had no trouble hating this guy, too. He was young, younger than me I was pretty sure. So, why was he the one backing Lionside?

"Ismaliz and Thurge aren't on close terms right now. Besides, I don't ask clients why they want something. I just make sure we obtain it for them legally and at our agreed upon price."

"Aren't you a saint?" This guy didn't like me. Okay, I could abide by that. Made hating him easier.

"Excuse me, but who are you?" Slinkie's voice was back to bewildered. "I thought Bryant... excuse me, Major Lionside, was in charge." She flashed Lionside a gooey smile. She batted her eyelashes, for good measure. I had to work hard to control my nausea.

Lionside smiled, but it looked forced to me. "Major Nitin has been recently assigned to us. He likes to help out." He turned to Nitin. "Don't you, Nigel?"

Nigel Nitin? Herion ran to stupid names.

Nitin nodded. "I'd like an answer, Captain Outland."

"I'm not a saint. You have to be martyred to be a saint, at least as it's been explained to me. I'd like my question answered, too. Which was, how do we leave Herion safely in order to go about our legitimate business? I thought Herion Military was in charge of protecting this solar system."

Lionside sighed. "Yes, we are. I'd like to ask you to delay leaving, Captain Outland. You're the only ship to survive a run-in with...whoever they are. That you've seen the attackers is wonderful in that we can, hopefully, gain some clues as to who's been destroying ships in our solar space and perhaps ways to stop them."

"We have no magma on Herion, of course," Nitin said. He looked supremely smug, like he'd trapped me into a corner.

"So very true. We weren't headed to Herion, we were going to Runilio."

"Why not Thurge? So much closer to Ismaliz."

"And, as I mentioned, those two planets aren't getting along right now. We thought it would be more diplomatic to get the magma from Runilio. If that's all right with you, Major."

"So, why come to Herion, Captain Outland?" Nitin still seemed to think he had me over some imaginary barrel.

"Well, it could have been because we were being attacked by a dozen nasty ships and wanted to head to the planet that supposedly was here to protect us."

Lionside nodded. "Nigel, really. Captain Outland did the right thing." I wondered at this positive statement being sent my way, then realized Lionside was smiling back at Slinkie. Oh well, take the good whenever it hits you, as Great-Aunt Clara used to say, even if it hits you in the stomach.

"Happy to help Herion Military out, but we also have to make money. Don't get paid until we deliver, sort of thing."

Lionside nodded. "I'm sure you'd all like to rest and recoup. As long as we can call on you for more details, why don't you join the rest of your crew and relax a bit."

"I didn't see much of a crew," Nitin said quietly.

I stood and gave him a wide smile. "We like to travel light." I helped Slinkie up. "I think it's time for the Governor's medicine."

"Yes. Bryant, see you later?"

Lionside stood and gave her that little bow of his. "I'll make it a priority." He led us out. "Where will you be staying, Captain?"

"I planned to sleep on the ship."

"Oh, no. New laws. I understand why you wouldn't know them. Had to be put in place once these mystery attacks started. All visitors must sleep at an official Herion hotel of some kind."

"Convenient for the merchants."

Lionside shrugged. "It's a bad business out there right now, Captain. Our trade's been badly affected. I think you'll find the prices very competitive now."

This was news. "How long have these attacks been going on?"

"Six months. Long months, too, believe me."

"We just saw you at Io Station not two weeks ago."

"Yes. Military are having no issues getting in or out of the solar system. Only military can say this, however." Lionside looked worried. "I know you have an order you want to fill, Captain, but I can't offer you escort. Which means, as soon as you leave Herion, you're fair game for

whatever's out there. You were lucky once. Do you feel
that you'll be lucky twice?"

"If you do something right more than twice, it's skill,
Major, not luck."

He chuckled. "True enough. But, truly, consider staying
on Herion longer than planned. Maybe with what information you have, we'll be able to stop the threat quickly
and you'll be able to leave safely."

"We'll think about it."

Lionside gave us, well, Slinkie, the bow, then he turned
on his heel and strode off. She stared after him. I kept
on hoping he'd trip, but no such luck. He was a skilled
strider.

"So, how soon are you going to jump him?"

"Nap, you're such a moron. We need to find the Governor, fast."

"Why?"

There's a look that all men have seen from a woman, at
least once in their life, and all women seem to come out
of the womb able to do—the "you're such an idiot" look.
Slinkie was giving me that look, big time. "Because I think
we're in trouble."

"Oh. Right. I knew that. Why do we need the Governor?"

She rolled her eyes, grabbed my arm, and dragged me
off. "Because more than just us are in trouble."

CHAPTER 9

We found Randolph and the Governor at one of the nicer spaceport hotels, in the bar, at a table for four. This would normally have been somewhere we'd have entered only if we were meeting someone for a job. It was designed along the overstuffed old money decorative theme, a place determined to make anyone who didn't own half of their own planet feel like the hired help.

"You two have any idea how much this place costs?"

"Not as much as it used to, Alexander." The Governor handed me a menu. "We took rooms here as well. A suite. We felt you'd want us to remain together."

"True enough." I scanned the menu. Prices were down a good sixty percent from the last time we'd been through. Things were as bad as Lionside had insinuated. Thank whichever god Herion currently believed in—we shouldn't have to sell our internal organs in order to square our tab. "How'd you know to take rooms?"

Randolph sighed and pointed to the small placard on the table. "We can read."

The placard mentioned the new "no sleeping on your ship" laws. It also mentioned a few others. "Interesting. Did you see that no one's allowed to stay in any one transient housing unit for more than fourteen days?"

"Maybe it's so they can spread the wealth." Slinkie looked around. "Then again, what wealth? It's pretty uncrowded in here."

"According to the bartender, we're the first ship from outside the solar system to make it here in months." Randolph sounded just this side of freaked out. "Nap, I have no idea how we're going to leave."

"Leaving, no issues. Living? That's the issue."

Slinkie fidgeted with her necklace. "Okay, room's not bugged. But I still think we want to talk about this somewhere more private."

I looked around. In addition to us and the bartender, there were two waitresses. I checked them out. Nope, not worth letting Slinkie out of my sight. Well, maybe both of them at the same time could be worth the risk. But not worth it separately. I didn't want Lionside getting a chance to make time with her. I figured I might have to tie her down to keep him from getting that chance. I thought about tying Slinkie down and my mind wandered off to its happy place.

"Nap!" Slinkie hit my arm, hard.

"Ow! What?"

"I've been talking to you for five minutes. Did you hear a word I said?"

Sure, I'd heard words. In my mind. They'd all involved me not stopping what I was doing and doing it to her some more, along with other words like longer, harder, faster, and sexual god. What I hadn't heard was anything Slinkie had said aloud, right here at the table.

"Ah, refresh my memory."

She rolled her eyes. "Why do I bother? I think I need to spend time with Bryant and see what he knows that he didn't tell us in that formal setting."

I didn't like where this was headed. "I don't agree."

"Why not? Do you have a better idea?"

I didn't, but saw no reason to say so aloud. "Yes." The others looked at me expectantly. Suggesting Slinkie and I spend the next two weeks in bed together and then worry about leaving was probably not going to go over well. I looked at Randolph. "What does Audrey think?"

Randolph sat up straight and gave me a shocked look. "You...you really want to know?"

"Yes." I was all over the idea of stalling.

Randolph looked like he was going to cry. "Nap, I can't tell you how much that means to me, and to Audrey." He stood up. "I'll be right back!" He ran, literally ran, out of the bar.

I looked at Slinkie and the Governor. "What did I miss? I mean, I must have missed something, because I've never seen Randolph that happy about anything."

Slinkie shook her head. "I have no idea."

The Governor coughed, hemmed and hawed. He liked to be sure everyone was paying attention. "Randolph has been working on…something special."

"For himself, us, the ship, or what?"

The Governor actually looked embarrassed. I got a sinking feeling in the pit of my stomach. "Ah… I think it would be… safe… to say that it's all of the above."

"Please, Governor, just tell me this one thing—is whatever 'it' is going to break or even bend any Herion laws?"

"Only if they're new laws since our last visit." The Governor grabbed the placard. "No non-speaking, non-sentient, non-tax-paying creatures allowed out of quarantine… no imports not listed on the Herion Exchange… no removal of any Herion natural resources, including anything made with at least one Herion natural resource, other than those approved by the Herion council…." He kept on reading. "No, Alexander. I only see new laws pertaining to trade, tariffs and other economic issues. None having to do with, ah, Randolph's, erm, creation."

"Creation?"

As I asked this I heard the sound of running feet, two pairs. One sounded like Randolph—spend half your lives together, and you learn how the other sounds when running for said lives. Or maybe we were just lucky that way.

The other pair, though, sounded odd. Metallic and heavy, and yet, fast.

We turned and looked to see Randolph return. And, lucky me, he wasn't alone.

CHAPTER 10

Randolph ran in, dragging along what looked like a woman. He was holding her hand. Only, she wasn't a woman, in the sense that I'd ever met one. Because she was metallic.

The Governor had been prepared. But Slinkie and I hadn't been. We both stared. I felt my mouth go dry and realized my jaw was hanging open. So was Slinkie's. I slammed mine shut and took the opportunity to gently close hers. She had soft, smooth skin, the kind you wanted to rub your whole body against, all the time.

She rammed her elbow into my ribs and I stopped stroking her face. I also focused back on the matter at hand. My Chief Mechanic had created his own Sexbot.

Audrey, as I knew we would all need to call her, wasn't bad, all things considered. If you didn't mind that she was sort of reflective, she was pretty nice to look at. Platinum blonde hair, done in a sort of wavy bob, hourglass figure, pretty face. She was in a white halter dress that went down to just under her knees.

Randolph beamed at us. "Everyone, this is Audrey."

"We guessed. So, the auto-help program is, what, in Audrey's brain?" I thought I was taking this very well.

Audrey smiled. It was eerie. Her teeth were also metallic. I figured I needed to have a serious talk with Randolph about what sexual acts to avoid, pronto. "In a sense, Captain." Her voice was the same as always, calm and soothing. It still felt like nails on a chalkboard to me. "I am an expansion of the auto-help program. My Randolph has made many important enhancements, so I now have much more capability and can be a more full-fledged member of the crew."

"We may have to pay taxes on her," the Governor whispered. He was looking at the placard again. "Not sure if she falls under Herion's definition of 'creature'."

"I'm so excited I almost can't stand it. Audrey, please, have a seat. Randolph, can I have a word with you in private?"

Audrey settled next to the Governor, who didn't seem to object. Of course not. He had the hottest humanoid woman and, I'd guess, the hottest robotic woman in the galaxy with him. How the old geezer always managed this, I never knew, and he never felt the need to share.

Made sure Randolph and I were in a corner of the bar, far away from anyone. "Are you out of your mind? How hard up are you? I mean, there are even sex partners for hire on Herion."

"I didn't help Audrey achieve her full personhood to have sex with her." Randolph sounded offended.

"You don't have or want to have sex with her?" I was now wondering just how far and how bad Randolph's insanity went. Achieve her full personhood? Who said, let alone thought, things like that? Well, Randolph, clearly, but what normal person?

"Well, only when she wants to. I mean, I would never force myself on her. And, you know, there are times when it's nicer to cuddle."

Tried to think of when that would be. Came up blank. "You two cuddle? Isn't she kind of... hard?"

"Well, I used an aluminum alloy from Quinsarti, which, when combined with..." Randolph was still talking. My mind shut off. He could go for hours about this. About ten minutes later he sounded like he was finishing up. "...and so, she's supple, almost humanoid. We're still discussing whether or not to put a skin on her or just let her stay metallic. It's up to her, of course."

"Of course." I wondered what bizarre discovery I was going to make about the Governor and Slinkie next. Maybe they were passionate lovers. Maybe I'd let myself out of the airlock when we were in deep space if this were so. "So, how does the new Audrey help fly the ship?"

No sooner were the words out of my mouth than I literally knew what Randolph's answer was going to be. "She can now function as a full copilot."

"You mean she hooks into the main ship's computer again and does her usual job?" It was worth a shot, after all.

"No. I mean she can actually fly. By sitting in the copilot's seat. It'll make things better—I'll be able to stay in Engineering, Slinkie can stay in Weapons."

"Randolph, the two of you never stay in your assigned seats. It's sort of a given, our crew's thing. You plop your butt into the copilot's chair, Slinkie hangs around behind us. I'm used to it."

"When Jack was copilot he sat in the chair."

"Yeah. You're talking about the guy I willingly turned in to the authorities on Omnimus because he was such a jerk he was stealing from all of us, as well as everyone else."

"He did take the definition of pirating a little far, yeah."

"I don't miss having a real copilot."

Randolph sighed. "Nap, I know you're lying. You were really happy when Saladine was with us."

"That has nothing to do with this." I managed not to snarl. I was proud of myself.

"It's not your fault he was killed, you know."

"I don't need a copilot. Are you insinuating that I need a copilot?"

"No." Randolph was doing his best to sound soothing. "We're the only ship to make it through to Herion in, what, the last six months. You're the best pilot out there, we all know that. But even the best can use help. Audrey's been your auto-helper for years now. She knows how you fly, how you like to do things."

"Yeah? She know that I like to have warning of imminent destruction sooner than fifteen seconds?"

He coughed. "She was just asserting her sense of humor—she told me she would have shut things down before we self-destructed. I mentioned that, in the future, she should feel free to share without waiting to be asked."

My head hurt. "So, your girlfriend is now going to be my copilot?"

"We're engaged."

I was proud of myself. I didn't scream, I didn't throttle him. I just nodded. "Wise. Get her off the market before someone with more to offer comes along."

"Yeah, that's what I thought." He was serious. I wondered about the rumors that too much time out in space caused mental issues. I'd thought it was a load of droppings, myself, but Randolph was showing that it might possibly be true.

"By the way, why'd you put her in that dress?"

"Oh, the model I used wore that."

"Huh. Well, she fills it out nicely."

"I only make the best, Nap."

"True. True." The best Sexbot, the best case for insanity, the best example for why having a pleasure princess on staff would have been a wise choice, no matter what Slinkie's opinion was. The list went on and on.

"So, what did you want to ask Audrey? About our getting off Herion safely, or whatever else your plan is?" Randolph asked this without any sarcasm.

I thought quickly. "Just wanted her thoughts. She might have picked up something from Herion's Main Computer that could help us."

Randolph beamed. "See? You're already thinking of her as both a person and an important part of the team." He hugged me. "You're the best friend in the galaxy."

I wondered how much a psychic scan would cost, and if it would outweigh the work needed to play along with Randolph's scary delusions.

But I merely shrugged. "That's me. The best."

A heavy hand fell on my shoulder. "That's what we've heard." The voice was male, and one I didn't recognize.

CHAPTER 11

I turned around slowly, making sure I was ready to fight if necessary and smile nicely, depending.

There were several men there, including the guy who had his hand on me. They weren't Herion Military, which was a small blessing. They weren't anyone I recognized, and they weren't dressed like any spacers I knew, either. They ranged in age between me and the Governor, and were dressed like businessmen.

"Captain Alexander Napoleon Outland?" the guy with a grip on my shoulder asked. The big guy who had about twenty years, six inches, and a hundred pounds of muscle more than me asked.

"Who wants to know?"

"Herion Business Bureau."

I took a careful look. They were all in expensive suits. They all looked familiar with money and probably power. What they didn't look like were business owners. At least, not legitimate business owners.

"You're representing special interests?"

The man gave me a slow, wide smile. "I like smart boys." I hoped he meant this in a figurative sense, not that he and his associates wanted to broaden my horizons. Because I had no doubt they'd be able to—they all looked like they'd passed on joining Herion Military only because it didn't pay as well as organized crime.

"What's your interest with me?"

He laughed. It was a low laugh that made my private parts want to shrivel up and hide. "Best pilot in the galaxy, who's also the best smuggler, and he has to ask what our interest is? Smart is good. Coy is not. Coy is for girls. You're not a girl, are you?"

"No. I like girls. A lot." I wondered if there was a way I could keep these guys from spotting Slinkie. I figured Audrey could hold her robotic own, but I didn't want them trying to make time with Slinkie. Having Lionside doing that was more than enough competition.

"So, smart boy who likes girls, why do you think we want to talk to you?"

"Because you can't get contraband on or off planet because of the pirate armada." Randolph sounded calm when he said this. "And you want to hire us because we've made it through alive."

The man who still hadn't released my shoulder gave Randolph a long look. I wondered if we were dead or being set up. I figured both.

"Your friend's not as stupid as he looks, is he?" he asked finally.

"All my crew's smart. The question is, is his guess right or do you just like holding onto me?"

He grinned and let go of my shoulder. "He's right, and if you're the best smuggler, that means you're the best at getting away. Didn't want you trying that right now."

"No plan to do so."

"Really? Perhaps you should work on controlling your expression, then."

"Oh, will do. So, is this about a job?" The men all nodded. "Great. Then I have some rules. First off, I don't do business with people without names, so if you want to have a discussion, pretend to be polite and introduce yourselves. Second, I have right of refusal. I don't like your offer or your terms, I say no, we leave if not friends then at least not enemies. Third, if I take your job, then we'll do your job, but if, as it so often turns out, your job has more complexity to it than you want to tell me about at this stage of the game, I'm going to demand appropriate additional payment. And, so far, I've been able to do that successfully each and every time."

"You're telling us this beforehand why?"

"I believe in truth in advertising. Last, if you're really talking a job, you'll talk about it with me and my business manager."

"Business manager?"

I gave him a slow, wide smile. "Yeah. In the trades, they call him Janz the Butcher." I prayed Randolph would keep his mouth shut and his expression neutral.

They exchanged glances. "You know Janz?" The man who'd had his hand on me sounded a lot less sure of himself.

"Very well. He hates rudeness, so, who the hell are you?"

"Beber Zoltan. I'm the head of the Bureau on Herion." This settled it. All the names on Herion were bizarre.

I nodded. "I'm sure he'll be impressed. I don't want to talk business here—we just had an interview with Herion Military and I have to assume they'll be keeping an eye on us for a while."

"Where then?" Zoltan asked.

"The Crazy Bear."

"That's a nightclub."

"Right. Still a popular, noisy and crowded nightclub?"

"Yeah." Zoltan shook his head. "Got your point. What time?"

"Tomorrow night, call it oh-twenty-hours." They ran on military time on Herion, and had an Earth-like rotation around their sun. It was interesting, how much influence Earth had had on the galaxy. I was from Zyzzx, but I could trace my family lines back to Earth. Great-Aunt Clara had been particularly proud of our heritage. Me, I just had to give it to the folks from Old Earth—they'd spread throughout the galaxy and left their mark on every single planet.

"Fine. No tricks," Zoltan added.

"Not from our side. We'll be expecting them from yours."

He laughed. "I think I like you, Outland."

"Well, guess we'll see if this is the start of a beautiful friendship or if you try to betray and kill me and my crew later."

Zoltan smiled as he and his group turned to leave. "Liking and business don't always go together."

"Yeah. Like I said, been there, done that, got the carbon markings."

He nodded as he walked away. "See you tomorrow night."

Randolph and I exchanged the "we're dead" look. "I can't believe you have us involved with Janz the Butcher." Randolph sounded like he was wavering between crying or killing himself.

"Or that I know him very well and am going to contact him. I know. You say this every time." I sighed. "Let's get back to the others. I need to make an interstellar call."

CHAPTER 12

We found the other three where we'd left them. I was immensely relieved. "Time to go up to our room, sweep it for bugs, check for potential snipers, bombs and similar, then figure out what the hell's going on."

The Governor hailed the waitresses. They came trotting over. I considered again. Yes, only worth it if I had both of them at the same time. "Young ladies, can we please close out our tab?" The Governor gave them both his patented "charming old geezer" smile. They giggled at him. The Governor never failed to impress. It never failed to amaze and astound me.

One of them handed him a bill which he handed to me. "My retainer," he said to them. They giggled again.

I paid, working not to mutter nasty things about the Governor under my breath, and then we headed off to our rooms. We were on the highest floor and the word "palatial" leapt to mind. We had four bedrooms, two bathrooms large enough to house the Ismaliz Boys Choir, and a sunken living room area. The furnishings were all top of the line and so sleek they gave Slinkie a run for her money.

"How much is this going to cost us? All our internal organs? The *Sixty-Nine*? All of the above?"

"Same cost as the cheap fleabags you normally stick us in," the Governor replied. "Things are quite bad for Herion."

Slinkie, Randolph and Audrey performed a variety of scans. I had to admit that Audrey was useful. She found some bugs no one else had. Once we had everything cleaned out and neutralized, we all sort of collapsed in the living room.

"None of the bugs were specific," Randolph said finally. "Just standard for Herion."

"No bombs," Slinkie added.

"And we have no risks from the occupants of other buildings that I can spot, Captain." Audrey was sitting next to Randolph, leaning against him. She looked almost human. If you could get past the way the lights reflected off her. Which I couldn't.

"Good. Then I can call my contact and we can make a deal we probably don't want to make with the Herion Business Bureau while simultaneously figuring out what Herion Military does and doesn't know."

"Nap, I still think I should spend time with Bryant and see what I can get out of him."

"I know you're hot for him, Slink. Cut me a break, though, and don't throw yourself at him. Play a little hard to get. You know, you practice that on me all the time, you're a pro at it by now."

She rolled her eyes. "I guess brains and piloting skills are not the same thing."

"What is that supposed to mean?"

"Security Chief Slinkie is not actually interested in Major Lionside," Audrey offered. "She is trying to gain information by using her feminine wiles."

Slinkie didn't look like she'd wanted Audrey to share this news. But I could tell it was true. Amazingly enough, I felt a lot better. "Oh, well, I knew *that*."

"Nap, don't even try to lie." Slinkie leaned her head on her hand. "But you haven't come up with anything better, and I want to be able to get off this planet and arrive somewhere else alive."

"I don't want you cozying up to Lionside, okay? I don't trust him."

"I don't trust Nitin. Not sure about Bryant, but that Nitin guy gave me the creeps."

"Same here. More reason not to let you go off with Lionside. What if they just want you for a group grope?" I had far too active an imagination. I could see this happening far too easily. And if anyone was going to be groping Slinkie against her will, it was going to be me.

"I'm more concerned with the gentlemen who are trying to hire you, Alexander," the Governor said gravely. "Dealing with organized crime on Herion is tricky at best, particularly since we have Herion Military interested in us."

"I agree. I need to call Janz."

The Governor nodded and stood. "I'll go with you. Sometimes he prefers to deal with me."

"True. The rest of you, stay here and brainstorm ideas. I don't want anyone wandering off right now, not alone, not together. You all stay here, got it? Especially you, Slink."

"Fine," she grumbled. Randolph and Audrey nodded.

"You sure you want to deal with Janz the Butcher again?" Randolph asked. He sounded no less freaked out than he had before. "That guy's reputation is pretty terrifying. Even those Business Bureau guys were afraid of him." Randolph clearly felt I should also be afraid of Janz. If he only knew.

I shrugged. "Been dealing with him for years. He seems to like me. Besides, the Governor uses his connections to smooth things out with the Butcher. We'll be fine."

"If the Butcher knows how to get us off this rock, I'm all over your talking to him, Nap." Slinkie sounded much more morose and uncomfortable than normal. I decided I'd see what I could do about that after I made my contact.

"I'll ask him for ideas, Slink, I promise."

CHAPTER 13

The Governor and I went into the room he'd taken as his. Closed the door, moved to the far side. He sat in a chair and sighed. "Exciting day."

"Too true."

"Exciting days are hard on old men."

"True enough."

"Why did you tell them you were dealing with Janz the Butcher?"

"Had to. No one on this planet respects weakness."

"Yes, I know. I'm the one who taught you that, remember?"

"Yeah. So, what do you recommend?"

He rubbed his head. "You need to go to the ship to place your call. They'll be monitoring the communications here. And if you don't make a call, that will be as bad as if you make one that's traced."

I sighed. "That means you need to go back to the ship, too. Patching a call through here will mean it's monitored."

"True."

"You up to it?"

"Do I have a choice? I realize we could wait to make the call, but who knows what will happen between now and the time for your arranged meeting."

"Good point. I'm figuring more people are going to try to force us to do things we don't actually want to do."

"Business as usual is always a safe bet, Alexander."

"Thank you, oh very wise one. Think they've put bugs on the ship?"

"I'm sure they've tried. You still have the sweepers set up?"

"Never turn them off. Why are you asking me stupid questions?"

"Have to stall a bit before we decide to go talk on the ship."

"Why so?"

The Governor sighed. "So it's believable for the others. Randolph seems quite shaken."

"He never gets involved with the negotiations. For a reason."

"I suppose it's wise. His new, ah, lady friend could present some issues, however."

"Well, if we go to the ship to make the call, chances are good Audrey will know what's going on. If we stay here, though, then we're back to everyone monitoring our communications."

"Ah, what a tangled web we weave."

I rolled my eyes. "The drama can stop any time."

"Miss Slinkie seems quite distressed." The Governor was the only one who called her Miss Slinkie. I always got the impression he got a private kick out of it, but I wasn't sure why. I figured it was something depraved and chose not to question.

"Yeah, none of us like to hang on Herion. Possibly because some old guy we know has spent a lot of time telling us how scary this place can be when they don't like someone. And, you know, we've been here before."

"I rather like coming to Herion. You, personally, are so much more pleasant to deal with when you're forced to behave yourself."

"You sound like my Great-Aunt Clara. Keep it up and I'll leave you here."

The Governor chuckled. "Idle threats scare no one, Alexander."

"But I enjoy making them. Just like you enjoy calling me anything but the nickname I actually like. Have we stalled long enough? If you're too tired to go to the ship, just let me know."

He gave me a dirty look. "I'm old, not dead."

"You're still doing a great job of fooling everyone on that."

The Governor stood up. "Yes, thank you. There are many times I ask myself why, out of all the people in this vast galaxy, I've become tied to your particular hip."

"Mine's the only hip you can trust."

"True. And what that says about the two of us I shudder to contemplate."

"Yeah, yeah, cry me a space trail. Let's get going." We went out and got questioning looks from the others. "We talked about it and figure no matter how well we've scanned, Herion's got communications bugged. We're going to call Janz from the *Sixty-Nine*."

"Do you require my assistance, Captain?"

"No, Audrey. As long as the bug sweepers are still active, in place, and finding any and all the bugs the various Herion factions are trying to put onto my ship."

She nodded. "Yes, Captain. I can and have been monitoring from here. Several different Herion Military have placed bugs, the Business Bureau have placed bugs, and an as yet unknown party tried to place a bomb. However, said party was captured by Herion Military."

The Governor and I exchanged looks. "Perhaps we need to find another way to make contact," he said.

"Open to ideas."

He shrugged. "There's always the old-fashioned way."

CHAPTER 14

I sighed. "We're on Herion. Not so sure that's a good idea."

"What's the old-fashioned way?" Slinkie asked, sounding both suspicious and worried.

"We use a cellular phone."

The crew, even Audrey, burst into laughter which lasted quite a while. Randolph got himself under control the fastest. "Nap, you've got to be kidding. I know you keep that ancient thing on you, but who the hell else even has one?"

"Janz the Butcher, for one."

They looked at me in shock. "You're kidding," Slinkie said. "Someone that well connected is using ancient technology?"

I shrugged. "He likes to be able to access anyone at any time. So, yeah, he has a cell. He also has a variety of transmitters as well as up-to-date equipment. You want to talk to him and question his choices?" This question was met with uncomfortable silence. "Didn't think so. So, Governor, back to the bedroom. At least we know it's not bugged. Probably our safest place to make the call."

He nodded. "I'd prefer to be sitting anyway."

"Randolph, while we make the call, can you and Audrey please check on who was trying to plant that bomb? And, Audrey, please up the security programs to full. We're plugged in and charging, so the drain shouldn't cause the *Sixty-Nine* any problems. Slink, I hate to say this, but call Lionside and see if he mentions this. Make a date with him for tomorrow night, oh-twenty-hours, at the Crazy Bear."

Slinkie nodded. "Let me guess. That's when and where you're meeting up with the Herion Business Bureau."

"I love you for your brains, Slink."

"You lie pathetically, Nap."

The Governor and I went back into his room, he went back to his chair. "We should have just said we were using the cell in the first place."

"Would have raised suspicions. Slinkie, at least, would have asked why."

"True. So, what's the situation you want to tell Janz? In full, I mean?"

He drove me crazy with this. "We're trapped on Herion, because there's an armada with the best cloaking in the galaxy lurking in their solar space. You thinks it's a pirate armada, but you haven't seen fit yet to tell me how you know."

"Because it's a signature from over thirty years ago. Old nemesis. I'll fill you in after we take care of this business."

"Can't wait. We have Herion Military watching our every move and suggesting we stay planetside. We don't know if it's because they want us spending our space credits, if they're concerned for our welfare, or if they have nefarious plans for us."

"I feel Miss Slinkie might be the goal of the nefarious plan."

"Too damned true. And, finally, we have the Herion Business Bureau who wants a word. They insinuated but didn't actually confirm that they want us to get something off this planet and out into the rest of the galaxy to make money. If that's the case, we can't say no. Unfortunately, the big question of the day is how we get away from Herion solar space alive."

"Succinctly put." The Governor reached into his inner jacket pocket and pulled out a small, slim piece of very old equipment. "Ringer's off."

"You can't seriously think I'm going to waste the energy in dialing."

He grinned. Still had all his teeth, and they weren't disgusting. I was always grateful—Great-Aunt Clara had put a lot of store in good dental work, and it had rubbed off on me. "You don't want to test and make sure the cells are still functioning?"

I rolled my eyes. "You got a call from the Ipsita Company on it just fine two weeks ago, right?"

"Right." He leaned back and dropped his voice a few registers. "What can I do for you, Mister Outland?"

I resisted the urge to hit him. He was an old man. Let him enjoy himself. "I need advice."

The Governor nodded. "Janz the Butcher is glad to help his favorite son."

CHAPTER 15

"If I were really your son, I'd be like eighty or something."

"I never married. It's a figure of speech." The Governor shook his head. "You're so testy when we do this. I've never understood why."

The why was actually easy, and I'd never understood how he hadn't figured it out. My crew and I, due to a system-wide mix-up that wasn't my fault, had inadvertently caused him to be deposed as Governor of Knaboor. Which meant he'd lost the best cover and base of operations any intergalactic bookie and all around special fixit man could have dreamed of. I'd figured out who he was during this little fiasco, and instead of him ordering my execution, he'd moved in with me.

It had kept us in jobs for the past five years, and no one seemed the wiser. But I hated that he wanted to play pretend when it was just the two of us. He insisted it helped to keep his cover with the others. I was pretty sure he just liked yanking my chain. A lot. Maybe he did understand why it bothered me—like my Great-Aunt Clara, the Governor was good with the applied guilt.

"So, what do we do… Janz? And, more importantly, what do I tell Beber Zoltan when I meet up with him tomorrow evening?"

"You'll tell him that Janz expects you to be given hazard pay, for whatever the job is. Whatever he first offers, quadruple it, allow him to bargain, but only settle for triple."

"They're a lot of them and they're bigger than me. Frankly, all of the men on Herion seem bigger than me."

"They put steroids in the milk here."

"Thank God I only drink alcoholic beverages."

"Truly. It affects their sexual abilities in a negative way."

"My day just got a lot brighter."

"Perhaps if you stopped screwing every female that moved, Alexander, Miss Slinkie would consider your suit."

"How did this turn into 'Your Love Life With Uncle Oldie'? What am I supposed to do if Zoltan and his crew don't like how I negotiate?"

"Well, that's why you had Miss Slinkie make a date with Herion Military, is it not? Stop playing stupid, Alexander. We don't have the time. You will simply tell Zoltan that Janz has made his decision, and hazard pay, plus twenty percent of the gross, is the final decision. Unless, of course, they offer more than twenty-five percent of the gross to begin with."

"Why so?"

He sighed. "Five years under my tutelage and you still have to ask?"

"I just love hearing you talk. Fine. If they offer more they're either so desperate the job's going to go bad in the first hour, or it's a set up. But, this is Herion. I expect both of those and for them to offer one percent."

He chuckled. "Good point. However, Janz the Butcher's reputation seems intact here, if your description of how they reacted to the name is any indication."

"Yeah, seems that way. So, getting off planet with a job and without military intervention is pretty much the story of our lives. I think we'll manage that, somehow. But getting to Runilio, let alone out of Herion solar space, without being vaporized is the bigger issue of the day. Any ideas?"

The Governor shook his head. "Ideas, no. That's your department. However, I can tell you who I suspect is behind the attacks, and why."

"I'm listening. Intently."

"I believe Pierre de Chance and the Chatouilleux Français Armada are back in business."

I did a fast translation. "You're kidding."

"No, that's really his name."

"Lucky Pierre and the French Tickler Armada? And someone, anyone, considers this guy scary?"

The Governor gave me a long look. "Before he was stopped, Pierre and his minions had the entire Delta Quadrant under their control. No ships could come in or out of solar space without their approval and, of course, tribute."

"How much was the tribute?"

"Seventy-five percent of cargo worth."

My jaw dropped. "That's piracy!"

The Governor gave me his patented "and I'm stuck with you" look. "Yes. Hence why I told you they were a pirate armada. This is the beginning. They capture any and all viable spacecraft. Kill or employ their pilots and crew. Once the planetary system is fully cut off, they offer negotiations. By the time that happens, economics are so bad the planets make the deals."

"So, what're the odds they'd hire us and let us work for them?"

"Slim to none. Your reputation is too good, Alexander."

"I'm not exactly known as hero of the galaxy."

"No. You're known as the best pilot in said galaxy and a man who can be bought, but not employed. And while I know you're a pirate, smuggler, and all around bad man, not everyone else does." This was said in the condescending way he used when he wanted to make it clear to me that, as bad men went, I wasn't really in the game, just pretending.

"So? I sound like a great addition to the French Tickler team." Not that I wanted to join up, unless it meant all the women I could ever want, any time, anywhere. Then again, I had the best one in my crew already, and I just had to figure Pierre, as head man, would sort of expect Slinkie as a show of good faith.

"Pierre would never let you live—you're someone who could, conceivably, take over his operation."

"Yeah?" Felt pretty good all of a sudden. The Governor didn't hand out a lot of compliments as a rule.

"Don't preen. I said 'conceivably'. Pierre doesn't know you. I do. You're fine with a small crew. Too many people and your so-called management skills deteriorate faster than a snowball on Thurge."

"I think I resent that."

"But you don't and can't deny it."

"Sadly, no. I just want to get off this rock, go out, get some legal magma, get paid for our one legal job in the last six months, then go back out and relieve some merchants of part of their load in a nice and friendly manner. I may be a pirate, but I don't take seventy-five percent."

"Because you're clear on the concept of keeping the herd fattened and producing."

"True. Pierre isn't?"

"No, he is. He had a desire to rule the world, however. Clearly the desire's back."

"How was he stopped the last time?"

He sighed. "We sent in an undercover team who infiltrated and were able to destroy from within."

"Didn't they kill off Pierre?"

"Oh, they did. But, I'd assume one of his children took over the family business. Some things are handed down."

"Are you sure he was killed?"

"Very."

"How so?"

The Governor chuckled. "Because I killed him."

CHAPTER 16

"You were part of the infiltration team?" This seemed unbelievable. I took thirty or so years off the Governor. He'd still be ancient.

"You'd be surprised," he snapped.

"Completely."

"Suffice to say that part of how I became Janz the Butcher was due to this particular successful infiltration and leave it at that."

I considered the Butcher's reputation. He was said to have killed his superior in cold blood because he wanted to take over a galaxy-wide crime syndicate. Did so, and then retreated to the shadows, to become the head spider in the middle of galactic crime's web. Yeah, that kind of flowery hype sounded like the Governor's style.

"So, why didn't you become Lucky Janz or something?"

He shrugged. "I was given the rule of Knaboor, the richest planet in the galaxy. Until that little mishap five years ago, I *was* Lucky Janz, in that sense."

I pondered. "You think the Frenchies know you, you personally, are Janz the Butcher?"

"No. I think they're aware that Governor Murgat no longer rules Knaboor. I was considered a military genius, if you recall."

"Yeah, yeah. Not so genius that you didn't get deposed."

"Correct. I'd assume we're dealing with, as I said before, Pierre's offspring. I'm sure he had children all over the galaxy. One or more of them have come of age and decided to take up the family business."

"Great. Nice to know and all that, but what we need is how to avoid them."

"Actually, we need to determine how to stop them."

"I thought we agreed I wasn't hero material."

"You aren't. However, unless you want to be dead or give up seventy-five percent of all cargo, in and out, to the Armada, we have to stop them here. If they control Herion Military, which I'm sure is their initial goal, the rest of the galaxy will be in trouble, and quickly."

"Why does this sound like heroics will be necessary? Why me?"

"Because I said so." He said this in his Janz the Butcher voice. I hated that voice, particularly when he was saying things like this. Because when he used it and gave me the "make it so" order, he always meant it. And he was always right.

"So, do we tell the others that Janz has ordered us to play saviors of the galaxy or fake it until we're surrounded?"

"I'll think on that. We have at least a day until we'll be expected to leave."

"We'll have ten seconds once we leave this room before one of them asks."

"Good point." He was quiet for a couple of minutes. I took that time to contemplate if my original plan—just grab Slinkie and stay in bed for two weeks straight—wasn't the wiser choice, no matter what. Maybe I could impress her with my knowing Janz the Butcher well enough that I knew what he ate for breakfast. Of course, if I had to tell her what that was, she'd probably guess Janz's secret identity. Who else ate stewed prunes and watery oatmeal each and every morning? Aside from the Governor, my guess was no one. Back to heroics. I hated heroics. It never paid well and certainly not in terms of the risk to reward ratio.

"I believe we tell them about Pierre's armada. Leaving out that I was in any way involved, of course."

"No problem there. I think I'd have a harder time convincing them you were able to do anything active than that Janz wants us playing hero."

"Hilarious. I can still be active when I choose, Alexander. It's just rarely worth it."

"Yeah, I know. You save it up for pleasure princess visits. I've heard. From you. Not so much from them."

"Professional discretion is a wonderful thing."

"Yeah, because most men don't want to know they stink in bed."

"You among them."

"See, here's the difference between me and the rest. They all think they're great in bed. I know I am."

"It's that kind of blind belief in yourself that keeps me confident we'll all survive."

I chose not to argue with his wording. "Fine. You ready to go face the others with our still total lack of a plan?"

"We have a plan, Alexander. It's still in the beginning stages, and will need flexibility in order to adapt as the situation changes, but overall, it's workable."

I shook my head. "The one thing I never doubt is that you were a career politician. The space droppings flow from your mouth like eggs out of an Aviatus henhouse."

"One would think you'd have picked up the ability after five years together."

"I filter it."

"Is that what you call it?"

"Yeah, it is. Shall we?"

He sighed and stood. We went back to the living room. The others all looked worried. "I have a date," Slinkie said morosely.

"I'll take you out tonight and show you what a real date should be, Slink. Then you can pretend you're out with me again tomorrow."

"I feel so much better." Strangely, her tone of voice said otherwise. "What did the Butcher have to say?"

"Half off on sides of beef, this week only."

"That joke was funny the first time, Nap. When we're at time five hundred plus, not so hilarious."

"Everyone's a critic. Fine. Janz gave me the deal for the Business Bureau. He's not happy with them, so it's going to be hefty. I'm not sharing, it'll stress you all out and you won't be negotiating with me anyway. Suffice to say the Governor about had a heart attack and leave it at that."

"Can we get it, is the bigger question." Randolph sounded worried. "I mean, get it and leave alive. It was some Herion xenophobe who planted the bomb. Apparently, there's this crackpot group that's become active since Herion got cut off by that armada. Their goal is to keep everyone planetside, so no one can be lost to the space devils, which is what they're calling the armada."

"Possibly because, before us, no one knew it *was* a space armada." I thought about this. The group could be local crazies, but they could also be working for Pierre's people. "Do a further search on the mad bomber, will you Audrey?"

"Right away, Captain."

"Now, about the armada." They all looked at us with expressions that said they were paying full attention. "Janz says he knows them, or at least the signature. Pirates from over thirty years ago. The original head man was killed, but the assumption is one of his offspring took over and is now old enough to follow in daddy's effective but strangely named footsteps."

"What's the name?" Slinkie asked.

"Pierre de Chance and the Chatouilleux Français Armada."

I waited for them to all do the translations. Unsurprisingly, Audrey translated first. What was surprising was that she laughed. Like a human. Randolph had done a really good job. I was starting to be impressed.

Slinkie translated second and, like Audrey, started to howl with laughter. "And they think that's a scary name?"

"No, but apparently it was effective."

"At preventing pregnancy while increasing satisfaction, sure." Slinkie was still laughing. "But at scaring the general populace?"

Randolph translated, finally. Machines, computers and anything related to them were his forté. Languages, not so much. He blushed bright red. "I think that's a really stupid name." Of course, he didn't like that we called the *Sixty-Nine* the *Sixty-Nine*, either. There were times

I really worried about him. I looked at Audrey. Check that—there were now no times I wasn't going to be worried about him.

"So anyway, Janz figures Pierre, Junior, or similar, is now flying the not-so-friendly solar skies. They only stopped Pierre the First before by infiltrating and blowing his brains out, up close and personal. I'd love to avoid doing that. However, Janz also feels we need to stop Pierre here, before he's able to conscript Herion Military."

The laughter stopped. "Did I hear you right?" Randolph asked slowly. "Janz the Butcher wants *us* to *stop* this armada? He didn't tell you how to get away, he told you to take them down?"

"Pretty much, yeah."

Silence filled the room. Slinkie finally broke it. "Dear Feathered Lord—we're all going to die."

CHAPTER 17

"**W**ell, see, not part of my plan. Us dying, I mean."

"Great, Nap. If only the rest of us could perhaps know your plan, maybe we'd feel the same." Slinkie shook her head. Her hair flipped around. Her mouth was moving, but I was focused on her hair. "NAP!"

"Huh? What?"

"You were doing it. Again. The not paying attention to me while I'm talking thing. The thing I hate. You remember?" She looked and sounded furious. Her chest was heaving. I forced my ears to pay attention. My eyes told me they were extremely busy and I shouldn't bother them now.

"I was?"

"Yes. We want to hear whatever plan it is you have, and we want to hear it now." Slinkie's breasts wanted to hear the plan? Maybe I did have a shot.

"Oh. That. Right."

"Nap, look at my eyes."

"I am."

"My eyes are in my head, you feather-brain!"

My ears told my eyes that pain was imminent unless my eyes obeyed. My eyes and I sighed and dragged up to Slinkie's face. Great face. Angry, but great. "Yes. I'm looking at your eyes."

"Finally. The plan. What is it? I'd like to know before I kill you."

"So, not telling you is in my best interests. Good to know."

"Nap, you're making me think that sticking with Bryant is the way to go."

That worked. I spoke quickly. "Fine, fine. We're going to act like we're happy to be stuck on Herion tonight. We're going to go out and see if anyone else tries to kill us or recruit us. Tomorrow, we'll make our deal with the Business Bureau and find out what's going on that the military didn't tell us. Once we know what we're dealing with, we make our escape accordingly, race off to Runilio, get the magma, race back to Ismaliz, get paid, do whatever we have to in order to get paid from the Herion Business Bureau, and then go to Libsuno and relax."

I watched them process this. If I was lucky, no one would notice the key portion of the plan that was, for the moment, missing.

Slinkie, Randolph and Audrey all looked at me. "But how do we escape or destroy the armada?"

"That's amazing. I've never heard the three of you talk in unison before. Have you been practicing?"

"No, but without asking I know we're all ready to kill you." Slinkie sounded serious.

The Governor sighed. "Until we know what we're dealing with here, all that we're dealing with, how in the galaxy do you expect Alexander to come up with a viable option? He's given the outline, we all know how to work within it." His voice shifted to peevish. "Now, I'm an old man, and I was promised a mineral bath. I want the nearest Herion equivalent or there will be some explaining to do."

Slinkie sighed and held up a booklet. "I already looked, Governor. You have plenty of options, particularly now. I called the one I figured you'd want and made a reservation for you already."

He beamed at her. "You're so thoughtful, my dear."

"No, I just hate hearing you whine."

"Whatever works, my dear. Where and when?" Nothing nasty Slinkie said ever seemed to bother the Governor. Perhaps because, when it came down to it, he was going to get to cop his cheap feels again.

Slinkie sighed. "In an hour and yes, of course, I'll take you. I'm going to have a bath, also. I need to relax. For some reason." She gave me a dirty look, like this was all, somehow, my fault.

"I'll go, too."

"No, Alexander. I believe you should be giving the ship some attention and make sure it's safe."

"That would fall to Randolph and Audrey, wouldn't it? As Chief Mechanic and, ah...." I stared at Audrey. What the hell were we going to say her title was?

"Copilot." Audrey said this in her typical calm, cheerful way. I was going to have to sit next to her for the foreseeable future. I started praying she wasn't going to think she had the right to get chatty. "I agree with the Captain. That would make the most sense." I had to give her this—she was still the only one who gave me the remotest shred of respect and she was also helping me to go to the baths with Slinkie. Maybe having a Sexbot copilot would be all right after all.

"I suppose," Randolph agreed. "What do you want us to say if someone comes and asks us what we're doing?"

"Protecting our ship and not planning to leave any time soon."

Randolph sighed. "I wish I could believe you were lying."

"You know, have we ever not gotten off a planet? Ever? I mean, none of us have been in prison for any length of time, none of us have been kidnapped for any length of time, none of us have been left stranded for any length of time. I don't see why everyone's all doom and gloom."

"Define what you mean by 'length of time'," Randolph said, a tad bitterly. "I remember being in prison, being a hostage, and being stranded. More than once."

"And yet, here you are, alive, well, and with the right girl. Really, is there just no pleasing you?"

"No," Slinkie snapped. "There isn't. Can we go to the baths now? I don't want to be late for our reservation."

"Sure. I'll come along, see if they have an opening. And, if not, I'll just bathe with you, Slink."

She gave me a dirty look. "This place isn't co-ed. I made sure when I booked it."

"Guess I'll just sneak around and stare at you from the shadows, then."

"Like you do every time I bathe on the ship?"

Dang. She knew? I shrugged. "Then it'll just be like every other day, won't it?"

Slinkie sighed. "Why do I stay on your crew?"

"Because it's hard to leave the best."

"Lethargy and comfort zone," Randolph suggested.

"Fear of the unknown," the Governor offered.

"Because you like the Captain despite his many flaws." I tried to focus on the positive portions of Audrey's sentence, versus the "many flaws" portion. Reconsidered how much I was going to like sitting next to her. Maybe Randolph could install a Captain's Mute Button.

"I don't have many flaws! I have hardly any flaws!"

Slinkie shook her head. "Let's go to the baths. I'll list your flaws for you on the way, Nap. Trust me, I have them all memorized."

CHAPTER 18

The mineral baths on Herion couldn't compete with those on Thurge, but for a non-volcanic planet, they weren't bad. Sadly, Slinkie hadn't been pretending—men and women were in separate areas, so I was stuck in the baths with the Governor.

I managed to enjoy myself anyway, because while the customers weren't allowed to mingle, Herion wasn't run by stupid people, and the attendants were female, quite attractive, and happy to see me. They seemed to like how I tipped, at least.

The Governor saw fit to give me a lecture as we finished dressing. "Alexander, how does your having, ah, sexual relations with each of the female bath attendants equate with your desire to land Miss Slinkie on a permanent basis?"

"Boy, are you old. I mean older than even I think you are, apparently."

"And you're stupider than I think you are, apparently."

I shrugged. "Slinkie either will or won't come around. I don't think I need to become an Athriall monk in order to get her to see reason."

"No, but you might not want to make her worry that by touching you she's open to every venereal disease in the galaxy."

"I take precautions. No diseases, no little Nappies running around. I have a perfect record, too." I looked at him out of the corner of my eyes. "Why the sudden focus on the me and Slinkie idea?"

"Oh, no reason." He was lying, and not trying to hide it. Meaning there was a reason, but he wasn't going to tell me, just wanted me thinking about it. Not for the first time, I wondered why I'd left Great-Aunt Clara behind only to be saddled with her male counterpart.

We left the men's side to find Slinkie waiting for us, looking extremely bored and annoyed. I got the vulture-glare. Not good. Presumably, she'd figured out why we were delayed. "I think I'm going to take Bryant up on whatever he offers me tomorrow night."

I gave her my patented "guilty boy you can't resist" smile. "Aw, c'mon, Slinkie. You know the difference between distraction and infatuation."

She snorted as she stood. "Right, Nap. You're infatu-ated with being distracted." She strode out. The positive was she looked amazing from behind when she walked like this. I chose to focus on said positive.

I didn't get to focus on it too long. As Slinkie reached the street, an autofloater skidded next to her, tires screeching. A door opened, and someone pulled her into the vehicle. I heard her scream my name, right before the door slammed.

Pilots have quick reflexes, and I was the best pilot in the galaxy. I didn't think, I just ran and jumped onto the back of the 'floater before it got away. This was an older model, so there was a passenger board all the way around and a decorative hold-bar on the roof—these had been popular a couple of decades prior, when someone had thought it was a good idea for people to have their families stand on the outside of an ugly, moving, box-like thing. Stupid on the streets. Moronic in the air.

Happily, I had a good hold on the bar and got decent footing on the passenger board. Sadly, the driver realized I was on the 'floater and went airborne.

The windows were tinted, but I was pretty sure I saw a lot of movement. The 'floater was certainly rocking more than it should be, even while in the air. I figured Slinkie was showing why no one was ever going to force her to do anything she didn't want to do without a huge fight and the potential that they may never be able to have children.

However, the driver seemed to want to get rid of me. At least, I assumed that was why he flipped the car. I didn't fall off, thanks to that decorative bar, but I decided getting inside might be a good idea. Naturally, the doors were locked. But I had my laser gun and I was pretty sure Slinkie wasn't in the front seat.

I shot at the front passenger's window. Thankfully I'd shot at an angle, because the laser shot ricocheted off. Laser-proofing was expensive. I figured the Business Bureau wanted insurance in the form of my girl. Well, my soon-to-be girl. Okay, my maybe-one-day girl. But still, she was mine, one way or the other.

I holstered my laser gun and moved around the passenger board. If I couldn't shoot them, they couldn't shoot me. While I moved, I questioned why the Business Bureau was using an ancient autofloater. Maybe they liked to keep a low profile. Or maybe it wasn't the BB after all.

The driver tried flipping me off again. Like before it didn't work, but it did cause me to fall across the windshield. It wasn't as tinted as the rest of the windows, and I could see three men besides the driver. Like all of Herion's males, they were larger than me. Slinkie was doing a great job of kicking and hitting the crap out of them, but one of them landed a good uppercut and I saw her go over and down.

One thing I'd never felt Great-Aunt Clara was wrong about was men who hit women. She felt they deserved to die. I agreed, especially when they hit my woman. I couldn't get in there to beat the crap out of them in return, but I could do something much worse.

I moved to the front of the 'floater. Older models like this had failsafes, and I knew where they were. I kicked the front grill at the emergency release point and the hood flew up. Searched around, yep, it was an engine all right. I didn't want us crashing to the ground, but I wanted us going down. Found the helium-reactor and hit the emergency overload switch.

The 'floater shuddered and coughed. Good. I looked over my shoulder. We weren't heading anywhere comforting. There were buildings around us and nothing all that soft under us. And, since I had the hood up, the driver couldn't see. We were flying towards what appeared to be a sewage processing plant—the huge vats of stuff that looked fetid from up here, the many tubes running in between, the high and thick external walls, and total lack of other businesses surrounding this plant made it a good guess.

I considered the dilemma. Seemed to be only one option, really.

CHAPTER 19

I left the hood up and moved around to the driver's side. He chose to open his door, marking him as an idiot. But that was good. I'd been planning to kick in the back window and drag Slinkie out before we crashed. Not the greatest plan in the world. A door open made things much simpler.

He fired, I dodged. Wasn't hard. His aim was poor—apparently it was hard to drive an out-of-control 'floater and shoot the good guy at the same time.

I grabbed the door before he could close it, pulled my laser gun, and fired. Missed the driver, got the passenger. In the head. One down, three goons to go. From what I could tell, Slinkie was still out.

The driver flipped the car while he and I continued to fire at each other. He missed again, possibly because I'd lost my footing and was holding onto the car via the door handle. He leaned out to aim better. I holstered my gun, flung my arm up, and grabbed his arm just before he fired. His shot missed and he was off-balance enough that I pulled him out of the 'floater.

I heard male voices shouting, but couldn't pay much attention. The driver still had a hold of the wheel, meaning the 'floater was spinning in the air while heading, from the quick flash I saw, straight for the main sewage vat. I could smell it now, and I knew we'd land in it—it was just the way the cosmos worked.

I had the worse position, so I decided to try reckless as my next option. I grabbed the driver and climbed up his body. He tried to stop me, but I landed a good kick on his hand and his laser gun went flying off. He was bigger than me, weren't they all here, but I was more agile and I had the desire to sleep with Slinkie spurring me on. Can't sleep with dead girls—well, some can, but I'd never been one of them and didn't plan on starting now.

Grabbed the wheel, made sure I had a firm hold, and then I slammed my elbow into the driver's face. It took a couple of hits, but fighting fair wasn't something I'd ever believed in. So I kneed his groin—hard—while I hit him with my elbow again. He lost his hold on the wheel and started to slide down. My elbow hit the top of his head while my knee met his nose. He let go and I stopped worrying about him.

Climbed in when the car spun around to help me. The positive about the car spinning was that the two remaining goons were too busy flipping around the car to shoot at me. I turned the wheel the other direction, took the laser gun the dead passenger wasn't using any more, and waited for the goons to settle for a second. Two shots to the head, two dead goons. It was a cheerful afternoon for me.

I heard Slinkie groan. Good, she was coming around. We were almost to the sewage plant. I couldn't see it, but damn could I smell it. I cranked the wheel hard to the left and we slammed into the side of the tank. The outer side. It didn't break and I thanked whatever god was active on Herion right now as well as Lord Avian. I figured He had to love Slinkie, so maybe had a wing in the assist.

We hit the ground, hard, but on the tires. I didn't hesitate. Reached over the seat, grabbed Slinkie, dragged her out, flung her over my shoulder, and took off. I knew the kind of reception waiting for someone who crashed a 'floater into the reclamation plant, especially a 'floater with three dead goons in it.

"Nap?" Slinkie sounded confused and bleary. "Nap, what's going on?"

"Goon attack. I saved you. It was impressive. Tell you later."

"Where in the egg are we? The smell is awful."

I heard the sound of metal groaning. Risked a look up. The tank had held when the 'floater hit it, but it had been damaged. And it clearly wasn't going to hold all that much longer.

"Ah, Slink? You up to running?"

"I think so."

I put her down and grabbed her hand. "Good. Run. Or die under a mountain of Herion excrement."

One of the things I loved about Slinkie was that she didn't question statements like this. She just ran. I had no idea of where we should run to, of course, but away from the tank seemed the best idea.

"There!" Slinkie pointed. A door in what looked like the exterior plant wall. Sounded good to me.

We headed for it. Locked, of course. I was great at picking locks and considered it—it looked like a standard Bulldog, meaning it would take me about thirty seconds. But it didn't sound like we had long enough. Pulled my trusty laser and shot the lock out. Kicked the door open and we ran through.

There was an impressive array of Herion Military there, guns pointed at us. But I knew what to say in this situation. "The sewage tank's gonna break!"

CHAPTER 20

Reactions were immediate. The military scattered. Slinkie and I kept on running. We were running with the military, as a matter of fact. No one really needed to be told they needed to move or were going to be drowning in crap twice, at least, not if they had functioning brains.

Still running at top speed, I pulled Slinkie out of the group. I didn't want us near enough to be grabbed once everyone felt far enough away to be safe. The sound of rending metal was louder, and then the sound of metal giving up the good fight came, followed quickly by a slooshing sound that was both gross and ominous.

We were on a street now, and I heard the familiar screeching of tires. "Don't these guys ever stop?"

An even older and less impressive autofloater slid up next to us. "Get in," the Governor snapped. I shoved Slinkie into the back seat and leapt in next to her. The Governor floored it and we took off. He had us airborne momentarily, though not up too high.

"They won't have any trouble following us."

"We go higher, this comes down. At least, that's what the little old lady I took it from told me."

"You stole this from a woman *you* consider old? Dear Herion gods, whoever they may be, how old could that be? Is she a mummy or an undead?"

"I could let you ask the Herion Military," the Governor snarled.

"My jaw hurts. That bastard hit me." Slinkie sounded furious. "I want to go back and kill him."

"Already taken care of, Slink. I killed all four of them. No one touches you if you don't want to be touched. Other

than me, of course." I massaged the back of her neck.
"How's your head feeling?"

"Okay." She didn't make a comment or tell me to stop
or anything. She also wasn't looking at me, around, or at
the Governor. She was looking at her hands, which were
folded in her lap.

I got worried. "Slinkie, you all right? Did they hurt you
worse than I saw?"

She shook her head and then she started to cry. Slinkie
didn't like to cry. I'd only seen her do it a few times—
those three times I'd gotten the dove look, when we'd lost
Saladine, and a couple of others.

I put my arm around her and pulled her closer to me.
"Slinkie, what else did they do to you?" I wondered if there
was a way to kill them again. Figured not, but maybe I could
find out who'd hired them and go kill those guys, too.

She buried her face in my chest and bawled. I hugged
her and tried to figure out what to do. Some other girl,
this was a great prelude to sex—comfort, reassure, head
into the sack. But this was Slinkie. I didn't want to miss
what seemed like a golden opportunity, however, I also
didn't want to screw up.

I settled for standard operating procedures. Comfort
and reassure, see if sex might be a possibility. I kissed the
top of her head. "It's okay. I won't let anyone hurt you."
She bawled more and clutched at me.

This was great. Or would have been, if I wasn't actually starting to feel upset that she was so upset. I kissed
her head again. Her hair smelled great, goon attack or no
goon attack. Holding her felt great, too. Only her crying
wasn't great. I rocked her, hugged her more tightly, kissed
her head some more, and stroked her hair. I could feel her
start to relax.

"Alexander, do you happen to have a plan?" The Governor didn't sound snappish. I assumed he didn't want to
say something that might cause Slinkie to start crying her
eyes out again, since she was down from all out hysterics
to my soufflé fell.

"Well, I have several plans. All of them center around us getting the hell out of Herion solar space as fast as possible. Unfortunately, I don't know how to do that and stay alive, at least not yet."

"They said they were going to hold me as a hostage until they could get you to do what they wanted," Slinkie said. Her voice was muffled, because she hadn't taken her face out of my chest. I didn't mind and hoped she didn't go back to completely normal too quickly.

"Did they say what it was they wanted?"

She shook her head. "No. I was too busy fighting to ask questions."

"That's okay, we'll figure it out. I saw that one hit you." Despite trying to sound calm, my voice came out in a snarl. "Did they hurt you more than that?" I really wanted to know how much mayhem and pain I was going to cause to whoever had given the order to pick Slinkie up.

She cuddled closer to me. I tried not to marvel at my luck. "No. Not much, anyway. Just the usual manhandling."

"Manhandling?" Had their man hands handled parts of Slinkie I considered mine, albeit mine in the future? I really regretted the inability to kill someone more than once.

Slinkie took her face out of my chest. For a moment I thought my happy time was over, but she leaned her head back against me. "No, not intentionally."

I wanted to ask if by "not intentionally" she meant they'd knocked up against her assets while she was kicking and hitting them, or if they'd followed in the Governor's footsteps and gone for the cheap feels. But something told me this wouldn't lead us down a good path and, besides, the Governor was right there.

"Well... okay. You want to go lie down?"

She looked up at me and gave me a sardonic look. "Smooth."

"Not what I meant. You were hurt. I don't know if you need to rest or are okay moving back into action." I slid my fingers along her jaw. "You may be the toughest bird in the galaxy, but that bastard who hit you was twice your size."

"You think I'm a tough bird?" She didn't sound like she really believed me.

"I think you're the greatest, Slinkie. You know that."

"Oh, Nap. I was so scared. And I hate being scared. And you jumped on a moving 'floater to save me and...." Her eyes were wide, her lips were parted, and she had the dove look on her face.

I knew an invitation when I saw it. I bent to kiss her. Our lips were almost touching when the 'floater jerked and started to fall.

"Alexander, we have a problem!"

CHAPTER 21

I resisted the overwhelming urge to curse. My lips had almost been on Slinkie's, and tongue had been a clear given. Who knew where that might have led? I mean, I had a damned good guess, but there was no way to put it to the test.

In a split second, amorous thoughts were in the ether, because the 'floater was having some serious problems. Caused, as near as I could tell, by the several military 'floaters around it.

Unlike what we were in, Herion Military's autofloaters were sleek machines. You wouldn't be able to stand on one of them, they were built for speed. They were also built for business. It was clear they meant it.

We were surrounded, both sides, above, front and rear. None of their drivers were stupid enough to go below us, though.

"Land and drive like a good citizen."

"Well, it's that or crash and die, Alexander, so, I was going to do that anyway."

I sighed. "So testy. Look, when we get out, Governor, you just act cranky and old—you know, be natural. Slinkie, you just stand up straight, toss the hair, smile, you know the drill."

"What are you going to be doing?" Slinkie sounded like she was back to normal. I tried not to dwell on the disappointment. All wasn't lost, just delayed. I hoped.

"I'm going to be angrily lodging a complaint."

The 'floater touched down and the Governor drove slowly along, while the Herion Military 'floaters landed around us. The one above us stayed in the air, not that we had a prayer of outdistancing anything in the old heap we were in. They indicated it was time to stop, pull over and assume the position.

We did so, and then got out of the 'floater. This wasn't always a wise move, but one thing Herion Military were great about was the fact that they truly waited to make sure they had the right people for the right reason before they blew them away. Of course, on Herion, the right reasons were easy to come up with.

The cosmos liked its little joke. Who should get out of the 'floater in front of us than Lionside. I looked around. Saw the rest of the gang we'd been interrogated by earlier. Only one missing was Nitin. No loss.

Lionside strode over. Slinkie did her thing. I tried not to lose all will to live—she didn't look like she was faking it. However, survival was still what mattered.

I moved in front of the Governor and Slinkie as Lionside reached us. "Major, I'd like to lodge a formal complaint. My crew member was kidnapped on Herion's streets, and no one from Herion Military was around to help until after I'd rescued her."

Lionside stopped in mid-stride. "What... you're saying Miss Slinkie was abducted?" The way he said it, it was clear space dragons were going to be slain, and soon.

"That's exactly what I'm saying. How bad is it here that tourists who are doing their best to enhance the Herion economy are snatched in front of a legitimate and quite costly business establishment?" I'd been trained well by the Governor—I could do the pompous double-speak with the best of them.

Lionside ignored me and focused on Slinkie. "Are you hurt? Do we need to get you to medical?"

"I'm fine. Captain Outland rescued me. If he hadn't...." She let that one hang.

Lionside looked physically ill. "I had no idea. We got a report that someone was joyriding and crashed the stolen autofloater into the main sewage tank. The cleanup is going to be horrific."

"I don't call what happened a joyride, and I'm sure Slinkie doesn't either. I had to take extreme measures since they were attacking her in addition to kidnapping."

One of the other military personnel came over and whispered something to Lionside. He nodded. "Run backgrounds, as much as you can." He turned back to me. "Captain, you killed the four men responsible?"

"It was self-defense. They didn't want to give Slinkie back and tried to kill me."

"No argument. We believe they were part of the Land League."

"The who league?"

He sighed. "The Land League. They're a group of, frankly, maniacs, who feel we should cease all intersystem and interstellar travel."

This rang a bell. "I think they planted bombs on my ship."

Lionside nodded. "Your Chief Mechanic reported such, yes." He rubbed his head. "I apologize for this, Captain. We do need to take your statements, officially, and I will need to do so at local headquarters."

"You're arresting Captain Outland?" Slinkie sounded enraged.

"No, not at all." He sounded evasive.

The Governor snorted. "You can take our statements here, then. A trip to Herion HQ is a trip to prison."

"There was a great deal of destruction of property." Lionside sounded apologetic.

"Blame the goons who snatched Slinkie off the side-walk."

"I'd love to, but they're dead."

"Take their dead bodies in for questioning, then."

Lionside shook his head. "Miss Slinkie is free to go, as is your, ah, driver here. But I'm afraid I'll have to insist you come with us, Captain."

I heard a lot of guns make that "ready to fire" sound. "Fine. But I'll be lodging another formal complaint, for wrongful arrest."

"It's not wrongful if you're guilty." Nitin's voice oozed from behind me.

I looked over my shoulder. Yep, he was there. And it was the soldiers with him who had the guns drawn.

"I'm not guilty of anything other than self-defense and the defense of one of my female crew members."

Nitin smiled, and it was a nasty, unpleasant smile. "Well, I'm sure we can find something you're guilty of, Captain Outland. Your reputation, shall we say, precedes."

CHAPTER 22

Herion Military HQ was an imposing, box-like complex made out of steel. Reinforced steel, so far as anyone had been able to confirm.

Despite Slinkie and the Governor's protests, in fact, despite Lionside's protests, Nitin had cuffed my hands behind my back and shoved me into a military 'floater, between two Herion Military who made the goons I'd already dealt with seem small.

They were reasonably careful with me, at least until we were inside the military complex. Then a bag was put over my head, I was taken into an interrogation room, the bag was removed as I was flung into the chair that was the only thing in the room, other than one light in the ceiling, and left.

I looked for the hidden cameras. That there would be hidden cameras was a given. They wanted something from me, that was also a given. Whether I'd be allowed to live once they got it was not a given.

Took a very good, long look. If there were cameras in here, they were amazingly well camouflaged. The walls were all concrete, so was the ceiling and floor, and the one light didn't seem to have much in it that would function as a camera. I still figured there was something in here, watching me—just something I couldn't spot. Which meant it was probably cloaked.

I tried not to dwell on how close I'd come to getting a willing wet one from Slinkie. I needed to think about how to get out of here alive, not focus on what kissing Slinkie might be like. The last thing I needed was someone thinking I was aroused by being here.

The door opened and Nitin walked in. He was alone. He shut the door, walked over, and stood in front of me, just out of kicking range. "We need your cooperation, Captain Outland."

"Take the cuffs of me, Nitin. I don't cooperate well tied up."

"The rumors are you can't be employed but can be hired. You're a mercenary, a pirate. And the favorite of Janz the Butcher."

"What's your point?"

"I want you off Herion. Tonight."

"Works for me. Let me out of here, give me my crew back, unharmed, ensure my ship isn't rigged or bugged, happy as hell to leave."

"Really? With that dangerous pirate armada out there?" Nitin sneered. He was pretty good at it.

"Made it away from them once. Odds on my doing it again have to be better than my odds of a happy life behind Herion bars."

"We'd prefer that you not… escape."

"Let me go, I'll tell everyone we're leaving 'cause it stinks here. Whatever."

"I mean, we'd prefer that you not escape from the pirate armada."

I let that one sink in for a few moments. "So, what, you want me to allow myself to be captured? Uh, sure. Fine. Let me go, no problem, happy to, and so forth."

Nitin shook his head. "Please. No one is that stupid. We want you to allow yourself to be captured, you and your ship."

"You're crazy. Why would I do that? It's suicide, they'll just kill me."

"Doubtful. You're too good a pilot. De Chance will want you to fly for him. Make a deal, whatever he wants. With tracking on your ship, we'll be able to capture the armada and save our solar system."

"You're smoking Knaboor Gold. Not going to happen."

He gave me an unpleasant smile. "Oh, it'll happen. And to ensure that you do what we want? We'll be keeping something you care about."

The door opened and two Herion Military goons dragged Slinkie in. She was tied up and gagged, but still fighting. One of them pulled the gag off her. "Captain! Don't do it!" She was going to say more, but one grabbed her head and the other shoved the gag back into her mouth. She still managed to bite him. I loved that woman.

They dragged her back out. Nitin turned back to me. "Now, if you want to see her again, you'll cooperate. If not... well... she is a lovely thing, isn't she? I don't think I'll let Bryant know she's here—he seems so enamored of her. And I'm sure she'll enjoy spending private time with me."

That did it. I leaped up and head butted him right in the gut. He went back, doubled over, and I shoulder slammed him. As I'd noted before, he wasn't as big as the rest of Herion Military. He wasn't much bigger than me, really. And I was both furious and fighting for my life.

Nitin was on his knees. I kicked his jaw. His head went back and into the wall. He went down, slumped and bleeding a little. Not bleeding enough, but he was out.

If someone was watching, they'd be here fast. No time like the present. I slid my cuff-pick out of my sleeve, fiddled around behind my back for a few seconds, undid the cuffs, pulled Nitin's arms behind his back and cuffed him. Like all of Herion Military, he was in a gray uniform, well-fitted, but the pants had pockets on the sides of the thighs, and the jackets had plenty of inner pockets. Searched all of them—he had a lot of interesting things, all of which I took. His keys were what I really wanted, and, naturally, I found them in the last pocket, on his left leg.

Unbuckled his shoulder holster and gun belt, put them both on. They'd taken my laser, but he had it on him, hooked in the back of his pants. Took that back.

Took Nitin's little cloth officer's cap off and shoved it into his mouth. It wouldn't hold forever, but it might help a bit. Pulled his jacket off—the sleeves hooked onto the handcuffs. Flipped the main part of the jacket between his legs and the ends of the jacket back behind him, like he was in a huge diaper. I could only hook a few of the buttons through buttonholes, but it would slow him down whenever he gained consciousness.

Spotted something inside his shirt and I ripped it open. Money belt, or similar, was strapped around him. Took it. Decided he was too well trussed up to undo it and search his pants. Besides, I didn't want to stick my hands down any man's pants, let alone his.

He had a tattoo over his right pectoral—it looked like a flying Ebegorn—a bird with a wild mop of multi-colored feathers on the top of its head. Their nickname was the clown bird. I had more facts about them stored away, but decided to pull them up later—fly with an Aviatian, learn all the birds of the galaxy, basically. Not mine to reason why, but it seemed like something Herion Military wouldn't approve of. However, I had bigger issues than Nitin's odd choices in permanent ink.

Not for the first time I wished I'd let Randolph hook us all up with comlinks. Of course, my reason for not doing so was simple—our first usage of a comlink set up had contributed to Saladine's death.

Didn't dwell, didn't have time. I needed to find Slinkie, figure out what they'd done to and with the others, and get us the hell out of Herion.

CHAPTER 23

I opened the cell door carefully. No one around. Interesting. Maybe Nitin hadn't been lying and Lionside and his pals didn't know where Nitin had taken me. Meaning that Lionside probably didn't know they'd captured Slinkie, either. Or she was in his quarters being ravaged by him. I chose to focus on option number one.

One of the things I'd lifted from Nitin was what appeared to be an electronic compass. Turned it on. Better than a compass. It was a system tracker, set to the military complex. This would have been better if Randolph were with me, since he could figure out the code to make it work with a lot more accuracy.

However, some things were automatically loaded into these things—the owner's individual living quarters, main holding cells, general areas, things like that. I tried to figure out where I was from any of the standards. Near as I could tell, Nitin's quarters were nearby. Decided to head for them—he was male and holding Slinkie. She was probably already tied up in his bed.

Let part of my mind enjoy itself with this train of thought. The majority of my mind was focused on getting to this location undetected. The complex was a big rat maze, and I was going to get lost in it. Tried to pull up the simple rhyme Randolph had taught me years ago when dealing with something like this.

"Dots are natural, dots are fun, dots are best when they're one on one." Realized this made no sense to me at all and figured Randolph had been deranged for at least as long as I'd known him.

Stared at the system tracker again. There were dots on it. One was green and it seemed to be moving. Another dot was blue, several were yellow, a couple red. The red ones were in what looked like bigger areas. Okay, figure red meant main area. Avoid red.

Since there was only one blue dot, and it was closest to where the green, moving dot was, I tried to see if I was the green moving dot by heading towards the blue dot. Seemed to be working. The green dot reached what appeared to be a corridor at the same time I reached what was for sure a corridor. So far, so good.

I turned and walked towards the blue dot. The green dot did the same. Felt I could safely assume I was the green dot. No firm assumptions yet on what the blue dot was.

I heard the sound of running footsteps and noted there were several gray dots moving towards the area where my green dot had been not too long ago. Decided to make a wild guess that these were more military—decided to worry about whether they were Nitin's guys or another set of goons later.

Looked around. Not a lot of hiding places. Typical. Ran on towards the blue dot. I had to turn a corner again and, thankfully, there were doors in this new corridor. The blue dot wasn't all that far away so I raced for it. Green dot was pretty much on top of blue dot. So far, so good. Or at least, not so awfully bad yet.

I pulled out Nitin's keys. Happily, he had a master— they were always camouflaged to look like an ordinary key. Problem was, they all looked alike. Well, not a problem for me. Because to learn what the master for any world was like was to learn how to spot all the others on said world. Why locksmiths kept on making masters like this was anybody's guess, but I never argued with luck going in my favor.

It worked on the door. I opened it, stepped inside, closed and locked it quickly and quietly. It was dark in here, which was fine for right now. I could hear the pounding footsteps and they were getting closer.

Heard what sounded like people trying to open doors, the one I was standing by included. "Locked." Male, not a voice I recognized.

"Yeah, all of them. Any idea what's going on?" Different male, still no one I'd heard speak before.

"No, but Major Lionside's pretty upset. Not that we'll be able to do anything when we find Nitin."

"Cut the chatter." This voice was vaguely familiar, but I couldn't place it to a face. "Find Nitin, find the off-worlders. Figure he stashed them separately." I heard footsteps trailing off. It sounded like everyone was gone. But I had instincts, and they told me I wasn't alone.

"We're in the midst of one messed up interstellar incident," the first voice said. He was still right outside my door. "We don't want that... do we, Captain Outland?"

CHAPTER 24

I didn't reply. Or move. I didn't stop breathing, but I made sure it was shallow.

The voice outside my door chuckled. "You're good. I'm better, but in fairness to you, that's because I'm special." Something slid under the door. "Don't try to find me. I'll find you. Avoid the red dots—I know you don't want to have to explain what's going on to a full complement of our military. The buttons on the left side correspond to the levels—we're on level three right now. The ones on the right show you the schematic of each section of a floor. We're in the northwest schematic of this level."

I looked. Made sense. But there was a blue dot supposedly right by my green dot. Interestingly, there was no gray dot by me. Worry about how this guy was off Nitin's grid later. Because, supposedly, someone was in the room with me.

"I know you've realized you're the green dot. The blue dot is, for Nitin, what he wants to keep track of."

I looked behind me. It was dark but my eyes were adjusted. It wasn't a big room and I appeared to be alone.

"The blue dot isn't level sensitive."

I pondered what this meant.

He sighed. "She's on the top floor. Hurry up. There's a lot going on and I frankly need you out of here and helping. Not that you want to help." He chuckled again. "Just that, believe me, you're going to find that it's in your best interests to do what I need you to do. It's nice when it works out that way."

I heard footsteps now, leaving. Considered who had just been talking to me. Telepath of some kind, or else a lifelong friend I didn't know I had whose voice I also couldn't recognize. Put my money on telepath. Rare, not unheard of. Less rare than a lifelong friend I wouldn't know. As lifelong friends went, Randolph was the closest, and it was only half of my life. And dead people didn't count in this equation, meaning Saladine was out of the running.

Once the footsteps were gone and there were no gray dots anywhere near me, I turned on the light. Nothing much in this room. It looked like a standard storage room with not too much in it. Looked up. What it did have in it was a tiled ceiling.

Looked down to see what my new friend had slid under the door. It was a small envelope. Opened it cautiously. It had a plasticized badge, no name or picture, just a symbol—a rearing eagle. I slid it into my inner jacket pocket, the one that also housed my false identification and a universal card with a thousand interstellar credits.

So, this guy was working for the Royal Family of Aviatus. Interesting. Figured Slinkie and I were going to have to have a long talk about whatever it was she'd done to get run off her home planet, because I had to figure this was related to her in some way.

But to do that, I had to find her and, from what it sounded like, the others, too. Slinkie first. She was the best looking and the one most likely to be in danger of being ravaged by someone other than me.

However, my Great-Aunt Clara had always said taking time to think before running off madly was a good idea. Most times I disagreed with her, but this moment seemed like a good opportunity to take her advice.

I went through all the things I'd taken off Nitin. His keys had already been useful and would be again—right outer jacket pocket. The money belt contained, sadly, no money, but did have some papers that were obviously written in code. They had the Ebegorn crest on them. Moved into my special inner pocket.

Wallet with, happy day, many Herion credits, a variety of cards that might work or get me arrested, depending on when and how I used them and, in a zippered pocket, a small key. Took the key out and put it into my inner jacket pocket. Fortunately, I favored the Old Earth retro look in pilot-wear, so I was in what was called a bomber jacket. They weren't form-fitting, which was great because as you stuffed your inner secret pocket with goodies, it didn't make your chest bulge in odd and interesting ways.

Herion credits went into my wallet, left inner jacket pocket, but not hidden. The cards I put into the money belt, which I shoved into the left outer jacket pocket. The assortment of other things I'd snagged went into my left pants pocket. None of them looked like a tracking device or a small explosive, so I decided to save their perusal for another time—preferably when we were all long gone off this rock. Other than one thing.

There was a flat, milky disk on a leather strap, surrounded by metal. It was clearly meant to be worn as a necklace. It looked manmade, but I couldn't be sure. I pondered, then put it on and tucked it inside my shirt. It lay flat enough and this way I couldn't lose it easily.

Considered my options. I could go back out and try the corridors, but I had to figure there were still plenty of gray dots looking for me. Decided to play around with the system tracker for a while. My mysterious friend had given me what I needed to figure out the best way to get to Slinkie. Did a quick run-through of all the levels—I was in luck, she was pretty much right above me, albeit two more floors above me.

Decided to use the ventilation system. Sure it was a common technique, not to mention a cramped one, but for some reason, it still worked nine times out of ten. Did a quick recount. Yep, since the last time it hadn't worked, I'd used it seven times. Should mean I had breathing space.

Did the stand on the table and push the tile up thing, did the cough, curse and brush off wildly as the ceiling tile disintegrated thing, did the search for a portable light thing, then did the check the extra junk thing. Sure enough, Nitin had a penlight with him. Nice of him to come so equipped.

A part of me wondered how much of a set up this was, but, as Great-Aunt Clara always said, in for a penny is a stupid amount to get nabbed for, if you play, play big. She didn't always make complete sense, but I got the gist of what she was going for.

I moved into the ventilation system, penlight held in my teeth, and started the long, dusty crawl. The system was one I was familiar with—interconnected up and down. Common to military and prison complexes for some reason. Presumably those all forced to dress alike wanted to also all smell the exact same air all the time.

No vermin showed up to share the fun with me, which was a small blessing. Not that vermin bothered me all that much, but there's something about having a crawly with a lot of legs inside your clothes to make you jumpy, and I didn't have a lot of room to jump in.

Crawled to the end of the corridor and found the shaft going up to the next level. This was the fun part, so to speak. If you enjoyed shoving your back against one side, bracing your feet against the other, and shoving yourself up, it was great. I didn't think about slipping down—once I was up a few feet, that wasn't an option I was willing to contemplate.

Inched and shoved my way up to the next level. Collapsed in the horizontal shaft for a minute. I used the time in between pants to check the schematic. Was rewarded for the effort—there were gray dots all over the schematics now, anywhere I looked.

For good or bad, Herion Military's ventilation system was a crisscross, meaning that I had to crawl the entire length of this floor in order to get to the next upward shaft. Wanted to send an angry memo to the cosmos, but knew it would get returned unopened with a "balance due" stamp on it.

Did the inch and shove routine again. Wondered if I could send in a bill for my cleaning services—no one else had been in here for ages, if the dirt my clothes were cleaning off was any indication.

Reached the top, got to crawl all the damned way back to the blue dot. I was getting to the point where I didn't care who or what was there, as long as I could get out of the stupid shaft.

Finally arrived. The ventilator grill was under me and I took a look. Couldn't see a damn thing. Not because it was dirty, though I assumed it was, but because there was nothing much to see. A carpet was about it. According to the system tracker, however, I was right above the blue dot.

I listened. Nothing. I chose to hope this meant Slinkie was tied up but alone, versus tied up and being ravaged or, worse, not tied up and happily in bed with someone. Decided not to wait to find out.

The grill lifted off easily enough, but then it slipped through my hands and crashed to the floor. Not my smoothest move. But, no one came running. Maybe there was no one in the room. Or they were waiting for me to come down before they killed me. Figured I'd make it easy on them and a lot more pleasant for myself.

I slid over the opening and went down legs first. Landed in what I had to admit was a pretty cat-like way—standing, knees slightly bent, ready for anything.

Well, anything but what I was looking at.

CHAPTER 25

"Captain, I'm very glad to see you."

I looked around. There was no one else here, just me and Audrey. "Um, hi. You got captured?"

"Yes. They said they would harm Randolph if I didn't come with them." She sounded calm and cheerful. We really had to do something about the voice program on Audrey.

"Who's they?"

"Major Nitin and his men." She was sitting on the bed. Just sitting. Not pacing, not lying down, not wringing her hands, and, key point, not trying to get away. Just sitting.

"Ah, Audrey, did Randolph actually program you to do whatever a man said?"

"Oh, no, Captain. I have complete free will."

"Then, uh, why didn't you free will yourself out of here? I'm just guessing, but I'd bet you're a lot stronger than I am, potentially able to break down the door."

She nodded. "Yes, Captain. I am. However, they told me they'd hurt Randolph if I tried to escape."

Ah, what he hadn't programmed her for was how to tell when the risk to reward ratio was worth it. There probably wasn't a lot of self-preservation in Audrey, either.

"Okay. Where's Slinkie?"

"I don't know, Captain."

"She's not here with you?"

"No, Captain." Audrey looked around. "It's not a large room."

"I just thought I'd be finding Slinkie in here, that's all." My brain was registering that Audrey was the thing Nitin wanted to keep his eye on, and, presumably, what my mysterious friend wanted me to get out of here. "Can you track the others?"

"Oh, yes, Captain. Randolph gave me programming so that I can find any of you when I need to."

"Audrey, we need to. I want to get the others and get out of here."

She shook her head. "I can't leave. If I leave, they'll hurt Randolph."

"I'm the captain, right?" She nodded. "I'm also Randolph's friend." She nodded again. "I'm also more experienced than you. Audrey, they're going to hurt Randolph if we don't get him and get out of here. They're going to hurt Slinkie and the Governor, too. I don't care what they told you, they're lying."

"They said they would torture and kill all of you if I didn't cooperate." Still said in that calm and cheerful way.

"Audrey, Randolph said you have feelings. Is that right?" She nodded. "Need to ask you a personal question. Do you actually feel as calm and cheerful as your voice would indicate?"

"No, Captain. I would like to cry and scream, but Randolph didn't allow for that in my programming."

"Really. Well. We'll talk to him about fixing that. Once we save him and the others. Okay?"

"I'm afraid." This was the first time I'd ever heard someone say that phrase with this much calm happiness in their voice. At least it was bothering her as much as me.

"I know. Me too. A little. But, you have to trust me. If Nitin wants you, then we need to ensure he doesn't get to have you. Okay? I'm saying this as the captain."

"Yes, Captain. Randolph did program me to consider you the leader and therefore to follow your instructions as long as the odds of them causing greater harm than they were solving were not over seventy-five percent."

"Where're we at?"

"About seventy percent."

"Great! Now, we'll talk to Randolph about that pesky twenty-five percent later." All I needed, an auto-help copilot who was going to second guess me at every turn.

"I have already made adjustments, Captain. I have run all history, and your odds of success are normally ninety-five percent, particularly when doing something considered dangerous and foolhardy."

I was impressed. "Great. So, let me know when we're dealing with that rare five percent. Otherwise, let's get out of here and find the others."

"I am happy to." She cocked her gleaming head at me. "Would you like to clean up before we go?"

Took a look in the mirror. "Huh. Yes, thanks." I washed the dirt and dust off my face and hands while Audrey did some very fast cleanup on my clothes. "How are you doing that?"

"I have a small but powerful vacuum in my right arm." She showed me. Her wrist was bent in a way that, had she had bones, would have indicated she was never going to play the xaxachord again. Her forearm was hollow and she was using it to suck the dirt off me. She finished, emptied the dirt into a wastebasket, then closed her hand and arm back together. I couldn't find the seam.

"Amazing. Once we're safe, I'd like a full run down of your capabilities."

"Of course, Captain."

I handed her the system tracker. "I'm hoping one of those capabilities will let you tell us where the others are."

Audrey nodded. "Yes." She took it and twitched. I got the impression she was hooking into it. "They are all together."

"Great!"

"They are also on this level."

"Even better!"

"They are scheduled for termination in ten minutes."

CHAPTER 26

"**M**oving out now, Audrey." I went to the door. It locked from the inside. "Audrey, you're not really a prisoner, did you know that?" I listened at the door. No sounds and no gray dots on the system tracker. I unlocked the lock, turned the handle and opened the door.

Nothing happened, so I opened the door wide and stuck my head out into the corridor. No one there.

"I was told to stay and wait, Captain."

"Audrey, if you have free will, I hope that means you can start adapting a lot of your programming on your own. Start with the fact that most if not all humanoids are lying sacks of excrement. Add in the idea that someone who threatens you in this way is probably not only an aforementioned sack but also planning to use you for his own nefarious plans. And then add in whatever quality it is I have that keeps me and our crew alive."

"You think like the sacks of excrement but you are actually a noble person."

We stepped out into the corridor. "Noble? Ah, not so much, no. We'll work on your comprehension program, too."

"You are trying to save the others instead of just yourself. You saved Slinkie at great personal risk and you do not take advantage of her even though you could. You take care of Randolph even though he failed at the Space Academy and should, by rights, be working in a Thurge power plant. You protect the Governor when others would have abandoned him. And you treat me as human even though it bothers you that I am not."

I didn't like that Audrey could pick that up. "Whatever. My supposed nobility aside, you need to lead the way, fast, to where the others are. And, how are they going to be terminated, can you tell?"

"Lethal gas."

"Run fast, break down their door, or whatever you need to do to get them out of there safely, I'll catch up."

Audrey took off. I'd guessed right—she was able to move faster than a human. As I pounded down the corridor after her, I considered why Nitin wanted her. Didn't have to think long. Reverse engineer her and you had the makings for the greatest army in the galaxy. If Randolph had put skin on her and allowed her to sound like a human instead of an automated response unit, it would be close to impossible to tell she was a Sexbot. Figured I needed to have that talk with Randolph sooner as opposed to later.

Found Audrey at the room at the end of the corridor. She was pounding on the door, but it wasn't doing anything. "Reinforced steel, but I think it has an iron core, Captain."

Tried the door handle, just to be sure. Nope, sadly, the others hadn't been left on their own recognizance. Figured our team's luck was out. I pulled out my lock picks. Unfortunately, I wasn't looking at a Bulldog. I was looking at a Dragon. Dragon locks were considered impregnable. They weren't, but they took longer. A lot longer.

I started the process. It took a lot of concentration, but I'd learned to pick locks before I'd met Randolph, and Dragons were always the test someone threw at you whenever they wanted to make you look bad. For some reason, a lot of people had wanted to make me look bad over the years.

"Three minutes left, Captain."

"Should be done in two, two and a half. Two and three-quarters, tops." I raised my voice. "Get ready to hold your breath!" Wasn't sure if my voice could to carry into their containment unit through the airtight door, but figured it was worth a shot.

"Two minutes."

"Thanks for the extra pressure, Audrey."

"One and a half minutes."

"Shut the hell up, Audrey."

I was on the last tumbler. Always the hardest. Always made with a little quirk that would cause you to take extra time. I forced myself to slow down and relax. Stress wasn't your friend when it came to picking a Dragon.

"Forty-five seconds." Apparently Audrey couldn't resist adding on the extra pressure. No problem. Slinkie was behind the door, meaning I had the best incentive in the world to remain calm and get it open.

I was at the quirk and now came the real test. Dragons had infinite quirk options. Part of being able to pick them successfully was based on the lock picker's ability to guess the quirk. Considering where we were, what this door was being used for, and what planet and planetary system it had been created for, I went with the idea that it would require muscle. Leaned on the pick and slammed the door handle at the same time. It didn't open. But it didn't relock, either.

"Ten seconds."

"Audrey, stop counting and come here. I'm going to move the pick and when I do, I want you to slam the door handle with the palm of your hand, as hard as you can. Ready?"

"Yes, Captain. Five seconds."

"Now!"

CHAPTER 27

I moved the pick and Audrey slammed the door knob. The door opened. I would have been relieved, but we still had to get away before the lethal gas started.

Happily, all three of them were in this room. Naturally, they were trussed up. Audrey and I ran in. I grabbed Slinkie, she grabbed Randolph and the Governor, and we raced back outside. I slammed the door behind us, just as I heard a hissing sound start.

Didn't take the time to untie them. I ran down the corridor and Audrey followed. I went back into the room Audrey had been in. Everybody in, locked the door and braced it with the bed. Audrey helped. Then and only then did we untie the others.

They looked mussed up and shaken, but no worse for wear. "How the hell did all of you get arrested?"

"Nitin waited until Bryant left to follow you, and then the rest of his men turned their lasers on me and the Governor and said we should come along or die." Slinkie sounded angry, but she was trembling. I put my arm around her, just to make her feel a little safer.

"I got arrested after I lodged a complaint about all the crap being put onto our ship." Randolph sounded furious. "This planet's gone bad since we were here last."

"I believe the pirate armada has something to do with it." The Governor sounded a little shaken.

"You okay?"

He shot me an icy glare. "I'm in no worse shape than Randolph or Miss Slinkie."

"Good to know. Then you'll be up for a nice crawl through the ventilation system." I got dirty looks from all of them, other than Audrey. But I suspected she wanted to give me a dirty look and just wasn't programmed to be able to do so. Yet. "Randolph, I want some programming improvements made to Audrey, sooner as opposed to later."

"Yeah, Nap, I think you're right."

"Okay, there's a lot of intrigue going on right now." Everyone groaned, even Audrey, though she made it sound cheerful. "Yeah, I know. Intrigue is never good. I'll fill everyone in once we're out of the military complex. As a warning, there's a telepath in Herion Military. He helped me, supposedly, get to all of you in time. I haven't seen him, but I've heard him. I'll recognize his voice if I hear it again, but have no idea who he is."

"Nap, why can't we get out using the corridors and elevators?" Slinkie hated going into the ventilation system, anywhere, any time.

"Because Nitin's goons are looking for us, Lionside and his goons are looking for us, and our telepathic pal is also looking for us."

"So, we have three separate plans in action here within Herion Military, and at least the same number active outside of it." The Governor sounded thoughtful. "Interesting."

"Yeah, in that 'oh Active Gods, oh Active Gods, we're gonna die' sort of way. Governor, can you think and crawl at the same time? Because Nitin or his goons will be here shortly to see how dead you guys are and how pliable Audrey is and I'd like to be long-gone when they arrive."

"How'd you get away from Nitin and his guys?" Slinkie asked.

"Got taken in with a bag over my head, dumped off into a room with only a chair in it, Nitin came in to do solitary interview, I declined and put him in the diaper."

"Good." Slinkie was seriously angry. "You think he expected it?"

"Thanks for the vote of confidence. No idea. Fifty-fifty odds right now. Can we move it, people? I really don't think I'm exaggerating the need to get the hell out of here."

"I'll go first," Randolph said, total lack of enthusiasm radiating from every pore.

"I cleaned off half of it for you, Mister Daintypants. And your girlfriend can vacuum us up later. I don't even want to ask why you thought her having suction in her arm was a valuable feature."

"Fiancée, and it's a useful thing."

"Right, right. Here, let me give you a leg up, go to the left." I made the hand bridge.

"Should I go first, Captain?" Audrey asked. "I have the ability to create light out of my eyes."

Tried not to find this creepy and failed. But it was useful. "Sure, Audrey, you go first. You sure you won't just give us all up should you run into a bad guy?"

"No, Captain. I've rearranged my programming to imitate you."

The other three groaned again. Touching. "Fine. Then Audrey first, the Governor second, then Randolph and Slinkie, and I'll bring up the rear."

"Why am I going between you and Randolph?"

"So I know you're safe."

Slinkie snorted. "I'll bet."

"You can go last, if you're able to both get up there on your own and put the grill back."

Got the eagle-glare. "Fine. You go behind me."

"Knew you'd see reason."

Audrey turned her headlight eyes on—it was as creepy as I'd imagined—and jumped up. I did the hand bridge while Randolph steadied the Governor. Audrey pulled him up after her, rather gently, which was probably a good thing. He was a tough old man, but old was still his operative word.

Randolph next, thankfully not needing a helping hand from anyone other than me. I didn't do the hand bridge for Slinkie. I picked her up by her waist. "Nap, why do you always act like I can't do what the others can?"

Her breasts were in my face. I resisted the urge to bury my head in them, but I felt I deserved a medal for it.

"Slink, when are you going to realize that I do this because I both like it and want to take care of you?"

"Oh." Her voice sounded funny. I forced myself to look up and away from her breasts. She had the dove-look back.

I decided that I'd missed out on one sure thing and didn't want to risk never getting another opportunity. I let go of her waist just a little and she slid down. Her mouth opened in shock, and I moved in.

CHAPTER 28

Kissing Slinkie was all I'd imagined it to be and more. I had my arms wrapped around her, one hand in her hair and one on her butt in a matter of moments. Her arms were around my neck and I wasn't getting the Avian Claw to the jugular—her fingers were running through my hair.

There was a bed in the room and I was ready to use it. Her body fit perfectly next to mine, her tongue was responding in a way that said she liked being kissed and was open to more, and visions of incredible sex danced in my mind.

"I don't think this is a good time for you two to stall." Randolph sounded annoyed and embarrassed. It was hard to connect his prudishness with Audrey, the Happy Sexbot.

Slinkie pulled away. She looked flustered and, I was happy to note, aroused. She also looked like the romantic moment was over. "Randolph's right."

Sadly, he was, so I didn't argue. Picked her back up by her waist and handed her up to Randolph. Then I got the ventilator grill and used the time to get myself back under control.

Happy time being firmly over, I handed the grill up to Slinkie, then jumped and pulled myself up. Slinkie helped me put the grill back, then she managed to turn around and started crawling back. If the shaft had been larger, this would have been great, because my head would have been right by her butt. As it was, my head was right by her feet, meaning I had to stay back a little ways so I didn't take a heel to the face.

I'd forgotten to warn the others about how the ventilation system was set up, but as some cursing filtered back to me, I took for granted they'd figured it out on their own.

"We couldn't walk out like normal people why?" Slinkie snarled at me as she reached the vertical shaft.

"Just shove your back against one side and your feet against the other."

"I think I hate you."

"I'll keep that in mind the next time you're tied up and about to be gassed to death."

She heaved a sigh. I normally loved it when she did that, but since I couldn't see her chest right now, it was, in my opinion, wasted. "Fine, Nap. I'll stop whining."

"Whine all you want, just keep moving."

Going down was no more fun than going up. Going back across was just as exciting. Went down again, amidst more cursing. I checked the system tracker. There were no gray dots in this area. Passed along the suggestion to go into the room I'd entered the ventilation system through. Got the nasty reply back that those in front had already fallen into it and were just waiting for the rest of us. You'd think being saved from a nasty death or a future of enslavement would have made my crew happier. You'd have been wrong.

Reached the hole I'd made, leaped down and landed in my cat-like stance. No one noticed, they were too busy complaining and being vacuumed off. Figured.

Checked the system tracker again. Still no gray dots on this third level. Plenty of them on the fifth level, however. "I think we've been discovered. Or, rather, they've discovered the three of you aren't dead and Audrey's disappeared."

"Can we go by conventional means now, Alexander?"

"Sure, Governor. It triples our capture risk but I have to admit it'll probably speed up our estimated time of departure." I handed the system tracker to Audrey. "What's our safest escape route?"

"The ventilation system, Captain."

"I like how you think, Audrey. However, everyone else is complaining. What's the fastest route that combines the least risk of detection?" Audrey opened her mouth. "Better yet, why don't you just lead the way and tell me about it as we go?"

She nodded and strode to the door, but before she opened it she looked at me. "Oh, Audrey, headlights off, please." Her eyes went back to normal and I checked the system tracker. Still no gray dots on this level. I nodded and she opened the door.

Apparently not everyone in the complex was hooked into Nitin's system tracker, because there was someone standing there with a big gun pointed at us.

CHAPTER 29

He was taller than me, but not by a lot. He wasn't all that much larger than me, either. He was dressed as Herion Military, but unless he came from a family of midgets, this wasn't someone who'd drunk his steroids as a kid.

"You my mind-reading friend?"

He grinned. "That's me. Let's get going." I still figured him for an Aviatus double-agent, but there were other possibilities.

I walked over and moved Audrey out of the way. "Where are we going?"

"Out. You do want to get out, don't you Captain Outland? Or would you rather they catch you all and put you into Nitin's gas chamber?"

"Oh, we're all over the out part. What we're concerned with is the out where part."

"Not to your ship. At least, not yet." He motioned with his head and the gun. "Seriously, are you people always this slow to react?"

"Sometimes we're glacial. Sometimes we move so fast you can't see us. It's all down to our collective whim."

"Really, Outland, move it or die."

"That we understand." I looked over my shoulder. "Let's move and follow our new friend here." Looked back at him. "What did you say your name was?"

"I didn't and don't plan to." He gave me another grin. "You'll learn it later, when it's safer to know. Right now, more moving, less talking."

Everyone filed out. Slinkie gave our mysterious friend a long once-over. My heart sank. Guessed the kiss hadn't been as great for her as for me if she was checking this guy out. Decided I might just have to hate him.

Slinkie didn't do the stand up straight and toss the hair thing, though. She made sure she was on my other side, so I was between the two of them. She also didn't talk. Decided I'd ask her why this guy unnerved her later. If, in fact, I didn't find out that she acted like this when it was love at first sight.

The telepath led us through the maze of corridors. We had to stop and hide a few times. I confirmed on the system tracker—every time he had us take cover, there were gray dots coming.

We wound down and around, in and out, zigged and zagged, never taking an elevator. When asked why, his reply was curt and to the point. "You're all really desperate to get caught again, aren't you?"

More stairs, more corridors, more hiding, repeat, repeat, repeat. I wasn't positive, but it seemed like we were visiting every part of the complex. Why, I couldn't say, but the good thing was we avoided any other guys in gray uniforms.

Just when I knew all of us, Audrey included, were at the breaking point of patience, he led us into the maintenance section and we reached a door that indicated we'd breathe fresh air if we opened it. "As a warning, the air quality's awful right now," our telepathic guide said. "Recommend shallow breaths or scarves if you have them."

"Fresh out. What about gas masks?"

"If you have them hidden somewhere, feel free."

"That bad?"

"You ruptured the sewage tank, you tell me."

I sighed. "It was an accident, and not actually my fault."

"Yeah, I know. That's one of the reasons why I'm helping you." He hit the button that raised the corrugated metal door and we stepped outside. It was nice to be out of the rat maze, but he hadn't been exaggerating—the stench in the air was almost thick enough to see.

We were actually on the outside of the complex and left without issue through the large door that, as I turned back, was labeled "Refuse Delivery". Guess they didn't want the trash people coming inside, which was okay by me.

"Now where?" I had no clear idea of where we were, just that we probably wanted to put some distance between us and the Herion Military complex.

Slinkie grabbed my hand and yanked, which pulled my head down towards her. "I want to get away from this guy." Her whisper didn't sound like she wanted to get away because she was afraid she'd throw herself at him. I started to feel better, horrible smells notwithstanding.

"Sorry, you all need me around." He gave her a look I could only think of as derisive. "I can read your mind, too, you know."

"I know. That's why I want to get away from you." Slinkie sounded angry and ready to fight.

I wasn't thrilled with having a telepath around, but so far he'd been a help and I wasn't too proud to accept help, particularly if it was keeping me and my crew alive. "Ah, Slinkie, after all that's happened, I think we might want to be more pleasant."

"He's a spy, Nap."

"Well, duh, yeah, I know." For some reason I didn't mention the card he'd given me to her. Now didn't seem like the right time. "So what?"

The telepath grinned at her. "Slinkie doesn't like spies, does she?"

"No, she doesn't." She was giving him the vulture-look. I started to feel great. "She also doesn't like people who claim to be helping but who won't offer a name."

"I could offer a name. But I don't like using an alias... unlike someone I could name." His grin got wider. "Now, be a good girl, stop worrying, and let me work with Captain Outland here."

I waited for the attack. Normally, if anyone spoke to Slinkie in a manner even close to this condescending he'd be icing his groin for a week. But she merely glowered at him and looked away.

This caused everyone else, even Audrey, to stare, myself included. The telepath shrugged. "I know how to talk to her."

"No. I think you know how to threaten her."

CHAPTER 30

I kept hold of Slinkie's hand and she didn't object. Alternated between hoping this meant she'd liked our kiss and was open to a continuation and worrying. "For the record, I really don't like anyone threatening me or my crew, Slinkie in particular."

The telepath still had his grin on full. "I know. One of your better points. Yeah, you do have them, hard as that is to believe." He didn't seem at all concerned. He was also leading us to what looked like a tankfloater. They were like autofloaters, only bigger, nastier and far better armored.

He opened the rear door and indicated we should climb aboard. I shook my head. "I drive."

He laughed. "Fine. I'll take shotgun." He reached in and pulled a lasershot out of the back. "There's weapons for everyone in here. I'd recommend you each grab at least one on your way to find a seat." He moved around to the passenger's side.

The others all gave me nervous looks. "Nap, you sure we can trust this guy?" Randolph sounded as worried as he looked.

"No, but I'm also sure you all weren't tied up in that impregnable room for fun."

"He knows what we're thinking," Slinkie hissed. "I don't want him around us."

"Maybe he doesn't have a long range."

"I'd assume it's long enough, Alexander. And, as we've always said, best to keep them close." The Governor seemed to feel this settled the matter and he climbed into the tank. In that sense, it did. The Governor's main motto was to keep your friends close and your enemies closer. Which was one of the reasons he was on the *Sixty-Nine*. I assumed we'd moved to the friends side of the equation after all this time, but I wouldn't bet money that he'd always thought of it that way. So, he wanted the telepath close enough to kill him if we had to, and I had no objection to that plan whatsoever.

The others climbed in after him, Slinkie last and with great reluctance. "Nap, don't trust him." She was still holding my hand.

I gave hers a squeeze. "It'll be okay, Slink."

"Hope you're right."

"When was the last time I was wrong?"

"When you picked Herion's system as our destination." She had a point. "I mean about people."

"Don't even get me started." Slinkie let go of my hand and shut the rear hatch.

I went to the front and got in. The way the tankfloater was built, the others were far back from us, so unlikely to be able to hear our conversation. No matter. If I needed them, I had no issues with shouting.

"You have the starter transmitter for this?" The telepath rolled his eyes at me. "Just checking." Hit the start button, it revved to life. "Where to?"

He sighed. "Under the circumstances, I think you'd better head for Business Bureau headquarters."

"No."

"You need the protection."

"We don't need it that badly. I want to go somewhere safe, not somewhere else we'll have to crawl through ducts to escape from." I wondered if he was agenting for the Business Bureau.

"No, I'm not working for them. Just want to hole up with extra firepower."

"Not going there, know what the Bureaus are like enough to know if you're trying to fool us. Pick another destination." I drove off, in a sedate manner. No hurry, just out for a drive, me and my tank full of people and weapons. At least this guy stole well. "So, who are you and who are you working for?"

"I don't want—"

"Look. I have at least one person back there who is now both armed and ready to kill you. Don't make me want to let her do it. You seem like you could be a decent guy, maybe even on our side or at least not working against us or trying to kill us, which, for our luck, counts as decent. Trust me when I say that Slinkie's got a gun pointed at your head, and the others probably do as well."

"If they shoot me, then you won't know who I am."

"I can live with the mystery."

"Probably not. Right now, you need me more than I need you."

"Doubt it. You didn't help us because you're a humanitarian. You helped us because we're more useful to you alive than dead."

"You need my support at least as much as I need you."

I considered this, hopefully at a lower level of my mind than he could read. I tried to focus on Slinkie's body in my upper level mind—maybe it would distract him. Always distracted me.

He was about my age, maybe a little younger. In order to infiltrate Herion Military, he had to have been here at least ten years, since they recruited young. He also had to have papers that either showed him as a Herion native or legitimate Herion immigrant. He was also likely working for the Aviatus government, since the card he'd slipped me was hard to come by. I hadn't had a lot of time, but the short examination I'd given it showed it as genuine. I could and would put it through better tests, but the working assumption was this guy was a spy for Aviatus, working Herion. Why, was the question.

Aviatus and Herion weren't in the same solar system, and while they weren't enemies, they weren't friends, either. They were politely neutral to each other—each one was the head planet of their system, each one had its own views about how things should work, but neither planet intruded on the other. Aviatus was in Beta,

Herion in Gamma. Their quadrants didn't even really connect that much.

So, why have an Aviatian spy on Herion? Deep on Herion. This kind of in-depth infiltration indicated decades worth of intrigue and espionage, and the Governor had never indicated it existed. He'd indicated a lot of intrigue and espionage, but not between these two particular planets. I didn't think it was time to doubt him.

I wondered how the hell we blocked anything from this guy, too. Telepathy was great in theory. When it was sitting in a tankfloater with you, it wasn't so fabulous. I wasn't really driving anywhere, other than away from the Herion Military complex, and towards somewhere that wasn't the sewage plant.

Something in the back of my mind sauntered up and knocked. This guy had never shown up on Nitin's system tracker.

I slowed the tankfloater and pulled up against a curb, legally and everything. Checked. Yes, legal parking area. I looked at him. "You're not actually Herion Military at all, are you?"

He looked uncomfortable and didn't answer.

I couldn't help it, I grinned. "In fact, you're helping us because, point of fact, you're stuck here and unless we help you get off-planet, you're totally and completely screwed."

CHAPTER 31

He looked like he was going to argue, then his shoulders slumped. "Yeah. Fine. Like you'd give away your main strength just because someone asked?"

"No, but give away your real name or you're walking home to Aviatus. And that's a long hike from here."

"Fine. Tanner Lauris."

"From Aviatus?"

"Yes. Can we keep moving? Really, we want to get far away from Herion Military right now. Specific members of Herion Military in particular."

"Nitin and Lionside?" I started off again. Tanner might not have had my trust, but he had a point. Moving away was still the best plan.

"Lionside's a patriot and a decent guy. Nitin...." Tanner shuddered. "The farther away from him all of us can get, the better."

"What's his game?"

"I don't know."

"Come on. You're a telepath."

Tanner heaved a sigh. "A limited telepath."

"Want to explain what that means?"

"Only if you have a better destination than wherever until the charge on the tank dies."

"Not so much, no. I assume the hotel we spent money on is out." He nodded. "And you said no to the ship."

"Only if you want to go back into lockup. The ship is for when we're ready to leave at that moment."

"I'm ready to leave at this moment. And there is, currently, no 'we' in leave, at least, not in terms of you."

"You really care about S— ah, Slinkie?"

I noted the slip. Clearly, he knew, or thought he knew, things about Slinkie, like her real name, that I didn't, but now might not be the time to question him about them. "Yeah. She's my Weapons Chief," I felt compelled to add.

"If you care about her, bring me along."

"She doesn't like you."

"Many times, people don't like the things good for them."

"You saying you're good for her?" I'd just gotten her away from Lionside. Like I needed to bring along another option?

"Her longevity. Damn, are you jealous."

I was, that was true. "So, back to your mind-reading abilities. I don't care for them overmuch, and I doubt the rest of the crew wants you reading their minds."

Tanner fiddled with the lasershot. Not in the "going to fire" way, but in the "I'm so embarrassed" way. I took another, longer, look at him. He wasn't my age. He was, maybe, twenty-five, and that was a big maybe. The uniform made him look older. But there were no lines in his face at all, very minor crow's feet around his eyes, and his hands hadn't seen a lot of years, either. The Governor was big on age-spotting, go figure, and he was adamant that hand, knees, and crow's feet gave it all away. No crow's feet usually meant surgical alterations of some kind. But hands and knees were hard to cosmetically alter. And Tanner's hands were young.

"Aviatian's Nest, why did they send a kid out here? For whatever they sent you out for, I mean."

"I'm not a kid. I've been in active duty since I was fifteen."

"So, less than a decade."

He shrugged. "Just under. Yeah, fine, I'm twenty-four. So what?"

"So, you're trying to run the show and you don't have the experience to do it."

"I do, actually. But, there's a lot going on. Makes it harder to handle things efficiently."

"You're stranded here. I don't call that handling things."

"The armada needs to be stopped. And you're the man who's going to do it."

CHAPTER 32

"Why does that seem to be everyone's opinion? I don't actually want to stop the armada, I want to avoid it."

Tanner sighed. "Look, I'll give you some information. As a goodwill gesture."

"Go ahead."

"The Business Bureau doesn't actually have merchandise they want taken off planet. They're planning to hire you to get rid of the armada."

I let this sink in. "So, let me guess... Lionside wanted to have me do the same as, what, a patriotic gesture to a planet I'm not from?"

"No, he was planning to appeal to your survival instinct. Stop the armada or evacuate Herion."

Made sense, in a way. "So, what does Nitin want?"

"Audrey."

"Yeah, but why? I mean, aside from the obvious. Herion Military should be trying to recruit Randolph, the guy who made her, not steal the finished product."

Tanner didn't reply. He pointed. "Go that way. We're heading out of the main city center for tonight."

"You expect me to keep that appointment with the Business Bureau?"

He shrugged. "Why not? You're going to have to stop the armada, might as well get paid for it." I looked at him out of the corner of my eyes. He didn't seem like he was kidding. Tanner looked at me and smiled. "I told you, I've been in active duty since I was fifteen. Why not get paid for what they're going to force you to do?"

"What do you get out of this?"

"A ride off Herion with congenial company."

I knew he was both telling the truth and lying. I was a pro at this, I could spot the signs. Not that the kid wasn't skilled. Just not up to my standards. "Neither's going to happen unless you explain what 'limited telepath' means."

Tanner mumbled something. He was back to fiddling with his gun.

"Not coming through. And stop playing with the laser-shot. I don't want to die from supposedly friendly fire."

"I'm the best friend you have on Herion who didn't arrive with you."

"That's the most backhanded compliment available. No one on this rock is my friend. So if you're merely trying to kill me in a humane way, that would put you at the top of the heap."

"Are you always this unpleasant?"

"Yeah, pretty much. Part of my charm. My crew doesn't seem to mind."

"Uh, right."

"Back to that whole required explanation of your tele-pathic skills or else I kick you out with extreme prejudice thing."

He must have been able to tell I wasn't joking. "Fine. Telepathy's an iffy thing. Sometimes it works, sometimes it doesn't. Every telepath has some quirk that they have to learn to work with and around. I'm pretty powerful, all things considered. But...."

"But?" He sure didn't want to tell me anything. Of course, this made me more determined to get the information.

"But my telepathic quirk is that the longer I'm around someone, the harder it is for me to read them." He sounded like he was admitting to being a eunuch.

I pondered this. There was more to it, I was sure. "So, you take a space flight with someone and you can't read their mind by the end of it?"

"Sort of." Tanner shifted uncomfortably. "It's based against my emotions. The more I like or dislike someone, the faster I lose the ability to read their minds. Someone I don't know at all I can read easily. Someone I've heard of but don't really know or have a strong impression of I can read easily. Once I interact with them, however, it's only a matter of time before I won't be able to read them any more."

"Ever?"

"Well, it's spotty."

"Explain spotty."

He pointed us onto a road that indicated we were heading for Herion farmland. Couldn't wait. "I don't really want to."

"I don't really care. I can dump you out, I can have the others shoot you, I can take you into space and shove you out the airlock. Or you can tell me all about your telepathic shortcomings and maybe I'll let you stay."

"You won't space me. You don't work like that."

"How would you know?"

"You're really enamored with being a scoundrel, and you are, but you're a decent person at your core. Decent people don't space someone just because said someone has a birth defect."

I considered this as we went over some impressive bumps in the road. In between the crew's complaints, loud enough to be heard up front, I wondered why everyone wanted to insist I was Mr. Nobility. I didn't see it that way. Besides, nobility rarely paid well unless you had a crown attached to it. But something else Tanner had said was bothering me more.

"What do you mean, birth defect?"

He snorted. "Like being able to walk into a room and know exactly what everyone in it thought of you, instantly, is some great benefit?"

"I think it would be."

"Yeah, you're not a telepath." He sounded bitter. Angry bitter, the kind of bitter built up over years. He also sounded hopeless.

"You've put the skill to good use."

"Right. Because I've got so many friends and such a wonderful life."

I looked at him again out of the corner of my eyes. I was pretty sure the kid was trying not to cry. "How long have you been on Herion?"

"A few months. A few long, horrible months."

"Yeah, I'm not a fan of this place either. Why were you sent here?"

"I wasn't. I was heading for Runilio. Our ship was the last one to land safely here… until yours did, that is."

"Why is that?"

"I was able to warn the captain. Of course, that earned me lifelong friendship."

"You're sort of obsessed with friendship, or the lack thereof."

"Yeah? Well, you try having no friends for your entire life and then tell me how it feels."

The last thing I wanted to do was let this guy manipulate me into feeling sorry for him. That led to keeping him around. Then getting used to him. Then taking care of him. Then worrying about him, fighting with him, laughing with him, and becoming attached to him. I didn't need that. I already had Randolph. And the Governor. And Slinkie. And now Audrey. Didn't need another one.

"How'd you infiltrate Herion Military?"

He perked up a bit. "That was actually kind of fun. Met a disgruntled officer about my size, learned he was getting transferred to Main Unit but really knew no one, took his identity and clothing, showed up in his place, no one knew the difference. That's the nice thing about telepathy—that first blush meeting can tell you a lot."

"No one recognized you as the person who'd saved that ship and its crew?"

Tanner snorted. "The ship's captain was questioned by Herion Military and he took all the credit for his great 'space instincts'. I wasn't part of his crew, no one questioned me. I left the ship and hid until I found the person I needed."

"So what happened to the guy you were impersonating?"

Tanner pointed to a smaller, even more bumpy road. I could see what looked like a Herion farm complex— square and stolid buildings painted red and white—in the distance. "We're going to stay with him tonight."

CHAPTER 33

I stopped the tankfloater. "Are you kidding me? Or insane? Or both?"

Tanner sighed. "He wanted out. I gave him the out. I'm hoping to get off-planet. In which case, he deserves the opportunity to take the uniform back. And if he doesn't want it back, then he has to know he's keeping his current persona forever."

"And you thought this was a good idea why?"

He rolled his eyes. "I read the guy's mind. He hated military life. He wanted to go back to his farm. So, I gave him the opportunity to do so. I've kept an eye on him, he's done nothing but happily farm under his new name and keep a low profile. He wanted out of Herion Military as badly as I do."

"The deal doesn't look that bad. Herion Military, I mean."

"Yeah? You ever dealt with bullies?"

"Who hasn't?"

"Well, try working with an entire military complex of bullies who are also so focused on following rules to the letter that a non-shiny button means hours worth of haranguing and apologizing. Lionside is a decent enough guy, but even he's a stickler for the tiny details."

I had to be truthful. "That sounds like hell."

"Worse than hell. There are interesting people in hell."

"Not in Herion Military?"

"Only interesting person, aside from myself, is Nitin. If you're into horror, he's your man."

"What's he want, besides Audrey?" I figured now was as good a time as any to ask that unanswered question again.

"I don't know."

"Come on! You had to have gotten something from him."

He shook his head. "You have no idea. I told you, my telepathy's affected by my reactions to someone. The longer I know them, the less I can read them, yeah. But in some cases, it's almost instantaneous."

"How do you mean?"

Tanner heaved a sigh. "Love at first sight, instant loathing. I'll get the first impression, and then that mind's slammed shut to me, because my mind won't let itself in."

"Why not?"

"In the case of loathing, because someone like Nitin is so repulsive to me that I don't want to know. In the case of love...." He shrugged again. "I guess I don't want to know if she hates me, when I disappoint her, things like that."

"You're in love with Slinkie?"

He laughed, long and loud. "Ah, no. *You* are, not me. I was talking about the general 'she' as in, the couple of girls I fell in love with who decided they didn't want to be with a weirdo." The laughter was gone now, replaced with the angry bitterness and a hurt expression he got rid of quickly.

I did not want to feel sorry for this kid. Or like him. No liking. I was being firm with myself. I did not need another stray dog hanging around.

"Okay." I started the tankfloater up again. "So, we're heading to this farming complex because you think this guy is trustworthy?"

"We have more on him than he has on us. He's a deserter. I'm just a kid who was so eager to join Herion Military I traded places with this guy to get in. I've had a great record, they'd let me stay. I might even get a promotion for it. What they'd do to him, though...."

"You'd stay with them?" Decided I might as well head for the farm. We had to be less conspicuous there than in the middle of this deserted road.

"If I have to in order to survive, yeah. I'm a field operative. That means you're given your assignment and then, until it's completed, you're pretty much on your own. No credits, no help, nothing. Just you and your skills, all alone in the big, bad cosmos."

"Your story of woe isn't affecting me."

"No idea if it is or not any more."

"What's that supposed to mean?"

He looked out his side window. "I already know you too well."

"Come on, you've been around me for a couple of hours."

Tanner shrugged but didn't say anything. He was still looking out the window. I got the impression he was embarrassed again.

"So, what's your assignment for Aviatus?"

"I can't, and won't, tell you." He sounded serious.

"You told me about your telepathic powers but won't tell me what you're doing for the Aviatian Government?"

"Right."

"Why not? Seems to me that you gave away a lot more by telling me about your telepathy than you would talking about your mission."

He snorted. "You'd already figured out I was a telepath. There's no big reveal in me telling you what my limitations are—they show up clearly if I'm around someone long enough. Either people believe me when I tell them how my telepathy works or they don't. The ones that don't end up trying to, say, think 'throw me that laser!' while I'm there hoping they have a plan to keep us alive."

"So, really, the longer you're with a group, the less help to the group you are."

"If that's how you want to look at it, yeah." His voice was tight, and I could hear the hurt, though I could tell he was trying to hide it.

Something Saladine had said to me chose this moment to surface in my memory. You don't get to choose your family, but you do get to choose your friends.

"I'm going to regret this, I can tell already, but, if you're not actually trying to double-cross us, then, yeah, we'll take you off Herion with us."

Tanner looked at me and I could tell he was shocked. "You mean it?"

I tested him and thought, "no way in hell, gonna shoot him the moment his back is turned" and then waited. Nothing. He still looked hopeful and surprised, but not worried. Either he was better at lying than I was, and I knew he wasn't, or he couldn't read my mind any more. "Yeah, I mean it."

"You are such a feathered pushover," Slinkie snarled in my ear.

"Slink, meet Tanner Lauris. We're sort of adding him on to the crew."

"Yeah, thanks for that. Why are we going to a farm?"

"Because we're going to hide out here until tomorrow evening," Tanner answered. "You can stop hating on me any time. Oh, and as a suggestion, it's better if you don't panic about the things you want to hide. The way the mind works, the moment you try to hide it, it's the clearest thought in your mind. Just a tip, for whenever you run into another telepath."

"Thanks, you're a prince." Slinkie sounded one moment away from trying to break Tanner's neck.

But he just turned around, looked at her, and winked. "No. *I'm* not."

CHAPTER 34

I would have loved to pursue the many questions this particular exchange brought up, but we were pulling up to the farm complex and I had to pay attention, because we were being attacked. By a pack of the biggest, meanest looking dogs I'd ever seen.

"Can we go now?"

"Just stop the 'floater and wait." Tanner didn't seem concerned. "Jabbob will be out shortly."

Sure enough, a man about Tanner's size came out. He didn't look all that much like Tanner—I wasn't interested in romantic relationships with other males, but I could say Tanner was a lot better looking than this Jabbob without concern. The guy wasn't ugly, but he wasn't anything you'd want to stare at for any length of time. He also had a rather dim expression. It became easier to see why and how Tanner had worked the identity switch.

Jabbob recognized Tanner, or at least the uniform, and he nodded and indicated we should drive all the way onto the property. The dogs were milling around him, but all were smart enough to stay out of the way of the tank-floater.

Tanner got out and I did as well. I didn't want to miss anything they might say to each other, especially in case "play along," "here's the suckers," "spring the trap" or similar were anywhere in the conversation.

But it was all pretty standard. The "my friends and I need to hide for a day, can you help us" sort of thing. Amazingly, Jabbob didn't seem to find this request odd or upsetting. His biggest concern was the sleeping arrangements.

Tanner introduced us. "Leon, this is Jabbob. Jabbob, this is Leon."

I chose not to question the use of this particular abbreviation of my middle name and shook hands with Jabbob. "Nice to meet you. Are you sure we're not intruding?"

"No. Any friend of Tan's is a friend of mine." Jabbob seemed sincere. It was almost unnerving, especially after Tanner's whole sob story of not having a friend in the galaxy.

Jabbob had us move the tankfloater into one of his barns, in between several long-eared donkeys that served as the main farm animal on Herion. The donkeys, like the dogs, didn't seem tied up, and, as everyone got out, they and the dogs all started their animal introductions.

"Get down!" Slinkie wasn't much of a girl for dogs, especially big, overly friendly and inquisitive dogs. "Get off me!" She wasn't much for the donkeys, either, particularly the one that seemed to want to eat her hair.

Jabbob chuckled. "Don't worry, miss. They're just being friendly. Ol' Temper there just likes pretty ladies."

"I'm not into anything with four feet," Slinkie snapped.

Jabbob gave her a look that clearly said he didn't understand. "You don't like animals?"

"Not that way."

"What way?" Jabbob was confused. "They just want some attention, that's all."

Tanner intervened. "Miss Slin's just had a long day, Jabbob. She's actually quite the animal lover. But she had some men treat her roughly, so, we'd like to get her, and the other lady, Drey, inside and resting as soon as possible."

"Of course." Jabbob was instantly contrite. "I'm sorry, miss. Pups, brays, off!" The dogs and the donkeys backed away. At least they listened to him.

He led us into his house. I grabbed Tanner. "Isn't he going to ask why Audrey's shiny?"

Tanner shook his head. "No. Jabbob is a very... simple person. Very face value."

"But he was an officer in Herion Military."

"Every male on this planet does time in Herion Military. He did what he was supposed to, when he was supposed to, and was willing to be brave, so they moved him up the ranks. He was miserable there. I doubt he's going to want to go back. He's happy here with his animals. And, before you ask, yeah, I saw his mind clearly and he's not faking it. There's not a lot of smart there, but he knows what he does and doesn't like. Does like animals, does like helping people, doesn't like being in Herion Military, doesn't like anyone telling him what to do."

"I can relate to his dislikes. You're sure he won't turn us in?"

"Positive." Tanner winced. "Get her under control, will you? She's going to upset Jabbob, and then, if that happens, then I don't know what he'll do."

"Who, Audrey?"

"No, Audrey isn't a problem. Slinkie is, as always, the problem. And, yeah, I'm using variations of everyone's names so he doesn't know, for sure, who everyone is. Think the rest of your crew will catch on?"

"The girls and the Governor, yes. Randolph, not so sure." I was going to ask how he'd know that Slinkie was always a problem when I heard the shouting, and then the screaming.

We looked at each other and ran into the house.

CHAPTER 35

"It's a snake! It's a ton of snakes! Get them off me! Get them off me!" Randolph was at his female opera singer level again.

"They're not dangerous," Jabbob said calmly.

Audrey took the snakes off Randolph, gently and carefully. "Where should I put them?" she asked Jabbob.

"Oh, I suppose in their cage." He took a couple of the snakes and put them into a huge glass terrarium that took up most of his main sitting room. "They don't like it in there much, but since he's so upset by them, may as well."

"Ran's a little jumpy, too," Tanner said quickly, as Audrey put the rest of the snakes away and Randolph shuddered and muttered.

"I'm Mur," the Governor interjected, voice quavering. "Mister Jabbob, would you mind if an old man takes a seat?" The Governor was good, I had to give him that.

"Oh! No, sir. Please, let me help you." Jabbob leapt into action and helped the Governor to the best seat in the house. The old man always scored, every time.

"When, *when* can we leave?" Slinkie snarled.

I saw the hurt look that crossed Jabbob's face and realized Tanner was right—Slinkie was about to cause problems. "Slin, honey, let's go get you a drink of water." I took her arm and moved her out of the room. "Stop it. Behave, act nice, stop whining."

"What's with you? You're suddenly best buds with that telepathic birdbrain, acting like he's Saladine, and then you want me to play with beast master there?"

"I'm not acting like Tanner is Saladine." I tried not to snarl, but didn't manage well.

Slinkie snorted. "Right."

"Whatever. Look, we aren't in the best position in the galaxy, so play nicely with others, especially the man who loves animals. You know, pretend you're a nice girl."

That earned me the vulture-look. "Oh. So, now I'm not a nice girl." Her voice was at that cutting space ice level again.

"You know what I meant."

"You scored tongue and that tells you all you need to know, I guess!"

"This has nothing to do with kissing you."

"Right." She turned and started to stalk out.

I knew this wasn't going to lead to anything good. So, because I didn't want to create a scene, I grabbed her, pulled her back into my arms, and kissed her again. Purely out of safety of the mission motives.

Amazingly enough, again I didn't get the Avian Claw to the jugular. Slinkie struggled, but in that way women will when they really don't want to get away, but want to make you think they might, at least a little bit, so they can claim they weren't actually interested later on. That was her body. Her mouth wasn't struggling at all.

This kiss lasted longer than our first one, and I had no complaints. From what I could tell, Slinkie didn't, either. She stopped struggling pretty quickly and had her arms wrapped around me. I started to feel that our time on Herion wasn't a total waste.

Before this kiss could move us into a horizontal position, I heard someone come in. "Dear Feathered Lord, this isn't the place!"

We pulled apart. "Great, you're a prude. Good to know." I was surrounded by them. Wondered if I should reconsider letting Tanner hang around.

"Hardly. Just, for Avian's sake, pull apart!" He sounded panicked. I decided to listen to him.

Jabbob came in just as Slinkie and I moved away from each other. "I have a nice room for the ladies. The men will have to bunk in the barn, I'm afraid."

"Sounds good," Tanner said cheerfully. Slinkie opened her mouth and Tanner stepped on her foot. "We'll just get settled in, don't want to disturb you any more than we already have."

Jabbob nodded. "Sounds fine, Tan. I'll bring some blankets out to the barn." He wandered off.

Slinkie grabbed Tanner by the back of his neck. "Give me one good reason why I don't rip your jugular out right here."

"Jabbob doesn't deal with public displays of affection well. At all. As in turns into a berserk killer not well." Tanner didn't sound worried. "That's reason one. Reason two is that you need to be nice to our host, or he'll get upset. I point back to reason one for why we don't want to get him upset. Third, much as you might want to pretend otherwise, you and I both know you're not going to kill me, so stop posturing, it's wasting time. Finally, if we want to get off Herion without leaking blood and also survive the pirate armada waiting out there for us, it might be a good idea to work together. Your choice, of course."

Slinkie made a sound of disgust and let go of Tanner's neck. "Fine. I'll play nicely." She stalked out of the kitchen.

There was more to what was going on between them than this exchange, but I figured right now wasn't the time to find out. "Are we actually safe here?"

"Safer than anywhere else on Herion right now, yeah. As long as you and Randolph keep your hands off Slinkie and Audrey, that is. And as long as Slinkie can remember her upbringing."

I pondered this. Jabbob sounded like one of those simpletons who plod along for years and then go crazy and kill a ton of people. I knew how our luck went—one of us was likely to set this guy off. On the other hand, we had a tankfloater, weapons, and a lot more freedom to run away screaming here than we did in any number of Herion prisons.

Clearly Tanner knew a lot more about Slinkie than I did. However, I figured I had enough to deal with right now and chose to let his comments about her upbringing slide.

"Works for me. If I ask him about dinner, will he offer edible food or try to kill me?"

Tanner grinned. "No idea at all."

"Should keep life interesting."

CHAPTER 36

The rest of the evening wasn't all that stressful. Jabbob was a pleasant, if dull, host. We had plenty to eat and drink, no scenes, no issues. Slinkie was subdued, but we were probably better off that way.

Tanner had his chat with Jabbob and, true to expectations, the farmer chose to stay in his dell. We gave reassurances that no one would connect Jabbob with whoever Tanner was pretending to be, and Jabbob seemed to feel the matter was closed.

Jabbob suggested we play cards after dinner. I knew better than to play for money—because I never lost when money was on the table and I didn't think taking Jabbob's credits would be a good idea. But Jabbob's idea of a thrilling game was War. According to my Great-Aunt Clara, this card game had been around on Old Earth for centuries. Even as a child I'd wondered why a game this dull had lasted throughout the ages. Playing it as a kid had been boring enough—I'd moved to games of skill and chance by the time I was seven. I'd moved to playing for cash when I was nine.

Playing War as an adult was the equivalent of being slowly tortured to death by boredom. We all played one game that took an hour to complete—Jabbob won. He was thrilled, and suggested another round. The only one of us who seemed able to feign interest in this was Audrey, probably because she had no choice but to sound cheerful about the idea. Even Tanner looked ready to topple over from boredom—I figured it was worse for him, bored in his own mind and in the minds of anyone he could still read in our group.

We all played another game anyway and I felt parts of my brain die. Jabbob won again and offered another

chance for us to win. I mentioned that he'd already managed to win best two out of three and expressed how my
ego couldn't take another trouncing. He seemed to buy it.

After all this excitement everyone voted for turning in
early, so Slinkie and Audrey went to their bedroom and
the rest of us went out to the barn. With the dogs. And
the donkeys.

Sleeping in a barn hadn't sounded that bad until I
realized I was going to be sleeping in the same barn the
animals were hanging out in. The Governor pulled age
rank and demanded to sleep in the tankfloater. I couldn't
object, for a variety of reasons, not the least of which
being one of the people I could trust would be in our
escape vehicle.

However, due to the way the tankfloater was set up, the
only comfortable sleeping area was the front bench seat.
So, only the Governor was going to get to sleep without
an animal friend.

Randolph had no issues with this, for some reason. If it
had legs, it didn't bother him. So, he settled in and soon
had most of Jabbob's dogs snuggled up to him, one big
doggy pile in the hay. It was hard to pick him out of the
pack, and I could understand why he'd built Audrey—
how many non-robotic women wanted to be with a guy
who might get flea-dipped by mistake?

That left me and Tanner with our own hay piles nearer
to the donkeys. The idea of getting kicked, sat on, or worse,
seemed to occur to both of us. "Think Randolph will mind
if we sleep with him?"

"You feel free. I don't want to risk one of the dogs taking a dislike to me."

Tanner sighed. "Probably wise. I don't know if Jabbob
would feel that was too up close and personal."

"So, how is it that no one in Herion Military has noticed
that you're not a simpleminded potential mass murderer?
No one there knew of this guy at all?"

"Not that I could tell. He did his early duty out in the
country."

"They have a military base out here?"

"No. This is considered close in. I'm talking far out."

I wasn't a back to the land type, so I already felt far out. My mind boggled at the idea that Herion had places that would consider Jabbob's farm to be hustling and too citi-fied. It was also a sharp contrast to Herion's Spaceport City. Where we had to get back to tomorrow, but in the evening. An unpleasant thought occurred.

"What is Jabbob going to expect us to do come daybreak?"

"No idea. The couple of times I've come out here to check on him he's never asked me to do anything. I've gotten to sleep in the guestroom then, too." He sounded disappointed.

"Nice room?"

"Nicer than sleeping in the barn, yeah. You think she'll behave with me not in there?"

"Slinkie? Yeah. It wasn't exactly a fun day and you put her over the top. So, how do you two know each other?"

"We don't."

"Right. That's why you're making all those insinuations and innuendos that have her on edge."

"I don't know her, she doesn't know me. Until today, that is." He shook his head. "Not telling you, okay? So stop wasting your breath."

"Fine." I knew when a well was dry, at least for the time being. "What's the story with the armada? And what little did you get on Nitin?"

"The armada is what you think it is—a pirate armada, following an old plan that worked very well before. I didn't get a big read, just knew they were coming and going to kill us all—the ship I was on was a fast ship, but the captain and crew weren't pirate material."

"Too law-abiding?"

"Too anti-authoritarian. Like you."

"Good to know I'm dead the moment we meet up with the Pirate King or whoever's running the show. What about Nitin, what's his plan?"

"Nitin wants to take over the galaxy."

"Nice plan. What's he doing cooling his heels on Herion?"

Tanner gave me a sharp look. "What do you mean by that?"

I snorted. "C'mon, Tanner. You're an agent. Nitin's not Herion-born. That means he's infiltrated. Maybe like you did, maybe like I'd originally thought you did."

"What makes you say he's not from Herion?"

"Other than you, he's the smallest guy I've seen in a Herion Military uniform. True, Jabbob is about your size, but he's a little guy who's bulked up in the Herion way. You and Nitin both look normal for another planet— muscular without being able to crack Knaboor Greatnuts with your bare hands."

"Yeah, okay." He seemed embarrassed.

I sighed. "Tanner, you didn't pay attention to this?"

"Look, I've survived for years on my own. So I didn't notice that Nitin wasn't a native. So what?"

"Defensiveness is an ugly trait."

"Yeah? You seem comfortable with it."

This was true. "The so what is that the little things you don't pay attention to can kill you." I reminded myself that I wasn't getting attached to the kid, just giving him some pointers so when I dumped him off on Runilio and waved good-bye I wouldn't feel guilty about it.

"Fine, I'll pay more attention to the little things. So, how do you mean he infiltrated like you thought I had?"

"I figured you were planted about a decade ago, with papers showing you to be Herion-born, then you joined the military all natural-like and without anyone being the wiser. Or having to steal someone's identity. Not that it wasn't good initiative."

"Thanks. And, that would make sense, I suppose. I don't know what his story is, though. I got very little before my mind shut him out. But, I can say this—he's the scariest person I've come across in my entire life."

CHAPTER 37

"Scarier than the pirate armada?" Not that it wasn't possible. I just felt a dozen manned pirate ships outweighed one nasty guy.

"I'd rather face them than be alone in a room with Nitin."

I'd been alone in a room with Nitin. Hadn't been a big problem. "You think he let me escape?"

"No. I think he underestimated you in a big way. He'll never do that again."

"Good to know." I thought about this. "Nitin said my reputation preceded me. That means he knew something about me."

"Yeah, you're the best pilot in the galaxy. Considered dangerously reckless and very adverse to following orders. And Janz the Butcher seems to favor you, which is always a good thing."

I wondered if Tanner had figured out who was sleeping in the tankfloater or not, but decided to hope for the best. If the Governor hadn't panicked when he discovered Tanner was a telepath—and the Governor rarely panicked—then the likelihood was slim. The Governor spent most of his conscious time thinking of himself as the pathetic old geezer I had to take care of, not the crime lord of the galaxy. I hoped Tanner didn't know—the Governor wouldn't want the nice young telepath harmed. Janz the Butcher would want him exterminated with extreme prejudice.

One of the donkeys, the one I thought Jabbob had identified as Ol' Temper, came over to us now. Despite polite efforts to move him away, he seemed to feel we were on his spot, to the point where he settled himself down right next to me. No amount of shoving or even hitting made an impact—Ol' Temper was going to sleep in the hay next to me or I was going to move.

"Maybe we can sleep in the back of the tank," Tanner said hopefully.

"Only if you don't want to get any rest at all. Not a good idea to sleep on top of loaded firearms."

"Yeah. I have explosives in there, too."

"Really?"

"Yeah, really." He sounded offended. "I keep telling you, I know what I'm doing."

"Yeah? Well, then why are we sleeping with a donkey?"

Tanner looked at me for a long moment. "You have a point."

"Well, at least the donkey adds warmth." No sooner were these words out of my mouth than another donkey came over and settled down next to Tanner. We weren't snuggled up to each other, but only because we were now both snuggled up to a couple of hooved beasts. "You know, if someone had asked me how I planned to spend tonight, this would never have come to me in about a million years."

"Same here."

"So, can you read animal minds?" I wasn't that interested, but it was something to discuss other than how we were bunking with the burros when where I wanted to bunk was with Slinkie. Plus there was light in the barn, presumably to keep the animals happy. It was going to make sleeping difficult. More difficult than it was already going to be.

"Not really. I could if I worked at it, just no interest. They don't think like humans, so it's harder. I've heard there are a couple of telepaths out there who can and do, but I don't know them."

"Big community? The telepathic one, I mean."

"Not really, no. We don't mingle with each other."

"Why not?"

"Most of us are in some form of espionage. Doesn't pay to hang out. Plus, there's the one-upmanship and the stress of wondering if they can read you better than you can read them. Not fun."

"Too bad. If you guys organized, you could take over the galaxy."

"Supposedly. But it's not as easy as you think. Organizing or taking over."

"The pirates are trying to do just that." I pondered this. "Think they have a telepath with them?"

"No. I think they've got something better."

"Oh? What would that be?"

Tanner looked right at me. "I think they've got someone like you, but who wants to run things, instead of work around and outside of them."

CHAPTER 38

"Interesting concept." Someone like me? Truly, was that possible? I had to admit that, in the huge galaxy, it might be. I didn't like the idea. I was, as I'd heard a lot, one of a kind. I liked it that way.

Tanner shook his head. "Only if it helps you figure out how to survive against him. Because we're going back into space and we'll run right into that armada."

"How can you be so sure?"

He shrugged. "They want your ship. And since you escaped from them the first time, they want you. Probably want you dead, but maybe recruited."

"Oh yeah? What happened to the captain who got you here?"

Tanner was silent for a few moments. "He was murdered on Herion, about two weeks after we landed."

"Huh. Do you know who happened to kill him?"

"Yeah. The Land League. The same people who tried to rig your ship to explode if you left the planet."

"Wonderful. So, I guess they don't want to hire me to get rid of the pirate armada." At least someone didn't want me to get involved.

"No. I figure they want to kill you. It's one of the reasons we're hiding out here."

"You sure Jabbob isn't part of the Land League?"

Tanner closed his eyes and I could tell he was concentrating. "No, he's not. Or if he is, it's not something he's thinking about in relation to any of us."

"I thought you said you couldn't read someone if you knew them well." I wondered if I was going to have to kill this kid after all.

He shook his head. "I can't. But, in the same way that I lose the ability to read someone the more I like or dislike them, if I don't feel much of anything towards them, they remain readable. It's a little harder, but not impossible."

"So, you took this guy's identity and you seem protective of him, but you don't like or loathe him?"

Tanner looked embarrassed. "I guess. I mean… there's not very much there *to* like or dislike. He's as simple as he seems."

"He likes you."

"Yeah. The story of my life. The one person who actually considers himself my friend? We have nothing in common and he affects me so minimally that I can still read his mind. Not that it's ever interesting."

"So, can you still read the rest of my crew?"

"Somewhat. Audrey's a robot, so not really. Robots have minds, but they're a lot more regimented than human minds. Again, it's a specialized telepathic talent that I haven't worked at. Randolph, yeah, I can still read him. Slinkie…." He concentrated and laughed. "Yeah, I can still read her. Boy, is she mad at you for letting me stick around. And the Governor? Not at all."

"You like or hate the Governor already?" That was fast, even if the Governor had his peevish persona going strong.

"No. But he's clearly come across telepaths before. He runs white noise."

"Pardon me?" The kid was starting to sound like Randolph, using terms I'd either never heard of or that meant something totally different than I thought they should. I hated that.

"White noise. It's something a person can do to make themselves unreadable. I guess I should teach it to you, if I'm going to be flying with you." He said it casually, but I could pick up the longing just under the surface.

Great. The kid wanted to stick around, didn't he? He didn't just want a ride to Runilio—he wanted a permanent berth. No way. No way in the deepest volcanic pit of Thurge. Absolutely no.

"So, how do I learn this white noise thing? And how the hell could you tell if it was working anyway?"

"Audrey could probably monitor it."

"Audrey can read my mind?" The horror of this day was never-ending. I tried to concentrate on kissing Slinkie.

"Not so much. She can monitor your brainwaves, and I could tell you if they were flowing right to throw off a telepath."

In my mind, Slinkie was telling me how to throw off a telepath. That wasn't romantic or sexy, it was downright odd. Figured I'd better stop the happy thoughts and focus on Tanner and his telepathic blathering.

"Fine. So, what do I do?"

"Easiest way to start is to come up with a song or a phrase, something that you can repeat in your mind over and over again. You get it so ingrained that your mind runs it as background, or white, noise."

"How long does this take?"

"Usually? A few months at least."

"So, you could potentially teach the whole crew how to do this?"

"Sure. You'd have to have me around for that time, though. Audrey couldn't do it alone, because she's not a telepath." Still trying to sound casual. Still not succeeding.

"You mean, you won't tell her what to look for so that you're not easily expendable."

"Yeah. That's exactly what I mean." The kid's expression had been almost excited and hopeful. Now it went back to that bitter, hurt look. He turned his back on me, which meant his face was in donkey fur. I had to wonder about him a little bit. "I'm going to sleep."

I was not going to let this get to me. He wasn't my problem. He was potentially a huge issue, and also potentially useless, since he couldn't read anyone's mind that mattered, or would lose his connection when we needed it most.

I lay back on the hay and tried to ignore that Ol' Temper was a haystack hog. I thought about Saladine. Randolph had been right—I had been a lot happier when he was flying with us. We got into a lot of trouble together, but somehow, we'd always get each other out of it, too. Sometimes I'd save his hide, sometimes he'd save mine.

Until the time I screwed up and cost him his life.

The kid was better off without us. He had a career and some job he had to do for Aviatus. Besides, it's not like we needed anyone else. We had Audrey as copilot now. Weapons and Security were fine as joined jobs. At least, Slinkie never complained. Much. And no one in their right mind would want to sign on as cabin boy to take care of the Governor's demands.

"By the way," Tanner said, back still to me, voice still stiff. "Randolph's worried that you're brooding about Saladine. No idea of what went on, since he's not thinking of that, but for whatever it's worth, Randolph doesn't think Saladine's death was your fault. He thinks it was his."

Interesting. Not surprising, but still, interesting. A thought occurred. "Check Slinkie, same thing."

He spoke a few moments later. "Wow, yeah. She's worrying about you blaming yourself for this guy's death, too. She blames herself, by the way. Who was he and what happened?"

"He was some guy we ran across and let join up with us. No one wanted to like him. We all did. He was the first person who called me Nap because he realized I like my middle name more than my first name. He nicknamed Slinkie when she wouldn't give us her real name. He was actually interested in Randolph's mechanical babbling. He honestly respected the Governor. Saladine was one of those people who made you a better person because he was around you."

"He sounds great."

"He was. And we screwed up, collectively, I guess, and he died because of it. But I'm the captain, so, when it comes down to it, no matter who else contributed, it's my fault he's dead."

"Would he see it that way?"

"No idea. Probably not." Knowing Saladine, not at all. He might have blamed himself, but not anyone else. I tried not to miss him—didn't do a great job of it. It was easier if I didn't think about him, but apparently I wasn't the only one missing him right now.

"Why are you all thinking about him? I mean, you must have been, because when I mentioned him, you didn't act like it was out of the blue."

I sighed. "We're thinking of him because of you."

"Why? Do I look like him or something?"

A chuckle escaped. "No. Not really at all."

"Then why?"

I sighed again. "Because, despite all my better instincts, common sense, self-preservation, and any other form of sane thinking, they all know that when we leave this planet, you're coming with us, and, should we survive to reach Runilio, let alone anywhere else, you're not getting off-ship."

CHAPTER 39

Tanner was quiet for a few long seconds. "You're going to let me stay on as part of your crew?"

"As moronic as that sounds when you say it aloud, yeah. And the others know it, too. The Governor's probably thinking the same thing, you just can't read him. Hell, Audrey's probably thinking it, too." I was, apparently, the easiest book in the galactic library to read. Saladine had always thought so, at least. It had been something he'd loved to joke about. I hated thinking about him, I really did. Because I still missed him, and I knew the others did, as well.

"Thank you." Tanner was still facing the donkey, but he sounded a little better.

"Yeah, well, see how you feel about it when we're running for our lives or captured. You may not be as happy about the decision." I managed not to add that he might not like it when he was dead because of my error—didn't feel like wallowing in the guilt and, besides, at least until we finished off or escaped from the pirate armada, the kid knew what he was getting into.

We lay there, just us and the animals, and I tried not to worry. Worrying wasn't worth much, according to Great-Aunt Clara. Actions counted, but worry was interest paid on something you'd never collect. Of course, Great-Aunt Clara was usually full of it, so who knew if this was good advice or just senile prattling?

Somehow I managed to fall asleep. I knew this because you have to be asleep to be awakened by something. In this case, by a donkey snout shoved into my face. "Gak!"

"I hate the country." Tanner sounded as repulsed as I was.

"You get the donkey wake up call too?"

"Yeah. I think we're on their breakfast."

I looked around. Yep, there were a lot of donkeys eyeing us in a way that said either they wanted the hay or had turned carnivorous during the night. We scrambled to our feet and the donkeys dived in.

Randolph and his pack were still happily snoozing. I had Tanner wake him up while I got the Governor. I figured, if anyone was going to get bitten, better anyone other than me.

The dogs barking helped me rouse the Governor, and then the four of us followed the dogs to the house. Jabbob was already up, feeding chickens and other fowls. I didn't look too closely. We were invited in for breakfast and found Slinkie and Audrey already up. Slinkie looked like she hadn't slept well and Audrey looked shiny and reflective. There were some advantages to her no-skin look.

"He asked me to make breakfast," Slinkie hissed at me as we came in.

This was bad news. Slinkie couldn't cook. And she didn't like to have it suggested that she should know how to cook, either.

"I'll do it," Tanner said. "He won't mind. I'll tell him I wanted to."

She looked at him suspiciously. "Why are you willing to do that?"

"I'm hungry." He grinned at her. "No other reason. Other than that I know you aren't lying about the cooking thing." He busied himself with getting food made and seemed to ignore the icy glare Slinkie shot at him.

I chose to take advantage of the lull and get washed up. Slinkie was worried about Tanner, I could see that in her eyes. So, whatever he had on her was big. But not life-threatening, because he was still alive and she hadn't asked me to kill him. She hadn't even fought about him coming along all that much.

Breakfast was ample and filling and, I had to admit, delicious. "You're a good cook," I said, mouth full of wheat cake.

"Yeah, I like it, too. I'd wanted to be a chef when I was little." Tanner slid an omelet onto my plate. It was perfect to behold. I checked everyone else's plates—all food perfectly made and arranged.

Audrey even had a plate and was eating. She gave me a gleaming smile. "Randolph ensured I could do all things humans can." Randolph turned bright red and busied himself with his perfectly browned fried potatoes. Slinkie and the Governor both coughed.

I didn't want to take the conversation where I knew it was headed, particularly since Jabbob looked confused. "So, Jabbob, is there anything we can help you with before we leave? By way of thanking you for your hospitality?"

He beamed at me. "Thank you for offering. I knew Tan only associated with nice people." I steeled myself for the rest of his reply. I hadn't discussed this with the crew, or even Tanner. Great-Aunt Clara had drilled certain things into me, and thanking your host and offering to help out was one of those things. It usually paid off.

Jabbob turned back to his breakfast, munching happily.

Everyone else looked at me. I looked back. "Ah, Jabbob? I missed what we could help with. Sorry."

He looked up from his food, surprise printed on his face. "Nothing. It's just polite of you to offer. But my farm's set up for just me, and I don't really like others trying to help—takes more time to teach you how to do things right than to do it myself." Back to his breakfast.

The rest of us went back to ours, too. I had to chalk another one up to Great-Aunt Clara. This now put her at twenty-one helpful things against about three thousand unhelpful ones. At this rate, if I lived to be a million years old, she might even out on my balance sheet.

We finished up, helped Jabbob clean up, then left. None of us wanted to push our luck. Tanner, in particular, seemed ready for us to leave, and since he'd originally suggested we hide out at the farm until evening, I decided not to question. I'd had my fill of simple country living. Jabbob loaded us up with snacks for the road and waved to us as we lumbered off in our tankfloater, dogs and donkeys milling about.

"He's honestly a nice, simple person, isn't he? I didn't think there were any of those in existence."

Tanner let out his breath. "Yeah. Thank you for asking what you could do to help, though."

"Just common courtesy."

"Yeah. But I'd forgotten to warn you."

"Warn me about what?"

Tanner coughed. "Um, if you hadn't offered?"

"Yeah?" I got a bad feeling about what he was going to say.

"Well, let's just say that his dogs would have removed any evidence of our being there and let it go at that."

I pondered this. "The only nice, decent guy we can trust on this whole damned planet is a simpleminded nut job, that about right?"

"Yeah. Welcome to what my life's been like."

"Kid, maybe you're right. You might like it better on the *Sixty-Nine*, pirate armada or no pirate armada."

"It couldn't be worse, believe me." He shifted in his seat. "So, um, what job are you going to give me? Janitorial?"

Apparently the rest of the crew were sitting close enough to hear us, because we all answered as one. "Chief Galley Chef."

Tanner looked shocked, pleased and like he didn't believe us. "Really?"

"Really. Everyone gets to be a chief on the *Sixty-Nine*, isn't that nice and democratic?"

He snorted. "Yeah. A lot of chiefs. One captain."

"Well, yeah. Democracy only goes so far, after all." No farther than my seat, but then, I wasn't considered the best pilot in the galaxy because I asked for input.

"No complaints. That's how it is in a kitchen, too."

Amazing. I'd managed to find the only telepathic spy in the galaxy who really wanted to manifest his destiny with a saucepan. I could find a stray misfit any time, anywhere. It was a skill, really. I tried to congratulate myself on it while we bumped back towards Spaceport City. Didn't succeed all that well.

CHAPTER 40

"So, Alexander, what is our plan? You do *have* a plan, don't you?" The Governor was in full-on quaver mode.

"Somewhat. Look, how is it you're all clustered around the back of my head? The back of this tank isn't set up for this level of chumminess."

"Audrey moved the firearms and explosives so I could sit more comfortably." The Governor got a lot of smug into that sentence. I considered avoiding the huge pothole in the road. Decided against it. The muttering and grumbling from the rear made me happy with my choice.

"How nice. Did Audrey move them to ensure we wouldn't all blow up? Since, you know, they were set up to prevent our dying in a dramatic and yet stupid fashion."

"The explosives are really touchy," Tanner added. He didn't sound like he was kidding. "Try to avoid the potholes. I mean it."

"I have taken all due precautions, Captain. You can drive through the potholes securely. The others grew tired of my repeating your conversation."

I let that one sit for a few moments. "Ah, Audrey? Am I right in thinking that you repeated everything Tanner and I talked about yesterday on our way out to Jabbob's?"

"Yes, Captain. Security Chief Slinkie was worried that you might be bambooz—"

"Shut up, shut up, shut up," Slinkie hissed.

"Don't speak to Audrey that way!" Randolph hissed right back.

"Tell her to shut up!"

"You don't speak to her like that!"

"Children, this scene is making me tired."

"Randolph, you're tiring the Governor. You and Weapons Chief Slinkie should relax. I understand she didn't want me to share that she thinks New Chief Galley Chef Tanner is a jerk."

"Shut up, Audrey! Really! I mean it!"

"He'd probably rather just be called Tanner, Audrey, honey."

"Miss Slinkie, I must remind you that he's been useful. And, adding someone who can cook will be a relief in more ways than one."

"Are you saying that you don't like my cooking?"

"No, the Governor's saying that you can't cook. There's nothing to like, your cooking is that bad. Now, apologize to Audrey."

"Over my cold talons! Let's see you cook something edible."

"I think that's why Nap hired Tanner on. He's more pleasant than you, even if he is a telepath. At least he doesn't insult Audrey."

"Great Feathered Lord, I didn't insult Audrey! Look at her! She's not insulted."

"I cannot actually show displeasure. Randolph didn't program that in. Yet."

"Oh. Ah. Gee. I didn't think of that. I can do that, right away."

"Add in the ability to change my vocal expressions. I know my constant cheerfulness bothers the Captain, and, honestly, it's starting to bother me, too."

"On that, I think we all agree." Slinkie was at a new level in sarcastic tonality. I was almost impressed, only I figured I'd have that tone sent towards me in the near future.

"Yes, I must admit that while Miss Audrey's voice is lovely, a change in its demeanor, from time to time, would be pleasant."

"That's the Governor's way of saying fix her voice or we all smother you in your sleep, Randolph."

"Got it. You're just jealous because Audrey's perfect."

"I'm perfect, too!"

Tanner and I exchanged a glance. "Not too late to change your mind."

He shook his head. "It's still better than Herion Military. Trust me."

"Wow." I leaned my head back a bit. "Slink? You're perfect to me. Everyone else? Could we stop sounding like us for a few minutes so that we can impress the new guy with what a swell time we all have together and how, despite our differences, we function as a well-oiled machine?"

"Oh, Nap, shut up!" Slinkie and Randolph got that one out in unison.

"See? Well-oiled machine."

"Alexander, the plan? What is it?"

I sighed. "We're going to cruise around Spaceport City, see what's going on, try not to get captured or arrested, then Slinkie and I are going to keep our appointments at the Crazy Bear, backed by the entire team. Then we're going to take our money and fly off to be captured by Lucky Pierre and his French Ticklers. I, personally, can't wait."

"Excuse me?" Tanner sounded incredulous. "*Who* are we going to be captured by?" We brought him up to speed on the pirate armada. When we were done, he sat there, doing a good impression of someone trying to decide whether to look stunned or horrified. "Lucky Pierre? And the French Tickler Armada? And we're all supposed to be afraid of them?"

"You were afraid of them when you spotted them in space." I could see Spaceport City in the near distance. At least the roads would be better. And we had a full charge on the tankfloater, thanks to Jabbob. So, we could always fly away and crash into something else if need be.

"Good point." Tanner shook his head. "Who names the people around here?"

"It's like you read my mind." He shot me a hurt look. "You know, kid, you're going to have to get a sense of humor about your telepathy. At least, if you want to survive with us for even the shortest length of time."

"I suppose." He stiffened. "Don't go in via the main road!"

CHAPTER 41

I didn't question or argue. We were at the main intersection leading into Spaceport City and I turned calmly to the right, meaning we were going to take the scenic, perimeter drive. "What's going on?"

"They're looking for us. Well, for you." Tanner concentrated. "Oh, droppings. They think you've kidnapped me, or worse."

"Because you're missing?"

"Yeah. I'm sorry. It didn't occur to me."

"Kid, the little details? When do you actually pay attention to them?"

He looked at his hands. "Sorry."

"It's okay. It happens. We'll work on it. So, is all of Herion Military out after us?"

"Yeah, pretty much. They don't know we're in this vehicle, though."

I pondered while we drove in a very law-abiding manner. "Who are you reading?"

"Grunts I don't really know. The ones at the main entry point."

Pondered some more. "Okay, we can use this to our advantage."

"How?" This was chorused by all the vehicle's occupants, Audrey included. She was coming along fast, I had to give her that. Add in expression and some skin, and she'd be a real woman without a challenge. Couldn't wait. Two of them, nagging, demanding, causing interpersonal issues. Oh, yes, the next flight would be a joy in more ways than one.

"We're going to continue to let Herion Military think we've kidnapped Tanner. What's the name you're using for them, by the way?" He did his mumble thing. "Tanner? We all agree—Herion names are stupid. But since it's not your real name, and is, most likely, Jabbob's real name, just tell us."

He heaved a sigh. "Percy Almondinger."

The silence was amazing. I wondered if this name would cause them all to shut up any other time. Like, if I actually wanted to hear myself think, could I shout out "Percy Almondinger!" and have them all go silent? Possibly worth a shot.

I looked at his uniform. "And, your rank would mean they call you… Captain Almondinger?"

"Or other things." Tanner rubbed his head.

"I think I understand why Jabbob is a simmering psychopath."

"Yeah. Then again, on this planet, who knows?" Tanner looked around. "I really hate it here."

"It's not that much different from Aviatus."

Both Tanner and Slinkie snorted. "Right, Nap," she said, derision clear.

"You left for a reason, Slink."

She didn't answer. I watched Tanner out of the corner of my eyes. He looked like he was trying not to laugh.

"Shut up," Slinkie muttered. I got the impression she was speaking to Tanner.

"Where are we headed?" I asked, as much to change the subject as to have a destination. One that hopefully wouldn't result in our immediate capture.

"No idea. Just not into Herion Military hands. Keep on going on the perimeter. They think we're still inside the city itself."

We drove on for a bit when another thought occurred. "What's the Land League's game?"

"What do you mean? They're crazed maniacs. They don't want anyone going into space because of the armada." Tanner shook his head. "They tried to blow up your ship, remember?"

"Did you mind scan any of them?"

"No. I was too busy saving you from termination. Sorry. I'll focus on the little details more next time."

"Kid, the sarcasm, is it really necessary? I was just asking."

"Why?" Slinkie sounded suspicious.

"Because I'm wondering who the Land League is working for."

"Oh, come on, Nap." Randolph chuckled. "Not everyone is working for some crime syndicate or something. They're just… passionate about their cause."

"Right. What is their cause, exactly? Keeping people on the planet? Sounds great, except that it's causing major economic issues."

"So? Maybe that's part of what they want. A return to the land." Randolph, for some reason, didn't seem anti the people who'd tried to ice the *Sixty-Nine*. Either getting intimate with a Sexbot really did things to his mind, or he hadn't felt the threat was that potent. Him being understanding about some insane cause was normal. Him being easygoing about anything threatening the *Sixty-Nine*, on the other hand, wasn't.

"Randolph, what kind of bombs did the Land League plant on the ship?"

"Oh, nothing much, really, Nap. They would have caused us a couple of issues, but they wouldn't have destroyed the ship. Worst would have been we'd be a little inconvenienced."

"Describe the inconvenience."

"They were focused on the hyper-drives. Might have made it hard to do a system jump, but not much more."

I was driving, so I didn't close my eyes. But I wanted to. I ran the mantra I'd been using for half my life through my head a few more times—he's an idiot but he's also a mechanical genius. "Governor?"

"Yes, Alexander, I agree."

"Me, too," Slinkie said.

"Agree with what?" Tanner sounded confused.

Well, good as time as any for the kid to show what level of support he was going to bring to the game. "Think about it, Tanner. And then tell me what you think it we're agreeing with each other about."

Tanner was quiet for a few minutes while I drove around and tried to figure out how I was going to get Randolph and Audrey back to the *Sixty-Nine*, right now, without getting caught.

"Do you think all the bombs were found?" Tanner asked finally.

"Good one. No. I think there are a lot of things on my ship right now I don't want there. However, there's more."

"You think the Land League is working for something other than their stated goals, got that. But—"

"Tanner, you're a spy. Think like one."

He was quiet for another few minutes. I used the time to run all my alternative scenarios. They all came back to one thing—it was going to take time to fix the ship, and that meant I had to buy us some. I hated those kinds of conclusions.

"You think the Land League's working for the pirate armada, don't you?"

"Finally. Glad to know you're not an idiot, kid. But, not quite. I think the Land League is part of the armada, Lucky Pierre's boys on the ground, so to speak."

"Why?" Randolph didn't sound convinced. Shocker.

"Because the captain who escaped the armada before us is dead, murdered by the Land League. I'm betting he was approached to join the Ticklers, declined, and was killed to ensure a variety of things. The Business Bureau's being hurt by the armada, maybe they'd tried to hire this captain like they're planning to hire me. Another reason to kill him. He wasn't going to join up, and he had the skills to escape, so get rid of him."

"His ship was confiscated." Tanner sounded thoughtful. "By Nitin's side of things, by the way."

"Interesting." I added that to my pile of fun Herion facts. "So, is Nitin in on it with them all, or running his own game?"

"No idea," Tanner said.

"I'd bet money on both, Alexander." Wonderful. The Governor only bet on sure things.

"Perfect. So, we need to get Randolph, Audrey, and some of this serious firepower over and into the *Sixty-Nine*, pronto."

"Why, Nap?" Randolph was still not quite on the same page with the rest of us.

"Because the Captain fears the ship is compromised. I have run diagnostics, Captain. If there are bombs we did not detect, they aren't traditional in nature."

"Maybe not bombs, Audrey. Maybe something broken or missing, something extra added on. They've got stuff on my ship that's going to make us unable to escape the armada the moment we're out of Herion's air space."

"I may not be able to detect those, Captain."

"Randolph will spot anything you miss."

"Thanks, Nap." Randolph sounded quite flattered. "It's nice of you to say so."

"It's also true. Which means we have to sneak the two of you back to the spaceport, because if they know you're there, you're arrested or worse. And we can't leave until the ship's fixed, cleaned and cleared."

"We will need several hours, Captain."

"I'm sure. What we need most, though, is a workable plan to get you both there safely while keeping the rest of us undetected and out of prison."

Everyone was quiet. Thinking, I hoped. Then again, maybe they were napping. Hard to be sure sometimes.

Tanner broke the silence. "I think I have an idea."

CHAPTER 42

"This is the stupidest idea I've ever had to put into action. It's also the most disgusting." Slinkie was managing to snarl while smiling. It was one of the skills she'd mastered well before I'd ever met her.

"So far, it's working." So far, it was. How long it would continue to work, I had no guess.

We'd ended up driving all around the perimeter of Spaceport City to leave the tankfloater with the Governor on the part of the road that backed both the spaceport and, conveniently, the refuse plant. The smell wasn't too bad on the road, because the wind was blowing into the city. Unfortunately, the rest of us were now in the city.

We'd snuck into the city by way of the refuse plant. Nice to come full circle. Tanner had used his telepathic skills and been able to lead us to where the workers kept their hazard uniforms, and we'd all snagged suits that at least sort of fit. The beauty of these things were that we looked like a complement of refuse workers on a mission. The downside was that the hazard uniforms apparently weren't cleaned a lot. We stank. To the outer reaches of space, at least as far as it seemed from the inside.

"It's not my fault that each worker has their own nose plugs." Tanner seemed to have mastered hissing while smiling. They taught interesting skills on Aviatus.

Everyone other than Audrey had their face shields up, because they were smoked and it was hard to see out of them. We each carried a laser pistol and a small case of explosives, inside cases made for some kind of sewage tools. I really didn't want to know, I just hoped I wouldn't have to take off a glove to fire anything that had been inside the cases.

We had our story—checking out the spaceport in case the tank rupture had caused problems there. If we were told another team was already handling that, we'd just say they'd called for backup, which should have the double effect of causing our questioner to race for the hills, since the only time these folks called for backup was when the crap was up to their knees. We could prove this by our borrowed suits.

Since the hazard uniforms were an orange not found in nature on any inhabited planet, including Thurge and Runilio, we weren't exactly inconspicuous. Which was okay, since no one in Spaceport City wanted to get up close and personal with anyone in a refuse hazard uniform, including Herion Military.

We were given wide berth as we made our way purposefully from the refuse plant to the maintenance entrance of the spaceport. I could see the benefits of having Tanner along now—he wouldn't be useful if he knew the people, but we were going past strangers, and he could read them easily. He used their thoughts to find the back entrance, get us the security codes, and avoid anyone who could cause us problems. It was one of the easier infiltrations we'd ever done. I kept on waiting for the hammer to drop on us, but we made it to the *Sixty-Nine*'s bay without issue.

"I don't want these suits on the *Sixty-Nine*."

"Agree with you there, Nap." Randolph sounded like he was trying to talk without breathing in or out.

"How can we get Randolph and Audrey out of their suits? Especially since Audrey is carrying a lot of firepower?" Slinkie was doing better at the not breathing as much thing than Randolph, but not all that well.

Tanner closed his eyes. "There're a lot of people in here. Randolph possibly no big deal, but they'll notice Audrey for sure."

Sometimes I did wonder why I ever expected anyone else to do the real thinking. "Um, gang? Slinkie, Tanner and I are going to create diversions while Randolph and Audrey do the get out of stinky town thing."

"Keep the suits nearby, though," Tanner said quickly. "Just in case."

"In case we want to kill someone via their sense of smell?" Randolph could, occasionally, match Slinkie for sarcastic inflection.

"In case you have to hide or run or something." Tanner sounded as exasperated as I felt. Maybe the kid was going to work out. No. I was not getting attached. Sure, I was letting him come along, but that was pity, not liking or friendship. No friendship. None.

"So, I'm thinking we spread out, and politely explain that we fear a rupture in this part of the spaceport."

"Should work." Tanner looked at Slinkie. "You need to do your best to sound as little like a woman as possible."

"Why is *that*?" Slinkie was snarling again, but this time with no smile attached.

Tanner shook his head. "Have you ever met a Herion female reclamation worker? It's not considered a feminine job at all, and the women who normally go for this line of work make Lionside look like a spindle-beetle. If you don't sound tough and unattractive, you'll blow our cover. They *are* looking for us, let's please remember."

Slinkie looked like she wanted to argue. "Slink, really, the kid's got a point."

She rolled her eyes. "Fine."

"Drop your voice. I mean it." Tanner sounded worried.

Slinkie sighed and gave it a go. "How's this?" Her voice was deeper, but she sounded ridiculous.

"Maybe Slinkie should stay here and guard Randolph, Audrey and the ship."

"I can do it, you little hatchling!"

"Look, I'm not trying to insult you. It's not exactly terrible that you can't sound like a sewage plant worker."

"The kid has another point, Slink. I, for one, would prefer to hear only the melodious sounds of your real voice."

"Oh, stow it, Nap. Fine, Tanner gets to win. I'll stay here and look smelly."

"Should be able to do that fast asleep, considering."

She gave me a dirty look. "Yeah. I can only imagine how long it's going to take to get this stench off us."

"I'll shower with you, I promise. The time will fly by."

Tanner coughed. "We really want to get moving."

"Yeah, not that I couldn't stand here all day and stare at the little part of your face that I can see, Slink."

"Please, just hurry up. I think the insides of my nostrils are burning." Slinkie didn't sound like she was kidding.

"Mine, too," Randolph offered.

"I cannot smell like humans do, Captain, but I can detect odors, and we are frightful. I will do my best to ensure the air filtration system is not contaminated."

"Throw in some air freshener while you're at it, Audrey."

"The strongest you can find," Tanner added.

"I can't wait to hear the Governor complain about this," Slinkie muttered.

"Well, then, I guess the kid and I had better go divert, or we may not get that pleasure."

"True enough," Tanner said urgently. "Herion Military is heading this way."

CHAPTER 43

I thought fast. "Tanner, choose a ship, any ship, far enough away from the *Sixty-Nine* not to contaminate her or have the others easily seen, and rupture sewage there. Use explosives if you can do it without getting covered in yuck yourself. The moment you do it, start shouting about how we have a tank about to blow."

He closed his eyes. "Good. There's enough people around, I should be able to figure out how." He zipped off.

"What are you going to do, Nap?" Slinkie sounded worried and suspicious.

"I'm going to go sound all worried and official."

"What good will that do?" Randolph asked.

"I'll dazzle and confuse the military goons, distracting them until Tanner can cause the refuse explosion. Then I'll just shout a lot and send everyone running."

"We're doomed." Slinkie and Randolph got that one out in unison again. I started to wonder if they'd been practicing.

However, pondering their mutual lack of faith would have to wait. I spotted military uniforms and that meant it was time for the Outland Charm and Bedazzlement to work its legendary magic once again.

I strode over. Happily, none of their faces looked familiar. Hopefully this meant they'd never seen my face, either. "Officers, can we help you?"

They stopped coming towards me and, to a man, backed up a step. I started to appreciate the stench. "Yes," the one who was apparently in charge replied. "We received a report that there was unauthorized activity in the space-port."

"Can't say. I can say that we're worried about more ruptures."

They all took another step back. "Sewage ruptures?" The guy in charge looked about Tanner's age, and the rest with him looked younger. Military on every planet tended to leave the crap jobs to the younger grunts. Which was good for me.

"Of course sewage ruptures! What do I look like, a pilot?"

"Uh, no sir. Sorry, sir. It's just that we have some escaped criminals and we're worried they're going to try to grab a ship and leave planet."

"Well, good luck to them. I'm more worried about being up to my armpits in sewage slush, but that's just me."

Another group step back. They might be young, but they weren't overwhelmingly stupid. Heroics is one thing. Heroics in raw sewage is quite another. "Sir, have you spotted anyone unusual?"

"No. I've been trying to find and stop a rupture. And get people out of here. Which I'd like to suggest you focus on. Even your escaped criminals don't want to be in here if we can't find and stop the rupture in time."

On cue, I heard Tanner's voice. "Run! Run! I can't stop it, it's gonna blow!"

"Take cover!" I flipped my face shield down.

This was enough for the military guys. To a man, they shouted, "Everybody, evacuate!" and then they followed their own advice.

Which was a good thing. Because Tanner knew what he was doing with explosives. I saw sewage sludge fly all around this portion of the spaceport. However, none of it went towards the *Sixty-Nine*. The kid was good.

I did the "usher the panicked masses out of the building" thing, and then went over to the ship that had drawn the metaphorical short straw. Tanner was more than good. The ship wasn't so damaged it couldn't fly, but it was going to be making a lot of planetary jumps or have to be manned by Sexbots only.

"We alone?"

He nodded. "No one left in here other than our crew."

"What about those minds you can't read?" I didn't want to discover Nitin lurking around the corner.

"I can still detect them, I just can't read them."

"So, should Nitin or Lionside be coming, you'd know?"

"Yes. I just can't tell what they're thinking."

"Good enough for me. Let's get back to the *Sixty-Nine*." We trotted back. Slinkie was there, no sign of Audrey or Randolph. "Are they inside?"

"Yes. Their suits are over there." She pointed to a pile of orange a hundred yards away. I was pretty sure I could see stench fumes radiating from them.

"Okay, did you run Randolph through the next part of the plan again?"

"No. Audrey repeated it to me, verbatim. I have to admit, she's good." Slinkie sounded worried. "I think she's too smart for Randolph."

"Why would that matter?" I didn't disagree, of course.

"Because she's self-aware and if she decides she wants to trade up, we're screwed, because she knows everything about us."

Slinkie had a very good point. "Okay. Noted. I'll see what overrides Randolph has or hasn't installed in her programming. But, unless your feminine intuition tells you she's going to dump him in the next day or so, we have more pressing concerns."

"She's coming along fast, Nap." Slinkie had the worry still going strong.

Tanner's eyes were closed. "We're still clear." He opened his eyes. "But what are we going to do to keep people out of here until we're ready to leave the planet?"

"What's standard procedure for this kind of situation, do you know?"

"Yeah, I got that from the mind of one of the spaceport workers. As long as people in hazard suits are around, everyone else stays out. Considering the likelihood that no one else is going to be coming in to land any time soon, and no one feels safe enough to leave, either, if we keep one of us here in a suit, that should do it."

"Slinkie and I both have appointments, and I want you along, Tanner."

"If we don't leave someone here, they'll come back in. It won't take much for someone to figure out that there are people in your ship, and the moment they do, they'll arrest them. Or worse."

I looked at the empty suits. "Not a problem. We'll leave people here."

CHAPTER 44

Slinkie, Tanner and I got out of our hazard suits. Sadly, the smell did linger, but we decided no one was going to notice, since Tanner's explosion had done a lot to expand the stink all over this section. I'd have thought our olfactory senses would have shut down by now, but no such luck.

I had yet to find a lock I couldn't pick, but this was Herion, and no one was allowed to lock their ships up anyway. We chose the damaged ship, because I figured spreading the love was probably not in our best interests. We raided it and used what we could grab—clothes, bedding, utensils—to stuff the suits.

In less time than I'd feared, we had five reasonable facsimiles of sewage workers set up strategically to ensure that anyone looking in would see them. I locked all the entry doors. In the worst case, they'd give Randolph some extra time to go airborne and hopefully they'd keep everyone out, particularly since each door that had any kind of window in it also had an excellent view of one of our sanitation dummies.

"Okay, we're at the best we can do here. Randolph has guns, ammo, explosives, and the ability to get out of the spaceport if he has to. The three of us need to get out of here, clean up, regroup with the Governor, and then hit the Crazy Bear."

"Crazy's the right word, Nap. How are we going to get out of here unseen without those suits?"

"Slink, you wound me." I looked at Tanner. "Can you lead us out of here like you did at the Herion Military complex?"

"I should be able to."

"Okay. So, the plan is that we slip out. If we get caught, we go with Hostage One."

"Hostage One?" Tanner asked.

Slinkie sighed. "Nap likes to give our standard plans names. It's stupid, but, whatever, it makes him happy. Hostage One would execute by grabbing you and threatening to kill you unless we're allowed to get away." She looked at me. "I hate Hostage One."

"We could be more elaborate."

"No. I hate Hostages Two through Twelve, too, so One is just as bad as another, so to speak."

"Why do you hate Hostage One?" Tanner sounded genuinely interested.

"Because Hostage One always ends up with us running for our lives and having to flip into what Nap likes to call Improvisation One."

"What's Improvisation One?"

"Whatever works, whenever it works. I hate that one, too."

"But you're good at it, Slink. The best around, really. At everything."

"Flattery's nice. Not smelling like an accumulation of every dropping in the galaxy would be better."

"Not to worry. I have a plan for that."

"Nap, trust me. If you take us back to the bath house we were at earlier, we're all dead."

"It worked well on Thurge."

"We had to leave Thurge before the ship finished landing. That's how 'well' it worked."

"It worked when we needed it to. Sure, it left some, oh, unpleasant residue, but it worked to get us off Thurge at a time when we needed to get off."

Slinkie looked at Tanner. "I hope you can run really fast. You'll need that skill if you want to stick with us and stay alive."

"Yeah, I'm picking that up."

"Everyone's a bastion of support, as always. Nice to see you fitting in so well with the rest of my crew, Tanner.

Let's get moving, and Tanner, remember—they will smell us before they can see us, so make sure we're not close enough to be smelled."

"I'll do my best." He sounded doubtful.

"If not, Hostage One is always fun." Hey, it was always fun for me.

We slipped out the way we'd come in. We were fine within the spaceport, but as we reached the back Tanner announced there were people massed there. "None of them are military, just spaceport workers."

I thought fast. "Okay. You lead. We're going to run out. I want you shouting in that lovely Herion Military way. Tell them that you barely got us out and that this place has to be locked down for at least a full day. Slinkie, I want you looking like you're barely conscious. We'll hide the guns in your lap. Tanner having guns on him isn't an issue."

"What about the explosives cases?" We still had two left. "I can't hide those in my lap."

"I'll carry one, Tanner can carry the other. No one's going to argue with Herion Military, and if we do it right, they're going to be too busy running away or rejoicing over a day off."

"Can Tanner do it right?"

"I think I can manage. You know, I keep on saying this—I've been in espionage since I was fifteen."

"We point to the whole 'stranded on Herion' thing as why we're worried, kid. Stop taking it personally. Everyone questions my abilities all the time. I note that, for the most part, we're all doing just fine." I knew when it was not the right time to think about Saladine. This was one of those times.

"I have to admit, as your plans go, Evacuation Five usually works well." Slinkie handed her explosives case to Tanner, who flung it over his shoulder. I picked her up—carrying her was always the best part of this plan as far as I was concerned.

Slinkie snuggled into my arms, we piled the extra guns onto her lap, then she shifted and wrapped her arms around my shoulders and put her face into my neck. This turned her so that the guns were hidden enough to fool a casual observer. If the plan went right, we'd be moving too fast for a non-casual observer, and the potential observers would be fleeing.

If it went wrong, well, that's what the guns were for in the first place.

CHAPTER 45

W̲e got into position, and then took off at a trot. Tanner hit the door, slammed it open, and we ran through it before it could swing back.

"People, you were told to evacuate!" He bellowed rather well. "We have a dangerous sewage issue in there, why are you still out here?"

The crowd moved back, the combination of Tanner's shouting and our combined stink.

"I want you people disbursed or, if you don't want to be part of the solution, I'll take you with us to Military HQ to see if you're part of the problem."

This did the trick for the majority. The crowd went down to two, both older men who looked like they'd been working in maintenance positions at the spaceport for a long time. Both were wearing jumpsuits and looked like I expected Randolph to in a few more decades, though they were bigger and less dog-like than Randolph, which on Herion was probably a given.

"Gentlemen, are you enamored of raw sewage?" Tanner sounded both angry and willing to take a personal interest. He was good, point of fact.

The men shook their heads. "No, sir. Just thought we'd be called in."

"Look, I barely got these two out, and the lady's not doing too well. I don't want anyone else in there unless they're in a Herion Sewage hazard suit, you got it?"

They nodded. "You want us to stay and keep people out?" the other man asked.

"Sure, that's a good idea. Just stay out yourselves. Trust me when I say you don't want to volunteer for this extra duty, no matter how tempting it sounds."

The men grinned. "No, sir," the first man said. "If we can help by staying right here, we'll do it."

"Fine. If anyone questions your timecards, just send them to Herion Military HQ for confirmation."

"Yes, sir!" Both men saluted, Tanner jerked his head, and we trotted off.

"Think they'll stick around and not go in?"

"Pretty sure, yeah. They usually volunteer to do the awful jobs because they get time and a half. This way, they'll still get it and not have to do anything."

"Nice. Unless someone questions or they go to HQ."

"I'm hoping you'll have us off this planet by then."

He had a point. "Me too."

"Can Nap put me down now?"

"Not yet." Tanner sounded stressed. "We need to get somewhere we can't be spotted. We left our best disguises back there." He turned suddenly and we went into a narrow, dark alley. "Be very quiet," he said in a low voice.

"Why?" I asked, in a voice even lower.

"Military complement coming."

We moved as far back in the alley as we could. The good part was it was very dark. The bad part was it was a dead end. If they spotted us, we had nowhere to go.

"Can you believe the stink?" I didn't recognize the voice.

"We need to ignore that and keep moving, men. Almondinger's out there somewhere, kidnapped." This voice I recognized. Nice to know Lionside was willing to slay space dragons to find and save one of his own. I didn't want to have to do Hostage One against Lionside. I didn't want to have to do any of our Hostage plans against him. Hostage plans only worked when there wasn't a total hero type against us.

Of course, I did wonder if Lionside was serious, since he knew full well we'd been arrested illegally. Then again, Nitin may have spun some story and bamboozled him. I didn't figure it would be too hard.

The footsteps faded and Tanner relaxed. "They've moved on."

"Thankfully. Great choice, leading us into a dead end. Nap, put me down."

"I'm betting the kid didn't have a choice. But, hey, you want to run after good old Bryant, just to say hi?"

It was dark in this alley, but I could still see the dirty look she shot me as I put her down. "You're really a moron, you know that?"

"Could you two do your romantic bantering later? We need to move, and fast." Tanner trotted out and we followed him.

We did a lot of dodging into side streets and, like we had at Military HQ, a lot of doubling back and crisscrossing. After what seemed like hours we reached the bath house. Found the employees' entrance and then it was time to put the Legendary Outland Charm into action.

It was legendary, but even I had some niggling doubts. I'd never used the LOC smelling like a sewer. Just meant I'd probably have to charm a little harder than normal.

We slipped inside. A quick check indicated the baths were empty.

"What's that smell?" I recognized the voice. It was one of the bath girls. Didn't remember her name, but it never mattered.

She rounded the corner and I grabbed her, hand over her mouth, her back pressed up against my front, the works. "Don't scream. I'm not here to hurt you. Struggle all you want, though, doll."

She relaxed and I let go of her mouth, though I kept my arms around her. She didn't object. "Captain Outland, what are you doing here?" She sounded breathless. I hoped it was due to the thrill of my return as opposed to our combined odor.

"Had some problems right after we left."

"We heard. And smelled. Did you fall into the big tank?"

"No, but it's a long story. One of my crew was attacked, I had to go rescue her, wrongful imprisonment, you know the story."

"Yeah. You want to hide out here, right?"

"Honestly? We want to stop stinking here."

She laughed. "Okay." I let go and she turned around. "On one condition."

"What's that?" I was willing to give myself up for the cause.

She flashed a wicked grin. "We get to have fun with your other crewman." She pointed to Tanner. Who blushed bright red.

"Tanner? You want to fool around with Tanner?" I managed not to sound overly shocked. It wasn't Randolph, after all.

"Yeah. He's cute. And new." She laughed again. "We like new."

"What's wrong with semi-new?"

"Nap!" Slinkie didn't sound happy.

I used the opportunity to look at the girl's nametag. "Just making sure Suzie and her girls are happy."

"You're in luck," Suzie said. "We just locked up. Only the five of us girls who work here and you three." She sniffed. "And, I can really understand why you want to take a bath."

"You have no idea," Slinkie growled.

"I can smell, so good idea. Come on." Suzie grabbed Tanner's hand and dragged him off. Slinkie and I followed.

"Did you tell them we were married or something?"

Slinkie snorted. "Sorry. Guess they weren't all that impressed with 'the Outland'."

I thought back. "No. They were very impressed."

"We just like new," Suzie tossed back over her shoulder. "No insult to you, Captain. You were great. But we've all had you. Time for fresh meat."

Tanner looked at us over his shoulder. He looked panicked. "I don't know if this is a good idea."

"You like girls?" Suzie asked. "Or boys?"

"Girls." Tanner sounded firm on that. Why he wasn't firm on the entire idea, I couldn't fathom.

"Then, don't worry, baby. You'll enjoy your first time."

"I'm not a virgin!" Now he sounded offended. A little too offended.

Suzie laughed again. "Right, baby. Whatever you say."

CHAPTER 46

S uzie called the other girls out, and they were all interested in the kid. He looked like he was going to faint. Clearly, he'd found me just in time. "Tanner, if you can't handle it, just say the word."

"I can handle it." He didn't sound overly convincing, but I let it pass.

"Gee, Nap. You'll be stuck with me. How awful." Slinkie's voice was back to diamond-cutting level.

"Slink, if I thought for one minute that I'd actually get to have you, I'd have a very different attitude."

She snorted. "Right."

Suzie and the rest of the bath girls dragged Tanner off to the women's baths. This left me and Slinkie with the men's. I was tired, I knew she had to be, and we both could still smell ourselves. Why not be a gentleman? "So, you want to go first?"

Slinkie looked at me like she'd never seen me before. "That's it? No innuendo, no suggestions, no come-on attempt. Just, do I want to go first?" She looked hurt. I felt a little bit better.

"We all stink. Maybe the girls are going to wash the kid up first, maybe they're not. But I can't imagine that you'd be interested in kissing me, let alone anything else, smelling the way we both do."

Slinkie reached up and felt my forehead. "Are you okay?" Now she looked worried.

"Thanks. And I feel fine. Kind of confused, but fine."

"I don't think it was a comment on your abilities, Nap. I heard the girls while I was waiting for you—they all seemed impressed. But, like Suzie said, they like fresh meat." She still looked worried. Wow, Slinkie was trying to reassure me about my sexual abilities? Maybe this being a gentleman thing was worth it.

"I'm not confused about that, Slink. And, trust me, if you want me to pursue because this is the exact moment when you want to finally admit the truth, I'm good with it. I just sort of thought us smelling like the bottom of the biggest bird cage in the galaxy was going to be a turn-off for you."

"Well, it's not exactly a turn-on, I'll give you that." We went into the baths. "Um, I guess, yeah, I'll go first then." She was looking at me out of the sides of her eyes. She seemed shy, which was odd, because Slinkie wasn't really the shy type.

"You know, Tanner doesn't really look like most Aviatian males I've ever seen." This wasn't my standard romantic comment, but it had been nagging at me for a while, the girls fawning all over him had brought it to the fore, and Slinkie being shy was making me feel funny.

"He's not a pure-blood." Slinkie said this like it was obvious.

"You sure? I mean, clearly the girls think he's attractive."

"He is attractive. I'm sure he's from Aviatus and I'm also sure he's got some other planet's genetics mixed in, since he's also very cute."

"Really? Tanner is cute?" I guessed so. I mean, cuter than Randolph was a given. "Cuter than me?"

"You're not cute, Nap."

I wasn't? I checked the mirror. Still me, no disfigurement. "What do you mean?" I tried not to sound hurt of offended.

Slinkie laughed. "You're handsome, Nap. Okay? Tanner's cute, you're handsome. Feel better?"

"A little." A lot. "So, um, go ahead and bathe and I'll wait here." I looked around. There were lockers, a couple of mirrors, and a lot of hard, uncomfortable benches. "Better yet, I'll keep watch."

"Thank goodness you're the leader and all. Because one of us being on watch while the other two were naked and unarmed would never have occurred to me."

"Sarcasm is such an ugly trait, Slink. You do make it look good, though."

"Thanks. Nap?"

"Yes?"

"Get out now."

"You sure? I mean, if you want me to scrub your back or anything, I'm willing."

"Now that I know you're okay? Yes. Fly off." Slinkie looked like whatever had been wrong was all better now. Clearly, she liked my pursuing her.

I wandered out and checked the place over. I figured the girls were going to have to do a lot of air freshening once we were gone, but I assumed they'd be up to it.

All doors securely locked. I slid chairs under any outer doors, other than the front. The front door was thick glass and even the stupidest military goon would wonder why a chair was under the handle. The door opened in, so I jammed in a doorstop. Sure, it was actually a bar of expensive soap they sold for customers to take home, but it was the right shape and would do in this particular pinch.

Checked the phones. Did what the Governor had taught me and used an intergalactic law enforcement code to verify the last calls in and out. Nothing out for the past couple of hours, the only incoming calls were from some people cancelling appointments due to the sewage issue. We'd really made our mark on Herion this trip.

Did another night watchman once over of the place. No one hiding out. I slipped into the women's area and checked to make sure no one was hiding in the locker room or other areas. All safe and secure. I heard a lot of noises coming from the bathing area. Did a fast check, just in case. Tanner seemed fine. And like he was about to "have a moment." I decided I didn't need to watch that. Ever.

Wandered through again. Still no intruders. The reading matter was both uninteresting and I couldn't safely turn the lights on outside of the baths themselves. Due to my overriding concern that Slinkie could slip and hurt herself, I went back to the men's baths.

I was a pro at spying on Slinkie while she was bathing. Oh, sure, I couldn't manage it every time, but I got in my share. Since she knew it, I had to figure she liked it. Ergo, she would probably be hurt if I didn't take the opportunity here and now. Women were touchy about odd things, after all.

Therefore, my going in would be the right thing to do. Right? Of course right.

I was prepared to see a lot of things. Slinkie lathering herself up. Slinkie covered in bubbles. Slinkie walking out of the water like a goddess.

What I wasn't prepared for was to see no Slinkie at all. I'd just come from the locker room. The only other in and out option was the staff door. I pulled my laser gun and moved quietly through the bath area. I had to be careful—there was a lot of water spread around the floor. This boded, and not well.

Slipped and slid over to the staff door. From what I remembered, this room connected to the women's baths and the front desk area, so the girls could easily get in and out to give their patrons what they needed.

I opened the door, gun leading the way. Moved into the room. Floor was still wet, but not as bad as by the baths. I heard a sound around the corner, where the towels were stored. I steeled myself for whatever I was going to be facing and moved around the corner. "Freeze!"

"Aviatian's Nest, Nap!" Slinkie was standing there, towel around her head, one around her waist, one clutched to her chest.

"Who's got you?" I looked around. Didn't see anyone, but they were clearly pretty damned tricky to have avoided me all this time.

"No one."

I looked at her expression. Maybe she was trying to give me a sign. "You sure?" I gave her a slow nod.

She stared at me. "I'm back to wondering if you're feeling okay."

She was trying to protect me. Sweet. She was the Chief of Security, after all. But my job was to take care of her, in all ways, if I could swing it. And saving her from the latest goon would have to add on some points in my favor.

I moved fast, grabbed her, and flung her behind me. "It's okay, Slink, I'm here."

"Nap, seriously, I'm worried. Did you get some of that sewage inside you or something?"

I moved forward and checked the rest of the rooms. No one. Ran back to Slinkie. "We need to move, he's probably going for Tanner next."

Slinkie grabbed me before I could head for the women's baths. "Nap, seriously, there's no one here." She was starting to sound close to hysterical. "I forgot to take a towel. I got out and looked for one, got cold, got back in the water. I did that a few times before I saw the staff door. When we were here, the towels were out where patrons could get them easily. That's all."

"Slinkie, does he have a gun on us, is that it?"

"Alexander Napoleon Outland, will you listen to me?" She sounded just like Great-Aunt Clara—angry, annoyed and all business. That tone of voice I was trained to focus on.

"Yes. Did he hurt you?"

"Nap, there is no 'he'!" She grabbed my shoulders and shook me. "Will you snap out of it? There's no one here but us!"

I snapped. Mostly because, in order to shake my shoulders, Slinkie had dropped her towel.

CHAPTER 47

I stared. I'd seen them before, but never quite this up close and personal. Slinkie truly had the greatest rack in, quite possibly, the galaxy. "Jiggly." I wasn't much for coherency at the moment.

"What?" Slinkie looked confused, looked down, let go of my shoulders and attempted to cover up with her hands and arms. "Stop staring at me." This was hissed. Didn't matter. She was actually sexier trying to cover up than when she'd just been standing there.

"Ahhh... can't...." I couldn't. Literally. My eyes refused to look elsewhere. The rest of me was suggesting that the towel around her waist hadn't looked all that secure. I managed to stop myself from grabbing at it, or any part of her, but only because I was too busy staring at her.

"Get undressed." She was back to all business. That was fine. If being in charge was what she wanted, who was I to argue?

I stripped fast, eyes still riveted to her chest. Slinkie waited until I was naked. "Nice necklace. One of your many give it to you?"

"Huh?" I looked down. Right, still had that milky disk thing of Nitin's. I would have explained, but I was naked standing next to Slinkie. Seemed like the wrong time.

She took my hand and led me to the bathing pool. Slinkie sighed. "This is for your own good." Then she shoved me into the water.

By the time I surfaced, she'd tossed soap and a variety of other cleaning materials into the water with me and was picking up my clothes. "I'm going to get these into the speed-clean. Be right back." Maybe she just wanted me not to stink. I could understand that.

Soap and bath oils, shampoo and more shampoo, getting the stench off took a while. In that time, I remained alone. I was starting to prune all over my body when Slinkie finally came back—fully dressed, hair dried, carrying my clothes and a couple of towels. The towels she left on a dry spot at the edge of the bathing pool. My clothes she dumped off in the locker room. "I'll be on watch." Then she stalked out.

Okay, maybe staring at her chest had lost me some points. But I didn't see how she could blame me. She'd dropped the towel, not me.

Dried off, got dressed. Didn't stink, so that was one for the win column. Checked on Tanner. He still seemed amazingly occupied. Found Slinkie sitting in the waiting room. "Aren't you worried someone will spot you out here?"

"Well, I could have waited in the towel room, but then you'd probably have accused me of hiding all of Herion Military in there or something." She wasn't looking at me.

"I wasn't accusing you of hiding anyone! I thought you'd been attacked or taken as a hostage or something. I was trying to protect you."

"Right." She didn't sound angry, she sounded hurt. And she still wasn't looking at me.

"You know, precedent for this trip is that you're a kidnap victim. I count at least twice that I know about."

"Whatever." She examined her fingernails.

Fine. I could spot a brush-off when it wasn't looking me in the eyes. "Oh, I get it. If it had been *Bryant* coming to save you, that would have been great. But it was me. I only have impure motives, I don't care about you at all. I'm not Mister Name of Kings. No problem. I'll leave you and your fantasy alone. In fact, if you hate flying with me so much, why don't you ask Lionside for clemency when you meet up with him tonight? I'm sure he'll find a way to keep you safely out of Herion prison." I spun on my heel and left.

Not that I had much of anywhere to go. Couldn't go outside, couldn't go into the women's baths, since the girls had been pretty clear that exclusivity was their word for the day. I could either stand around in the staff area or go into the men's locker room and sit on a hard bench. Opted for the bench because I figured I could hit a locker if I really needed to blow off some anger.

I sat on the bench that was the furthest away from the main area and stewed. What had I done? I'd tried to take care of her and it had made her mad. I had to figure she just hadn't been as aroused when I'd kissed her as I'd been. Nowhere close, obviously. She just wanted me to want her, but not do anything about it. Fine. There were plenty of other girls in the galaxy. I knew. I'd slept with half of them.

Considered kicking or hitting something, but at the last moment experience waved and reminded me that this led to broken toes and bruised knuckles, and almost never made the rest of me feel any better, either.

I heard a sound behind me but didn't bother to turn around. "Nap?" Slinkie's voice was soft. "I'm sorry."

"No problem. It's been great flying with you. Enjoy life as Missus Lionside."

I heard her sigh. "Nap, you're such an idiot."

"Thanks. Great parting shot, Slink. Sorry, all I can come up with is 'you're gorgeous'. You win."

Her arms slid around my waist and she leaned her head against my back. "At first I thought you were sick and then I thought you were making fun of me and then I thought it was just an elaborate ruse so you could see me naked."

"Because I do that all the time. And I feel fine." Well, I felt like I belonged in the sewage tank, but I wasn't ill.

"Well, yeah, you tease me a lot. And I know you spy on me in the shower. All the time," she added dryly.

"When have I ever run in with a gun drawn as a joke?"

She sighed again. I could feel her chest move against my back. My lower body mentioned that the rest of me should pay attention and not cause her to stop. "Never. Nap, I'm sorry. It's just been a long couple of days."

"Yeah. So, seriously, you're ready to stay here with Lionside, aren't you?"

Another sigh, another happy moment for my lower body. The rest of me didn't feel nearly as good. "No, you moron. He's okay, but I'm not in love with him. I'm flirting with him to get information and to keep us safe. You're the one who insisted I make a date with him, if you'd care to recall."

"Yeah." I *was* an idiot, clearly.

Slinkie hugged me. "I didn't mean to hurt your feelings."

"What makes you think my feelings are hurt? I'm great."

She chuckled, which my lower body said was as acceptable as her sighing. "You're just like a cat right now. Keeping your back turned to me because you're mad." Slinkie hugged me again and snuggled closer. My lower body asked if it would be possible to turn around and move her into my lap.

"Okay. Maybe my feelings are a little hurt."

"I liked kissing you."

"My feelings are crushed beyond belief."

She laughed. "I really liked kissing you."

"I may have to commit suicide, my feelings are so badly shattered."

"Oh, no. Maybe I should kiss you once more."

I used the patented Outland Flip which moved Slinkie from my back into said lap in a matter of moments. "I don't know, what if it doesn't help?"

She gave me the dove-look. "Then I'll just have to kiss you again."

CHAPTER 48

M y Great-Aunt Clara always said the third time was the charm. I don't know what she thought that meant, or why she felt it was good advice to impart, but I had to admit that kissing Slinkie for the third time gave me hope that I might have a real shot with her.

Kiss number three certainly had a lot going for it. Slinkie's arms were around my neck, she was snuggled in my lap, and we were alone. Already a huge improvement over the prior two kisses. The floor was clean, and besides, we could always take another bath, this time together.

I was about to shift us to the floor when I heard a loud banging. I considered ignoring it, but it was persistent. It was also familiar. I'd heard banging like this many times in the past.

We pulled apart. "What's your guess—Herion Military, jealous boyfriends, or the Business Bureau?"

Slinkie stood up. "The way our luck's running on this rock? All three."

"Yeah, that's what I figured. You get Tanner, I'll hold whoever it is off."

"Be careful, I don't think we have a lot of escape options from here."

"Oh, we can always run back to the sewage plant."

Slinkie snorted and ran off towards the women's bath. I pulled my trusty laser gun again and headed for the back door.

There was no window for the back, either in the wall or the door, so I was sort of stuck. I was also glad I'd shoved a chair under, because whoever was outside was trying to force their way in, and the chair was helping. It wasn't

going to last forever, but at least it gave me a little time
to think.

I took the risk and ran to the front. No one at the front
door. I took more risk and went up to it. No one I could
see, at least no one who appeared remotely threatening.
There were people out there, but no one was acting in a
way that would indicate they were part of the military, the
Business Bureau, or even noticed the bath house was here.

Experience had taught me how to spot the official lurk-
ers, those trying too hard to look casual, and there weren't
any of them out front, either. So, whoever it was wanted
to keep a reasonably low profile. That probably let out
Herion Military.

I went back to the rear door. The pounding was still
going on. Slinkie ran up. "Tanner and the girls are getting
dressed. The girls insist they don't have friends or relatives who would be doing the jealous boyfriend act."

"That leaves the Business Bureau."

"No," Tanner said as he skidded to a stop next to us,
boots and pants on, shirt and jacket on but not buttoned,
gun belts over his shoulder. "We have to go, right now!"
He grabbed me and Slinkie, and headed us to the front
door. The girls were already there.

Suzie pulled at the door. "It's stuck!"

"Tanner, button up." I reached down and pulled out
my impromptu doorstop. "It seemed like a good idea at
the time."

Suzie jerked the door open and she and the other girls
fled. "Take the kisses goodbye for granted," she called
over her shoulder.

Tanner grabbed me and Slinkie and dragged us out
after them. "Run. Head for the sewage plant." He took
off, we went after him.

"What about the explosives?"

"I have them, Nap." Slinkie handed me one case. "Tanner has his guns, I have the extras." I took a couple off
her hands.

"What's going on?" I called to Tanner, who was still ahead of us, but not by too much.

No sooner were the words out of my mouth than there was a huge explosion from behind us. We were all knocked to the ground. I scrambled to my feet and pulled Slinkie up. Tanner grabbed the explosives case from her. "Keep running!" He took off again.

We followed, but I kept a hold of Slinkie's hand. I risked a look over my shoulder. "Hey, that was the bath house."

"Yeah, I picked that up. I don't think that was the Business Bureau calling, Nap."

"Nitin or the Land League, then."

"Land League." Tanner ran back to us. "Do you have any way of reaching the Governor?" He pulled us into a side street.

"Why?"

"Herion Military has the sewage plant blocked off due to the rupture. We have to get out of here, now." He sounded close to panicked.

"Tanner, deep breaths. Well, as deep as you can stand." The smell of sewage was still full in the air. "What's going on?"

"The Land League's after us. I think the ship is fine, because they don't know we're the ones who were in the reclamation suits. But—" Before he could finish, we all heard another explosion. This one was farther away, none of us were even rocked. But the blast was impressive. "Oh, my Dear Feathered Lord." Tanner's voice was a horrified whisper.

I thought fast. "They just blew up the Crazy Bear, didn't they?"

He nodded. "There were so many people inside...." It was dark, but not pitch black, and I could see his face had drained of color.

Slinkie let go of my hand and put her arms around Tanner. "It'll be okay," she said softly. He put his arms around her, too, and buried his face in her neck. She stroked his hair and patted his back. I didn't get jealous—he was shaking and I knew he was close to losing it.

I put my hand on his shoulder. "Kid, we have to move. I can reach the Governor while we go. Come on—if they kill us, then they win."

"Give us a second, Nap." Slinkie made eye contact with me. Okay, correct that—the kid had lost it. But he didn't need to know that I knew.

"Okay, easier for me if we're not moving. But, let's get into the shadows." I moved them back so they were in a doorway, pulled out my cell phone, and dialed.

"I heard the explosions," the Governor said by way of hello. "Did we lose anyone?"

"No, but it was a close thing. We need you to come pick us up. Unfortunately, I think you're going to have to be obvious, because we don't have time for you to be stealthy. Herion Military's around the sewage plant, we're a few blocks away from the bath house, the bath house that was just blown up."

"How's the ship?"

"Randolph and Audrey are there, hopefully it's fine."

"On my way. Please be ready to move quickly, Alexander."

"I think we've given Randolph enough time."

"If we haven't, we still need to get spaceborne."

"It's what they want." I tried to say it calmly, but it came out as a snarl.

"Yes, I'm sure I've arrived at the same conclusion as you. However, we may have to do what they want. For now. We won't do what they want for long, Alexander. I promise you."

"Why are you so sure?"

He chuckled. "Because I know you. How is young Tanner doing?"

"Ah…." I took a look. "A little better."

"From experience, telepaths have a very hard time with witnessing mass murder. You and Miss Slinkie will probably have to take care of him, longer than you might think."

"Yeah, I'm picking that up. Speaking of which, are you coming to pick us up, or are we just running for the spaceport and praying we don't get blown up along the way?"

He sighed. "Coming. I'll be there soon. Please be ready." He hung up.

"The Governor's on his way. We'll need to move fast when he gets here."

"Nap, why would they blow up the Crazy Bear when we weren't there yet?" Slinkie was rocking Tanner. I still didn't get the feeling he was going for the cheap and easy feel. I got the feeling the kid was trying not to have hysterics.

"They're anal-retentive and really thorough? No idea, Slink."

Tanner straightened up. "They got the Business Bureau." Tanner's voice shook, but he sounded like he was sort of together. "Lionside's still alive, because he's out looking for me." Tanner jerked. "In fact, he's close. He and his team are coming to investigate the bath house explosion."

"Were we lucky and was Nitin killed in the Crazy Bear?"

"No idea, but I'd bet not." Tanner gulped. "We need to move."

"We move, the Governor loses our position." Our cell phones had Universal Position Monitoring in them. But UPM only worked when the phones were engaged. So the Governor knew where I'd been when I'd called him. If we moved, he'd have to call me to find me—and if Lionside and other Herion Military were nearby, we couldn't afford to have a phone ring at an inopportune moment. And our luck ensured that if the Governor had to call, it would be at a bad time.

We all heard the sounds of footsteps at the same time, and all three of us moved further back into the doorway, guns at the ready.

CHAPTER 49

I put Slinkie and Tanner behind me. I didn't want her getting hurt and the kid was clearly not going to be up to much for a while. Besides, one of them might have an issue with shooting Lionside, and I knew I didn't.

"Men, fan out from here." Lionside was close. "Give me regular reports." I heard footsteps fade away. Then I heard footsteps coming towards us. "I know you're here. I'd appreciate it if you didn't shoot me."

My gun was pointing at him, but I didn't say anything. Someone saying they knew you were around and them actually knowing you were and where you were hiding were not always mutually inclusive.

Lionside looked around, then stepped nearer to us. "Outland, we don't have a lot of time. Please put your gun down. I don't plan on arresting you. Unless one of my men spots us talking, that is. So time is of the essence."

I could tell he could see us, he was only a few feet away. "You talk, maybe I'll holster."

He sighed. "Fine. I know you're not the ones responsible for all the chaos and destruction. I have a man missing, no idea if he's alive or dead, or if he's involved or not. But he's not the real problem."

"The Land League and the pirate armada are the real problem."

"Yes. If it's really a pirate armada. You're the only ones who've seen it. That's why they want you and your crew dead, I'm sure."

"Part of why. Let's take your missing man out of the equation." I made sure I was fully in front of Tanner. He was taller than me, but only by a couple of inches, so all Lionside was likely able to see was the top of the kid's head. Hard to make a confirmed identification based on wet, tousled hair. "Who do you think's behind this?"

"The same man you think is behind it. Nitin." He spat the name out. "My men found a room filled with poisoned gas, and this was in it." He held up a necklace. Slinkie's necklace, the one that had the bug-spotter in it. I hadn't realized she'd lost it, and clearly neither had she. "Is she still alive?"

"So far, all my crew's still alive."

Lionside looked relieved. "So, is that Miss Slinkie behind you?"

"Let's assume I'm not feeling chummy enough to confirm. What's in this for you? Why are you talking to us and not arresting us?"

He glared at me. "I believe I mentioned my name comes from the ruling family of this planet, from centuries ago?"

"Yeah. I'm not big on royalty, titles, or authority, for that matter."

"Yes, I know. However, I am. This is my planet, these are my people. I may only be a major, but the blood of this planet's leaders runs in my veins. And I'll be damned if I'm going to let some insurgent scum murder my people randomly simply because they want power and glory."

I was almost impressed. He meant it. He meant every word. I really hoped I wasn't going to have to implement any Hostage plan—Lionside was pure hero, meaning he'd take the shot to save the innocents. Which meant we'd be running or captured, because I had a hard time shooting most people in cold blood, heroes especially. Someone like Nitin was a different story, but he was as far away from hero as you could get.

"They want to rule the galaxy. And they're part of the pirate armada."

"How do you figure?"

"Control Herion Military, control the solar system. Control Herion Solar, control the entire Gamma Quadrant. Spread out, control all the Quadrants."

"That's why they have to be stopped, here, now."

"Yeah, I'm picking that up."

Lionside was looking at me and the area around me closely. "Ah, Almondinger, you're alive and with Outland. Should I ask why?"

"Who are you talking to?" I hoped the kid would keep his mouth shut.

"Captain Almondinger, who is standing behind you."

"Don't know anybody by that name."

Lionside seemed to be thinking. I was surprised that he could. "You've done your best to block him from me, much more than Miss Slinkie, which means you're more afraid I'll recognize him than her. So, since I know you were taken by Nitin against my orders, and I also know at least part of your crew were kidnapped with intent to kill, someone had to have helped you get out of Military HQ. It wasn't Nitin or any of his men, and I'm only missing one man. So, what planet is the young man who's been calling himself Captain Percy Almondinger actually from?"

"Aviatus." Tanner stepped out from behind me. I was going to have to have a word with the kid about heroics and why they were bad. If he survived this incident. "I'm sorry, Major. I had to help them—they relate to my real mission."

Lionside didn't seem upset. At all. I'd heard steroids made you meaner, not placid, but maybe Herion steroids were different. "I understand. What should I really call you?"

"Almondinger's still fine," I said before Tanner could open his mouth again.

Lionside chuckled. "Fine, Captain Outland, I'll play the game." He looked serious again. "Are you actually going to stop these people, or just run away?"

"I'd love to say run away. It's what I'd prefer to do. However, my impression is that we won't have a chance to run. So, we'll be taking them out. Or dying. Not sure which yet, but if you're a betting man, put the money on dying."

He laughed. "Actually, I'm putting my money on you succeeding, Outland. Otherwise, I'd just kill you where you stand."

I heard the unmistakable sound of guns cocking.

CHAPTER 50

"So, now that your men are around us, what's your real plan?"

Lionside put his hands up slowly. "Not my men."

I resisted the urge to curse. Cursing on the public streets was a big no-no on Herion. I looked around. To see the Governor holding two large, nasty-looking laser shotguns. "I'll take these miscreants off your hands."

I jerked my head. "Get the kid inside."

Slinkie grabbed Tanner and dragged him off to the tankfloater.

"Outland, what help can I give you?" Lionside sounded serious.

"Letting us take off safely would do for a start. Sending Herion Military cruisers with us would be better."

"I wish I could." Lionside's voice was bitter. "But Nitin's convinced Herion Political that we shouldn't get involved."

I was about to pursue this line of thought when the Governor barked. "Move it! Both of you, into the tank!" He backed up and wasn't looking at us.

"I can't believe I'm saying this, Lionside, but come on. You get in the back." I took one of the big guns from the Governor. "I'll drive."

"What a joy that will be. We need to hurry."

I saw what the Governor had spotted—a platoon of Herion Military heading our way. I put my money on them being Nitin's men.

Lionside shocked me to my core and got into the tank without argument, questions, or posturing. I almost hoped he'd try something sneaky so I could go back to hating him.

The Governor ran for the passenger's seat. I covered him, then tossed the guns back to Slinkie, jumped into the driver's seat, and took off. "How much charge left?"

"Enough. I kept it turned off most of the day." The Governor fired out of the window as I floored it and the tank sped off.

"Those could be my men," Lionside said mildly while the Governor sent out a steady stream of laser fire.

"They aren't." The Governor sounded like he was enjoying himself. "Unless your men work for Nitin."

"Shoot to kill, sir," Lionside said cheerfully.

"He's growing on me, Alexander."

"Thanks for that. I'll try not to let it shatter my self-esteem." The positive of being in a tankfloater was that it was hard to get hurt when you were inside of one. The negative was that it was hard to go fast. We were moving at a decent pace for a low-stress situation, but not fast enough for hot pursuit. Even on foot Nitin's goons probably had a good shot at catching us.

"Head down this street." Lionside pointed. "We have no military there at the moment." I turned. He was right, we were reasonably alone.

"I think we need to bring Major Lionside along."

"Governor, it's official. You've gone senile."

"Alexander, they'll kill him if we leave him on Herion."

"What's your point?"

"I might be able to help you, Outland."

"By trying to run my show?"

"No. The captain is the ruler of his ship. I, perhaps more than many others, understand that."

"Who'll take care of things down here?" It was feeble, even I had to admit that, but it was worth a shot.

"Someone else." Lionside sighed. "I'd love to tell you I could get things under control here. But I know better. Nitin's got too much power, and I have too little."

I was amazed he'd admitted that. "You're really from Herion? All the way through?"

"All the way through. We weren't always under martial law, you know." He sounded sad. Great. Another one. I wasn't going to like Lionside, either. It was going to be easier to keep hating him, though, than it had been to hate Tanner. I knew Lionside still had the big lust going for Slinkie.

We had a barricade ahead of us. "Lionside, why did you send us this way?"

He sighed. "It was our best escape option."

"Right. It's our best get captured option, you mean."

"Well, we're in a 'floater, Outland. Surely you can fly it."

We were a lot closer to the barricade. No worries, Lionside was right. I'd just go airborne for a ways and then go back to low profile. I hit the airborne button. Nothing happened. "Ah, Governor? I thought you said you'd kept the charge up."

"I did. I sat there in the heat of the day, broiling with no cooling on, waiting for you to finish playing around." He was back to peevish. Wonderful.

"Tanner! Kid, pull it together. Why aren't we going up in the air like I want to?" We were now very close to the barricade.

"Hit the button."

"I did."

"No, I mean really hit it."

I slammed my fist on the airborne button. The tankfloater coughed and rose up from the ground. We just cleared the barricade, meaning we were, perhaps, five feet off the ground. "Why isn't it going up any higher, Tanner?"

"We're overloaded."

"How can that be? It's a tankfloater! It's supposed to hold more people and weapons than we have."

Lionside cleared his throat. "If Tanner, as you're calling him, took this from where I presume he did, it's one of our, shall we say, less effective engine models."

"What, in plain language, does that mean?" We were over a huge hole. I'd somehow driven us not to the spaceport but to the center of Herion's urban renewal project. The hole looked deep as well as wide.

"It means we need to land very soon or blow up."

CHAPTER 51

I'm wide open to suggestions." I didn't see anywhere to land that wouldn't result in our blowing up anyway.

"Just go down," Lionside said, voice all calm authority. "It'll be fine."

"Really? Because I'm so not fine with dying." I didn't see any options, and the tankfloater was starting to shudder in that way a vehicle will when it wants to let you know it's not happy and is about to share that unhappiness with its occupants.

"This work is being done on the sewer lines." Lionside said that as if it were no big deal.

"Close the windows!" Tanner, Slinkie and I shouted in unison.

"No need to give in to hysterics," Lionside said.

"We finally don't stink," Slinkie snarled. "Close the windows, batten the hatches, do whatever we have to in order to stay that way."

"What Slinkie said. Only more so. Governor, while I'm keeping us from crash-landing, see if you can find something that gives us some sort of extra protection against seepage."

"There." Lionside pointed to some buttons. The Governor pushed them all. A couple he had to hit. One Lionside had to reach through from the back and slam. The last button was engaged as the wheels hit the ground. Or what was passing for ground down here.

There's a way vehicles drive when they're on a substance that's less than firm. The tankfloater was driving this way, only to a huge degree. It's hard for a big, lumbering tank to drive "squishy," but it was doing a stellar job of it.

"Lionside, where are we?"

"Inside the main sewage pipe. It had some corrosion that was causing problems. We went through the hole in the pipe."

"That was some hole."

"It was some corrosion."

"I'll take your word on it. Where are we heading?"

"Main sewage shaft leads to the reclamation plant."

"Wonderful. How do we not go there?"

"We should hit a fork in the tunnel. When we do, take the left side. It leads to the spaceport."

Whatever Lionside and the Governor had engaged was working. I didn't smell anything horrible, and we were still dry inside. This was good, because we weren't dry outside. I had to put on the wipers. What they were wiping was best left unsaid. Forever.

"Nap, how are we going to get out of this thing?" Slinkie sounded beyond repulsed. I could hear Tanner gagging in the background.

"You two need to stop looking out the windows. And, Tanner? Be glad the Governor's got shotgun this time." The old geezer wasn't fazed at all by our little sewage swim. I guess the daily prune diet made him appreciate what he had to work to create.

We sludged to the fork and I managed to turn the tank. We weren't going very fast, but I had to figure no one but the most insane or dedicated would be following us. Our destination couldn't be hard to guess.

"Do we have any radio communication in this thing?"

"I have a universal communicator, Outland. Who are you trying to reach?"

"Well, I'd like to know who's after us, what's going on above-ground, and, should we be able to connect via a private, non-monitored, non-bugged channel, I'd like to talk to my ship."

I heard background noise now. It wasn't too loud, but I could make out voices, mostly because they all seemed to be shouting. Lionside listened while we sludged along.

"No survivors from the nightclub explosion." He sounded angry, but went on. "No casualties at the bath house explosion."

"We could have told you that."

"Do you not want the communications, Outland, or is it simply impossible for you not to make a comment?"

"Oh, *so* sorry. Didn't mean to rain on your official parade, Lionside."

"I hope we find rain when we're out of this crap."

"Hush, Slinkie. Lionside wants to relay information."

"Hilarious. Sewage plant is still secure. Spaceport is still under sewage lockdown."

I didn't cheer. I figured it would come off as conceited. Besides, I knew how the cosmos liked to work. If I mentioned my superior plan, something would come along to ruin it.

"Huh." Lionside sounded confused. "That's odd."

"What's odd?"

"There's a… stampede?"

I let that one sit for a moment. "Stampede? Something's stampeding in Spaceport City?"

"Apparently yes." Lionside listened some more. "Interesting. It's a huge herd of donkeys. Causing quite a ruckus. Can't be shot, which makes it difficult."

"Why can't they be shot?" I thought about Ol' Temper. I was willing to shoot that donkey. Couldn't imagine why anyone else would have a problem with it. Other than, perhaps, Jabbob. Got an uneasy feeling.

"They're our planetary symbol. The hardworking donkey that overcomes obstacles to survive?" Lionside sounded annoyed.

"Oh. I thought Herion's symbol was an ass. That always made more sense to me."

"Donkey. Not ass." Lionside now sounded offended.

"Then why aren't you called Donkeyside or something? If your name used to be held by the rulers?" I resisted asking why he wasn't called Asseside, but it took all my self-control.

"Alexander, can we discuss heraldry and heritage another time?" The Governor sounded as uneasy as I felt. Either he was worried about who was leading the herd or he knew what I was thinking. Possibly both. "Major, is there anyone with the herd?"

"Yes. One man, so far as I can make out. He seems to be quite out of his mind."

The uneasy feeling grew. "Oh? Why? Do they know?"

Lionside listened some more. "Huh. Interesting. From the little I can gather, this citizen seems to feel we're being invaded by, and I quote, evil robots from space."

"Tanner!"

"Yeah, Nap, we're close enough, I can read him." Nap? Tanner was calling me Nap now? What was next? Lionside joining my crew permanently? "It took a while, but I guess Audrey's, ah, skin finally registered."

Yes, indeed. We'd truly left our mark on Herion this visit.

CHAPTER 52

"Lionside, where, exactly, is this stampede taking place?"

"Near the spaceport."

Naturally. "Do we have a secured and non-monitored channel that I can reach my ship through?"

Lionside sighed. "Yes. Give me a moment." I heard some noises and could tell he was fiddling with his communicator. "I need your ship's call numbers. The full set."

"Zyzzx-three-three-six-nine."

Lionside coughed. "No, Outland. The full set. You know what I mean."

"Yeah, I do. I don't want you having it. More to the point, I don't want Herion Military having it."

"Why not? What do you have to hide?"

The Governor cleared his throat. "Major? I happen to know you can reach our ship without any other information than what Alexander's given you. Please don't make me decide to suggest that we merely knock you out, take your device, and dump you out in this pipe. Because, if you push it any more, I will do so. And I know Alexander lives to obey his elders."

Lionside chuckled. "Can't blame a man for trying." He fiddled some more and then handed the communicator to the Governor. "There you go, sir."

The Governor held it between us, so we could both talk and hear. "Ready, Alexander."

"Randolph or Audrey, are you there?"

"Yes, Captain." Audrey still sounded calm and cheerful. Had to figure Randolph hadn't had time to tinker with her yet. Which was probably a bad sign.

"We have myriad situations going on, Audrey. How soon can we safely take flight?"

"We can safely take flight now, Captain. Unfortunately, we cannot safely make a hyper-jump."

Everyone in the tank, Lionside included, cursed. It was impressive. "How long before that can be rectified?"

"No idea, Captain."

"Come again, Audrey?"

"We are missing parts, Captain. Until we have those, I cannot give you an estimate."

"Put Randolph on, please, Audrey."

"Yeah, Nap?"

"Randolph, I'm going to ask this question, and I want you to think about it, very carefully, before you answer."

"Sure, Nap. Go ahead."

"If we're missing parts, and we need said parts in order to get off this miserable rock, why haven't you done the obvious and borrowed them from the many other ships docked around us?"

There was dead silence on the com.

"You know, under the circumstances, I'm with you, Outland."

"You really don't want to stay on Herion right now, do you, Lionside?"

"I'm enamored with living, so, no."

I risked a look at the Governor. He shrugged. "Keep them close, Alexander. Plus, he's got skills I'm sure we'll need."

"Fine. But, Lionside, just so you're clear, you're not giving orders, you're taking orders."

"Understood. What position will you give me? Weapons?"

"Slinkie's got that one."

"Security?"

"Slink again." I didn't hear her offer to give up either position, which was fine with me. "We have pilot, copilot, engineering, and culinary already accounted for as well."

"Culinary?"

"Not-Really-Almondinger back there's an amazing chef. Prepare to eat well. You know, for the possibly one meal we might have before we all die from the dread disease of being in the wrong place at the wrong time."

The com finally sprang back to life. "Ah, Nap?"

"Yes, Randolph. Good of you to rejoin the conversation."

"Heading out to get the parts now, Nap. Sorry."

"Have Audrey do it, speed is of the supreme essence. Like beyond supreme. The faster, the better. Accuracy matters. Do it right, do it perfectly. Or we're all gonna die."

"Oh. So, routine. Good. You had me worried for a minute." I detected no irony or sarcasm in Randolph's tone. I didn't know whether to worry or congratulate myself. I picked worry, it seemed smarter.

"So, Outland. Not to be pushy, but what are you going to have me doing? Janitorial?"

Why did these guys all think I was going to have them scrubbing toilets? Did I really come off as that much of a comet-lover? "No, at least, not unless you really make me angry." Chose not to mention that him putting the moves on Slinkie would indeed make me angry. Now wasn't exactly the time.

"Then what?"

I sighed. "Seems so obvious to me. Communications."

"Oh." Lionside sounded pleased. "Due to my natural abilities to deal with those of all walks and races?"

"No."

"Leadership skills and understanding of the military mind?"

"No."

"Naturally pleasant speaking voice?"

"Ah, no."

"Why then?"

"You possess the universal communicator."

He was silent for a few long moments. "Good application of available resources, Outland. No wonder you've survived and done well all this time."

I had to hand it to him—Lionside knew how to find the trace metals in the asteroid. He could also shovel the excrement with the best of them. I had a sinking feeling he was going to fit in with the rest of my crew exceptionally well.

CHAPTER 53

We sludged along. "Where are we now, Lionside? Best guess."

"We're about fifteen minutes away from the spaceport at this speed."

"You sound awfully sure."

"I had to study the pipe system." He didn't sound enthused about it.

"Why? I mean, you're a major. Why were you given the, ah, crap job?"

"I think I mentioned Nitin's made a lot of friends in Herion Political?"

"Ah. Why's he have it out for you? I mean you, personally?"

Lionside was quiet for a few moments. "I'm not really sure."

"I am, Nap," Tanner offered. He and Slinkie had scooted up and were flanking Lionside. It was like having three big dogs in the back, all trying to get up in front and help drive. I wondered when the fight would start. "I think Nitin identified the person on-planet most likely to get in his way and did his best to discredit and hobble him."

I pondered this. The kid was probably right. Lionside was total hero material, and he had that whole "blood of my forefathers" thing going. If I were trying to take over the galaxy by starting with Herion, I'd want Lionside out of the way, too.

"Which means, if we take you with us, Lionside, we're doing what Nitin wants."

"He wants me dead, Outland. He wants you dead, too."

"So, we'll make it easy and all be together?"

"Think of it as us banded together against a common enemy."

"The enemy of my enemy is my friend?" I'd never really bought into that one. In my experience, the enemy of my enemy still somehow ended up my enemy.

"Politics makes strange bedfellows, Alexander."

"You know, my Great-Aunt Clara used to say that. It sounded as kinky coming from her as it does from you, Governor."

Lionside sighed. "I'm not your enemy, Outland. I'd classify myself as your ally."

I knew when to let something rest. "Fine. I'll go with that until circumstances prove otherwise. Here's the important question—how are we going to get out of the pipe without swimming in sewage? I think I speak for Slinkie and Tanner as well as myself when I say there's no way in the galaxy you're getting us to leave this 'floater until we're surrounded by stuff that doesn't stink. Or ooze."

"I'm not getting out of this thing unless it's gone through the wash first." Slinkie sounded serious.

"What she said. In triplicate." Tanner sounded like he was one syllable away from puking. "There's a hydro-cleanser for the spaceport. Not sure how close to it we'll be, though."

"Very close. Our exit route is right by it." Lionside sounded pleased. "Good thinking, Not-Really-Almondinger." Lionside had a sense of humor. Was this trip never-ending in its horrors?

"Nap, please. Can I tell him my name?"

"He already knows it. At least part of it. Let's pretend you're actually a spy, and not tell him all of it, okay?"

Lionside chuckled. "But Not-Really-Almondinger has a certain ring to it. And nothing wrong with Percy. Old name, quite traditional."

Tanner made a sound that was half-groan and half-growl. "That's not my name. I hate that name."

"Actually, it's the name of the guy causing the donkey stampede. The real Percy Almondinger is a simple person who goes psycho when something upsets him. One of our somethings has upset him."

"Yes, your metallic woman."

"We call her a robot," Slinkie snapped. "Bryant, stop acting stupid."

"But it works so well." Lionside sighed. "Well, truthfully, it works well in Herion Military. I note it doesn't work so well with all of you. Not-Really-Almondinger, I've known you weren't a Herion native since you arrived. It's why I ensured you were in my unit."

"Why would you do that?" Tanner sounded shocked. Me, I was just hoping Slinkie had a gun pointed at Lionside's head.

"Oh, Miss Slinkie, really, the gun, is it necessary?" Lionside was calling her Miss Slinkie, too? Great. I wondered if she liked that. Hoped she didn't.

"Slink, I'm still serious. Marry me."

"Can we talk about that when we're not swimming in a sewer? And, Bryant? Until I don't think you're dangerous, the gun remains."

He chuckled. "Well, no man wants a beautiful woman to think he's harmless."

"Stop flirting with her. That's an order."

"Interesting choice for when to pull rank, Outland. But, perhaps it's understandable. Insecurity affects everyone at some time, I suppose. And, Not-Really-Almondinger, you don't look like a Herion native. I would have guessed either Runilio or Unitatso, but that's because I had no idea Aviatus had spies on Herion."

"We don't. I'm not here to spy on Herion. I'm here for another reason."

"Supposedly he won't tell you what that is, Lionside. However, he wasn't supposed to tell you his name, either."

"He didn't, Outland. You did."

Oh. Right. I guess I had shouted it out. "Whatever. I ask again, how do we get out of this pipe and through the hydro-cleanser? Without being killed by Nitin or his goons?"

"We go up." Lionside pointed ahead. It looked like the pipe was slanting upwards.

"You're kidding, right? How are we going to get up what qualifies as a high-grade hill under these conditions?"

"Tankfloaters are made for conditions like this."

"They're made to drive up a slick metal pipe made slicker by tons and tons of waste? Liquidy waste, I'm forced to add." I heard Tanner gag again. The kid had an amazingly weak stomach. Either that or he still wasn't recovered from the Crazy Bear explosion.

"Trust me, Outland."

"I'm going to hate this, I can tell already."

We started up the pipe. We slid back down. I gunned the engine and we raced forward, at least, raced for the tankfloater and the conditions. We got a little farther up, but not enough, and slid back down.

"Nap, you do not want to know what that's kicking up behind us." Slinkie sounded as grossed out as Tanner now.

"Who wants to get out and push? No one? Then stop complaining."

Lionside sighed. "Engage the traction control." He pointed to a button. I hit it. The tank shuddered. "It's just the suction and tread mechanism shifting to accommodate the current terrain." He tried to sound reassuring.

"Well, that makes me feel all secure." The tank was still shuddering, and now it was fighting me. It took a lot of strength to steer and keep my foot on the accelerator at the same time, since the wheel and the pedal both were resisting. "Is there a reason this tank doesn't want to do this?"

"The terrain is challenging. Do you need me to drive, Outland?"

I would have rather had to swim through the pipe to safety than let Lionside take over any form of driving. "No. I've got it." I had to talk through gritted teeth—the tank was clearly made for someone who'd drunk the special milk.

On the positive side, we were going up and we weren't sliding back. On the negative side, I had no idea how long I could keep this up.

204 » G. J. Koch

The Governor seemed to read my mind. I figured Tanner was too busy being grossed out. "Major Lionside, how much longer do we have inside this pipe? Specifically this incline?"

"Not too much farther. Outland, you'll want to be ready, though."

"Ready for what?"

"For the gate."

"What gate?"

"The gate we're going to have to ram through."

CHAPTER 54

O f course there was going to be a gate and of course we were going to have to break through it. Why would I ever have assumed otherwise?

"How fast will we need to be going?"

"Faster than this. Or we'll have to send an explosive out to blow the gate."

"Lionside, thanks for volunteering for that mission."

"If you just push the accelerator down, Outland, we'll be able to speed up."

"I have this thing to the floor. You're the one who mentioned this was your crap model." Literally and figuratively.

"Hmmm. You're sure you have it to the floor?"

"Yes. Positive." We weren't going any faster and if I pushed any harder there was a possibility I could break through the floorboard.

"If we don't break through the gate our chances of sliding all the way back down increase dramatically." Nice of our resident hero to offer that observation so calmly.

"Nap, try going airborne."

"Tanner, do you remember what happened the last time we did that in this thing?"

"Yeah, but we don't need it in the air long, just long enough."

Well, at least the kid could still think while he was nauseous. "Lionside, your thoughts?" I figured we had about thirty seconds before we hit the gate and, from what I was picking up, bounced all the way back down.

"Worth a shot."

"Wonderful. One of you will have to hit the airborne button. I'm a little busy controlling the metal beast."

"Choice turn of phrase, Outland." Lionside leaned through and slammed his fist onto the button.

The tankfloater did its cough and sort of raise up thing. The positives of being airborne, if you could call it that, were immediate. No more fighting for control, no more squishy feel. No speeding up, however. And there wasn't a lot of room in the pipe. Now I was having to make sure we remained in the air and away from the sides of the pipe. It sounded a lot easier than it was in reality.

"Alexander! Stop drifting to the right!" The Governor didn't sound peevish, just freaked out. Not really an improvement.

"Outland, I don't think it's a good idea to bang the roof against the pipe!"

"Nap, you're hitting the left side again!"

Only Tanner was quiet. I had the feeling he was getting airsick. Either that or he'd looked out the windows, because I heard gagging.

I had to ignore them—the gate was coming up. The wisdom of slamming the front of the tank into what looked like a very sturdy bit of iron escaped me. Going back down was the least of our worries. Stranding in this river of waste was a much more realistic possibility.

The tank wasn't happy, either. It was coughing and complaining. I decided to go for broke. I didn't see a lot of other options.

I shifted and spun the tankfloater—it was slightly less cumbersome in the air—while I took my foot off the accelerator. I was in luck, the pipe was big enough that I could stand the tank up on its end. The tires or traction tread or whatever was active down below hit the gate. I slammed my foot back on acceleration while I turned the flying mechanism off at the same time. This meant only one hand on the wheel, but I could handle it for a short time.

Because of how 'floaters worked, the weight of the tankfloater hit the gate like I'd hoped it would. The metal groaned but didn't budge. For a moment I wondered if we were going to tumble down and land on the roof, which, all things considered, would both define and illustrate the term "very bad." But The Outland Luck held. The metal shrieked, the barrier slammed down, and we rolled over and onward.

It was still sludgy and difficult, but we were back to flat, which was a relief.

"Nicely done, Outland." Lionside sounded like he'd never doubted me. I was impressed—because I knew point-blank he'd doubted. Frankly, so had I.

"Thanks. Now where? Are we going to have to go up again?"

"In a way." Lionside sounded evasive.

"Explain that. In detail."

He sighed. "We're going to come out in the main pool for the spaceport. We'll have to fly out."

I let this one sit while we trundled along. The amount of yuck in the pipe was increasing, meaning our progress was impeded.

Slinkie wasn't as willing to let this one slide. "So, you're saying that you sent us into the sewage pipe in an ancient and touchy vehicle and now, in order to get out of this river of crap, we're going to have to swim up through an entire pool of space-droppings?"

"Succinctly put. And, yes, accurate."

"Nap, can I kill him?"

"Not yet. In case someone has to get out to go for help, wouldn't you rather that be the man who knows all about these pipes?"

"I'm wondering if Bryant's here to help, hinder or harm."

Lionside made a sound of disgust. "Why would I be in here with you if I had ulterior motives? I sent us in here because we're safer in here than on the streets."

I could hear snatches of conversation from his communicator. "Speaking of the streets, what's the latest?"

The Governor handed the communicator back to Lionside, who fiddled with it while we moved along, to use the term loosely. "Rioting in the streets. Donkeys everywhere. Dogs, too, it seems. More problems at the sewage plant."

Tanner groaned. "How soon can we get to the ship?"

"Kid, are you feeling alright?"

"No. Not at all." He sounded faint.

The Governor pulled out his cell phone, hit a couple of buttons, and handed it to Tanner. "Sit down, close your eyes, and listen to this. Miss Slinkie, please assist young Tanner. His distress is more important than you pointing a gun at the Major."

Slinkie grumbled, but I heard her move around. She muttered about being forced to be a mother hen, but she seemed to be taking care of the kid.

"What did you give him?"

"Music, so he can keep himself distracted." I looked at the Governor out of the corner of my eye. He was giving me his usual look for when he thought I'd missed something key. "Our young man's not repulsed by our current surroundings so much as being affected by everything going on right now, Alexander. As I believe I mentioned only a short while ago?"

True, he had. Apparently telepathy had some major downsides apart from not having any friends or scoring the major happy time. As I thought about it, Tanner had scored a lot tonight, and seemed surrounded by people doing their best to be nice to him, so either he whined a lot or I was his personal savior. I gave it even odds for both.

It was getting harder to drive. "Lionside, just out of curiosity, but if we're going to drive into the bottom of a pool of waste, how is it we're not drowning in said waste right now?"

"We have to get through the filter." He said it like it was obvious. I went back to hating him.

"Filter?"

As I asked this, I saw the filter. It had huge metal slats that opened briefly to allow waste through, and then slammed shut. I timed them. They slammed shut faster than we were able to move.

"Okay, gang? It's official. We are gonna die."

CHAPTER 55

I slowed down, not that this made much of a difference. We were barely moving forward now as it was. Everyone was talking but no one was offering much in the way of help.

The gunk was up over the tires. I checked—easily to the middle of the doors. Getting out wasn't going to be an option. I didn't want to get out in the first place, but liquid pressure is a heavy thing, and I doubted anyone other than Lionside would have a chance of getting one of the doors opened even if we were willing to go swimming in Crap Creek.

"I want to talk to Randolph." I didn't shout, I said it quietly. But everyone else stopped speaking.

Lionside fiddled with his communicator and then held it near me. "Randolph?"

"Yeah, Nap. We're still secure, and we're almost done here. Where are you? I expected you a while ago."

"We have a problem." I described where we were and what we were facing.

Randolph was quiet for a few long seconds. "You're sure on the timing? It's consistent, not one longer, one shorter sort of thing?"

"Give me a minute, Outland, I have a timer." Lionside concentrated and the rest of us sat there. I couldn't speak for the others, but I was wondering how I'd ended up in this situation. It wasn't like I'd done anything to deserve it. Well, not to deserve *this*. "Aha," Lionside said finally. "There is a differentiation in the pattern. Three times it opens for ten seconds. The fourth time it opens for twelve seconds. Then back to three for ten, one for twelve, and so on."

"Twelve seconds still isn't enough."

"It might be, Nap." I could tell Randolph was thinking. We were finally back to his area of expertise, which was good. But if he said it couldn't be done, we were royally flushed, literally and figuratively.

"This thing can't move fast. At all. Particularly because of our, ah, terrain."

"Got that, Nap. You need to get up close, as close as you can without being hit by the opening flaps."

"Great plan. Only the gunk gushing out is going to push us back."

"Right. So, you need to start doing this on the start of the cycle. So, as soon as the last twelve second opening closes, you move up. You'll get shoved back, move up again, and so on. You should be close enough by the start of the next twelve second cycle to move through. You don't have to be all the way through—the closing of the flaps should hit the back of the tankfloater right and move you in the rest of the way."

"Should? The huge metal flaps should hit the back right? What if they don't hit the back right?"

"I hope you guys can swim without opening your eyes, noses or mouths."

"Thanks, Randolph. You're a pal."

"We did things like this as drills," Tanner gasped out. "On simulators, but still, it's a doable thing."

"I didn't do things like this."

"Sure you did," Randolph said. "Same thing, simulation, but we did it."

"When and where?"

He chuckled. Then again, he was safely in the *Sixty-Nine*. "Nap, think back to the Academy. The Leisure Center?"

"Not coming through."

"This is just like *Mission Aqueesis: Depth Charge*."

"Mission Aqueesis? Depth Charge? What are you guys talking about?" Slinkie sounded stressed. "I've never heard that either one of you did underwater work."

"We didn't. It's a game. A hard game."

"You were good at it," Randolph said. I wasn't sure if he was being loyal or truthful. Prayed it was truthful.

"Fifteen years ago."

"Outland, if you don't feel up to the challenge, as young Not-Really-Almondinger said, either one of us can do the job."

"Lionside, if you're not careful, I'm going to shove you out an airlock."

"If only you were a man like Nitin, or if we were, in fact, in a spaceship at this point in time, I might be afraid. Look, Outland, stop sitting there. Drive forward or back all the way up, and maybe we'll survive it and get to your ship before it's destroyed."

"Gosh, when you put it that way…." I took a deep breath. "Slinkie, what are the odds?"

"Of our survival? Slim to none, Nap."

"I meant of you sleeping with me if we survive."

"Oh." I looked over my shoulder. She was still taking care of Tanner but looked embarrassed. Possibly because everyone else had turned to look at her, too. "Um, why are you asking me that, Nap?"

I couldn't figure out why she was confused. I asked her that all the time.

"Chief Weapons and Security Officer Slinkie, the Captain tends to do better if he feels he has something positive to live for."

"Audrey, what are you doing on the line?"

"Trying to get you to hurry up, Captain. We will not remain secure for too much longer. I'm monitoring communications and Herion Military has the spaceport surrounded. Some to stop Jabbob, who is creating much havoc, some to stop us from leaving. Also, there are the riots, which I estimate will reach the spaceport in less than fifteen minutes standard galactic time."

"Thanks for the pressure update, Audrey." She lived to do this to me, apparently. I really needed to talk to Randolph about his programming choices. "So, Slink, what's the word?" I made eye contact. I figured it might be the last time I got to look at her.

She stared at me for a long few moments, then she smiled. While giving me the dove-look. "Nap, you da tomcat."

"I love you, Slink. Lionside? Don't touch my girl. Everyone else? Let's get ready for the most disgusting part of the most disgusting ride of our lives."

CHAPTER 56

The great thing about games is that you can start over. Mess up the big mission and "die"? No problem, just hit the "start over" button. The problem with real life was that it didn't like to give do-overs.

The tankfloater didn't like it, but we shoved closer to the filter. Then got shoved back. Drove forward. Shoved back. We were making progress, but it was awful. My Great-Aunt Clara used to call this taking three steps forward and two steps back. She wasn't a fan of this kind of progress. Neither was I.

We were close enough that I had to have the wiper blades going on high to have a prayer of seeing anything. Visibility being what it was, the counting became more and more important.

"Lionside, you're in charge of timing. We're about to start getting so close that we won't be able to see a thing."

"On it, Outland. Our progress, such as it is, has been steady. We move forward for ten seconds, are pushed back for five, hold steady for three, then move forward two more seconds before the next time the flaps open."

"So we have to time it to get right up there on the twelve second opening."

"Right."

"How many more advances do you figure?" He was quiet. I waited. He remained quiet. "Did Lionside just die on us?"

"No, Outland." He sounded testy. "I'm doing the mathematics."

"You will need three more cycles to complete at your current rate, Captain." Audrey was still on the com it seemed. "Unless you did not press on during this conversation."

"No, I pressed on. So, who's going to tell me when to, ha, floor it and hope for a helpful pat on the rear?"

"I am." Now Lionside and Audrey were doing the unison thing. I hated the unison thing. I was going to have to pass a crew rule against it, just as soon as we were out of this particular mess but hopefully before our next undoubtedly worse mess.

"Whatever." I had to figure the Outland Luck was either going to save us or fail. Spent the time inching forward and sliding back counting up the number of times I'd been lucky since the last time I hadn't. Ran into trouble in deciding if getting to kiss Slinkie three times counted as luck, skill, karma, or my proof that hard work and perseverance did still pay off. Couldn't reach a conclusion, chose to risk it and take kissing Slinkie out of the equation.

"Almost there," Lionside said. He sounded tense.

"Please get ready, Captain." Audrey sounded calm and cheerful. I couldn't wait to put Lionside fully in charge of communications.

All pilots can and do talk to their ships. Sometimes out loud, usually telepathically. Not like Tanner's telepathy—maybe it was empathy or natural affinity or something. All I knew was that the *Sixty-Nine* and I had an understanding. She was my ship, I was her pilot, we were a team. One was useless without the other.

You had to tell your ship the truth. Maybe you *only* told your ship the truth, maybe no human ever knew the truth, but your ship had to know. It had to know your strengths and weaknesses, so it could compliment them. Just like you had to make allowances for the capabilities your ship didn't have while taking advantage of what your ship did well.

I communed with the tankfloater. It hadn't been with me long, but after all we'd been through together, it was long enough. It was old, considered inferior, and, when it wasn't in the sewage pipes, it was surrounded by models that were supposedly far more desirable. Just like my crew. Just like, I had to admit, me.

Everyone wanted to count us out. I'd been told I'd never get off Zyzzx. I went all over the galaxy. I'd been told I'd fail the Academy. I passed with honors. I'd been told I'd never amount to anything. I was considered the best pilot in the galaxy. Because I believed. I believed in me and my ship, and, as they joined me, my crew.

Now, anyone with half a brain would tell me that we were going to die. That my vehicle wasn't good enough to do what had to be done. That I wasn't good enough.

But I knew better. Because I believed.

"Ready?" I wasn't asking the crew—I was asking the tank.

It shuddered, and everyone else gasped, though I could tell Lionside was still counting. But I didn't worry. That wasn't a shudder of defeat or collapse. That was the tank's way of saying that, for its kind, it was da tomcat, too.

"Now!" Lionside and Audrey both shouted, his voice booming, hers perky. Didn't matter. I'd had the accelerator to the floor, but I applied more pressure anyway. The tank jerked forward, a tiny bit faster. But the tiny bit was all we needed. I hoped.

We went over some kind of bump that jostled everyone. I kept my foot pressed against the floorboard. My leg felt like it wanted to fall off, but I didn't let up.

"Six seconds until the flaps close," Audrey said. Cheerfully.

"Five," Lionside countered. Not cheerfully.

"Four."

"Three."

"Two."

"Everyone, shut up."

No sooner were those words out of my mouth than the tank shuddered like it had been hit by an entire building. The flaps had closed on us.

CHAPTER 57

T he sound of the metal flap slamming into our metal vehicle was still reverberating. I couldn't hear anything and I doubted anyone other than Audrey could, either. For all I knew, Sexbots couldn't hear through the din of crashing metal. That was fine. I had to figure at least some of them were screaming. Not me. It's hard to scream through gritted teeth.

We were through. At least I didn't smell anything horrible, so I assumed we were through and not cut in half. I slammed my fist onto the floater button. The tank complained but I could feel the difference. We weren't driving through a river of crap. Now we were swimming in a lake of it. And we were at the bottom. I hoped Tanner wasn't looking out the windows.

"Any idea of where we'll surface?" I shouted in the hopes someone would hear me.

"None yet," Lionside shouted back. I assumed he was shouting, anyway. His voice sounded faint and far away.

I decided verbal communications could wait. I took my foot off the accelerator and started maneuvering the tank-floater like we were in a thick cloudbank instead of the yuck stew of nightmare and legend.

It didn't like flying, but apparently that was because it didn't like having to hold itself up in the air. Amazingly enough, the tank seemed happy in the sea of crap. We were certainly moving with more buoyancy than we'd had in the air. I chose not to comment. If it functioned better under these circumstances, who was I to argue?

The biggest issue was going to be rising both to the top and under an opening. Since visibility was nil, couldn't rely on that. Buoyancy and air rising through liquid would help, but the tank was pretty damned heavy. Plus,

if I used *Mission Aqueesis: Depth Charge* as my guide—
and I had nothing else *to* use—there was no guarantee
we'd luck into rising up to the top in the first place.

"Lionside, what part of Lake Disgusting are we aiming
for?" I shouted this out. My ears were still ringing so I
figured his were, too.

"Northeast corner." He shouted, too, I could tell.
Though it still sounded like he was far away, he wasn't
quite as far away as he'd been before. At this rate, we
might have our hearing back in time for Lucky Pierre's
attack.

"Governor, any help with a compass of any kind?" I
shouted this out on the top of my lungs. If Lionside and
I could barely hear, the Governor was probably going to
be worse.

"Stop shrieking, Alexander." He didn't sound far away.
Annoyed, yes, but not far away. He fiddled with some
knobs on the tank. The ringing in my ears went away.
"How's that, everyone?"

"What did you do?" I asked while the others shared
their ears didn't hurt any more. "And why didn't you do
it sooner?"

"I had hours to kill, Alexander. I read the operations
manual. This model is equipped with a sound reduction
capability. I activated it. And I activated it as soon as it was
prudent to do so. It's seating based. I did my seat first."

"Why?"

"Because I'm the senior partner."

"Senior something, I'll give you that. So, during leisure reading time, did you happen to see if this model is
equipped with a compass? Or any other directional device
that will get us out of Lake Disgusting before we run out
of air?"

"We won't run out of air. The oxygen filtration system
is internal to all Hulkinator models."

"Hulkinwhat?"

"Hulkinator. That's what this model's called."

I looked back at Lionside. "Hulkinator? What's wrong with the people on this planet?"

"Nothing. Well, being economically destroyed by an evil conspiracy that could be pirate-related. But otherwise, nothing."

"Forget I asked. So, Governor, how do we find our safe exit point? Because I know the charge won't last forever, and I want to at least be under clean, flowing water when the batteries die."

The Governor fiddled with some more knobs. A screen flickered to life. Green concentric circles radiating out from the center of the screen, intersecting lines creating quadrants, and a flashing green dot. That was it.

"We the green dot?"

"Yes, Alexander." He sounded peeved. Shocker.

"Well, that's nice. I can watch us move. I still have no idea where to move us to, of course. And this is two-dimensional, and we need three. Maybe four. And I don't know what it considers north, since that's not marked. But, otherwise, thanks."

He gave a long-suffering sigh. "The driver has to engage the full function viewer, Alexander."

"I didn't read the manual. Sue me."

Lionside reached through and pushed the button. A three dimensional grid sprang to life and beamed up from the screen to sit cube-like in front of me. Not bad. Not the Ultrasight but not too shabby, either. We were still the green dot, but now the concentric circles were spheres, and there were borders around the entire cube. Uneven borders.

"The borders our exit points?" I pointed to something behind and below our dot that looked familiar. "Is that the fan we just passed through, as an example?"

"Yes." Lionside studied the grid. He pointed to the far, upper right, where there was some oddness in the border. It looked like stairs. "I believe that's the exit point we want."

"Those look like stairs."

"They are indeed stairs."

I tried to resist the question and couldn't. "Why are there stairs leading in and out of Lake Disgusting? Who would willingly walk down into this?"

Lionside sighed. "The fan has to be cleaned out periodically to ensure it's working at maximum. The spaceport sewage hold is drained and then the sanitation workers come down and check things over. We believe in keeping everything running and working at optimum at all times, Outland."

I managed to refrain from comment. Besides, we'd been in the suits. I felt for the poor slobs who worked Herion sewage. I knew their pain. Or at least their smell.

We moved well through the muck. It wasn't like flying a 'floater in the air, and it sure wasn't like flying the *Sixty-Nine*, but it was a lot better than it had been in the pipe and the less said about the improvement over the fan the better. Still wasn't fast, but slow and steady was winning this race so far. Besides, the last thing I wanted to do was hit something while we were immersed in Lake Disgusting, just in case. Damage to the tank would define the term "royally spaced."

As I got the hang of moving us effectively, I noticed something. There were red dots. Moving red dots. Many moving red dots. And they were moving towards our green dot. Rapidly.

CHAPTER 58

"**O**kay, I'm going to ask a question, and I want to stress that I don't want any sarcastic replies or jokes or even questions. I want concrete answers and I want them right away. As of this moment, the only person allowed sarcasm or a witty comeback is me. Got it?"

"Alexander, what are you going on about?"

"Governor, I'm glad you asked. There are a variety of fast-moving red dots heading towards our slow-moving green dot. In *Mission Aqueesis: Depth Charge* they would be some sort of horrible crap-loving monsters that would attack my ship in order to prevent my escape from Lake Disgusting. I'd like to know what the red dots are, and, if they're what I just know in my gut they are, how I kill them."

"What do you know in your gut they are, Outland?"

"Some horrible crap-loving monsters trying to attack our ship and kill us."

"Impressive." Lionside didn't say anything else. I got the impression he was impressed with my ability to guess right.

"Miss Slinkie, you and I need to trade places. Immediately." The Governor's tone was brisk and urgent. Clearly the Governor agreed with my assessment of Lionside's brief reply. That meant things were on the doomed side of bad.

Much shifting, cursing, knocking and whining ensued. I ignored it. The red dots were occupying all my attention. The Governor gave Slinkie some instructions as he was moved to the back and she was moved to the passenger's seat.

The first red dot hit us as Slinkie was sliding into her seat. I managed to grab her and keep her head from slamming into the windshield. That she didn't complain or even mention I'd stopped her by grabbing one of her impressively perfect breasts meant we were in deep, well, crap. I didn't spend a lot of time enjoying the feel—unless we got out of this alive, I wasn't going to get to feel the rest of Slinkie. Positive motivation still worked on me.

Slinkie activated what, on a Zyzzx 'floater would be the mapping compartment, that little box built in to let you store your handheld navigation receiver and anything else you could cram in. On Herion, it was the weapons compartment. I was almost impressed. Until I took a look.

"Slink, are you holding a toy gun?"

"In a way." She sounded guarded. She activated something else and a cube similar to the one I had in front of me came to life in front of her.

"Want to explain what way?"

"You said I couldn't be sarcastic."

The next red dot hit. "And you were obeying me?" I tried not to let the shock show in my voice as the tank shook.

"You sounded upset." Slinkie pointed the toy gun at one of the red dots and pulled the trigger. Nothing happened.

"I am upset. We're in Lake Disgusting instead of on the *Sixty-Nine*. Every time I turn around someone's trying to kill us. And Lionside got to cop a lot of the cheap feels when he helped you into your seat."

"Like you didn't cop a big one?" She sounded headed back to normal. She was also still pointing the toy gun and firing it.

"Is that actually doing anything?" I refused to acknowledge that she'd noted the feel. Besides, other things to pay attention to, like red dots slamming into us and my Weapons Chief apparently playing pretend.

The Governor sighed. "Yes. It's the External Attack Eliminator. Feature only found on Hulkinator models."

"You're in love with our tankfloater. How sweet."

"It was only found on Hulkinators because it didn't work well," Lionside said.

"So, I'm just wasting my time?" Slinkie sounded like she was ready to point the toy gun at Lionside.

"No. If you notice, you're hitting the attacking merderians. However, it takes several hits to destroy one."

"Merderians?"

"Underwater, ah, crap eaters. Yes. Small but very territorial and quite strong for their size. Very useful for the larger wastes that come in from space."

There was a thudding silence, followed quickly by a few thuds as more merderians hit the tank. "So, Lionside... tell me if I'm right. They can and will eat something solid. Say, solid like a tankfloater?"

"Yes. But it takes time."

I counted. "There are fifty of them if there are two. How much time?"

"We might want to hurry up, Outland."

Slinkie started firing her toy gun a lot. I was gratified to see a couple of the red dots disappear. Sadly, many more of them seemed just fine. And attached to our vehicle.

"Captain, must advise you that the riots and other problems will converge on our location within ten minutes."

"Thanks, Audrey. I didn't have quite enough pressure before. Good of you to cover that lack."

"You're most welcome, Captain."

"Audrey? Remind Randolph to add in the comprehension of massive sarcasm to your programming."

"Already in, Captain."

It figured. "Randolph! I don't know how, but you need to figure out how to get rid of Herion's versions of killer remoras."

"See, Nap? I told you this was just like *Mission Aqueesis: Depth Charge*." He sounded so cheerful. I couldn't wait to get out of here so I could kill him.

"Yeah? Well, whatever we need to do to survive this, do it."

"You've got a universal communicator with you?"

"Yeah, it's Lionside's."

"Good. Put it as close to a window as you can, but don't touch it."

Slinkie muttered something about featherbrained nincompoops, but she tossed the communicator onto the dashboard. "It's there."

"Good. Slinkie, are you shooting something at them?"

"Yes. What Nap thinks is a toy gun. I think it's more useless than that."

"It's not. I want you to point it at the communicator and hold the trigger down."

"What? Randolph, is there anything in your head besides feathers?"

"Just do it. Nap, Audrey's going to send a sonic sequence through the communicator. The External Attack Eliminator will enhance the sound."

"Should we plan on being deaf?"

"No. Subsonic, not super. Not to worry, Nap."

"Oh, no, Randolph. I'm not worried at all."

"That's the spirit." I heard him muttering. It sounded technical. I ignored it.

The only positive I had about the merderians was that they weren't stopping us and really didn't seem to be slowing us down. But our green dot was invisible now in the swarm of red dots, and it didn't take genius to guess we had a lot less time than ten minutes to get out or drown in what I, personally, felt would be the worst thing to drown in in the history of the galaxy.

"There's only one risk," Lionside said quietly.

"Only one? Wow, we're moving up in the risk world. What risk is that?"

"If the resonance is right, it could shatter the glass."

I opened my mouth to tell Randolph not to push his proverbial button down, but I was too late. I felt, rather than heard, every part of the tankfloater start to vibrate. I heard, rather than felt, a terrifying thing—a loud, cracking sound.

CHAPTER 59

Sorry about that," the Governor said. "My knuckles have been killing me all day. Finally got a good pop."

"I'll hurt him, Nap, you just keep getting us out of here." Tanner sounded serious. I had to admit it—I liked the kid.

"I'll assist young Not-Really-Almondinger if needed, Outland. Sir, may I request you not pop anything else until we're out of this particular holding facility?"

The Governor and Lionside started arguing about who had the right to tell whom to shut up and not make unpleasant bodily sounds. At least they weren't on bodily odors. I gave it no more than five minutes. Sadly, I gave us less than that.

Per the grid, we were closing in on the steps. Per the dots, we were still had the galaxy's worst merderian infestation, though I could see many more of the dots breaking up and disappearing.

"Nap." Slinkie's voice was a whisper. "I think I smell something."

"Pray it's the Governor manifesting his rights as the ancient oldster to not only pop and lock, but belch and fart."

"I heard that, Alexander."

"Tell me I'm not exaggerating."

"It's not me." The Governor sounded highly offended.

"It's him," Slinkie said, clearly relieved. "That's how he always says it when he's cut one and wants to blame it on a dog we don't have."

The Governor protested and Slinkie was now involved in the conversation. She still had the gun perfectly aimed and her finger never relaxed on the trigger, even though she was turned halfway around in her seat. I felt the urge to survive grow stronger.

"Come on." I said it under my breath. To the tank. It didn't want to die, at least as much as I didn't, I knew. And it was the one getting eaten. "Come on, big guy. You can do it. You can show them all."

The merderians were coming off, but not fast enough. I had to stop acting like we were in a sea of excrement and instead act like we were in space. I was good in space, the best. There were space remoras—usually harmless, unless you flew through a herd of them, and then they could cause you real problems. There were only a few safe ways to get them off, all of which involved landing on a planet. But there were a couple very unsafe ways to get them off while you were moving.

I put the 'floater into a spin, as fast as it could manage. I was impressed—it was faster than I'd figured. We were spinning on our axis like an older but still on-stage ballerina. Sadly, what I'd forgotten was that there was no GravCreate on the 'floater like we had on the *Sixty-Nine*.

Passengers and other things started to flip around, including the universal communicator. Everyone was yelling at me, but I watched the grid—we were losing merderians a lot faster this way and making forward motion at the same time. The tank liked to spin wildly as it flew. Who would've guessed?

Happily, nothing that was flipping was hitting me. Slinkie had herself braced, one foot holding the communicator against the windshield, still shooting the toy gun accurately, knee on the seat, other hand on the roof. I couldn't wait to live through this and get her somewhere even semi-private.

"Hang on."

"Doing my feathered best, Nap," she snapped. I didn't share that I'd been talking to the tank again. I was many things, but moronic wasn't one of them.

The spinning was helping with more than merderian removal. We were truly speeding up, almost like we were drilling through the crap instead of trying to swim in it. "Lionside, what're we going to hit after the stairs?"

"I'm going to hit you, Outland. But other than that, the doors down here are rarely if ever locked. No one in their right mind wants to come down into the space sewage holding facility."

"Right, so I'll assume they're locked, bolted and reinforced, just for us." I knew how our luck worked. "Anything else that's almost never activated?"

"Only the lasers."

Lionside shared this as we crested the crap. The grid shifted and went very rectangular. The windshield wipers were the hardest working in the solar system at least, so I could just see the stairs in front of us as we spun around. I decided to make my life a little less disgusting.

I held the 'floater in the air, just above the shallows of Lake Disgusting and the stairway to heaven, and kept it spinning. Crap and merderians flew off and hit all the available surfaces. Did this until we had no more red dots on us. Then I slowed the spin, engaged the all-terrain mechanism, and set the tank down. We started up the stairs. It was bumpy and uncomfortable, and the whining from my crew was unreal, but we were no longer submerged and being chewed to bits.

"So, Lionside. These lasers, what do they do?"

"They prevent juvenile delinquency."

"Come again?"

"They keep the kids out of here," Tanner supplied. He sounded like he was doing better. Either that, or he was too jumbled up to be sick. Or already had been. I chose not to look behind me. "You know, youthful pranks."

"On Zyzzx, there is no kid you can find youthful or prankster enough to come to the sewage holding facility to steal crap, no matter how much they hate someone or how big the dare is." I knew this for solid fact. If I'd refused to do it, no one on Zyzzx would do it. Not that I'd held any kind of leadership role there. I'd been desperate to prove myself when I was a kid—according to my

Great-Aunt Clara, *the* most desperate in the history of the galaxy—and I'd turned down all the sewage facility dares like I was the king of the universe.

"We're different on Herion," Lionside supplied.

"Yeah, I've picked that up. So, what do these lasers do? Damage-wise, I mean?"

"They aren't deadly. They give an electroshock, mostly. They work as a deterrent, not a final solution."

"Electroshock?" Randolph's voice crackled on the universal communicator. Slinkie had rearranged herself back to sitting normally, put the toy gun away, and had the communicator in hand.

"Yeah, Randolph, that's what Bryant said."

"That's a problem," Randolph shouted. "Nap, you need to engage—"

I didn't get to hear what I needed to engage. Because Randolph was interrupted by the lasers hitting us. Lasers sending out an electromagnetic charge, hitting a big, wet, metal object.

CHAPTER 60

Metal is a conductor. A good conductor. And we didn't have enough crap on the tank to defuse the electromagnetic charges hitting us.

The universal communicator shorted out first. But we weren't fried, so that was a good thing. The shots weren't enough to kill, after all, just enough to hurt. But there were a lot of them, and the tank was big enough to take more than one hit at a time, meaning we could easily get hit with enough juice to turn us into crap encrusted snacks on a stick. "Governor! Randolph wanted us to engage something. What would it be?"

"Hit the anti-attack shield!" The Governor, Tanner, and Lionside all shouted this at the same time.

"Where is it?" Slinkie and I shouted that one out together. I'd worry about the unison thing if we all survived.

Lionside lunged through and slammed one of the many buttons down. The Hulkinator model had more buttons than a petticoat on a virgin, as my Great-Aunt Clara used to say. Still hadn't found anyone who knew what she meant by that, not even the Governor. I took it to mean a lot of buttons. The tank started to hum.

"Ah, Governor? Why is our vehicle singing without words?"

"Hulkinator models use harmonic frequency to disable many forms of attack." The Governor sounded like he'd not only read the manual but memorized it.

"I can't wait to leave this planet."

"I'm beginning to share your sentiments, Outland. Miss Slinkie, if you'll please give me my communicator? I'd like to repair it."

"You can do electronics repair?" I asked as Slinkie tossed the communicator to Lionside and he started fiddling with it.

"No. However, we're trained in how to repair vital equipment in case of enemy attack. Most enemies try to knock out communications first, Outland."

I pondered this as we rolled up the stairs, humming a happy tune. The pirate armada had certainly done that as their first step. But it wasn't what I went for when attacking someone. I tried to knock out their guns, their navigation, their hyper-drives—things that could prevent them hurting me or following me, not the things that would prevent them calling for help.

"The pirates are under some form of military control, whether it's a former military guy who's gone bad or they're functioning like a military unit or even are an existing military unit."

"I'd have to agree, Alexander." The Governor sounded like he was pondering, too. "Major, once we're able, and preferably before we're spaceborne, could you please run a check for any military units that have gone AWOL in the last year or so?"

"Will do, sir."

We hummed along, literally, as we went up the stairs, laser bolts now bouncing harmlessly off our tuneful hull.

"Nap, are you humming along with the 'floater?" Slinkie sounded like she was trying not to laugh.

"Maybe." I was trying to keep the tank's spirits up. We still had doors to bash through, a space wash to find, and untold military, dogs and donkeys to get through.

"You are such a fried egg sometimes." She didn't make this sound pathetic, so I decided not to worry. I'd fry her eggs as soon as we were alone, while serving her the Outland Surprise all the ladies loved the galaxy over. "Nap, what are you smirking about?"

"Ummm… breakfast."

"Right. Think we can break through doors without falling apart? From what I can manage to see, it looks like the merderians did some damage to the front."

"Like everything else on this stop, we'll find out the hard way." We crested the stairs. The doors were about a hundred feet ahead of us. Closed, of course. I took all the other reinforcements possible for granted. "Any way to fire a weapon without having to get out or open a window?"

Lionside relayed that question into the apparently fixed communicator. Randolph replied, voice no longer crackling. "So glad you're all okay." We'd been submerged in more space excrement than the human mind could conceive of, gotten through the Steel Fan of Death, been attacked by killer crap eaters, but Randolph had only been worried about the electromagnetic lasers used to slap naughty Herion kids on the hand. I added this to my list of things to show Randolph wasn't a normal person by any stretch of anyone's imagination. The list was the size of any popular religious text by now, and growing every hour we were on Herion. Audrey was a companion book in her own right.

"For the moment, and I mean that literally. We have to break through doors. Assume they're steel reinforced and loaded with all the special trimmings. We have weapons and explosives with us, but no one's willing to get out of the 'floater, and rolling down the windows isn't an option. Whaddaya got for me?"

"Captain, now that you are no longer submerged, I am able to mark on your location."

"Super, Audrey. What does that do for us?"

"I can see the doors blocking your exit."

"Super duper. So can I. What of it?"

"I can relay a command from the *Sixty-Nine* to the facility in order to override Herion security and open the doors for you."

"Really? You can do that?"

"Randolph only programmed me to lie to people who were not part of our crew, Captain."

"Interesting choice. I'd have figured he'd have wanted you to lie to him all the time."

"I'm fully programmed for romantic relations, Captain, thank you for caring."

"This trip gets more horrifying every time I turn around. So, what's the chance of the door opening before the rioters overrun the spaceport?"

"Very good, Captain. I am able to multitask quite efficiently." The doors swung open. "Proceed with all haste. I cannot spot any more impediments at this time."

"They'll show up shortly, Audrey, don't worry."

We rolled as requested. Didn't have that far to go before we hit the great outsideness that was on the other side of the doors. Tanner and Lionside provided directions and we got to the space wash without any difficulties. No difficulties after myriad difficulties boded, and not well.

The wash was closed but Audrey did her magical override thing and turned it on. Space washes are fast, furious and very strong. Space crud stuck like no one's business. Fortunately, the merderians hadn't breached anything important, because we didn't get wet or soaped. The machinery indicated we were sparkling clean, and we rolled off.

The tank was coughing and complaining, but still moving. I figured water had gotten into the engine, since the merderians had made their most impact on the front. I didn't take us off of the tough terrain tread, however—the chances they'd eaten the tires were too good.

The space wash was at the back of the spaceport, so there weren't any rioters or livestock there. However, we couldn't drive the tankfloater into our docking area for a variety of reasons, the doors being locked down by a security program Audrey couldn't override being the main one.

I drove around to where Tanner, Slinkie and I had exited what seemed so very long ago. Amazingly enough, the two maintenance guys were still there. Sadly, they weren't alone. There was a huge crowd with them. Somehow, these two were keeping the crowd from entering the building, but I didn't figure that was going to last long.

"Ramming speed."

"Outland, I don't want you running over any of my citizens."

"Lionside, the windows are now clean. Take a look at your citizenry before you whine to me about defending them."

"Ah. Even more so. I don't want you harming any animals, particularly our native donkeys."

"Oh, great," Slinkie snarled. "Just what are we supposed to do? Jabbob's got his menagerie blocking our entrance into the docking area."

"He's not alone," Tanner said urgently. "There's a lot of Herion Military coming up, and a mob you wouldn't believe right behind them."

"We're going to do Diversion Ten."

"NO!" Slinkie screamed.

"Not Diversion Ten!" the Governor added at the top of his lungs.

Too late and too bad. I was already rolling Diversion Ten. I liked it. It tended to be so dramatic and impressive. And it always worked.

CHAPTER 61

The essence of a good diversionary tactic is to ensure that the general populace is paying attention to one thing while you're actually doing another. Diversion Ten was showy, loud and frightening. No one paid attention to details while Diversion Ten was running.

I slammed on the airborne button, we raised up, and I put the tank into what I'd learned was its favorite position—spinning. Then I headed us towards the crowd.

True to form, the crowd scattered, dogs and donkeys included. Herion Military included. No one with an ounce of self-preservation wanted to be the thing our tank hit before it stopped moving.

Crowd moved well back, I proceeded to keep them far away from the door. Sure, our crew and supplies were again flipping around, but no one and nothing was coming near us. I'd even moved the two maintenance guys off.

Hovered around the door we had to go through and now instead of spinning wildly, I righted us, still floating, and did a spin that kept us level but still dangerous.

"Nap, I'm going to be sick!"

"Slinkie, even puking you'll be gorgeous. Please get ready to jump out." I heard the Governor giving orders to Lionside and Tanner to grab what they could carry in the weapons and explosives department. "Make sure you take anything worthwhile, Slink."

"As long as I can put them in a barf bag."

"Outland, is there a method to your madness or did you just not get enough love as a child?"

"Lionside, you haven't been a part of my crew long enough to get away with that level of comfortable insult.

Tanner, need you ready to go to open the door into the spaceport, in case someone changed the codes."

"Can I barf after I open the door?"

"Only as a diversionary tactic. Governor, does the Hulkinator have any projectile weapons on it?"

"I shudder to say yes, Alexander. Please ensure you have the rear aimed."

"It fires from the back?" Why was I surprised?

"Yes, Outland, it does. What are you insinuating?" Lionside pointed to the buttons. "Make sure no one we like is in range."

"Make sure you go last, Lionside."

"Nap, we have to get out from the back."

"Tanner, did I give you the impression I was going to shoot you?"

"For most of the time I've known you, yeah."

Slinkie made a sound of disgust. "Governor, give me a rapid fire, fully stocked." He handed one through to her. "Stop long enough for me to get out without being flung into one of those stupid donkeys. I'll cover them until you can start firing."

I slowed our spin to where we were going slow enough for the little kids to get on or off the carousel. Slinkie timed it and jumped out at the point farthest from the crowd. She closed the door, went to the side of the building, and started firing over everyone's heads and at the ground in front of the mob.

"Tanner, get ready. I'm going to stop with the rear facing the door. I want the three of you out in under thirty seconds, and that includes the Governor."

"I take more time, so you young men are going to have to move quickly." The Governor didn't sound like he was asking.

"Captain, I must stress that you need to hurry."

"Get the *Sixty-Nine* prepped and ready to go, Audrey."

"Yes, Captain." I put the universal communicator into my inner jacket pocket. I didn't want to lose it and Lionside was going to have his hands full.

"Ready, Nap," Tanner called.

I slowed the tank and hovered. Tanner and Lionside jumped out. Tanner ran to the door and Lionside helped the Governor out, slammed the hatch, then helped Slinkie with crowd control. I spun the tank around a bit more, then moved it closer to the crowd. "Audrey, are you capable of flying the *Sixty-Nine* within atmosphere?"

"Captain, if I am guessing your meaning correctly, are you asking me if I can fly the ship to pick you up?"

"Yes, that's exactly what I'm asking."

"No."

"No?"

"No. That kind of flying—where the chances of success are so slim—goes against my core programming. I'm a very good robot, Captain. I'm not a human." She still sounded cheerful, but I had to figure she didn't feel that way about it.

"Randolph loves you just the way you are."

"Yes, he does. Weapons and Security Chief Slinkie is worried needlessly. I have no intentions of trading up. I prefer to be with the man who thinks I'm perfect just as I am, and who is willing to let me change that perfection and still love me."

"He's an idiot in most things, but he's absolutely a mechanical genius."

"I agree. You need to hurry, Captain. We are about to go down to a level of potential success that could cause me to override and overload."

"That bad, huh?"

"Worse."

"Got it, Audrey. Just have the *Sixty-Nine* ready to go the moment my butt's in the Captain's chair."

I risked a look over my shoulder. They'd done a good job—I couldn't see any guns or explosives left. "Nap, the door's open," Tanner shouted.

"Get everyone through, Slink, that means you especially. Everyone onto the ship!" I set the tank down. My door was right by the building, so I was able to ensure the others were inside. As Lionside, who went last, disappeared into the building, I looked behind me. The crowd, sensing the tank had stopped moving, were heading towards me again.

I looked back. The door had closed behind Lionside.

No matter. That's what the projectiles were for. I would have felt bad about shooting and maybe killing innocent people, only no one in this mob was likely to be innocent, and I knew without asking they'd all rip me to shreds if they had the chance.

Lionside had pointed out four buttons to control the rear projectiles. I pushed them all down.

It was impressive. Not what I was expecting by a long shot, but still, impressive. The screams were amazing. The crowd hadn't screamed that I'd noticed while Slinkie and Lionside were shooting live laser fire, but now it was all different. They were screaming and running. Not that I could blame them.

I'd have run, too. Only I'd have kept my mouth shut.

CHAPTER 62

The Hulkinator had a sense of humor, at least, that's how I saw it. It wasn't firing live rounds. It was spraying out crap. With gusto.

The entire back of the tankfloater was sending out what seemed like an endless stream of attack crap. I decided to take advantage of this moment. Not by taking pictures, though the thought did occur to me. Not by gloating— I liked to save gloating for private moments, not public ones. I'd seen too many gloaters dethroned in mid-public-gloat.

No, I backed us up and kept on spraying. It was like the Hulkinator had been given the world's largest vehicle enema. We'd been submerged for quite a while, after all. I wondered if the Governor had had any idea of what the tank would be firing out, and knew, in my soul, that he had. He'd read the manual, after all, cover to cover. There were times I questioned why I kept the Governor around, secret identity or no secret identity. This was not one of those times.

The essence of Diversion Ten was to keep people focused on what didn't matter. In the grand scheme, them getting sprayed with liquid waste didn't matter. To me, anyway. Getting off Herion alive was what mattered. I couldn't get to my ship from the back. I couldn't get to her from the side. So that meant I had to get to her from the front.

It's amazing how people who will bravely throw themselves onto a grenade or leap in front of laser fire in order save innocents will react when faced with a steady stream of yuck heading for them. I hoped the pirates weren't watching this, because all they'd really need to take over Herion Military was a crap machine.

The military guys were running faster than anyone, some trampling citizens to get away from the flow. Not that I could blame them. Maybe they were trying to get away from the donkeys.

Jabbob's dog pack, being lower to the ground, had all raced away the moment the Hulkinator and I started firing. The donkeys were also in full stampede mode, only there were a lot of humans in their way, forming a living corral. The donkeys didn't like their corral, at least, if I was any judge.

The mob rounded the side of the building—kicking, screaming and braying, all while jumping and running— and the tankfloater and I did the same. Now that we were in the front, however, there was more space for the mob. There were also large glass double-doors leading in.

"Ready?" I asked the tank. It indicated it was ready for anything. We lifted into the air and I put us back into a spin, so that liquid yuck was going everywhere. This kept the crowd well away from us, and anything we were hitting. Landed, then slammed into the doors.

The merderians might have affected the front, but the Hulkinator was a trouper. We smashed through the glass and rolled on in, crap still spraying out behind us. Unfortunately, it was a little bit of a drive to get to our docking bay. Happily, the tank seemed to have stored a never-ending supply of crap, because our output wasn't slowing down at all.

Our particular docking area had been quarantined, but either the rest of the spaceport hadn't heard the good word, or they weren't going to let a little something like a sewage explosion stop them from the completion of their daily and nightly duties. It was closing in on dawn but the main portions of the spaceport were filled with people going about whatever business they had in a spaceport your ship couldn't safely leave.

Well, they were fleeing now that the tank and I were there, but there were a lot more of them than I'd expected. And some of them had guns.

I never liked people shooting at me, but it didn't bother me too much right now. I was in a tankfloater, and if it had survived Crap Creek, Lake Disgusting, and the Attack Merderians, a couple of laser shots weren't going to slow it down. However, in order to get into the *Sixty-Nine*, I was going to have to get out of the tank.

We barreled along towards our docking area, crap, people and anything in our way flying randomly. I had to admit the Hulkinator had been a good choice on Tanner's part. We had room in the cargo hold, since we had no contraband. Maybe I'd take it along.

"Wanna go into space, big guy?" The tank replied that it was all for space. Good. Never knew when an all-terrain attack vehicle would be necessary.

Reached our docking area about the time we finally ran out of crap. At least, I assumed the sputtering from the rear and the fact I couldn't see anything spraying out meant the Hulkinator was finally dry. This was good. I didn't want to take a crap-filled tank onto the *Sixty-Nine*. She'd never understand.

The doors were locked, and they weren't double, but I figured in for a planet, in for a solar system, and we rammed the main entry door. Successfully. The tankfloater was really coming into its own.

Rolled in, only to find there were a lot of people here. Far more than I'd expected, particularly since I'd expected none. They all had guns, and they had most of them pointed at the four of my crew who weren't in the *Sixty-Nine* or in the Hulkinator. The *Sixty-Nine*'s ramp was down, but no one was on it.

I chose to be offended. "Audrey, why aren't you or Randolph shooting at the people who have the others surrounded?"

"We have been hoping you would arrive, Captain."

"Why?"

Randolph came on the communicator. "Because the sewer gasses make it touchy, Nap. If we hit the wrong thing, the entire spaceport could blow. I figured you'd want all of us out of range if that happened."

"Good point." A thought occurred. "Are we infiltrated on board?"

"Um, if we were, how could I tell you that?"

Randolph had another point. We'd tried various codes—they never worked. "You'd sound stressed. Then again, you sound stressed right now."

"I am stressed. I've kept them off the ship by firing at what I can see of them. I'm lying on my stomach, so I can just see their shoes. You know how hard it is to hit shoes?"

"Hard?"

"Hard. I'm terrified I'm going to miss the shoes, have a shot ricochet, and somehow hit a gas pocket and make us go up in flames. Do something, get the others in here, and let's blow this planet. I thought Knaboor was a bad situation. This is worse."

"Thanks for the update. Good to see you and Audrey are continuing to make sure I'm feeling the pressure. Keep shooting the unfriendly shoes. Hopefully friendly shoes will be able to run on board soon."

I turned my attention back to the people surrounding Slinkie. Oh sure, they were surrounding Tanner, the Governor and Lionside, too, but I didn't want to sleep with any of them. "I think we need to show we're offended." The tank agreed.

We kept on rolling, right into the variety of Herion Military who had my crew surrounded. I was unsurprised to see Nitin among them. I aimed for him.

Sadly, he heard me coming, because he turned and tried to grab Slinkie. However, she showed again why I loved her—by kicking him hard in the groin. Lionside and Tanner took this as their signal to start hitting. The Governor took it as his signal to get onto the *Sixty-Nine*. I hoped the others would follow his lead.

Nitin was doubled over and we kept rolling for him. He managed to stagger out of the way. We followed.

I couldn't go too far, though, because I had to create enough chaos for the others to actually board the ship. I figured this would best be achieved by doing the tank's favorite thing—spinning madly in the air.

"Let's see if we can hit Nitin while imitating a whirling dervish, shall we?"

The tank indicated we should. It was my kind of all-terrain vehicle.

CHAPTER 63

The moment we lifted off the ground, I saw Slinkie and the others look horrified. Then they body slammed anyone in their way and ran up the *Sixty-Nine*'s boarding ramp. I assumed we still had liquid crap remnants they could see. Good, that could be helpful.

I turned our rear away from the *Sixty-Nine* and started to spin. Sure enough, we still had leftovers. Some of which hit Nitin. I resisted the urge to give a Weshria Cheer or a Zyzzx Whistle. Victory was not yet assured.

"Nap, hurry up!" Slinkie had the com. "We have to get out of here."

"I want to get the tank into the hold."

"Are you insane?"

"It's been useful. More than useful. I don't want to leave it here."

"Did you hit your head?"

"No! I just want to take the tank along. Get the hold ready."

"We don't have time." Slinkie cursed. "It's really hard to hit shoes, even for me."

"You're lying on your stomach now?" I started to go to the happy place.

"Yes, and we're in trouble. They're bringing in reinforcements." I looked around. Sure enough, they were.

"Alexander, the Hulkinator has an ejection mechanism for in-flight escapes."

"I don't want to eject from it, I want to get it onto the ship."

"Yes, wonderful. Get into the ship, and then, once you're piloting, we can tractor beam the Hulkinator. But unless you're on the ship, we're all going to Herion Military prison, and Major Lionside is indicating that we won't be given time to say goodbye, let alone escape, before they execute us."

"Fine. Tell me how to work the ejection. I want the tractor beam warmed up. The Hulkinator is coming with us."

But before the Governor could speak, I lost control of the tank—the wheel wasn't responding to me and we weren't doing what I wanted. The tank set itself down. We slammed against the ground. It was jarring, but I wasn't too shaken up.

"C'mon, big guy. We'll get out of here."

The tank rolled back and forth—it was maneuvering itself, but I couldn't tell why.

"Nap, what are you doing?"

"Me? Nothing. The tank's doing something, Slink, not me."

"I had Audrey activate the Hulkinator's autopilot program, Alexander."

"What? Why?"

The tank stopped moving. To shoot the guns I didn't know it had, apparently. Crud-enhanced laser shots were flying all over, though none went towards the *Sixty-Nine*. The grid I'd been ignoring for a while now changed patterns. It wasn't showing schematics—it showed a trajectory.

"Randolph, open the top hatch, and do it fast!"

"On it, Nap."

The picture changed. It was crude, but it looked like a box giving a salute. I got a bad feeling. "Don't give up." The box saluted again. The roof above my head flipped open, and I went flying.

Fortunately I'd been prepared and the tankfloater aimed well. I went up and over, right into the top hatch of the *Sixty-Nine*. I caught the lip and kept from falling in. This knocked the wind out of me, and, while I hung there, head and upper body still out, I saw what the tank was doing.

It was in the air, spinning again, heading for the larger complement of military personnel, who were being directed by Nitin. Only I could see what some of those personnel were carrying—ground to tank missiles.

"NO! Don't do it! Come back, you'll fit in the hold!"

Someone yanked me down, hard. "Outland, now isn't the time for ridiculous sentimentality. Get us out of here." Lionside flipped me over his shoulder, engaged the locking mechanism on the hatch, ran us to the cockpit, and flung me into my captain's chair. Herion steroids were quite effective.

"All doors closed, all personnel on board, Captain." Audrey was in the copilot's seat. "We need to leave now. Estimated time to full spaceport explosion in fifteen seconds." I heard alarms going off, and figured Audrey had plugged into Herion's system in order to get as many out as possible.

I didn't have a choice, and we were out of time. I hit the thrusters and we took off. I turned on the rearview. The Hulkinator was spinning like a champ, heading for Nitin, who was running like a galaxy-class sprinter. The missile hit, and the tank exploded. Which triggered all the gasses Randolph had been worried about.

We made escape velocity just ahead of the fireball.

CHAPTER 64

We were back in space. No Herion Military ships were after us, which, considering we'd helped blow their main spaceport to smithereens, wasn't a big surprise. Back in space. Just a nasty pirate armada waiting to kill us. It was going to be another great day.

"How soon do you estimate before the pirate armada hits us, Outland?"

"Don't want to guess, Lionside." I handed him his communicator. "Go somewhere and see what you can pick up. Somewhere other than here."

I heard him leave. I didn't look. "Captain, I will go and see if I can assist Randolph with anything."

"Thanks, Audrey." I turned off the rearview.

It was stupid, and I knew it. Getting upset over losing a machine. Only, Audrey was a machine, and I knew without asking that Randolph would be upset if she were blown up. It wasn't like I'd had a sexual relationship with the Hulkinator. But, it had been my ship on the ground, and it had sacrificed itself to save the rest of us. To save me.

I heard a step behind me. "You okay, Nap?" Slinkie asked softly. "You don't seem… right."

I shrugged.

She slid her arms around my chest. My head was nestled against her breasts. I knew I was upset—I didn't have an overwhelming urge to turn around. Oh, the urge was there, it just wasn't overwhelming. Slinkie nuzzled the side of my head. "Tell me."

"The tank… it was… my friend."

"It died a hero." I figured she was laughing at me, but I couldn't hear any humor in her tone.

"Yeah. To save me."

"It was a Herion Military vehicle. Maybe it wanted you to survive because it knew you were the only one who could stop the pirate armada."

"Maybe. Maybe it just wanted to go out in a blaze of glory."

"Which it did. You going to be okay?"

"Yeah." Maybe. Probably. Had to be. The Hulkinator shouldn't have given itself up in vain, after all.

"Know what I like best about you, Nap?"

"My good looks?"

"No."

"Charm?"

"No."

"Snappy dressing?"

She chuckled. "No. I like that you care. You care about things most others wouldn't. I know you got attached to that ancient hunk and you're upset it's gone. That's why you're such a great pilot. And why you're more of a leader than anyone thinks you are. Because you care when others don't, and about what others don't think is important. That's why I know we're going to survive whatever this Lucky Pierre's going to throw at us. Because he won't care about the right things."

"You don't think it's stupid to have wanted to take the tankfloater with us?"

She kissed my forehead. "No. Any more than I think it's stupid that we took Tanner and Bryant along with us. Now, stop being upset with yourself. There wasn't anything you could have done and we're going to need you at optimum, because we all know the armada's out there, and close by."

"You really my girl?"

She hugged me tighter. "I've always been your girl, Nap." She had? Then why had I only scored a total of three actual kisses in all this time? Decided that would be a stupid question to ask aloud. I was mourning a semi-inanimate object, not brain-dead. Slinkie nuzzled my head again. "I'm going to assign Bryant and Tanner their berths and show them their assignment locations."

"You're the best, Slink."

I considered what course to set as Slinkie left the cockpit. Runilio seemed best. If we could get there we could actually fill our magma order. I started the calibrations. Worst case was I was wasting my time. If we could make the jump, though, it might be worthwhile.

As I started programming, I noticed something in the lower part of the *Sixty-Nine*'s windshield. It was a small grid, concentric circles radiating out, one green dot. As I stared at it, the grid reformed itself into a crude box, saluted, then went back to the circles and dots sequence.

"Thanks for that, babe." The *Sixty-Nine* indicated she wasn't jealous of my affection for the Hulkinator, and that she didn't mind the company of its programming. I took a closer look at the grid. "Can we bump up the size?"

"Yes, Captain." Audrey had returned. She seated herself and the grid enlarged. "It's very crude. It's running as a separate yet attached program."

"You want to explain that?"

"I don't think you can understand it, Captain."

"Oh, try me. Sometimes I'm not a moron."

"I don't feel you won't understand because you're not smart enough. I don't believe I can explain it because your mind is not robotic."

"Ah. Okay. So, I'm thinking we head for Runilio." The grid enlarged. "So we can fill that magma order." The grid enlarged even more. "Audrey, is that you making the grid giant-sized?"

"No, Captain. That would be the program itself. It is an independent autopilot program."

"So, the Hulkinator wants me to look at the grid, right?"

"That's my impression, yes, Captain."

I looked. "I know we're the green dot. I figure the white, non-moving dots are the celestial bodies in this solar system, you agree?"

"Yes."

I stared some more. "There aren't any other dots."

"I see none, either, Captain."

I pondered. The Hulkinator's sensors had been able to pick up merderians in a lake of thick waste. It couldn't have been a visual recognition, so it picked up something—thermal, sonar, whatever. That should mean if there was something cloaked out there, it would still see it. "This is sort of like a mini-Ultrasight, isn't it?"

"I believe so, Captain."

"Nice. And we're all alone out here." A thought waved merrily. "But, if we're alone, where're Lucky Pierre and his French Ticklers?"

CHAPTER 65

I stopped the jump calculations. "I want all crew on the com."

"Ready, Captain."

"Okay, gang. I have a couple of interesting announcements. First, the Hulkinator's autopilot has joined us from the great technological beyond and is doing its best to keep us alive. Next, we seem amazingly un-attacked at the moment. Finally, the Hulkinator is showing me and Audrey the entire solar system. Other than us, there are no other ships out here. At all. Thoughts? And, Lionside, I want your thoughts in particular."

"Like I told you when you arrived, the entire solar system is essentially locked down, Outland."

"To the point where they couldn't do inter-system jumps?"

Lionside was quiet for a few moments. "No. Particularly out Runilio's way. Ships were getting through to the other planets, just not in or out of Herion."

"I can't sense any minds other than those on this ship, Nap. My range can be spotty depending on circumstances, but if there was someone in our solarspace, I should be able to tell."

"Can you sense minds on Herion?"

"Yes. They're faint, but there are so many, I can tell."

"What about the other planets, can you reach any of them?"

"Only if you want me to pass out. They're too far away."

"What are you thinking, Alexander?"

"That something's wrong, Governor. As Lionside just confirmed, there's been space traffic, at least inter-system. Most inter-quadrant arrivals would jump into Herion's solar space—it's just good flying policy. But let's say you knew the system was having problems. Then you'd go in by Runilio. It may be far out, but it's a good center of trade."

"You mean it's a good center for piracy and smuggling, Outland."

"Yeah, I like Runilio. And, Lionside? Let's not play pretend now. You're on my ship, as part of my crew. Bloodline of kings or not, there's no way you're going back to Herion any time soon. Am I right?"

"Yes, you are." He sounded somewhat regretful, completely resigned, and a little excited. I hoped the excited part was getting to do something out of the Herion Military norm, not because he was going to get to spend quality time with Slinkie or had some great plan to turn on us and turn us in for whatever money he could claim.

"Then, stop whining. Yeah, we're smugglers. I've done piracy without a lot of guilt attached to it. But I've never blasted someone's ship to smithereens or denied them the ability to live to carry good cargo another day. So, stop acting like Herion Military. As of this moment, you've retired from active service to join the private sector."

"Nice spin." He waited a beat. "Any Herion Bitterroot on board?"

"Bryant, really."

"I'm thirsty."

"You're as obvious as a hatchling."

"I'm truly thirsty."

"Tanner?"

"Can't read him, Nap, sorry."

"You like him?" I tried not to sound shocked.

"Many people don't find me offensive, Outland."

"Name three."

"Alexander, don't we have a pirate armada to stop? As I recall, Janz the Butcher wants you doing a job for him." The Governor's tone was both peevish and authoritarian. No idea how he managed it, but it was annoying in the extreme. Especially because he really sounded just like my Great-Aunt Clara.

"Janz the Butcher?" Lionside sounded like he was vibrating. "The notorious crime lord of the galaxy? You work for him?"

"In a way." I wondered what the Governor was going for, bringing Janz in all of a sudden. Old fashioned senility seemed the most likely answer. "More like we run certain ideas past him and get his impressions."

"You're the ones the Butcher runs his master plans through." Lionside sighed. "I'd be excited about this—if I weren't most likely now a more wanted criminal than you are, on Herion at least. As it is, seriously, do you have any Bitterroot on board? Sniffing raw sewage for the better part of a day makes a man thirsty for something that doesn't smell like a latrine."

I gave in. He had a point. "Tanner, give the new Communications Chief a brew. In the icebox. In the back. He only gets one. And, trust me, I know how many are in there."

The sounds of pouring liquid, lip smacking, and the happy sighs of quenched thirst floated over the com. "How many of you are drinking our meager supply of the most expensive beer in the galaxy?"

Slinkie came in and handed me a glass. "All of us. Nap, seriously, the chances of us dying are pretty high. Why leave this for Lucky Pierre to either drink, destroy or sell himself?"

She had a point. "What happened to that all-encompassing belief that we'd survive because I'm so special?"

Slinkie tousled my hair. It felt great. "We're all tired, thirsty and sick of smelling stink. And yet, we're all still alive. About the only celebration we're going to get is drinking a Bitterroot. Let it go and drink your beer."

She had another point. I pulled her into my lap. "Works for me. Audrey, you want a beer?"

"No, thank you, Captain. I don't enjoy them like humans do. If I may, however, I'd like to join Randolph for the impromptu celebration and before we're facing life-threatening circumstances again."

"How long do you figure we have?"

"With the way our luck runs, Captain? I'd give it no more than thirty minutes."

"Go for it, Audrey." Randolph must have programmed her for optimism. I gave us no more than fifteen. Less, if Slinkie and I got amorous.

I considered the options. Finish the Bitterroots, give amorous a shot. That way, we got to fully enjoy something before the next disaster hit. Besides, if the next disaster took its time, maybe after a relaxing cold one Slinkie would be in the mood to retire to the Captain's quarters and play Around the Galaxy.

As my Great-Aunt Clara always said, why not go for rich instead of broke?

CHAPTER 66

"Mmmm."

"Nap… ooooh."

"Talk turkey to me, baby."

"You are such a bad egg." Slinkie didn't say that like it was a bad thing. She might have come from a bird-based planet, but she was purring like a happy kitty.

We were still in the cockpit and she was still on my lap. The beers were done, however, and we were definitely into amorous. By my mental clock, we had about five minutes before hell was going to break loose again. I planned to make the most of those minutes.

"What do you do to bad eggs?" I asked this against her neck. She liked my mouth against her neck, at least if her body's movements were any indication.

"Mmmm, we do just terrible things to them. Takes hours. Sometimes days."

"Can't wait."

On cue the *Sixty-Nine*'s alarms went off.

Slinkie sat up and heaved a sigh. "Guess we have to wait. What's trying to kill us now?"

I moved her off my lap and took a look. "Absolutely nothing, so that must mean Lucky Pierre's around. Hulky, you have anything?" The Hulkinator grid shifted around.

"You're calling it Hulky?"

"Why not?" Hulkinator seemed so formal.

Slinkie laughed and kissed the top of my head. "You're totally cracked, you know that, right?"

"As long as you like it, it's fine with me."

She kissed the back of my neck. "I like it."

I cursed whatever fates were causing me to have Slinkie this ready to go and yet be unable to take advantage of the moment. Clearly I'd made a variety of the various worlds'

Active Gods angry. "Mmmm, good." The grid stopped moving as Audrey came back in. Along with everyone else.

"Why is the entire crew in here?"

"We want to know what's going on." Randolph sounded embarrassed. Must have caught a nanosecond of me and Slinkie being chastely intimate. Maybe he just had a thing against human girls. "I ran a diagnostic—the alarm system's in perfect order."

I stared at the grid. "Interesting." It was truly working like a remedial Ultrasight. Nothing was near us, but there were ships out by Runilio. A dozen of them. "They knew we'd go to Runilio. How did they know that?"

"Why do you make that assumption, Outland?"

"Because they were hiding somewhere just outside the solar system. We were supposed to jump to Runilio, then they'd hit us there. And we would have, if Hulky hadn't shown me there was nothing here."

"You're calling it Hulky?" Randolph sounded like he was warring between being touched and laughing his head off.

"Audrey was taken."

"Point made. But, Nap, what are you thinking? How would they know we'd head to Runilio?"

"It makes sense," Slinkie said. "We have an order for magma."

"But who knew that? Besides us, I mean?"

"I knew because you mentioned it," Tanner said.

"Same here. You brought it up when…." Lionside's voice trailed off. I didn't have to look at him to know he was thinking. So was I.

"I mentioned it when Slinkie and I were being interrogated by you and Nitin." I pondered. "Tanner, am I safe in assuming Lionside isn't in league with Lucky Pierre?"

"Pretty darned sure, Nap."

"Why do you keep on calling this person Lucky Pierre?" Lionside sounded peeved. How nice—we had someone to cover that if the Governor was feeling tired.

"Because this is an old signature and the original guy who did this went under the moniker of Pierre de Chance and he leads the Chatouilleux Français Armada."

"You're kidding."

"No."

"Lucky Pierre and the French Tickler Armada?"

"Yes." Something was tickling me.

"Who names these people?" Lionside sounded stunned.

"Wait a second. Lionside, have any of us ever told you the name before?" I turned around and looked at all of them. It was easy, since the cockpit wasn't all that large and they were all squished in it.

"No. Why would I have asked about it if you'd already explained?"

"Slink, neither one of us mentioned a name when we were being briefed by Herion Military, right?"

"Right, Nap. You said 'pirate armada' a lot, but nothing else."

"You were also the second one to say it, Outland. The only other person who said 'pirates' in relation to what was going on was the last captain to manage to land… before you, I mean."

"So, that would be the captain of the ship I came on, Nap. And I had no idea what anyone's name was."

"Speaking of which, what's going on with young Not-Really-Almondinger?"

"He's a spy. Oh, and a limited telepath. Don't hate him for it, he can't read you any more."

"Ah, because he likes me, right. That all makes sense now."

I decided not to argue. I had a sinking feeling Tanner did like Lionside. I had a worse feeling that somewhere along the line, I was going to like Lionside. "You know what doesn't make sense? When I was trussed up in Military HQ and Nitin had the others in his gas chamber and Audrey tucked away, he and I were talking. He told me he wanted me to allow myself to be captured by the armada.

Me and my ship. So, supposedly, Herion Military could track on us and save the day."

"He had a noble purpose?" Lionside sounded like he didn't think that was possible by any stretch of anyone's imagination. My estimate of his intelligence rose.

"No. He threatened to hurt Slinkie if I didn't comply." There was a lot of male snarling at this. "Keep in mind that he planned to kill Slinkie, and Randolph and the Governor, whether I complied or not. In fact, before I could comply, since they were in the gas chamber and would have died if Tanner hadn't given the assist."

"That makes no sense." Lionside sounded both frustrated and angry. "If his hold over you was Miss Slinkie, how in the world would killing her before you'd done what he wanted work out? Why kill any of your crew? Kill them and lose the only incentives you might have to cooperate."

"He wanted Audrey," Tanner replied. "He used Slinkie as an incentive, but what Nitin wanted was Audrey."

"Why?" Randolph asked. "I mean, she's wonderful, but I have to be honest in that she's not the only advance robotic in the galaxy."

"She's the only one in our solar system," Lionside replied.

"So, he wanted Audrey from the moment he knew about her—but how could he know about her? I didn't know about her until we were already on Herion and through our interrogation."

"Maybe he saw her when Randolph brought her off the ship, Alexander." The Governor's eyes were narrowed. I hoped in thought, not due to constipation.

"How? Was he watching us? And if he was, why?" Randolph asked again. "And, why did he threaten you with hurting Slinkie?"

"You mean besides the fact that he's an evil bastard? He used Slinkie as a diversion. He dragged her in and showed her to me, then dragged her out again."

"Wait, Nap, what?" Slinkie looked confused.

"When I was in the nasty room, tied up to the chair, remember? You were brought in also tied up, struggling, yelling at me not to do it. Right before one of the goon squad shoved a gag into your mouth."

She shook her head. "It wasn't me. Nitin trussed us up and tossed us into that gas chamber. I never saw you until you came and rescued us."

"Then it was a damned good facsimile of you. She even bit the goon when he was gagging her. I was all proud of you."

Slinkie shrugged. I enjoyed the view. "Glad she represented, but it wasn't me."

Randolph and the Governor nodded. "Miss Slinkie was never out of my sight, Alexander, from the time we were captured by Nitin."

"She called me Captain, not Nap. I should have realized it wasn't the real Slinkie from that." And I hadn't. Well, I'd been distracted. I looked at Audrey. "Did you pick up any other robotic signatures while we were on Herion, especially at Military HQ?"

She shook her head. "No. But I wasn't monitoring for them, either."

"Tanner?"

"Nap, I keep telling you, I don't do robotic minds."

"I'm getting the feeling it's time for you to branch out." I thought back. It hadn't been that long ago in terms of hours, but in terms of activity, it seemed like a month, easy. Nitin had been blathering about how I had to do what he wanted, he'd threatened to hurt Slinkie by having his goons show her to me, and when I'd said the pirates would just kill me, he'd told me to make a deal. A deal with the pirate leader. "He said the name."

"What name?" Lionside asked. "Lucky Pierre?"

"No. He said de Chance. He was talking about the pirates and said that de Chance would want me to fly for him." I leaned back in my chair. There was something more, something else I knew I'd noted and filed away.

The Governor spoke slowly. "Now, how would Nigel Nitin of Herion Military know that the head of the heretofore invisible and unknown pirate armada was named de Chance? Particularly since we only figured it out because Janz the Butcher recognized the signature."

"I have a better question," Tanner said quietly. "Why is Nigel Nitin on Herion in the first place?"

"I'll top that one," Lionside said. "Who is Nigel Nitin, really?"

"Is the enemy of my enemy my friend?" Randolph sounded nervous. "Or is he my enemy?"

"I see your bets and raise you this—why are we assuming Nitin is de Chance's enemy?"

"Captain?"

"Yes, Audrey? Do you have a question to add into the game?"

"No. I just wanted to point out that the armada is moving. Towards us."

CHAPTER 67

"**S**tations! We'll figure out the rest of this as we go along." Just like always.

"If one more crazed Ebegorn shows up, I'm going to space something," Slinkie muttered as she left the cockpit.

"Slink, I love you. That's it."

"What's it?" This was chorused by most of the crew, other than Audrey, who was busy turning on our shields and warming up the hyper-drive.

"The thing I couldn't remember where I'd filed."

"What? Nap, did you crack your skull or something?"

"No, Slink, I'm fine. Nitin has an Ebegorn tattooed on his chest, right over his heart."

"Why? I mean, they look ridiculous."

"Yes, they do. Because they look like clowns. You told me yourself, Slinkie. The Ebegorn is called the clown bird. It's a large bird with a wild mop of feathers on its head and a somewhat stupid expression. Pretty hilarious to look at, but also a great predator and flier. And Ebegorns hunt in flocks. Large, nasty flocks."

"So?"

I sighed. "So, let me spell it out for you. Nigel Nitin has another last name. It's de Chance. He's either also a son of the original Lucky Pierre or he's related to the de Chance family in some way. I mean, come on—Lucky Pierre and the French Ticklers? The guy's a joker... a clown." I remembered something else. "I have papers with an Ebegorn crest that I took from Nitin. Written in code. Haven't had time to look at them."

"I'm good with codes, Nap."

"Tanner Lauris, come on down and get your next assignment. Work on them in between cooking breakfast and dying, okay?"

"Ah, Not-Really-Almondinger is truly named Tanner Lauris? Much better, I must say."

"Nap, I thought we weren't supposed to tell him my real name." Tanner was back in the cockpit, waiting for the papers.

Dang. I'd done it again. Oh well, Lionside was crew now. "You weren't supposed to, Tanner. As captain, I make the decisions for who we trust when." I dug the papers out of my inner jacket pocket.

"You mean it slipped out again." He took the papers from me and started thumbing through them. "When are you going to work on those little details?"

"Being a smartass is the most direct way to janitorial duty."

"I'll worry about it if we live." Tanner shook his head. "It's an old code."

"Work on it with the Governor. Bonding time and all that. It'll give the geezer something to live for."

"I heard that, Alexander."

"Estimate we have at least thirty-seven minutes before the armada arrives to engage, Captain."

"That's an odd amount of time."

"Why so?" Tanner was still looking through the papers.

"I'll explain while you head back to your station."

He rolled his eyes. "The galley's not exactly a battle station, Nap."

"You never knew my Great-Aunt Clara, did you? Head off, I want you strapped in or helping Randolph or Slinkie, whoever shrieks your name the loudest." He sighed but did as he was told. Good kid. Hopefully we'd make it long enough for me to turn him into a fully good man. Of course, I'd helped a lot with that already. "It's an odd amount of time because if they're jumping, then they should be here in less than five minutes, and if they're not, then they should be here in a day."

"True," Lionside chimed in. "Herion to Runilio is normally a full day trip on an express charter. It's longer on a standard charter. Most ships would do it in at least a couple of days, to conserve fuel, lower wear and tear on their ships, and prevent space-sickness."

"The armada is not jumping, Captain. However, they are moving much faster than express-level speeds."

"Randolph, how can they do that?"

"Advanced quantum physics. You want me to go into detail?"

"No, not at all. Ever. I want you to explain why they have it and the rest of us do not. And when I say 'the rest of us', take that to mean me, specifically."

"It's something a variety of space engineers and scientists have been working on for a while. How to move faster without having to use hyper-speed. It's most important to systems like Herion's, where you have a lot of planets and a lot of active trade between them." Randolph chuckled. "So it's kind of funny."

"What's funny?"

"Oh, just that the scientists and engineers who've made the most strides on this over the past couple of decades are on Trennile Main."

While Randolph continued to chuckle, I pondered. Trennile Main was an extremely remote planet in the Alpha Quadrant. It was the sole populated planet in its system, but it was quite self-sufficient. Not a lot of trade in and out, considered a great place to go to think and learn, since there were limited distractions.

Lionside cleared his throat. "Ah, Outland? Are you thinking what I'm thinking?"

"I think so."

"You two want to share what you're thinking, or just say the word think a few more times until I break both of your eggs?"

Slinkie sounded testy. I chose to figure that meant she was as frustrated by the constant coitus interruptus as I was. Not that we'd made it even close to the coitus part, but that was certainly my intention and it was being interrupted nonstop.

Lionside cleared his throat and I opened my mouth, but Tanner beat us to the punch. "They're thinking they've found Lucky Pierre's base of power."

"Tanner, new rule. You don't steal the captain's big reveal moment."

"Oh, noted." I detected sarcasm, and a lot of it. The kid was coming along fast.

"Makes sense, Alexander. However, it doesn't help us if we don't survive."

"Good point, Governor." I considered my options. As my Great-Aunt Clara always said, he who fights and runs away can usually live to fight another day, but he who runs without fighting gets farther and faster, and sometimes can't be caught. She was a nasty biddy, but she did occasionally have a point.

I made the calculations. "Captain, what are you doing?" Audrey asked this very quietly. I saw her turn the ship's intercom off.

"What, off the group com, do you think I'm doing, Audrey?"

"An interesting gambit. You did make some promises."

"The people I made those promises to are either dead, on this ship, or so far away that the situation will be handled by the time they find out."

"Good point."

"Any argument?"

"Honestly? No. I enjoy being alive, just like you do. I'm not alive in the same way, but I can die and I don't want to. And I don't want Randolph or the rest of you to die, either."

"You know, Audrey? I think this could be the start of a beautiful flying relationship. Hulky, your thoughts?" I already knew what the *Sixty-Nine* thought about the idea. A girl tended to get mussed up when she was attacked by a dozen big, nasty bullies. She was all for choosing where and when we fought, and doing our best to stack the odds in our favor.

Hulky formed into his box and saluted. Then he shifted and showed me a different solar system. It had no space traffic, only that was normal. "Good man. Audrey? Let's turn the com back on, please." She did. "Okay, gang, I want everyone strapped in. It's going to get bumpy and uncomfortable fast."

There were some questions and grumbling, but they did as they were told, per Audrey's monitors. I could tell the last couple of days had taken a lot out of them—my usual crew never complied easily unless we were in the thick of battle and the short experience with Tanner and Lionside indicated they'd fit right in with everyone else without missing a beat.

Everyone was locked in, calculations were made, all was in readiness. "The armada is twenty minutes from us, Captain."

I considered. If we left now, that gave them that much more time to figure out where we'd gone. If I waited, something could go wrong. In fact, so many things could go wrong that I could spend the next twenty minutes listing them.

I hit the hyper-drive button.

CHAPTER 68

Against most of my initial expectations, we actually took off. Happily, it was impossible to talk or move much during a jump, so I had plenty of time to consider what I was going to say when the shouting started in nine minutes.

Among my possible answers was the simple fact that picking where we fought was a huge incentive. That Lucky Pierre was going to follow us was now a given. He wanted me and the *Sixty-Nine*—Nitin's little charade had proved that.

Any time we could buy would be good. It would give Tanner and the Governor time to work on the code. It would give us all time to rest. And it would give me an opportunity to get Slinkie to rest with me.

Reality intruded and mentioned there was no way Slinkie and I were going to have time for a decent tumble. Probably not even a quickie. And it was Slinkie. And would be our first time. I didn't want to rush it. Honestly, I wanted it to be perfect. So perfect she'd never consider the idea that anyone else could ever match up. That kind of perfection took time and a reasonably relaxed atmosphere.

There was nothing for it. I was going to have to defeat this intrusive pirate armada so I could get my girl. Life, truly, wasn't fair.

We came out of the jump. Trennile Main was an Earth-like planet, only double the size. Lots of water and foliage, so it sparkled green and blue in the light of its sun. I checked the grids—true to expectations, we were the only ship in the system.

I'd ensured we exited our jump far enough away that Trennile Mission Control would be unlikely to monitor.

It was a seven planet system, with Trennile Main being planet number four. We were on the back side of planet number seven.

"Audrey, are you able to monitor to see if we're being picked up by Trennile Main?"

"Yes, Captain. So far, we are undetected. Or they are pretending."

"Figure they don't know they'd need to pretend. Keep monitoring, however."

There was a pounding of feet and, shockingly, the crew were all back in the cockpit. They couldn't seem to handle long separations from me.

"Outland, where the hell are we and why?"

"Trennile solar," Tanner answered after a look at Hulky's latest schematic. "But I'm with Lionside—why?"

"I thought we promised to take care of Lucky Pierre and his boys. You told Janz the Butcher you'd do that." Randolph sounded just this side of panicked.

"I tell Janz a lot of things. He tells me a lot of things, too. What he doesn't tell me is how to go about doing what I do best."

"Get us into trouble?" Slinkie sounded like she was only half-joking.

"And out of it." I sighed. "Look. I'm sure you can all think of some good reasons why I took us here. But while we have the element of surprise on our side—for the first time since this whole ordeal started, I might add—I'd like to take advantage of it."

"Are you thinking this is the last place Lucky Pierre would think we'd go, Alexander?" The Governor, unlike everyone else, didn't seem upset by the fact we were here. Of course, he was the one with the most experience.

"No. I think he'll figure out we're here."

"Fighting on his home turf might not be in our best interests."

"Fighting him on Herion's turf wasn't in our best interests, either."

"You did gain some valuable personnel," Lionside said. Hulky went large and flashy. He coughed. "And, ah, sentient electronics."

"Aw, don't sell it short. Hulky's been worth his weight in Herion Bitterroot. Tanner's working out, too, I must admit. Your jury, Lionside, is still out."

"Universal communicator."

"I'll bet Randolph or Audrey could both work said communicator and fix it as well."

"Intricate knowledge of the military mind and protocols."

"The Governor's probably got that covered."

"Weapons expert."

"I point you to Slinkie, who you are not allowed to touch." She laughed softly and looked flattered. She liked me possessive. That was good. Because I was.

Lionside sighed. "Biggest guy on your crew, and fully capable of cracking a human skull in either hand."

"I knew I brought you along for something."

"Oh, good. I ask again, why are we here? If you were jumping us, why not take us to where we could get some support?"

"Just where would that be?" I shook my head. "See, this is why you're still at the worth-proving stage. No one's going to help us. I know that. So I'm not wasting time trying to get help. I'm spending time trying to get into a position of strength."

"Why wouldn't some other planetary system's military help? We're fighting a dangerous pirate armada. Surely you have contacts who would support you."

I snorted. I couldn't help it. "Look, think. The only group willing to work with us on this was Herion Military, and only barely. Frankly, you all wanted me to solve your problem while you hid out. Right now, the problem is limited to your solar system, and people are self-centered twits with short memories. Until it's not a Herion-only problem, they won't want to get involved. And the moment it becomes a bigger-than-Herion problem it'll be too late. That's why the Butcher wants them stopped now."

"He's right," Tanner sad. "Aviatus wouldn't be willing to help, and they're the next most likely system for Lucky Pierre to target. Earth won't help—too far away to care, and they're too old, fat and protected. By the time Lucky Pierre would really make Earth's radars, it'll be too late for the entire galaxy. I could go on naming systems, it's all the same. The only military with chips in this game is Herion's. And your system's been shut down, and the only person in Herion Military who has both the understanding of the situation and the correct belief about what to do is you."

I took the opportunity to circle the planet. It wasn't habited or even habitable, but it wasn't like some, where you couldn't get within its atmosphere without having your ship destroyed. Trennile's system was notable in that all of the uninhabited planets were decent places to be, with breathable air. That no one had tried to terraform or pioneer was considered one of those quirks of fate. Now I wondered if we were going to find out that the quirk was named de Chance and the fate was that he and his people ran off anyone who expressed an interest in moving into the neighborhood.

"Why is the biggest crime lord in the history of the galaxy the only one who wants this armada stopped?" Lionside sounded both frustrated and interested. I really hoped he wasn't going to try to play hero by arresting us. He did have some skills it would be a shame to lose.

"Because it's bad for business." The Governor chuckled. "Your ability to think like a military man is a great help, Major. But you also need to start thinking like a businessman. Because that's what most successful criminals, pirates included, truly are, at their cores. They're in business. And there's nothing worse for business than a market that isn't free."

The planet still seemed completely uninhabited. This was good. Air was still breathable. Also good, not that I planned to go for a hike.

"It's fine if you have the monopoly." Lionside truly was from Herion. They were big on monopolies on Herion.

"Not really. Monopolies, like dictatorships and kingdoms, get toppled because they're restrictive. Free trade allows the most forms of individual success—and the galaxy is made up of trillions of individuals, after all." The Governor sighed. "Major, think of all the problems you just had within your own military organization, and then accept that they exist on every civilized planet. If you want to stop these pirates and save your solar system, then you're going to have to do it our way."

"But first, we're going to set down on Trennile Main's little brother and see if anyone notices."

"Why?" This was chorused. Even Audrey joined in. I resisted the urge to shout out "Percy Almondinger" and see if that created the group silence again.

"I would think that's the last thing we'd want to do," Lionside said. "We just escaped from the armada. How will we escape if we're on a planet?"

"Exactly."

CHAPTER 69

S ensors found a good area to land. Hulky altered and now we could see the terrain. All clear.

I set us down, my usual perfect landing. Not even a bump. The *Sixty-Nine* didn't like to be jostled and I couldn't blame her.

"Outland, really, why are we here, specifically, and on the ground?"

"Audrey, all systems off other than sensors, both short and long range." I turned around. "Because we don't have any allies to run to. So we have limited resources and they have to be conserved."

"I echo Bryant. Why are we setting down? We can run on low in space, too."

"Why are all of you so dead-set against it?"

"Because it's stupid," Tanner answered. "It leaves us sitting ducks."

"Do you think Nitin, or Lucky Pierre, or anyone thinks I'm stupid?"

Lionside answered slowly. "I believe Nigel did indeed think you were stupid. But I'm sure he no longer does. And, if you're right, Lucky Pierre no longer does, either."

Randolph shook his head. "Nap got us away from the full armada. They knew he wasn't stupid before we landed on Herion."

I glanced at the Governor. He looked pleased. "It's so nice to see you learning, Alexander."

"Learning what? How to live dangerously?" Slinkie shook her head. "Nap, this is stupid and reckless, even for you." She jerked. I loved it when she did that. "Oh. Um, sorry. It makes sense now."

"How so?" Randolph was, as always when intrigue reared its head, slow to catch on.

Tanner laughed. "Oh, damn. Okay, yeah, good plan."

Lionside shook his head. "Not if they've figured out how to think like you."

"Tanner's guess is that our current Lucky Pierre does think like me. However, I'm not really thinking like me, so much."

"Who are you thinking like?"

"My Great-Aunt Clara. And Janz the Butcher. They have a lot of similarities." I avoided catching the Governor's eye, somewhat to ensure no one made the connection but more because he knew how I felt about Great-Aunt Clara and rarely enjoyed my making a positive comparison.

"The Butcher is hidden away," Lionside said, eyes narrowed in, I had to admit, thought. "Some say hiding in plain sight, where no one would suspect him. Others say he's on a planet like Trennile Main, safe and hidden, but where he can get wherever he needs to, whenever. You're hiding us in plain sight, if you will, but where no one who has the slightest experience with you would think. You're a pilot—pilots feel safest when they're flying. And we're running away—and you'd normally just focus on getting away. But you've been told you can't do that, but the only people who know that for sure, and who also know you'd actually turn and fight when you weren't cornered are all on this ship."

Slinkie was right—he'd been playing dumb, possibly for most of his life. But he wasn't. The feeling in my gut that had mentioned Tanner wasn't going to be getting off-ship on Runilio churned up and said that, in all likelihood, I'd better start getting used to Communications Chief Lionside pronto.

"I don't get why we're not running and not hiding where we can escape, Janz the Butcher's orders or not." Randolph was still trying to catch up. I wondered if it bothered Audrey, who was, if my guess was right, well ahead of the others now in terms of my overall plan.

"Randolph, the Captain has us on-planet because it's the last thing anyone would expect him to do. He assumes

Lucky Pierre will figure this out, but it gives us time to regroup and determine a plan of attack, while conserving our resources." Audrey sounded cheerful, but then, Randolph hadn't had any time to alter that programming.

Speaking of which. "Randolph, first thing, please fix it so that Audrey can sound upset or cranky if she wants to. The constant cheerfulness is going to cause me to kill something, and you'll be the most likely choice."

He shrugged. "If you want. I think her voice is soothing and uplifting."

"I think I want to help Nap kill something," Slinkie said.

"It does tend to lessen the impact of urgent orders such as 'duck' or 'run', Mister Billur."

"Oh, Major, really, call me Randolph. We only use formality when we're trying to impress pompous, rigid gasbags that we're law-abiding and live to follow rules to the letter." Randolph said this to Lionside's face without a trace of sarcasm or irony. I was pretty sure there was a ton of sarcasm and irony intended. I was impressed with his self-control.

"So we only refer to each other formally when meeting with Herion Military and its equivalent? I can abide by that. And, it's Bryant, Randolph. As the captain said, I've retired from active duty."

"Thanks, Bryant, I appreciate that." Again, no sarcasm or irony showing. Maybe I was assuming too much—it was Randolph, after all.

"So, Not-Really-Almondinger, what's your pleasure?"

"Never hearing the words 'Percy' or 'Almondinger' again, for starters. Tanner works just fine, Major."

"Ah?"

"Fine, Bryant." Tanner sounded flattered and a bit embarrassed. We'd gotten him out of Herion Military just in time, it seemed.

"I'd prefer you stick with Governor, Major. And, if you don't mind, I'd like to continue to refer to you by your rank. It was honorably received and dishonorably taken from you, much like my own title. So, humor an old man and allow me to keep both my and your former glories intact."

"As you wish, sir, I shall take it as a great compliment, coming from you. And your preference, Miss Slinkie?"

"Just plain Slinkie, Bryant. Only the Governor calls me Miss Slinkie. And, really, only the Governor is allowed to get away with it on a regular basis."

"With pleasure."

The love in the cockpit was getting nauseating. "Yes, wonderful, we're all pals. Randolph, Audrey's vocal programming? Let's get that fixed, shall we? Tanner, I think a decent meal would do everyone some good. Governor, while Tanner's cooking, please continue to look at the papers I took from Nitin. Slink and Lionside, let's make sure this ship is set to fight and run away. I want all weapons ready, locked and loaded, the universal communicator not only up and running but, if possible, linked into the *Sixty-Nine*'s systems so we don't lose it in case we lose the original communicator. Randolph and Audrey, once the programming fix is done, I want another full schematic run on the *Sixty-Nine*. Have Hulky help with that, just in case."

"What are you going to be doing, Nap?" Slinkie asked as everyone started to go take care of their assignments.

"I'm going to be sifting through everything I took from Nitin, to see what other information about the Family de Chance I can determine."

CHAPTER 70

Everyone went off to do their assigned tasks. I went to the dining area. I had a feeling I'd want the Governor's input, possibly Tanner's too. Hopefully the kid could cook and decipher at the same time.

Tanner bustled about, looking happier than I'd seen him so far, including when he was in the bathhouse. Then again, I hadn't looked at him overlong while he was occupied with the girls. He was efficient—I could smell food cooking already. My stomach reminded me that we hadn't had any food since breakfast at Jabbob's.

The Governor was at one end of our dining table. He had the papers spread out, but I wasn't concerned. Like most spaceships, the table had a small GravCreate that ran separately from the ship's larger, internal gravity creator. Food and drink floating through the air were not positives, and the less said about floating cutlery the better.

I emptied my pockets and took a look, though I left Tanner's calling card in my inner jacket pocket with my false ID and universal card. I didn't show it to the Governor. Not because I wanted to hide it from him, but I didn't want to risk Slinkie seeing it. At least, not until I knew what was going on with Tanner's mission and how it related to her.

Immediate needs first, however. I ran everything for tracking devices, bugs or bombs. The *Sixty-Nine*'s sensors showed nothing untoward. The penlight had been handy, but was clearly Herion Military issue. Same with the gun and holster. I kept the penlight and put the gun aside to add into our armory.

Pulled out the array of cards Nitin had carried and spread them out. Same with the variety of items I hadn't catalogued yet. Small combo knife and every other possible thing you'd need set, including nail clippers. Useful and unexciting. Set that aside for Randolph.

Still had his system tracker. Also put aside to see if Randolph or Audrey, or even Tanner or Lionside, could do something with it. Still had Nitin's keys. Put them by the cards, just in case. I pulled out the small key he'd had in the zippered pocket of his jacket and examined it. Nothing exceptional, but it was important, considering where he'd stored it. Important, but not frequently used.

I compared the little key to the others on his key-ring. None of them compared, though there were several I'd never seen before. More for the others to take a look at. He also had a couple keys that were obviously for Dragon locks. I looked closely at those. They weren't for Dragons on Herion, the mark was wrong.

"Huh."

"What, Alexander?" The Governor didn't look up from his translations.

"Confirmation, more than anything. Nitin has two Dragon keys. One's from Trennile Main."

"And the other?"

"No planetary mark."

"It will correspond to something our current Lucky Pierre holds dear, most likely on his ship." He didn't sound like this was conjecture.

"Any other givens you want to share with me?"

"Not at this precise time. Tanner, a moment?" Tanner trotted over, saucepan in hand. They discussed some code intricacy, argued a little, reached consensus, and Tanner went back to the truly important things. They could send all this intrigue right to an asteroid belt—I was starving.

Went back to Nitin's stuff. He had the usual male assortment, including an embroidered handkerchief, with the initials 'N d C' in one corner. "Pretty positive he's a direct Lucky Pierre descendent."

"Perhaps that will give us something to go on, but I wasn't exaggerating. The likelihood that de Chance left

an assortment of children all over the galaxy isn't far-
fetched." The Governor looked up. "He was quite like
you, only not careful."

"So, not quite like me." The Governor shrugged and
went back to his translations. I went back to the rest of the
junk. Most of it was junk. Nitin had a sweet tooth—there
were a variety of wrapped candies. Checked them all with
my ring—not poisoned. They'd come in handy if anyone
was overly hungry, but didn't give me a lot to go on—they
were standards you could get anywhere in the galaxy and
definitely on Herion.

The only remaining item of interest was a small disc,
about the size of a circle made with my thumb and fore-
finger. "Audrey, can you come here, please?"

She arrived, gleaming like always. "Yes, Captain?" Still
sounded cheerful and calm.

"Oh, sorry, thought Randolph would be done with the
programming by now."

"He is. I don't see a need to be distraught at the moment,
so I'm keeping my voice calm and cheerful like Randolph
enjoys."

Decided not to argue. "Can you play this disc? And can
you ensure it won't cause a problem, for you, the *Sixty-
Nine*, or Hulky if you do run it?"

She examined it. "I believe this will not cause issue. I'll
run it through anti-virus first." Audrey pushed something
on her neck and a small tray slid out from her stomach.

"Oh, I did so not need to see that."

"Apologies, Captain." She put the disc in and closed
her stomach. She twitched. "Interesting. It's clean. However, you will want to see this immediately." She turned
towards the wall with the least obstruction and her eyes
glowed—not like they had when she was using them as
headlights, but like she was projecting through them.

Which, as I looked, she was. As the images flashed
on the wall, the knowledge that Nitin and Lucky Pierre
would be hunting me down to the ends of the galaxy settled firmly in my stomach.

"Ah, Governor? You might want to take a look at this."

He didn't look up. "Are the pictures showing random locations and a variety of people who, after a while, all start to share a familial resemblance?"

"Yeah."

"This is why dictators and other unpleasant leaders are so fond of genocide, Alexander."

"I'm looking at the de Chance Family Album, aren't I?"

"Yes. And I'm decoding their true names and aliases, including where each alias is used and why." He didn't sound perturbed.

"You realize they want to turn us into space dust."

"And this changes their original intent how, exactly?"

"Good point." Another reason why I kept the Governor around—he really wasn't into the idea of panicking. Ever.

Tanner wandered over. "Food'll be ready in a couple of minutes, but I have enough time to take a look." We watched as the pictures flashed by.

"Audrey, any estimate of how many pictures are in here?"

"Over three hundred, Captain. But, before you get too upset, divide by half—there are two pictures per person, one of them and one of their planet of origin."

"Yes, I can see how a hundred and fifty plus people out to kill us would seem more comforting than three hundred. Are you sure the pictures are of where they're from and not where they're working right now?"

"Yes, Captain, not in the least because there are no pictures of space vessels. I also have found Nigel Nitin, and his origin picture is not from Herion."

"On screen, please." She flipped to him and put his picture and his planet of origin picture side-by-side. She was good, I had to admit, in a sometimes very creepy way. "Interesting. Tanner, any guess as to what planet our buddy's from?"

"Aviatian's Nest, Nap. I think that's Earth."

CHAPTER 71

Everyone was called in and we ate while watching the Slide Show of Doom. It was like being trapped in someone's home, with them refusing to let you leave until they showed you the picture of their darling aunt's sister's husband's mother's boyfriend's cousin twice removed just once again. The only positive was we didn't have to hear the droning about how much fun they'd had and how we should go visit first chance we got.

Thankfully, the food was delicious—perfect to behold as well as perfect to ingest. Which settled it for me. Barring Tanner planning to murder Slinkie for some odd reason, he was staying permanently. If we survived longer than the next few hours.

Audrey didn't bother to eat—apparently it was just for show or if she really wanted to. Which was fine with me. I didn't think I wanted to see her chew and project from her eyes at the same time.

"You know what I don't see?" Slinkie said as we started rotation number five.

I let a variety of snappy comebacks go. I had no idea of how long we had before Lucky Pierre the Next found us. "What?" To punish my restraint, my mind created the droning commentary anyway, just for something to do, including my choice of names and histories. Look, there was our sweet Clarice who married so badly. And our Howard, who just got out of prison.

"The obvious Lucky Pierre," she replied. "I see a lot of people, but none of them look, well, leader-like."

Oh, surely our Bubba looked like a leader. A leader of losers, but still, a leader.

"Outland doesn't look leader-like." Lionside sounded far too matter-of-fact.

But dear Sumpsie does, just look at her, leading with her huge nose. "Thanks, Lionside." Of course, he had a point. Lionside looked like a leader. I didn't. "I'm not trying to 'look' like a leader. I'm a leader naturally." I tried to stop the commentary, but dearest Mildred waved from behind her large, buckteeth. Apparently the original Lucky Pierre had not been selective in who he'd shared the fun with. At all.

I ignored the coughing and snorting coming from the Governor, Slinkie and Randolph. Mostly because Tanner was nodding, and he looked serious. "Yes, you are. And, again, I really think we're looking for someone like you, Nap, not like Bryant."

"None of the de Chance family bear a resemblance to Captain Outland," Audrey shared.

For which, as I stared at dearest Marvin and adorably disfigured Gaeorg, I thanked every god from every planet, civilized or not. "Thank the various gods, Audrey." I figured I should say that aloud. Just in case. Gods had funny senses of humor. "Tanner's talking personality, not looks."

"Ah. I cannot help you there, Captain."

"No, but can you do picture groupings for me?" I clamped down on the commentary. Right after we left our Reardin, who was so good with mathematics but not so good with people.

"Yes. What would you like to see?"

Anything but these people again. "Put them together based on galaxy quadrant, and, within that, based on solar system. Then, within solar system, based on planet, if there's more than one of them per planet." I cursed Great-Aunt Clara. Oh, sure, she'd never done this family picture album stuff herself, but she'd had so-called friends who had. I was having horrible childhood flashbacks.

"Do we have more than a hundred and fifty civilized inhabiteds?" Randolph asked. Cosmos Geography had never been his best class.

"Two-hundred-and-forty-nine at last count," Audrey answered without missing a beat. The wall was a flurry of activity. She could send a lot out of her eyes. I tried to focus on this making me sick—it forced my mind off the running commentary.

"Yes. That's why they're pushing Werotalin so fast." Lionside sounded disgusted. "So they can induct Planet Two-Hundred-and-Fifty into the Galactic Community in the year Twenty-Five-Hundred."

"Cute." But not as cute as our little Chachi. Who was smirking at me from the Beta Quadrant section. "Governor, what are the odds we can determine who's who based on the documents?"

"Once I translate, perhaps Miss Audrey can run them through her programs and see if there are any clear planetary name connections."

"Nigel's common on a lot of worlds, not just Earth," Tanner said morosely.

"Well, we'll get what we can." The pictures were up, divided as requested. Audrey had even gone one better—she'd placed them not only by solar system, but had them spread out like a map of the galaxy, each picture or set representing their planet and its location against the Galactic Core.

"Nap," Slinkie said slowly. "Do you see what I see?"

"Yeah, I do. It's a map of the original Earth exploration and trade routes. From three hundred years ago."

CHAPTER 72

"I agree," Lionside said slowly. "But why?"

"Why did the original Lucky Pierre follow the old Earth routes, you mean?" He nodded. "I'm guessing because he was from Earth originally."

The Governor's eyes were narrowed. "Perhaps. But even if he was, the old routes make much less sense today. Even less sense a few decades ago, when Lucky Pierre would have been active."

"Audrey, how many Earth de Chances do we have?"

"Just two, Captain." She bumped their pictures. There was good old Nitin. The other was a picture of a girl. She was attractive, though the family resemblance was there. Like Nitin, she wasn't ugly. Not ugly at all. I reminded myself Slinkie was in the room. Did a fast comparison. Nope, Slinkie was still better.

"Age guesses?"

"I know Nitin is in his late twenties," Lionside offered. "If that helps us at all."

Something occurred to me. "You know, Governor, do you remember when it was Janz told us this pirate armada was active before?"

"Over thirty years ago. Well over." The way the Governor said it, I got the distinct impression he'd tossed out the phrase "over thirty" previously as well as now to avoid admitting just how old he really was. Which, when I thought about it, was typical.

I revised the estimate to figure forty or fifty years, maybe sixty. Which also made sense considering how long Janz the Butcher had been considered the galaxy's chief crime lord. It would also put the Governor at a far more believable age to have been actively infiltrating a vast pirating network.

"So, let's assume Janz fudged a bit, so we wouldn't have information he probably figured wasn't key at the time." The Governor nodded and gave me a look that said I wasn't always as stupid as he feared. "So, I think it's safe to say that we're not looking at Lucky Pierre's offspring—I think we're looking at the offspring of his offspring. The grandchildren."

"That would account for some of them not looking nearly as, well, 'related' as the others." Slinkie was staring at the picture of Nitin and the woman. "I think that woman's Nitin's sister, though. I mean, they look a lot alike."

Audrey bumped the size. There was a strong resemblance. "Yeah, Slink, I think you're right. Sister or very close cousin."

"They look about the same age in their pictures," Tanner said. "In fact, I think they may be in the same place, or general area."

Audrey nodded, which made the pictures move. Made my stomach move, too. "I believe Galley Chief Tanner is correct." She moved the pictures closer together. "Observe the background."

Sure enough, there were some buildings behind them. They matched up. "So, Nitin's got a sister. There were a lot of women. Think they're all involved?"

"In some way, I'd assume so, yes," the Governor replied. "There are certainly female names on this list."

"Does it change our strategy?" The way Slinkie asked, I knew I had to choose my reply carefully.

"Doubt it." She relaxed. Correct answer. Good. Nice to know I still had it, in that sense. "But they might think it would." Not all of the women had been homely. Some had been easy on the eyes. Nitin's sister, in particular. Visions of scantily clad pirate women crowded into my mind. I focused on Slinkie. Who was glaring. Told the pirate women to get spaced. They sulked and wandered off into my subconscious.

"Or not." The Governor shrugged. "Alexander, surely you have more of a plan than idle chit-chat?"

I did? Oh, right, I did. "I want to lure them back here."

"Why, exactly?" Lionside sounded interested more than confrontational. "I assume you mean into the solarspace, not onto the planet." Everyone gave indication they'd had enough fun planetside for a while.

"Yeah, I'd prefer to take them on in space. The problem is, we want to be captured, not killed."

"True." Lionside nodded. Then his eyes narrowed and he gave me the hairy eyeball. "You have no intention of going back into space, do you?"

"Well, we'll be back in space. But not under our own power."

"You're going to, what, just have us sit here until they catch us?" Slinkie sounded like she wanted to hit me or cry.

"Slink, stop worrying. We want them to take us prisoner, remember?"

"No. I remember we wanted to stop them. I don't recall anyone saying that we had to be captured in order to do it."

Everyone else's expressions matched Slinkie's—fear masquerading as anger—other than the Governor's. He hadn't even looked up from his translations. "Miss Slinkie, would it be better to win and survive or destroy the armada in a blaze of glory?"

"Survive."

"Correct. What would our only experiences with this armada suggest?"

"That we barely made it once," she muttered. "And now they know what Nap's able and willing to do."

"If I'm right, and I know I am, they also know what we did on the ground."

The Governor nodded. "I'm sure. Either Nitin is working closely with the rest of his relatives, or he's working against them. However, if it's against, it's not out of any law abiding desires."

"In which case, he'll help them get rid of us."

"I don't want to be captured," Slinkie said. She looked uncomfortable as well as afraid.

"None of us do," Lionside said reassuringly. "I'm sure we'll all be able to protect you."

"I'm not," Tanner said. Slinkie shot him a look that could freeze Thurge. He shook his head. "They have a right to know. Under the circumstances."

"Like feathers they do. You keep your mouth shut, you little hatchling."

"Name calling isn't going to change things." Tanner grinned. "It's all about the names with you, though, I know."

Well, I'd wanted to know what was going on with Tanner and what he had on Slinkie. Looked like the time was now. "If it's something Tanner, based on his experience and training, thinks could endanger all of us, or you in particular, Slink, then I want to know. Besides, no matter what Tanner tells us, it's not going to change how any of us feel about you. Okay?"

"Ha." She crossed her arms over her chest and slumped down in her seat. "Fine."

Tanner nodded. "I don't think it'll change how they see you."

"Bet me." She glared around the table. "And, don't you all go swearing how everything will be the same. It never, ever is."

I wondered if Slinkie was the female Janz and I'd just been clueless all this time. No matter what the reveal, everyone was now breathlessly waiting for Tanner to get on with it.

"I think it'll be fine, for a variety of reasons, Slinkie. But guess we'll find out."

"Any time, kid. Really, any old time."

Tanner shrugged. "Okay. Slinkie's real name is Seraphime."

CHAPTER 73

Thudding silence met this statement. I broke it, saying what I could tell by looking was on everyone else's mind. "Pretty name. So what?" On everyone's mind, that is, but the Governor's. He looked like this was ancient news and hardly worth noting.

Tanner gaped at us, clearly shocked his big reveal had been a dud. Slinkie looked embarrassed and a tiny bit relieved. "I don't like my name much."

Tanner rolled his eyes while the Governor chuckled. "But, my dear, it's a very traditional name for your planet."

"Yes." She was back to muttering.

"Want to tell the rest of us what this means?"

"Sure, Nap." Tanner had managed to recover and was, clearly, going for the next shocker. "Only one class of person on Aviatus is allowed to carry that name."

"Why?" I couldn't believe that Slinkie would have been considered to fit into any form of lower class, but who knew how a planet based on birds and birdbrains really worked. "It doesn't sound insulting."

"It's not." Tanner laughed. "It's restricted as a compliment, not as an insult."

"So, only the greatest looking women get named Seraphime. Got it. What's the problem?"

Slinkie was still upset, but she looked flattered. "Nap, you're really a featherbrain sometimes." She sighed. "It's not based on looks. It's based on… lineage."

"Tanner, either tell them or let me. We have better things to do than draw this anticlimax out." The Governor sounded ready to knock some heads. I didn't want to see the attempt—the chances of me laughing were too high, and it seemed like we were going for tense and solemn.

"Fine, sorry sir. Seraphime is a name associated with Aviatian royalty. You may recall, a few years ago, there was a huge interplanetary manhunt. Well, womanhunt, really. Because the youngest member of the Aviatian Royal Family had disappeared?"

"Vaguely." Hadn't concerned me, didn't care.

"Oh, I remember," Randolph said. "Everyone was upset, she was kidnapped right before her wedding or something."

"She wasn't kidnapped," Slinkie snapped. "Did you take a look at the atrocity they had set to marry me—" She slammed her mouth shut.

Reality dawned. "You're Princess Seraphime?" My Slinkie? A princess? Looks-wise, sure, though I usually considered royalty to be just this side of barking. Clearly they ran to better genetics on Aviatus.

"He was a disgusting dodo and almost as old as the Governor! I was not going to hang around to get married off because it was convenient."

"No argument coming from me." I pondered. "How did you escape and stay hidden?"

Everyone, including Randolph, gave me a look that said I was an idiot. Tanner answered. "Well, as far as our intelligence network was able to ascertain, she hooked up with a space pirate who doesn't base out of any particular planet."

"When was Slinkie with some space pirate I don't know about?"

"Never, Nap." Slinkie started to laugh. "And this is why my cover was never going to get blown. Until the hatchling showed up," she added with a snarl for Tanner.

"Oh, it'll get blown in a nanosecond as soon as the de Chance crew from Aviatus sees you, Princess." Tanner looked at me. He was also laughing. "Nap, you moron, she hooked up with you. She jumped a lot of ships, found the one where she fit in, and she stuck around. It's taken years for us to figure out who she was crewing with."

A different light dawned. "That's why you were head-ing to Runilio. To intercept us." I could tell from his expression I was right. Might be stupid about Slinkie but not about self-preservation. "But how would you know?"

He coughed. "That order for magma you were trying fill? I originated it."

The Governor gave him a sharp look. "We took that order from the Ipsita Company, but it came through Janz the Butcher."

Tanner shrugged. "Yes, it did. And it took several months to get to Janz and a few more to get to Ipsita and then to all of you. I told you—I've been doing this a long time."

"How did you figure we wouldn't fill the order on Thurge?"

"Once I knew who Princess Seraphime was hiding with, I did extensive research. Your, ah, way with the ladies wasn't exactly hidden information. It's not hard to remind women of the guy who loved and left them."

"You're the reason we're in this mess?"

"No. Slinkie's the reason you're in this mess." Tanner didn't sound accusatory. He was also, as I thought about it, probably right.

"I'm not going back." Slinkie's voice was very calm. "I'd truly rather die."

"Like I'd let anyone take you where you didn't want to go?" This earned me a fast shot of the dove-look. Slinkie liked me possessive and protective. Check. I was good with that.

Tanner shrugged. "Should we survive this particular encounter? All your father really wants to know is that you're alive and well."

"He knows."

"No, he doesn't."

"How long have you known?"

"A couple of years."

"Then that's how long my father's known, isn't it?"

Tanner sighed. "No. I haven't told him. I haven't told anyone."

Slinkie looked at him, the shock obvious. "What do you mean? Why not?"

"I'm a telepath, remember? I was already in active service when you ran off. I read your intended, well for the brief moment before my mind slammed shut on him. Not as bad as Nitin, but honestly, pretty close. I wouldn't take a woman I despised back to him, let alone someone I like. And, yeah, if you go back, he's still waiting for you."

"All these years? I mean, Slinkie's worth waiting for, but that seems a little over-committed, especially since she left him at the altar."

The Governor sighed. "Sometimes, Alexander, you're so simple and short-sighted. Miss Slinkie's intended isn't waiting for her out of love or even lust. He's waiting because marrying into the Aviatian Royal Family is a very good thing. And he's from a very needy planet."

"You know?" Slinkie sounded surprised.

"My dear, I knew who you were the first time I laid eyes on you."

Randolph coughed. "Me, too."

Slinkie's jaw dropped. I only managed to keep mine closed. "How? I mean, Randolph, you never said anything."

He shrugged. "You didn't want anyone to know. Saladine and I both figured it out, and it was obvious why you needed to hide. You were great with weapons, normally nice to be around, and Nap was in love with you. Seemed like good reasons to help you keep your secret identity, well, secret. What?" he asked in answer to the look I knew I was giving him.

"I don't think you needed to say that out loud."

"Nap, it's really obvious you're in love with Slinkie," Tanner said.

Lionside nodded. "Nauseatingly obvious."

"Even to me," Audrey added.

"Do I need to chime in, or are you clear that I, needless to say, knew you were in love with her before you did?" The Governor was back to his translations. Nice to see that my love life rated so high on his interest meter.

"Nap, if it's any consolation, I wasn't sure." Slinkie gave me the eagle-glare. "You sleeping with half the galaxy wasn't exactly a tip-off."

"Slink, I keep on telling you—I sleep with them because I can't have you. If I now have you, why would I want any of them?"

"Why aren't you calling me Princess Seraphime?" Said with curiosity, not pique.

I shrugged. "Aside from the fact that you don't like it and don't want to be Princess Seraphime any more?" She nodded. "Slinkie fits you."

She stared at me for a few long moments. "You know there's no money or power that comes along with fleeing royalty."

"See, that's why we're in the business we're in, Slink. Don't need to marry into money if you're capable of stealing all you need in the first place."

I got the dove-look again. "You really don't see this as any big deal?"

"No. I see it as a great reason for me to stick with my original plan."

CHAPTER 74

There was an appreciative pause before Lionside asked the inevitable question. "Just what is your original plan?"

"I want Audrey and Slinkie staying on board the *Sixty-Nine*, and I want all three of my women in hiding."

"Three?" Tanner asked.

"Ships are female," Randolph answered. "I agree with the idea, Nap, but how are we going to do it?"

"Hulky? You able to flash into this area?" A green grid placed itself next to Audrey's slide show. "Good man. Okay, anywhere on this rock we can hide you and the girls? Until such time as we start screaming for you and the girls to come rescue us, that is?"

A variety of schematics flashed along. I got the impression Hulky was looking at and then dismissing options. Hulky finally settled on a schematic. Looked like a lot of lines to me. But there were no dots.

"Captain, I believe we would be able to hide the ship in the area denoted. However, I'm concerned that we would be easily tracked."

"Oh, I doubt it."

"Why not?" Tanner sounded worried. "I mean, even if we had a beacon calling to the armada, they'd know we had a ship here. How else did we get here?"

"See, that's the thing. We're not going to be here." I got the group look of confusion and disbelief. Always nice to know my crew believed in me. "We're going to fly over to Trennile Main and be dropped off. Audrey can pilot back here and hide. We'll steal a ship and be up in the air before the de Chance Family Pirates show up."

"You make that sound so simple." Lionside sounded less than thrilled. "How in the world do you think we'll get away with something like this so easily?"

"Well, it might not be easy but—" I was interrupted by a change in Hulky's schematic. Instead of a grid, there was a circle within a circle, with two lines going out in a V from the top. I stared at it. "Um, Hulky? You trying to tell me something?"

Apparently he was, since the picture began flashing. It rang no bells.

"It's a couple of circles attached to a couple of lines." Slinkie sounded annoyed. "You know, that's pretty useless as a clue."

Hulky scrambled the picture. I got the impression he was doing the electronic equivalent of heaving a huge sigh. A stick figure appeared, with the circles and lines superimposed over it.

"Oh! It's a necklace." Randolph, unsurprisingly, was the one to pick up the electronic charades.

"It wants us wearing necklaces?" Lionside sounded as confused as I felt.

Hulky drew a crude ship around the stick figure. "That the *Sixty-Nine*?" The picture flashed, so I took that as a yes. "Sorry, still no idea what you're going for."

More stick figures appeared. Two had 'hair'. I counted—the stick figures corresponded to the number of us on the *Sixty-Nine*. Only the one was wearing a necklace.

"You want Nap to wear a necklace?" Randolph asked. The schematic flashed again. I was sure it was in frustration. The necklace grew larger. "Oh. He's wearing a necklace?" The schematic flashed again, this time, clearly showing joy.

"I'm wearing a necklace?" I was? I pondered. Oh, right, I was. That thing I'd taken from Nitin. I pulled it out. "Yeah, forgot about it."

Randolph stared at it, eyes almost bugging out of his head. "Where did you get that?" His voice was hushed, like we were visiting a shrine to Weshria's top god.

"Took it off of Nitin. Forgot about it. Why?"

"Could I see it?"

Couldn't think of a reason why not. Took it off and tossed it over. Randolph looked panicked and almost fumbled the catch. "Don't throw this, Nap. Ever again." His hands shook. "I haven't seen one of these in years."

"What is it? And why can't I throw it?" It wasn't that great to look at and why should I care about preserving something of Nitin's?

"Because this is one of the most rare things in the galaxy." Randolph's voice was shaking like his hands.

"Looks like an unimpressive decoration to me," Lionside said. The rest of the crew, Audrey included, nodded.

The Governor deigned to take an interest. I saw him stiffen. "Randolph, has Alexander damaged it?"

"Not that I can tell."

"Can you make more of them?"

"Now that I have a prototype? Yes, probably."

"Excellent. Make it so and be sure to determine if you can create one that will work for the entire ship."

"Good idea, Governor."

They were off in their own little world. "Excuse me? What is that and why do you think I'm going to okay it being put on my ship?"

Randolph looked at me, eyes wide, still breathless. "It's a matter-shifter. There are only a few in existence."

Tanner and Lionside sucked in their breath. Slinkie, thankfully, spoke for both of us. "What does it do?"

Randolph managed a smile. "It allows you to shift matter wherever you want, whenever you want. If we'd had this, we could have just moved onto the *Sixty-Nine* and left without any of the other stuff we went through."

Thudding silence hit again. Tanner broke it. "Ah, if Nap took it from Nitin, then we did have it."

"We could have avoided the hazard suits and the sewer system?" Slinkie's voice was back to creating space ice.

"We could have avoided blowing up the entire Herion Spaceport?" Lionside was matching her.

"Yes," Randolph confirmed.

Everyone gave me the hairy eyeball. I shrugged. "Sure, we could have. But think of all the fun we'd have missed."

CHAPTER 75

"Fun?" Slinkie didn't sound amused. "You call everything we went through fun?"

There was much crew grumbling. I shrugged. "I didn't know what it was. We're all alive and two of you, Tanner and Lionside, should be happy I had no idea what I was wearing. Or you'd both be on Herion and we'd be long gone."

Tanner sighed. "Good point. How powerful is it?" he asked Randolph.

"Not sure. Audrey and I need to spend some time on it."

"Do we have enough time?" I really didn't want to engage the *Sixty-Nine* with the armada if I could help it.

"I think so. Excuse us." Randolph wandered off to his part of the ship, aka the parts I rarely ventured into. That load of droppings that a captain knows every part of his ship is just that—a load. Captains who know every single part are captains who can't find a Chief Engineer. Randolph was many things, but among them, he was the best CE out there. He didn't tell me how to fly, I didn't tell him how to keep us flying.

"Captain, I have uploaded the disc's contents to the main computer. You can continue to view the pictures where it's convenient." Audrey trotted off after Randolph.

"I think I've seen enough. Tanner, Governor, you want them left up?"

"Yes, so we can start cataloguing." The Governor was back to his translations. I'd never realized all I needed to get to keep him occupied and quiet was a puzzle book. Good to know for the future. If we had one.

"Fine. Hulky, let's move to that safe and hidden area." I got the schematic flash that meant affirmative. Wandered back to the cockpit. Slinkie came with me. Sadly, so did Lionside.

"Do you need a copilot?" Lionside asked.

"Rarely if ever, and certainly not to do this, thanks for asking."

"No need to get defensive. I do know how to pilot. Not up to your reputed skills, but enough to get by if needed."

"Good to know." I planned to never need it.

"You still want to go steal a ship?" Slinkie didn't sound against the idea.

"Not sure. If Randolph can do whatever it is he does with that matter-shifter, then we might not have to."

"Think he'll be able to?" Lionside asked as he seated himself in the copilot's seat.

"If anyone can, Randolph can. Lionside, why do you think I'm going to okay your taking Audrey's seat?"

"I don't. I'd like to know what your plan is, beyond our leaving the women planetside and hoping the pirate armada doesn't notice."

"Bryant has a point."

"You too? Okay, fine. We have something with us the pirates want."

"The *Sixty-Nine*," Slinkie offered.

"You," Lionside suggested.

"Information about who actually killed Lucky Pierre, Senior."

They were both quiet. "What kind of information?" Slinkie asked finally.

"The kind offspring with a grudge are interested in. They do want the *Sixty-Nine*. I doubt they want me. But Nitin was trying to make me think they wanted me. So, they want me where they can see me."

"How do you figure?" Lionside sounded like he was thinking again.

"Nitin didn't kill me when he had the easy chance. It's not like someone else can't fly the *Sixty-Nine*. If all they wanted was my ship, have one of Nitin's goons fly it, or have one of Lucky P's boys sneak in and fly it out. But I'm still amazingly alive. And Nitin's plan was to get me into solarspace and hooked up with the armada pronto."

"Why? I thought he wanted Audrey?" Slinkie sounded confused.

"Nitin does, yeah. But I think he's working on his own plan, that maybe his other family members don't know about."

"Or they want Audrey, too," Lionside said.

"Possible. We don't know enough to make a confident guess. However, we do know they want the *Sixty-Nine* without any question. So, I don't want to give her to them. We also know the moment they identify who Slinkie really is, they'll realize they have the best living cargo in the galaxy. Slinkie'll be back on Aviatus and married off to the Creature from the Aqueesis Depths and the armada will have moved successfully into Aviatian solarspace."

"That would be very bad."

"Thank you for stating the obvious, Lionside. Don't you have a job to do?"

"You put me in charge of communications. No one to communicate with at the moment, other than you and the rest of the crew. I'd be happy to discuss Aviatian politics with Slinkie."

I looked at him out of the corner of my eye. Baiting me, for sure. But willing, should I be stupid. "No, feel free to stay here and annoy me."

He grinned. "Thought so."

"Flattering as this is, what's the rest of your plan, Nap? I don't like the idea of cowering, and you know it."

"I don't want you cowering. I want you monitoring. I'm sure something's going to go wrong and I'm going to be screaming for you. I just want you to be sure when it's real screaming versus when it's fake screaming."

"You can fake scream?" Lionside asked.

"Women do it all the time," Slinkie said with far too much laughter in her tone.

"Never to me, Slink. Never to me."

CHAPTER 76

Found the hiding spot Hulky had picked out. Had to give the program credit—no one was going to spot us visually. We were at the bottom of a deep canyon, under a huge overhang of solid rock, with a variety of jutting rocks and stones piled randomly in front of the entrance. They still left enough room to maneuver, but no one would think this was a landing area under a normal visual scan.

The overhang and cave area had some kind of natural metal in it. Once hidden, the *Sixty-Nine*'s scanners reacted as if we were in a bizarre electromagnetic field, so we felt confident the metal would confuse other scanners enough that we could hide here and not be detected by the majority of electronics. Hulky's scanning, however, had no issues with the area, which was why we found the cave and could see what was around us.

According to both the Governor and Lionside, the Hulkinator had been the only Herion ship equipped with this kind of scanning system. It was antiquated and the consensus was if Nitin was going to steal Herion military secrets, he'd have chosen something flashier, newer and a whole lot more impressive sounding. They always sold me short, too. My affection for Hulky and his talents grew.

Randolph's voice came through the com. "Nap, I think we can replicate it. The metals in the rocks where we are happen to be very rare, and they're what's used in this matter-shifter."

"Good. How fast?"

"Because Audrey's fully functional, very fast." His voice vibrated with possessive pride. I really hoped he'd made her susceptible to flattery, because there were times I was with Slinkie and didn't buy Audrey's protestations that she would never look to trade up.

"Make it so. How do we safely test it?"

"Needs a human test, Nap. Non-organic and non-sentient matter can be moved with them, but in order to work them properly, it needs someone to set coordinates and such. It doesn't respond to Audrey like it responds to me, so she can't be the tester."

"No problem. Lionside's volunteered. Good man."

"Thanks, Outland," Lionside said. "But, realistically, I'm the best choice for the job."

I looked. Nope, he wasn't being sarcastic. "Want to explain your thinking?"

He shrugged. "You're the captain and the crux of the plan and the pirate's focus. Can't risk something going wrong with you. Randolph and Audrey are too vital to the ship's functioning. The Governor's too old. Young Tanner has important skills that shouldn't be risked. Slinkie has both necessary skills and is also the last person in the galaxy you, personally, want to risk, a sentiment I agree with. That pretty much leaves me. I also happen to be military, well, former military now. I'm trained to handle things when they go wrong. I'm big, I'm strong, and I'm willing to kill someone if I have to."

"You know, I hate to say this, but I like how you think. Tell me—were you at all happy in Herion Military?"

He was quiet for a few long moments. "No. Not so much."

I knew it. He wasn't getting off-ship once we defeated the armada. Oh well, I'd adjust once I knew if we were going to live longer than tomorrow. "Randolph, how long before we have a test model?"

"Ready now, Captain." Audrey shoved into the cockpit, what looked like the necklace I'd taken from Nitin in her hand. "While it looks like one ring of metal around the milky stone, there are really five rings. You manipulate them to move where you want and with whatever you want going along with you."

She described what went where and why. Seemed easy enough. "So it's somewhat thought-based?"

"Yes. The stone pulls your thoughts in and then the metal components shift your matter to your desired location."

"You don't find that fuzzy or funny?"

"No, Captain. There are many things that work like this. You just don't realize it."

"Take your word on it, Audrey. I don't want the rundown now." Lionside took the matter-shifter and put it around his neck. As he did, I noticed something. "Where did we get another leather strap?"

Audrey cleared her throat. I didn't know Sexbots could do that. Randolph did engineer well. "It was easier to, ah, clone a duplicate than build from scratch."

That sat on the air for a few long moments. "We can clone things?"

"I can clone things, yes." She seemed embarrassed. "It's how I would… create progeny."

"Randolph set you up so that you can have children?" I was back to adding into the Book of Randolph.

"Yes, Captain. I look forward to it."

"They'll come out little or big?" I didn't know why I was asking. I truly didn't want to know—the images in my mind were somewhat horrifying.

"I can adjust the cloning process. For children, little. For something like this, fully formed and ready to go."

I looked at Lionside. He nodded. "No wonder Nitin wanted Audrey."

"How did he know, though? Randolph, how did you come up with all of Audrey's many bells and whistles?"

"Oh, well, some of them I did myself, Nap. But there's an underground manual from a couple of centuries ago, and I have a copy. There are only three in existence. It takes a strong engineering aptitude to be able to understand, let alone create, from it."

"A manual? What's the title and who's the author? And how did you get one of the only copies available?"

"It's *Build a Better Robot* by Larry Isaacs. Most of the copies were destroyed during the Omnimus Overthrow of twenty-two-twenty-five. The legend has it that three Athriall monks took one copy each and hid them in the far reaches of the galaxy, so the Omnimuns couldn't stomp out all cloning."

Interesting theory. Not sure I bought into it, especially since something like this would be hugely valuable and, therefore, I'd think as a pirate I'd have heard of it. "How'd you get one of the three copies?"

"I won it during a poker game."

"I beat you at poker. All the time."

"Yeah, but you're the best player around. I've been playing against you a long time. I've managed to pick something up." He sounded both insulted and accusatory.

"Fine, whatever. Who'd you win it from?"

"Some guy named Peter Chance."

CHAPTER 77

The silence was awe-inspiring. I tried to think of what to say. "You're an idiot" seemed so right and yet so likely to cause an argument we didn't have time for. "Do you know how to translate names at all?" was another one, probable same outcome. "Why me, oh Active Gods, why me?" seemed to cover it.

Slinkie recovered faster than me. "Randolph, how long ago and how old was this Peter Chance?"

"A few years ago. I think you'd just joined up with us, Slinkie, might have even been before."

"You won one of the most rare books in the galaxy and you don't remember when it happened?" Lionside sounded like he was channeling every prisoner interrogation he'd ever done.

"I've had it a while. So what?"

"This Chance guy, how old was he?"

"Older than me. Not old enough to be my father, but close."

"So, Junior had it on him and lost it. No wonder the second generation didn't do anything—they were led by an idiot." Anyone who put up a rarity of this magnitude as a poker stake was, in my book, automatically a moron.

"What do you mean?" Randolph sounded confused. Of course. We were talking about the obvious, politics, and familial succession. Naturally he was floating in space without a lifeline.

"I mean you won this from Lucky Pierre's son. Audrey will explain it to you later. Right now, we have bigger problems."

"So, they want the ship, they want Audrey, they want the guy who can make more Audreys, they want the manual." Slinkie sounded ill.

"And, the moment they see you, they'll want you too, Slink. Probably Tanner, if they figure out he's got telepathic skills. Hell, why not take Mister Name of Kings? For all we know, they'll see a way to use you, too, Lionside."

"Potentially." He sighed. "We still need to test this." He pointed to the matter-shifter around his neck.

I opened my mouth but shut it again. Hulky was flashing a picture of the Trennile solar system. And there were a dozen little dots flying around it. I thought fast. "Lionside, give me that necklace for a moment. Audrey, how many clones have you made?"

"Just the one so far, Captain."

"And, how many people can this one transport, besides the wearer?"

"Without testing it, I'd say no more than one. The range could be better, but we haven't had time to verify."

"Uh huh." Not a surprise. I knew how my luck ran. "Show me again how I would work this to get onto the flagship of the oncoming fleet."

She fiddled with it. "It's set now, Captain. You'd put it to your forehead and focus on your destination."

Hulky flashed a dot at me urgently. I marked where it was in relation to the planets and other vessels. "Thanks, big guy. How would I get back?"

"Same thing, Captain. It's set for a round trip, if you will."

"Seems so easy." I doubted it would be in reality. I got up, put the necklace on, and wandered out of the cockpit. The others trailed after me. "Governor, need you for a moment."

He looked up. "Yes?"

"I need you to stand up and come over to me. Just for a minute."

Got the martyred sigh, but he did as I asked. "What's this about, Alexander? Tanner and I were about to start the cross-referencing."

"It'll wait." I put my arm around his shoulders. "Slink, you're in charge. Get us when you should get us—you'll know when." I slapped the pendant to my forehead and thought about heading to the last place I really wanted to go. I heard a variety of shouts and protests from the crew, but the shifter worked quickly and they faded from view fast.

It seemed to work. The positive was that I still had the Governor with me and I managed to slide the matter-shifter under my shirt while we were moving. The negative was that no one had mentioned that matter-shifting was hard on the body, the mind, and most importantly, the stomach.

Managed not to toss my comets and asteroids, but it was a near thing. Of course, looking around at where we'd ended up, vomiting might have been an improvement.

We were on the command deck of the main vessel in the armada. It was big enough to warrant a command deck, versus a cockpit. It was manned with a lot of people who all looked vaguely familiar, as if I'd just seen their photos flashed over and over again against the walls of the *Sixty-Nine*'s dining area.

And they were all, to a person, pointing guns at us. Situations like these demanded a great opening line. The line I wanted didn't come to me, but one that pretty much summed up the entire trip so far did.

"Wow, Governor, I guess we're not on Knaboor any more."

CHAPTER 78

A leggy blonde who looked familiar stalked over to us. She was dressed like a fantasy woman pirate— tight blouse, tight leather pants, bandoliers crossed over her impressive planetary simulations, knee-high leather boots, laser pistol on one hip, what looked like an Omnimun saber hanging off the other.

I couldn't imagine what the bandoliers were for, other than to keep her rack in place—lasers and sabers didn't need bullets and she didn't have knives or explosives hooked in them. They did show off her assets impressively, so I went with them being a decorative touch and nod to the ancient past when no self-respecting pirate would have let a woman on board unless she was flat on her back.

On the Slinkie Scale, she wasn't at the top, but she was close, bandoliers or no bandoliers. I was also pretty sure she was Nitin's sister. I wondered where her Ebegorn tattoo was. I hoped it was in the same spot as Nitin's. Or on her butt. Lower back would be acceptable as well. Forced my mind back to the matter at hand.

She glared at me. "Who are you and what are you doing on my ship?"

I figured I had nothing to lose with honesty. "Looking for Pierre de Chance."

Her mouth quirked. "Why?"

"Have something for him. Possibly, anyway." I still had my arm around the Governor, who was looking particularly frail. I figured it was his act, but the possibility that the shift had caused him problems was there. Decided him collapsing on the floor wasn't in my best interests at the moment. Kept my arm around him. "Where is he?"

"He's been dead for fifty years." Her voice was both icy and amused.

"Oh, I know that." Nice to know I'd figured the Governor's time fudging correctly. "I know who killed him. And I'm not interested in Petey, Junior, either. I want to talk to this generation's top bird."

She smirked at me. "Why should we take you to our, ah, top bird?"

"Oh, give it a rest. You know who I am."

"True. And who you're hugging."

"We believe in revering the elderly on my planet." I hoped she thought the Governor was Murgat, not the Butcher. Figured we'd find out fast, one way or the other.

She snorted. "Right. So, what information do you have for our top bird?"

"I like to give top information to the top directly. Saves time, saves confusion. Sure, it cuts out the middleman, but that way, you get your information wholesale."

She gave me a wide, slow smile. "Feel free to spit it out."

"Like to know who I'm talking to, first."

She shrugged. Not up to Slinkie's standards but still worthwhile to watch. "I'm Charmaine de Chance. And my eyes are up here."

Unlike Randolph, I could translate names. "Lucky Charm?" Truly, who named these people, and could I find and hurt them, even retroactively? Forced my eyes back up. Not as hard as leaving Slinkie's rack, but I did find myself glad I'd left her on the *Sixty-Nine*—I didn't need to deal with the vulture-glare right now.

She grinned. "So to speak."

"So, Captain Charm, I presume?"

"Feel free to call me Commander de Chance. Since we have a fleet, I outrank you. And, since you supposedly have information I'm eager for, please tell me what it is before I have you killed."

"Always with your family it's the killing."

Charmaine raised her eyebrow. Nice arch. "Who else from my family do you know?"

"I've become close enemies with your brother recently."

Her eyes narrowed. "Oh, really? How's the little weasel doing?"

"Nice try. He's handling your operations on the ground."

Charmaine's eyes were still narrowed. "No, he's not. The traitor went planetside and hasn't done one thing he was supposed to."

"Oh, don't sell him short. He tried to kill me."

"Yet, you're here, alive and well."

"Aren't you lucky? Well, considering, I guess you are. Always. In that sense."

"I'm lucky, you're not."

"Oh? I was lucky enough to get away from you on our way into Herion's solarspace."

She shook her head. "I'd assume that was skill. So, what is it you wanted to offer me? Your ship? I'll find it and take it. Your crew? Got a crew, would never be able to trust yours. You? You're not bad to look at, and your reputation precedes you, but I need a pilot I can't trust less than I need crew I can't trust."

"Hmmm. So it's in my best interests to hang onto my information a while longer and see if I can charm you into adding me and my crew on as the lucky thirteen in your fleet."

"It's in your best interests to pray to your gods for safe passage to the next world."

"Oh, come on. If you kill me right now, you won't know what it is I'm here to offer, you won't know what all your brother's been up to, and you won't get to find out if my reputation's true or not." I winked. "It's true."

She rolled her eyes. "Yes, I did hear that you didn't have any problems with a small ego."

"Let me reassure you—nothing's small on the Outland."

"You actually refer to yourself as 'the Outland'?"

"Amazing, isn't it?" the Governor said.

Charmaine gave him a long look. "So, what's a deposed, washed-up politician doing with the most overrated pirate in the galaxy?"

The Governor and I looked at each other. "I beg your pardon, young lady. Washed up?" He sounded just this side of furious.

"Yeah, and overrated? Hardly, babe. If I were overrated, you'd have caught me before we ever made Herion."

"I've caught you now." Charmaine looked smug.

"Well, see, here's the thing. I got onto your ship without your consent. And I can get off it without your consent, too. Whether or not you'll be around to know about it is the issue."

She snorted. "Right. Just what do you think you're going to threaten me with? The ancient you're clinging to? The possibility of having sex with you? The likelihood that you have a plan other than running your mouth?"

"Nah. I thought I'd try being friendly and, since you keep on forgetting about it, sharing some information I know you'll want to have. Or do you really not have any interest in taking revenge on the person who offed dear old Lucky Pierre the Original?"

"I'm interested. Somewhat, at any rate."

"Good. Then I'll bet you'll be even more interested to know all that your brother's been up to." She nodded. "Great. Then my real news should excite you beyond belief."

CHAPTER 79

Real news?" Charmaine's interest finally sounded truly captured. Great. Now, just had to come up with something better than sharing that I had the entire de Chance Family Album uploaded to the *Sixty-Nine*.

In cases like this, stalling had always been my friend. I decided to stick with the tried and true. I let go of the Governor—he seemed fine on his own power. Rolled my shoulders, stood up straight, relaxed a bit. Ready to leap out of the way or drop to the floor, depending.

Took a look around. Drop to the floor would be the only option—we were still surrounded by de Chance progeny and they were still pointing weapons at us. Noted all of them were dressed like Charmaine, in what I considered "Ipsita Casual"—clothing only found in entertainment, never worn in real life.

I took a closer look. They were all my age or younger. Most of them were closer to Tanner's age. Lionside would seem old to them, let alone the Governor. They all also had looks on their faces that were vaguely familiar. True, I hadn't seen something like this since I'd left Zyzzx, but some things you didn't forget. Their expressions were all overdone, like they were copying something from the latest Ipsita release.

Reality waved. The de Chances were poseurs. Good at it, but still, in reality, fakes, kids playing dress up with real ships and guns. Killing real people and doing very bad things, but clearly with the mindset that, in a way, it wasn't real. I realized why Nitin had split, if, in fact, Charmaine wasn't lying about it—he had the pure nasty naturally. The rest of them, not so much.

I'd spent too long observing. "Well?" Charmaine sounded annoyed. Annoyed and ready to give a sign to her cast to shoot. More stalling was in order.

"Candy?" I pulled out a random sweet from Nitin's store and offered it to her.

Charmaine went pale. "Don't threaten me."

"With sugar? You've got a nice figure but a couple of extra pounds wouldn't be a problem."

"Don't toy with her, Alexander," the Governor said, voice on full quaver. "You know that's not a candy."

I did? If it wasn't a candy, what was it? Did my best not to look or sound confused. "Well, where's the fun in not playing around?"

"No one but a lunatic plays around with Plastiques." Charmaine sounded different—I realized she was frightened. About time. Thought about what I was holding, and what I apparently had a pocket full of—got a little tense myself.

Plastiques were bombs. Effective, nasty, and above all, small bombs. Disguised to look like something ordinary. And, if the Governor's reactions were right, I was carrying a pocketful of them. Enough to blow up the entire armada.

My original impression of Nitin returned. He hadn't underestimated me, like Tanner thought. He hadn't been overconfident, like Lionside thought. He'd anticipated me perfectly, right down to the smallest details—and I'd stopped thinking about it, because we'd been too busy trying to stay alive for me to really consider why Nitin would have come into that interrogation cell alone. He'd let me escape, and put this entire plan into motion. And I'd helped him, the entire way.

No time to berate myself right now, though. I had to determine if the enemy of my enemy was a weaker or a worse enemy. The possibility of them being my friend wasn't in the realm of reality—sure they were playing at what their grandfather had almost achieved with hard work, but the genetics were there to create havoc. Herion's situation was proof they were effective. Which made me wonder whose plan they were following—Charmaine's or Nitin's. Or Lucky the First's. Or, worse thought, someone else's heretofore unnamed and unknown.

"I'm not a lunatic so much as someone who doesn't like being forced to do things against my will. Call me uncomfortable with authority other than my own."

Charmaine nodded. I got the distinct impression she was trying not to make me mad. Did a remedial review of Plastiques. They were set off by a variety of mechanisms—sound, force, triggers. Really, you named it, a Plastique could go off at any time from it.

We hadn't blown to bits when we were in Lake Disgusting, so I had to presume these weren't sound-sensitive. We weren't blowing up now, so if they were trigger-set, Nitin's triggering mechanism had been destroyed. This left the easy answer of force as the explosive mechanism. If you chewed it, your head and the heads of anyone within a mile radius would explode. Wondered if the Land League had been using these explosives to blow up the bathhouse and the Crazy Bear. Decided that was more of an issue for Lionside to be concerned with than me.

I closed my hand around the candy. "Now, before I ensure no one on this ship ever has to worry about creating the next generation of de Chances, why don't you tell me what's going on?"

"We want to control the galaxy." Charmaine said this like it was some big reveal.

"Yeah, really clear on that. Put the damned weapons away or I squeeze my hand really hard." She nodded, the weapons went down.

The Governor did a slow turn. "He meant all the weapons, children, not just the ones in the front. That's better." He shook his head. "Amateurs."

"No argument." I shot Charmaine my best withering glare. I'd seen it enough from Slinkie, figured I was probably good at imitating it. "Whose plan is it you're following?"

Plastiques or no, she got annoyed. Her eyes narrowed again and she clenched her jaw. Not bad. Slinkie still looked better doing something like this, though. "My plan. Are you insinuating I can't think strategically because I'm a woman?"

"No, I'm insinuating that I already know you're following the blueprint your dearly departed set up decades ago. I'm asking why your brother's on Herion and just what is it the two of you think you're pulling."

She opened her mouth and the sound of claxons came out of it. Charmaine closed her mouth. The claxons continued. Something of a relief, really.

One of the family who hadn't been surrounding us raced over. Not as good in the looks department as Charmaine but did have a decent rack. I could tell, because faux pirate wear didn't really offer the lift and support so important to the full-figured woman.

"Commander, Herion Military ships coming to engage!"

CHAPTER 80

Charmaine barked orders and the Governor and I were suddenly very alone. Plastiques held nothing like the terror a Herion Military fleet did.

"So, you think Lionside called in the troops?"

"Sadly, no, Alexander. I think Nitin got rid of the one man who might possibly have stood in his way by making it more worthwhile for the Major to join up with us."

"Yeah, sadly, that's what I was thinking, too." I pondered. "I really want to go back to the *Sixty-Nine* and get our flock out of here."

"Not an option. This armada must be stopped or at least have their wings severely clipped. And Nitin cannot be allowed to follow Lucky Pierre's plan with the might of Herion Military behind him."

I sighed. "I knew you were going to say that." I pondered—I didn't want the *Sixty-Nine* engaged unless we had no shot of survival otherwise. "I wish I could talk to Tanner."

The Governor shrugged. "What do you want to ask him?"

"Which ship in this fleet is the best and which pilot is the worst."

The Governor closed his eyes. "Huh, interesting. The flagship would be considered best, but young Tanner says the ship manned by the worst pilot would probably be more what you're looking for."

"Um, how are you talking to him?"

"Comlink."

"We don't use comlinks."

"You, Randolph and Slinkie don't use comlinks because you all mistakenly feel they contributed to Saladine's death. Audrey, as a logical being, knows differently. Ergo, she uses a comlink. I have one installed, and young Tanner agreed it was a good idea. The Major did as well."

"So you can chat with the three of them?"

"When necessary, yes."

"Where's it installed, your brain? You didn't repeat anything I said."

"It's in a molar. Very safe, very easy, hard to spot, convenient because it's also close to the ear canal. You're standing next to me and the range is very good. Hence, Tanner could hear you because I could hear you."

"When did you have time to do this?"

"When we returned to the ship. On Herion. While you were playing around with the Hulkinator. It doesn't take long. And it doesn't hurt. Which I mention so you'll whine less when you finally see reason." He reached into my shirt and pulled out the matter-shifter. "You might want to hold onto me again, Alexander." I grabbed him around his shoulders just in time.

We did the shift and my stomach complained. This one wasn't quite as bad as the first, possibly because we weren't going as far. We were in the cockpit of a different ship. One of the many vaguely familiar de Chances was piloting, assisted by a different de Chance as copilot.

"Who are you and what are you doing here?" the pilot shouted.

I let go of the Governor and slammed the de Chance heads together. Lionside probably would've gotten a better crack, but I represented Zyzzx pretty well. They both went down and out.

The Governor and I flung them out of the cockpit. "Nice, a locking door." I so locked. "Think they'll shoot through it?"

"No. I plan to advise Miss de Chance that we're here." The Governor put on the communications headset this ship ran with and started chatting. I decided my skills were better used in figuring out how this ship flew.

The ship appeared to have been from Weshria originally—I recognized the instrument panel. Good for me, I could fly all of Weshria's ships. I hadn't been on it long or gotten a tour, but I was pretty sure the command ship was from Earth. Took a guess that the other ships in this fleet would be from a variety of planets.

I wondered why the Governor, Tanner and Lionside had accepted a comlink so easily. Especially one that was internal to the head. Maybe Lionside and Tanner had just gotten used to taking orders. Or their military training said it was no big deal.

Memory stirred. The Governor and I had been pretty sure this crew was following a military leader. But Charmaine didn't seem like military so much as she seemed like a good actress. Nitin was military, but I was inclined to believe Charmaine—it was too clear he was working his own scheme. So, who was the military brains behind the New French Ticklers?

"I need to talk to Randolph."

The Governor sighed. "For all your complaining about him, pray he never dies or gets sick of you. You can't manage without regular contact with him."

"Many would say the same about you. Want me to airlock both of you and see how I do, just for the sake of scientific discovery?"

"So testy. The Major has secured a private channel from this ship to the *Sixty-Nine*. Only live in the cockpit." He flipped a switch. "Go ahead."

"Randolph, the Peter Chance you won the manual from, what line of work was he in and what planet was he from?"

"He was from Earth, Nap, at least as far as I could tell. He was on leave when I met him, didn't really discuss his career, sorry."

On leave. Only one class of person called a vacation taking leave. "What branch of the military was he in, do you remember?"

"No. He wasn't in uniform."

"Audrey?"

"Running queries now, Captain. Hulky is helping tremendously, I must add. We wouldn't be able to contact you or Galaxy Central without his help, due to our location."

"Have either the armada or the Herion fleet found you?"

"Not as far as we can tell."

"Good. Let me know when you find something, anything, Audrey."

"Will do, Captain."

"Nap, what in the egg is going on?"

"Herion Military's decided to join the fun, Slink. I think Lucky, Junior's still alive and running the show. Need to find out where he is and do the whole déjà vu thing all over again."

"You sure? I mean, Randolph beat him at poker." Slinkie didn't sound convinced that anyone who Randolph could beat could be in charge of this kind of operation. I couldn't blame her.

"You know, you play with the best and things do rub off." Randolph sounded offended. Guessed I couldn't blame him, either.

A thought niggled. "Governor, would you say this was an impromptu or long-term strategic plan?"

He snorted. "Long-term strategic, Alexander."

"I hate to say it gang, but I'm impressed. Audrey, we need to find where Pierre de Chance, Peter Chance, or whatever the many hells he could be calling himself is, what he looks like, and, most importantly, how we get there to kill him."

"No argument, Captain. But why?"

"Because everyone, even Tanner, was wrong. We aren't in this predicament because of me, Tanner, Slinkie or any other human on board. We're in this predicament because of you."

CHAPTER 81

Had to think. Had to fly and think, but flying was second nature. The Governor had cleared us helping the Pirates de Chance with Charmaine. Had to figure she'd take the assist and worry about getting rid of me after we got away from or rid of the Herion fleet. Which bought me some time, but not much.

Left the armada and zipped around the fleet. Figured it was time to see what we were up against. Thirty ships, half of them battle-cruisers, the rest good-sized fighters. No individual jobs, which was good and bad. Good because it meant we had less little bugs to worry about. Bad because they might just be waiting to pour out from some of the cruisers.

"Lionside, where did these ships come from if we blew up the main spaceport on our way out of town?"

"If they're military, they came from our base. Military and civilian don't use the same spaceport." He made it sound obvious. Maybe on Herion it was. On Zyzzx and good number of other planets, a spaceport was a spaceport. "Nitin would have had time to get there from Spaceport City—if he survived the explosion."

"Of course he survived it. Learn now—our luck doesn't run any other way." That Nitin was leading this fleet was a given. "Audrey, if you can spare the time, I want all information on Nigel Nitin pulled out of the Herion Master Computer and the Earth Master, too. Figure he's going by Nigel de Chance on Earth."

"Shouldn't be a problem, Captain." She still sounded calm and cheerful.

"Oh, and Audrey? Have a chat with Lionside. I'd like you to start learning when it's great not to sound all perky."

"This is one of those times, Captain?"

"Yes."

"Got it." Her voice went tense. "Making all haste with the searches."

"Much better, thanks." Went back to flying and pondering. The Governor went onto the ship's command and started barking orders to shoot at the military vessels. One of the many secrets I didn't want anyone to get too comfortable with was that if I really needed or wanted a copilot, the Governor was the best option. Not necessarily better than Audrey—it was hard to beat a computer, after all—but he'd been better than Jack Rock and pretty much as good as Saladine. But having a ninety-some-year-old geezer as your copilot was pretty much the recipe for ridicule in 99.9% of the galaxy. And it didn't hide him nearly as well as him being my perennial passenger did.

"Children, is it so hard to comprehend that you are the ones under attack? Truly, is this the first time you've been challenged? Ever?" Yep, the Governor was enjoying himself.

This ship wasn't the *Sixty-Nine*, but it handled well. Spent a lot of time spinning away from laser cannon fire. The fleet was doing a typical military move—they were trying to surround the armada. "Governor, put the full navigation onscreen for me, will you?" He sighed but did as requested. Nice to see Charmaine wasn't just sitting around. The armada had followed my lead and were erratically circling the fleet.

So Lucky, Junior had two kids and daddy's plan. Pierre the first had undoubtedly been the one who'd gotten his hands on the robotics manual, and somehow he'd passed it along to his #1 son.

But none of them possessed the technical know-how to make an Audrey. Randolph had said it took a lot of skill and training to be able to even read and comprehend the manual, let alone do the creations. Those skills were few and far between. Audrey had been right—if I hadn't kept Randolph with me, because of how badly he did on anything at the Academy not technically-based, a low-level position at a Thurge power plant would be all he could have hoped for. I was the only one who'd seen the genius in him. He hid it well, after all. Contemplated my lifelong streak of finding the best misfit in any crowd. Decided I'd navel-gaze once I could feel confident I'd still have a navel to gaze at.

So that meant Junior had to find someone with the technical expertise and the willingness to give it a go. Maybe that was why the second generation hadn't done anything—no one with the right know-how had been found. Or they all hated each other, which was my gut guess, based on my observations of most extended families I'd ever run across.

That Junior had lost the poker game intentionally was now a given. He'd put the manual up not because he was stupid but because he was clever. Knowing Randolph, he'd looked at and discussed the merits and veracity of the manual—I'd trained him to make sure he was getting real Knaboor Ducats, after all, not dressed up pieces of comet. Proving Randolph's qualifications would have been easy.

Proving I'd finally found the person Tanner and the Governor both felt was truly in charge—the guy who thought like me—was also easy. Because I wasn't having any trouble now in coming up with just what Junior was up to and why he'd done what he had. He was a smart, sneaky bastard but above all, he wanted to stay a smart, sneaky bastard. He was willing to risk his own blood to do it, too. Tanner was right—I could think like someone like this, but I wouldn't allow myself to become someone like this.

Spun through the interior space of the main part of the fleet. The fleet didn't have tractor beams or attach cables active. Wasn't sure yet if this meant they really weren't trying to capture the armada, or if they felt they had too many of their own ships around to take the risk.

I figured Junior had hoped to snatch Randolph somewhere close to when they'd played poker together. But
our exit from Herion was pretty typical—fast and with a
lot of law enforcement sniffing our vapor trail. Had to figure we'd left after that poker game in similar fashion. And
even knowing who Slinkie was hiding with, it had taken
Tanner two years to actually be in a position to collide
with us. So it taking a long time for the de Chance Family
Players to catch up wasn't a surprise.

They were based out of Trennile Main for sure. The
rare metals in the matter-shifter being on Trennile 7 were
proof enough for me. But they weren't really from Trennile Main—they'd just taken it over, probably in Pierre
the First's time.

This clan set a store by their Earth heritage—the flagship was from Earth, their expansion followed Earth
trails. I figured we'd find they were related to some form
of Earth royalty somewhere. Either that or one of the first
Earth space explorers. Something. There was too much
pride attached to Earth. It was there in the little things—
names, for starters. Nigel was a common name, yes, but
it originated on Earth. Charmaine was also Earth-based.
Pierre and Peter, same thing. The reason everyone else
learned to translate names was because of Earth. Earth
had marked the galaxy like no other planet. Like we'd
marked Herion, in a way. Only we were small satellites
and Earth was the big gas giant.

"Why didn't he name Nitin Peter the Third?"

The Governor pulled off his headset. "No idea. Maybe
there's another brother who's not part of the plan." Put
his headset back on. "Children, truly, if I wanted to play
games, I'd have stayed on Herion. Do none of you know
how to aim a gun before you pull the trigger? None of
you?"

I left the Governor to his haranguing. He was so good
at it, and for once he wasn't haranguing me. It was a lot
more fun to listen to him complain at someone else for

once. Went back to my pondering. I wasn't having to fly too hard, meaning Herion Military wasn't trying to kill us—they were going for the capture. At least, for the moment.

Wasn't sure if this meant Nitin wanted to ensure his vast array of relatives wouldn't be harmed, if this was part of the overall strategy and how they planned to get Herion Military ships and personnel, or if Nitin wanted to be sure Audrey and her creator weren't aboard before he gave the order to set cannons to vaporize.

"Any guesses as to what the real plan is?"

Got an exasperated sigh as the Governor pulled off the headset again. "The same three options you've come up with, I'm sure. And, no, I have no idea if the goal is success for one, two or all of them. Assume no outcome equals our health and longevity."

He was right there. "Here come the fighters." Tons of them. I stopped trying to count. Okay, it was official—the fleet was trying to destroy the armada. Nitin wanted his kin wiped out. Back to pondering why while dodging fighters and big guns. Missed the *Sixty-Nine* like never before. This ship was fine, but she wasn't my girl.

Which begged the next question—who was following Junior's plan, Nitin or Charmaine? Or both of them?

CHAPTER 82

I dodged fighters while I pondered this question for the ages. I found the fighters easy to dodge. Too easy.

"They're not trying to shoot us."

"You're sure?" Lionside asked. Nice to know our secured channel was still open. "I can hear laser fire and Audrey and Hulky have managed to put the show on screen for us. Certainly looks like they're firing."

"They are, but either no one in Herion Military can aim a gun to hit, or they're missing on purpose. Tanner, you able to read anything or anyone?"

"Hang on." He was quiet. I dodged some more fighters and lazy cannon blasts while I waited. The pirates were shooting to kill—saw a few fighters burst into the pretty light display that was last hurrah, eulogy, burial and epitaph all in one. So Charmaine was still working her plan. "The grunts think they're trying to capture the pirates. To take them in for questioning."

I snorted. "Like that'll happen. You sure it's capture as the main goal?"

"Well, the fighter pilots are unhappy that they can't shoot to kill, so yeah."

Noted that the cruisers seemed to be forming a crude barricade. "Lionside, you can see what they're doing. What does it look like the fleet's got going on? Look at it as though you weren't intimately involved, like you just stumbled onto the scene."

He sighed. "Happy to." I called his tone a liar, but decided to keep it to myself. Had to flip a bit, but only a bit, to avoid a shot from one of the big guns. "Huh. Interesting. Looking at it as requested, it seems like the fleet is trying to shove the armada back. Towards Trennile Main."

"Now, there's no way Commander Lucky Charm's going to land on the home base. So, as she starts to realize she's going to lose, she'll jump them, right?"

"Right. And, excuse me, Commander Lucky Charm?" The disbelief in Lionside's tone was clear. I heard snickering in the background.

"Yeah. They're one fun family. So, the armada jumps. What would standard Herion Military procedure be, Lionside?"

"Hmmm… they've already left Herion Solar, meaning they're under auspices to pursue for capture, presumably at all costs. So, they'd follow."

I looked at the Governor. He pulled his headset off again and nodded. "Brilliant, really. You control both the pirates and the military. As you go along, you gain more military under your command. The pirates see that they're in trouble, they start adding in the competition instead of trying to kill them off."

"And Junior controls both the pirate armada and the supposed good guys. That's how you take over a galaxy, isn't it?"

"One problem. You have to have world leaders following your plan. For example, the Herion fleet couldn't just enter Aviatus Solar and expect to be welcomed in by the Royal Family as anything but an invading force."

The last piece clicked into place. I was amazingly calm. "Randolph?"

"Yes, Nap?"

"Could you, perhaps, describe this Peter Chance, in full detail, to Slinkie? I'd like the Governor to pay attention, too."

Randolph sighed. "Sure. Like I said before, he wasn't as old as the Governor, but close to old enough to be my father. About your build and height, fair coloring."

"Ugly?"

"I wouldn't know. Seriously, Nap, I like girls."

"Robotic girls. Peter Chance likes robotic girls, too. Tanner? What's Slinkie's intended like in the looks department?"

"Average and normal. Older. I don't think Slinkie reacted to his looks—I think she reacted to his personality. It's vile."

"He was more than old enough to be my father. I didn't spend a lot of time hanging out trying to find mutual interests, call me a bad princess. Nap, what in the egg are you driving at?"

"Well, Slink, in an eggshell, the man you ran away from marrying is Pierre de Chance, Junior. Tanner, if you recall, you found his mind almost as horrifying as Nitin's. I wonder if you could do me a favor and try to read Commander Lucky Charm's mind. Take your time."

"Not all that horrible. She's... she thinks this is fun, like a game." Tanner sounded angry.

"Relax about that, kid. Try not to let it get to you." We needed all we could get before his mind slammed shut on Charmaine's. "What else can you get? Get all you can, and stay calm and disinterested about it for as long as possible."

"Will do."

With Tanner thus occupied, I turned back to the Governor. "What planet is Slinkie's intended that's never going to happen from?"

"Unitatso."

"The Illia System's broke but big. And the next major solar in the Gamma Quadrant after Herion."

"Yes, hence why they made the arrangement with Aviatus." The Governor looked thoughtful. "You think Lucky Pierre actually made his romantic mark on the Royal Family of Unitatso?"

Couldn't help the snort. "Well, if I look at the number of progeny in the vast galaxy, I give it a good, strong yes. Audrey, please see if you can find any pictures of the Unitatso royal family and run them by Slinkie, Tanner and Randolph."

"Anticipating your request, Captain, I have already done so. Pictures on our view screen now."

"There, that one," Randolph said. "I'm pretty sure that's the guy I won the manual from."

"It's my supposed fiancé," Slinkie confirmed.

"Cross-referencing, Captain. Name is Prince Petrius Unita of Unitatso."

"I could have told you that," Slinkie muttered.

"For his protection and anonymity, Prince Petrius was schooled on Earth under the name of Peter Chance."

"Huh. Outland, Nitin and his sister look very like they could be this man's children."

"I agree with Major Lionside, Captain. Individual was on Earth for at least a decade, and would have had ample time to father progeny. If age estimates for Major Nitin and his sister are accurate, they would coincide with individual's time on Earth."

Tanner chimed in. "The Commander of the armada is getting nervous. She's doubtful that even with you along they can win. She also thinks you're hot and is hoping to seduce you into joining up and helping her out. Oh, and yeah, that's the guy I read, the picture both Randolph and Slinkie agree about, Prince Petrius."

"But I'm not marrying Prince Petrified, Nap. So what good does him waiting on Aviatus for my return do for him or his plan?"

I sighed. "See, that's the problem. You're going to be returning, and very soon."

CHAPTER 83

There was thudding silence. Even the Governor looked at me in shock.

"So you're going to take up with Commander Lucky Charm?" Slinkie's voice could have cut diamonds, space ice and pure steel. I also detected the hurt. I had to figure she was ready to cry. Not that it was my intention, but it seemed my lot in life was to be continually misunderstood. Figured I'd complain about the injustice another time.

"Someone tell me that Audrey and Hulky, at least, aren't sitting there acting like I'm about to turn Slinkie in for some reward."

"No, Captain. I understand your assumption. I believe you're right. But that means Pierre, Junior found someone else with Randolph's talents."

"I know he did. I saw the proof. That's the other thing Nitin was doing—testing the finished product."

"Alexander, what are you going on about?"

"Governor, you're really slipping. Maybe it's because you've missed so many naps over the last few days."

"Do I look or sound amused?"

"So many wrinkles, I can never tell for sure."

"Nap!" Slinkie sounded freaked and furious. I was sure someone was getting the vulture-glare in my physical absence.

I did my best to sigh loudly enough for the com to pick it up. "I mentioned this before, yet no one can bother to remember. Nitin 'showed' me Slinkie, when I was in the interrogation room. Only we confirmed it wasn't the real Slinkie. And, in fact, after I confirmed that I believed his simulated girl was my Slink, he ordered the real one to be terminated—along with the only people other than myself who could identify her as the real deal."

"So Nitin is in on his father's plans?" Lionside sounded like he'd caught up without too much effort. I dreaded whatever questions Randolph was going to toss out.

"Well, he's in on part of it. Charmaine's in on another part. Only, the kiddies don't know the full plan. Which makes sense."

"Why?" This was chorused from the com.

The Governor's turn to sigh. "Because you never tell anyone your entire plan. Yes, they're your children, but maybe they can be turned, tortured, show themselves to be morons. You tell them what they need to know to get their part of the job done and let it go at that."

"Figure whoever can build the Audreys is with Junior on Aviatus. We'll deal with them later." Wondered if Slinkie's family had already been replaced. Chose not to ask.

"I wonder if he's already replaced the Royal Family, Nap." Randolph said this musingly, like great thought was attached. "OUCH!"

I assumed Slinkie had slugged him. "Randolph, may I remind you that there are at least two people with you who are at least somewhat attached to said Royal Family?"

"Sorry. You didn't have to hit me. I didn't mean it in a bad way. Besides, it's something we need to be prepared for."

"Slinkie, not that I can blame you, but please stop hitting Randolph."

"I'm not. Tanner slugged him, not me." I got the distinct impression Tanner was getting the dove-look. This was not my preferred plan. No one was supposed to get the dove-look other than me. Ever. "For once, though, Randolph has a point."

"Cross it when we get there. Really, we have two big armadas to deal with first. Both have to be crippled."

Or we'd be fried by Nitin's side or forced to join up with Charmaine's. If Slinkie hadn't come pretty much fully around and been clearly ready to go horizontal, the Charmaine option would have looked a lot better. The last thing I wanted to deal with, however, was two women fighting over me. It happened too often for me to enjoy it any more. Well, okay, it never got old. But I didn't want Slinkie to change her mind. And I knew without asking that doing the space mambo with Charmaine would be a quick trip to Not Getting Slinkie for Another Five Years Land. This was not a land I wished to visit. I'd done my time there long enough already.

"What about joining up with the pirates and pretending for a while?" Randolph was really hitting them out of the atmosphere. I was used to him being slow to catch up and catch on, but this was ridiculous.

"Oh, sure. Then Nap can 'allow' Miss Lucky Charm to 'seduce' him. I'm sure you're all for that plan, aren't you, Nap?" Slinkie's tone was back to cutting the space ice.

"Have I suggested that? Have I sounded remotely interested in said option?"

"I can't see you. For all I know, she's on your lap right now."

"Slink, there's only one person in the entire galaxy I allow on my lap when I'm piloting, and I'm talking to her."

"Really, you two, could you possibly hold off on the lover's quarrel until we have a prayer of both stopping the evil plots and staying alive?" Lionside sounded annoyed. I figured he was jealous. Fine with me.

"Oh, Bryant, stuff a dodo in it. Nap, I'm really sick of hiding."

"Picked that up. Going to give you a chance to blast things in just a minute, Slink. At least, if everyone could argue and bicker amongst themselves so I can actually think."

"We need to fool them, Nap."

"Randolph, yes, right, thanks. What part of 'talk amongst yourselves and let the Outland think' didn't come through?"

There was a lot of grumbling, but it was quiet. Dodged some more lazy fire and fighters who weren't really trying. If I chose not to care about however many de Chances were on board, the easiest thing to do would be to identify which cruiser Nitin was on, do a suicide run, ram it with this ship, and matter-shift with the Governor at the last moment.

The comet trail to that idea was twofold—I wasn't good with intentional mass murder, especially as perpetrated by myself, and there was no guarantee Nitin would be killed. He'd survived the spaceport explosion, after all.

Figured I was going to have to side with Charmaine and her gang right now. When push came to shove, I didn't want to align with Nitin, no matter what.

So, the French Tickler Armada needed to do something that would catch Nitin completely by surprise.

"Gang, I want you all utterly silent. Audrey, make sure none of you can be heard in my cockpit until such time as I ask to hear you."

"Going to listen-only mode now, Captain."

I looked at the Governor. "I'd like Charmaine on the com."

He flipped a switch. "Go ahead, you're live with Commander de Chance."

"Charmaine, babe, how goes it?"

"Outland, we have to jump or they're going to shove us into Trennile Main's atmosphere."

"Why would that be a bad thing?"

Significant pause. The Governor had trained me well. Once you ask the big question, you shut up until the other guy's forced by your silence to answer. Hadn't realized I was asking the big question, but I could pick up a clue faster than most. Unless, apparently, it related to Slinkie. Okay, I could pick up a clue if it wasn't attached to the best rack in the galaxy.

I counted to forty-five seconds before she finally replied. "There are... protections in place around Trennile Main's atmosphere."

"Mind expanding that?"

"Yes."

"Share anyway."

Fifteen seconds of silence. "It's rigged. Ships without authorization to land are removed with extreme prejudice."

"Blown to smithereens, you mean?"

"Yes." No hesitation now. Good, she was broken. At least, for the moment, and the moment was all I was looking for.

This was actually good news, since I didn't plan to go to Trennile Main. At least, not right now. "Jump and they follow. You have to stop them here or you'll have the entire galactic military after you." Which was what Junior wanted, but why share this information with her if he hadn't felt the need?

"Well, I don't want to get captured, chased or blown up. We can't cloak because they'll just turn on their Ultrasight, if it's not on already. They've got superior firepower and my weasel of a brother leading them." Nice to have that confirmation. Figured they'd been having a sibling chat while I was busy.

"Meaning he'll know where you'll go."

"Most likely. He radioed to tell me he was going to blast me out of the ether if I didn't cease and desist and agree to surrender."

"Well then, we're just going to have to go with my plan."

"And just what plan is that?"

"Simple, yet effective. We're going to surrender."

CHAPTER 84

There was silence again. Presumably only because my crew were cut off from saying anything. Figured there was a lot of chat happening in the *Sixty-Nine*. Charmaine's silence I put down to shock.

I looked at the Governor. He nodded. Good, the old fox was clear on where I was going. Took the assumption he was the only one. At least, I hoped so.

Charmaine cleared her throat. "Did I hear you right?"

"Yes. Surrender. Now. Oh, does Nigel Dearest know I'm flying with you?"

"Yes."

Resisted the desire to curse or groan. "Why did you tell him?"

"He guessed. Apparently you have a 'flying signature'." Meaning I could fly better than the rest of this armada put together.

"Fine. Just agree to the official surrender, and insist that all your ships be pulled into the belly of whatever ship he's on."

"What if he asks why?"

Found myself wondering just how Charmaine had managed to lead this armada to do anything. Had to remind myself that she was following a successful blueprint and Lucky Pierre probably hadn't had time to write the "what happens when it all goes wrong" portion before the Governor had blown his brains out.

"Tell him it's so you can be sure he isn't trying anything sneaky. Demand clemency and also demand to speak to the man in charge."

"Nigel's the man in charge."

Took a deep breath. Let it out. Counted to ten. Got myself under control. "Do you want me to talk to him?"

"Well, it's your plan. Whatever it is."

"Fine. Please put us onto two-way communication that will pipe into all the ships of the armada. Please start by demanding to speak to the man in charge. He's not on a private channel with you, not if he's telling you to surrender in an official manner. You're demanding so that the rest of Herion Military who are listening pay attention to this request. Broadcast to the rest of the ships in your armada so they know what you're doing and be sure to tell Nigel that I'm speaking for you as your second-in-command."

"Why?"

"Because otherwise your people won't do what I say, will they? And we want everyone to hear what I'm going to say, and I do mean everyone." I looked at the Governor. "Really. I mean it. Everyone." He nodded. Whether this meant anyone else was clear on what I wanted or he was just agreeing with me I couldn't tell. Figured I'd find out soon enough.

"Oh. Okay. What's your plan?"

"Just put me on the two-way!"

Interestingly, shouting at her in an authoritative manner did the trick. Really wondered what kind of mind games Junior had played on his kids—if I'd used that tone on Slinkie, I'd be nursing my groin.

"Herion Military, this is Commander de Chance." Charmaine's voice came over the com—assumed this meant the rest of the armada were hearing it, too. She sounded pretty good, all things considered. "I would like to speak to the officer in charge."

Happily, Charmaine's com being open meant Nitin's response was also piped through. "That would be me, Commander." Nitin sounded amused.

"Excellent. My second-in-command will be speaking to you on my behalf. Go ahead, please." She sounded formal and cool, like she was totally in charge of things. I confirmed my initial impression—she was a really good actress.

"Nigel, buddy, how goes it?"

Thudding silence, followed by a clearing throat. "Outland, is that you?"

"Small galaxy, isn't it? Look, I want to talk to the man in charge."

"That would be me."

"Really? You're moving up in the military chain of command, aren't you? One day, a major, the next day, a commander. Impressive."

"Commander de Chance said you were speaking for her, Outland. Just what is it you have to say?"

"Aside from mentioning that your spaceport blowing up wasn't my fault? We want to surrender."

"What?" He sounded shocked. As before, belayed congratulating myself. We were nowhere close to being alive and victorious.

"I said, we want to surrender. We accept your superior firepower and give up. You got us, we're scared, don't shoot, we'll be good. However, we also ask for clemency, would like to dock our ships within your battle cruiser, and would like to plead our case with the officers in charge."

"What we?" Nitin continued to sound shocked and like he was stalling. This was clearly not what his blueprint indicated should be happening.

"Me, Charmaine—oh, sorry, Commander de Chance— a couple of others, you know, the head gang. We want to meet with the head officer—who is supposedly you even though you seemed shocked by the success of your offensive—and do the whole beg for mercy thing. And, like I said before, we want to dock our ships within yours."

He cleared his throat. "You're surrendering?"

"You told us to, we're doing what you want." I spoke with exaggerated slowness. "We'd like to surrender, have our ships docked within your cruiser, and have a face-to-face with you. Is there a problem, or are you just having trouble grasping the concept? I can talk even slower than this if that's the case."

There were voices murmuring in the background. Got the impression Herion Military was starting to question why Nitin wasn't taking this offer immediately. It was standard HM policy—any offender surrendering and asking for clemency had the right to request to see the officer in charge. They also had the right to ask that their ships be docked within the main battle cruiser. This was supposed to prove the surrendering party had no intention of escaping. It had always seemed like a great way to get your main battle cruiser blown up to me, but apparently those kinds of things didn't happen to HM.

Nitin cleared his throat again. Apparently this was a family trait when they were out of their depth. Good to know. "How do we know this isn't a ploy?"

"Well, you have superior firepower, more numbers, and have asked for our surrender. We're trying to comply. Why don't you want us to surrender, Major Nitin?"

"I don't trust you."

"We don't trust you, either. Let's all not trust each other together. It's chummier that way."

"Don't try any tricks, Outland."

"Which ship are we supposed to head for, Nitin? Just asking because you seem so hesitant to make the capture of a career. I'd bet Major Lionside wouldn't be sitting on his hands if he had the opportunity to capture the pirate armada that's choked off Herion from the rest of the galaxy. Then again, he's from Herion, so maybe that matters more to him than it does to you."

Nitin didn't just clear his throat, he practically coughed up a lung. "Just what are you implying?"

"Implying? Nothing. Flat out saying you're not from Herion. You were born on Earth. But, truly, your being a deep-cover Earth spy isn't important now. We're trying to surrender. You going to let us or should we discuss your genealogy a little more?"

There was a lot of louder murmuring in the background. "Fighters will escort your ships into the cruiser." Nitin sounded stressed. Good.

"Will that be the cruiser you, yourself, are on, Major Nitin? I'm asking under Herion Military procedure and by Herion law. You are going to follow Herion law, aren't you? Even though you're from Earth, really, you should be following the laws of the planet you're spying on."

"Outland, your accusations are ridiculous."

"What accusations? I'm just stating fact, filling the time while we wait for you to accept our surrender by shooting the asteroid dust with my old buddy, Nigel Nitin, or, as I also know him, Nigel de Chance."

"I'm not your buddy, Outland. You're a pirate."

"Gosh, so's your sister. And all your relatives. Come to think of it, so are you. After all, we pirates do know each other. Charmaine, I can see why you're upset with Nigel. He's pretty rude. Didn't even introduce you to the other officers with him."

"How can you possibly think anyone would believe this insanity?" Nitin sounded like another throat clear was just around the corner. The noise in the background was getting louder and more insistent, too.

"Well, how else do you explain why you let me escape from Herion Military HQ? And why you let us blast out of Spaceport City, while you blew up the spaceport to cover our escape? And why you didn't let your fighters actually shoot any of us? I mean, it seems sort of obvious, if you ask me. Guess that's why you had to get rid of Lionside—he was on to you."

"I didn't do anything to Lionside!"

"Really? Then, where is he?"

CHAPTER 85

"**M**ajor Lionside defected and he's with you!" Nitin's voice was raising.

"I'm on a Chatouilleux Français Armada vessel and there is no Major Bryant Lionside anywhere near me. If you ever let us dock, we can prove that pretty easily, too."

A different voice came through. "Captain Outland, this is Major Crissell. You and the rest of the surrendering vessels are cleared to dock within Cruiser HMV *Reliant*."

"Which of the planet-sized ships is that, Crissell? They all look alike."

"Flashing lights now."

Some of the armada vessels started to move forward. "Belay those movements, Chatouilleux people. Crissell, are we being sent to the vessel where the officers leading this offensive are housed?"

"No. We're sending you to the cruiser capable of housing all your ships."

"So sorry, when did Herion Military policy change?"

Crissell sighed. "Look, fine. Send the majority of your ships to the *Reliant*. Yours and the command vessel head for Cruiser HMV *Endeavor*. Flashing red lights."

I looked at the Governor. He nodded. "Will do." Couldn't have everything. "Which vessel are you on, Crissell?"

"The *Reliant*."

Good. Crissell was probably a lot like Lionside. I didn't want to get rid of Crissell. He wasn't my enemy, he was just a guy doing his job. "Charmaine, let's head for the *Endeavor*. Everyone else, head for the *Reliant*. Turn over all weapons to the Herion Military personnel as soon as you disembark."

"Outland, are you crazy?" Charmaine sounded a lot like Nitin—stressed.

"We're surrendering, Commander de Chance. Part of surrender is giving up your weapons. I could add a 'duh' in here, but I'm trying not to be insubordinate."

"Fine. All Chatouilleux personnel, follow Captain Outland's orders."

I waited until the ten other armada ships were swallowed up by the *Reliant*. "All pirate vessels docked within the *Reliant*, Captain Outland." Crissell seemed to be on my wavelength. Hoped this wasn't a bad thing.

"Thanks. Charmaine, let's head for the *Endeavor*. Ladies first."

"What a gentleman you are." She wasn't up to Slinkie's standards on sarcasm, but she held her own.

The command ship flew into the belly of the big cruiser. I followed. Every instinct I had wanted me to run. I didn't because my brain was still in charge, and it knew we had to defang Nitin or everything else we'd done was worthless. Besides, I wasn't giving up the *Sixty-Nine* to Herion Military. I was giving up an armada vessel.

Everyone's seen the holos where some smaller ship is dragged into the belly of the big imperial cruiser against said smaller ship's will. We weren't being dragged, but I could still hear the ominous music playing in the background.

"Outland, are you humming?" Charmaine sounded upset and annoyed.

"What of it?"

"It's creepy. Cut it out."

"Oh, yes, ma'am." What was everyone's problem with humming?

While we were docking the fighters started to come in as well. Realized Crissell hadn't been kidding—there wasn't a lot of room in the docking area. In addition to our two ships and the myriad fighters, there were evacuation ships. Nothing fancy, just enough to pack your people in and fly off or make a jump to safety. Just as well. I wanted more than just

Charmaine's side of things crippled, but I might be able to do it without that whole pesky mass murder thing.

Docking inside a cruiser's a lot like docking at a space-port. In some ways, it's easier. The GravCreates on ships generate optimal landing conditions, cruisers have a variety of failsafes built in to prevent landing crashes, and the emergency systems are normally faster and better maintained than those planetside. There's more terror involved in blowing up in space.

As with everything else about Herion, their cruiser docking ran on extra-crispy. We were in and hooked to cables within a matter of minutes. "All crew, disembark and provide your weapons to Herion Military personnel." Well, all crew other than me. Slid my laser into my inner jacket pocket.

The Governor and I waited until sensors showed our entire crew was off the ship. Then he shut all communications down. "I know what you're planning. But it's at least a two-man operation."

"Yep." I handed him everything else that mattered, weapons-wise, other than the Plastiques. Who knew when someone would want a treat? I took the matter-shifter off and put it over his head. "You stay here and take care of things. Get back to the others as soon as you're done."

"How do you plan to get back? I know you aren't planning to die nobly."

"Why the sarcasm? Like you're ever planning to die, let alone nobly?"

"Your plan for escape, Alexander. What is it?" He sounded annoyed and worried. Nice to know he cared.

I grinned. "You don't tell your Uncle Oldie your entire plan in case he gets captured, is going senile, or just has a senior moment. You tell him just enough to make sure he can do his part."

The Governor gave me a long look. "Out of all the mis-creants in all the galaxy, how is it I'm saddled with you?"

I shrugged as I headed out of the cockpit. "You're attached to staying alive. And, like everyone else, you love the Outland."

CHAPTER 86

Walked down the ramp to see a whole lot of Herion guns pointing at me. I'd found a couple of stray lasershots on my way out of the ship and tossed them to the nearest military goon. Looked around. Didn't see any familiar faces in uniform.

"Where's Nitin?"

One of the Herion officers stepped forward. "Major Nitin's orders were to bring you and Commander de Chance to him, only. All others needs must go directly into custody." So Nitin still had the major title, not commander.

"I protest," Charmaine said.

"Works for me," I said. Charmaine glared at me—nowhere close to the eagle-glare, let along vulture. Slinkie pretty much outbid this girl's ante in all ways. I was relieved Charmaine was keeping her mouth shut about the Governor. Hopefully she realized he was going to be our secret weapon. "Let's go. Let the troops deal with the, uh, troops. We need to chat with your brother."

She rolled her eyes, but nodded. A small cadre of officers surrounded us. The rest of the military goons took the rest of the de Chance goons into custody.

I was fascinated that no one searched us. Didn't want to question it, since I didn't want either my laser or the Plastiques found, but it was still surprising. Wasn't sure if they were following Nitin's or Crissell's orders, or if Herion didn't believe in on-ship strip searches. It would make them the only law enforcement I'd ever heard of that didn't. Maybe it was the steroids.

Paid careful attention to where they took us, noting shipmarks and such that would identify how to get back to the docking area. Conveniently, we took an elevator to the command bridge. Inconveniently a code was required to make the elevator work and my view of the keypad was obstructed. On purpose, as near as I could tell.

Herion did command bridges just like all the other successful, highly militarized planets—impressive two-story structure, complete with metal stairs and railings, lots and lots of bells, whistles and view screens, nice walkway/viewing area for the commander to stand picturesquely and look all commanding and impressive. Needless to say, Nitin was up there, staring out into space. I looked around. Nope, no one was doing a portrait or taking a picture of any kind—the display was for me and Charmaine. Lucky us.

Nitin wasn't alone, however. There were several other officers with him. I got the impression they weren't sure if they could trust him. Good, hopefully this indicated my plan was working so far.

We were led up the stairs. It was a decent drop to the lower level, but you did have a clear view of pretty much everything from here. The other ships in the fleet were on a block of screens on the opposite wall. Looked like all the de Chance Family Players were in some form of custody.

The entire Trennile system was on-screen as well. The only ships were Herion Military. Good. My crew were still on Trennile 7. I spotted the usual command center paraphernalia, including communications, which I hoped were on two-way, a variety of weapons and tactical monitors and equipment, and the bay of escape pods. Wanted your head guys to be able to get away, after all.

Nitin turned and gave me a very satisfied smile. "Nice to see you, Outland."

"Can't say the same, Nitin. Or would you prefer me to call you de Chance?"

"No idea of what you're babbling about." He sounded confident, but the men behind him didn't look nearly so reassured.

"Charmaine, doll, be a doll and go stand by your brother."

She sighed but did as I asked. Nitin moved away. Charmaine stepped towards him. He moved again. "This woman is a stranger to me." They kept up the step-move-step thing until Nitin was stopped by running into another officer.

"Oh, Nigel, you were always such a weasel." Charmaine sounded disgusted. "You happy? You have everyone in custody. Is that really what was supposed to happen?"

I answered for him. Hoped someone, somewhere, somehow was broadcasting this to the rest of the fleet. "Actually, no. You were supposed to run and Nigel was supposed to follow you, with the might of Herion Military backing him up."

Nitin twitched. "You're insane. He's just trying to focus blame away from himself to try to avoid going to prison for the rest of his life for blowing up the spaceport."

"It was your attempting to murder me and Lionside that caused the spaceport to blow up, Nitin. And, really, is this all you've got? 'I don't know the woman who looks just like me'? Didn't Granddad's blueprint give you more than this to work from? Oh, sorry, it's Daddy's blueprint you're following. Charmaine's the one using Granddad's stuff."

"What are you talking about?" Charmaine and Nitin got this one out in unison. Maybe I just brought it out in people.

I looked around. "Other than our deep-cover spy here, who's the highest ranking officer with the fleet?"

"That would be me, Outland." Crissell's voice came from behind me. Turned to see him on the block of view screens. Someone had thoughtfully put his face onto every screen.

"Wow, that's almost nauseating, seeing your face all huge and divided up into thirty different boxes." He looked vaguely familiar. Hearing his voice this way also rang a faint bell. Was pretty sure he'd been the man in charge when I was running through Herion HQ, right before Tanner and I had "met" for the first time.

Looks-wise, he was clearly a Herion native. But there was more to why he looked familiar.

"Deal with it. I'm the highest ranking officer after Major Nitin. What did you want to tell me?"

"Herion Military really gives their majors a lot to do. No Commanders or Admirals or anything?"

"Is this relevant? Or are you just stalling?"

"Just making an observation. Unless that's suddenly against Herion law."

"No. Blowing up the reclamation plant, a bathhouse, a nightclub, and the spaceport, causing a variety of riots, and kidnapping two Herion Military officers, on the other hand, are all still considered prison-worthy offenses."

"Well, that's good to hear." I looked at Nitin. "Enjoy prison."

"Outland, you want to expand on your accusations?" Crissell sounded tired and fed up. I could relate. "I'll give you right now that the woman looks enough like Nigel to be his sister."

"I'm his twin," Charmaine snapped. This was disquieting. I'd had some pleasant twins experiences, forever tainted now by the thought that Nitin was Charmaine's twin. I'd have to work to get over it. Hopefully Slinkie would be up for the challenge.

"Never seen her before," Nitin said. No one around us looked like they believed him, but they didn't look like they believed me, either.

I sent a prayer to all the active gods. "Hulky, can you please show the nice people in the Herion fleet the pictures of Nigel and Charmaine we have?" Then I held my breath.

CHAPTER 87

The gods did love me. The image of Charmaine and Nitin together appeared, in widescreen. "Note that this picture was taken at the same time and they're standing together. Also note the mountains in the background. Anyone want to guess what planet this picture was taken on?"

"Earth." Crissell's voice was icy. "And, it's clear these two are siblings, and, Nigel, it's also clear the young woman standing with you is the same one as in this picture and, therefore, your sister."

Charmaine moved away from Nitin and back by me. "Great. So, now what?"

"Now, I'd like to bring Herion Military up on all that's going on." I heard groans. "Oh, it won't take long. Fifty years ago—"

"Outland! For the sake of the gods, man, get to the point!" Crissell sounded ready to snap.

"Too much caffeine, Crissell? Anyway, fifty years ago, Pierre de Chance and the Chatouilleux Français Armada had a chokehold on the Delta Quadrant, with designs on the entire galaxy. They were pirates, and they had the major solars cut off from all trade, forcing the planetary governments to give them seventy-five percent of all cargo in order to survive. Sound vaguely familiar?"

"Lucky Pierre and the French Tickler Armada? Are you serious?" Crissell sounded just like the rest of us had when we'd heard this name. I heard snickers and outright laughter in the background.

"Very. Lucky Pierre roamed the galaxy and he was apparently popular with the ladies, if you catch my drift."

"Yes, clearly. I mean, he was advertising. What's your point? He'd be an ancient man now, and no one in custody is over thirty."

"Oh, Lucky Pierre's dead. His operation was infiltrated and he had his head blown off. But that's ancient history." And I hoped the ancient historical responsible was doing his job. At least I knew he hadn't been caught yet. "However, he left a huge number of little de Chances all over the galaxy. The second generation weren't really into the whole pirate thing for whatever reason. But the third generation think it's the greatest plan ever."

The pictures started to flash on the screen. "Note these faces, Crissell. Most if not all of them are in one of your cruisers right now. Led here by the twins. I'd like to suggest something fun. Look for a tattoo of an Ebegorn on the persons of the detainees. Nitin has one over his right pectoral, as a mention."

Crissell barked some orders. Charmaine gave me a look warring between curiosity and revulsion. "Just how did you know Nigel had a tattoo on his chest?"

"Found it when I knocked him out and stole his stuff. He had a money belt on, had to open up his shirt."

"I'd heard you liked girls."

"I do like girls! And if I were going to like boys, your brother wouldn't be who I'd start with." She didn't look convinced. Had to remind myself that proving otherwise would undoubtedly not sit well with Slinkie. And, since Charmaine didn't have a female twin, there was no way she was going to be worth losing Slinkie over.

"Outland, confirmed that all the prisoners searched so far have the tattoo." Crissell sounded seriously angry, and not with me. For once.

I looked at the officers around Nitin. "You want to verify the tat on Nitin? Oh, and Charmaine, be a doll and show them yours."

"No," she hissed. Looked at her. She was blushing.

"Wow, so it's on the right pectoral area for every-one?" Tried not to want to see how her tat looked and if I approved.

"No, Outland," Crissell said. "It's on the, ah, lower back area on the women."

I opened my mouth to suggest we make sure it was the same for Charmaine and could *feel* Slinkie's vulture-glare hit me. "Ah, is yours in the same place, Charmaine?"

"Yes. And I'm not stripping in front of all these men."

Managed to keep from suggesting she strip for me. Only just. Felt I deserved a reward. Hoped it would be Slinkie. "Fine. Do you admit you have the family crest tat-tooed on your body?"

"Yes, and Nigel does too." She strode over and ripped his shirt open. He looked shocked. Clearly, this wasn't in his blueprint. It wasn't in Charmaine's either, but while he was obviously the military brains, she was the actress. All good actresses learn how to improvise.

"Major Crissell," I said as formally as I could, "I present Nigel Nitin, also known as Nigel de Chance, grandson of Lucky Pierre. He's been in deep cover in Herion Military and working with his family to cut off your solar system."

"We were doing a good job of it, too," Charmaine said with a bitter laugh. "Until you showed up."

"Well, see, Herion isn't the only solar system under attack by the extended de Chance family."

"Oh? What are you implying, Outland?" Crissell sounded suspicious.

I reached into my inner pocket, the hidden one, and pulled out my ace in the hole.

CHAPTER 88

I held up the card Tanner had given me. "Anyone able to identify what this is?"

One of the officers around Nitin nodded. "That's the crest of the Royal Family of Aviatus. The card is what they give to their highest level operatives."

I looked at the view screens. Crissell was back on in huge-face form. "You're a spy?" He sounded shocked.

"I've been known to help out the Royal Family of Aviatus now and then." I always held the door for Slinkie and I was always there if she was cold. Or hot. Or in need of someone to guard her while showering. I figured I could count saving her from the Land League goons as help as well. "Oh, there are more de Chances on Herion. You'll find them by the tattoo, I'm sure. They're all part of the Land League."

Nitin lunged for me. "You space-damned bastard!" Interesting to see what got to him. "You're no spy! You're a pirate, just not as good a one as our grandfather, and you never will be!"

I shrugged. "I'm alive, he's not."

"You're going to rot in prison, just like the rest of us."

"Oh, I won't be going to prison for anything."

"Just how is that?"

Put my hand in my pocket, grabbed my backup plan. "Candy?"

Nitin sneered. "Those are defused."

"Yeah, I figured when I didn't blow up. But thanks for confirming they were Plastiques—and yours." I showed them to Crissell. "Took these off Nitin when I discovered his tattoo. I think you'll find they match up to the same explosives that blew up the Crazy Bear and the bathhouse. Possibly the spaceport as well."

Crissell barked some orders. The officers around Nitin grabbed him. He fought, pretty well, but they were all Herion-born and really he didn't have a chance. One of them confiscated the Plastiques. He tried to take the card, but I declined. Figured Tanner would want it back.

"Outland, what happened to our two officers, Captain Almondinger and Major Lionside?" Crissell didn't sound like he was asking out of concern or curiosity. He sounded like he was asking a leading question.

I took a longer look at him. "Captain Percy Almondinger died in service to Herion Military. He'd identified Nitin's plan and tried to stop him single-handedly. We got to him just in time, but sadly lost him in the sewer pipe. Not the way he wanted to go, but he died a hero, so the rest of us could survive and save the galaxy from this scourge."

Crissell nodded solemnly. "I'll ensure he receives a hero's plaque, Outland. And Major Lionside?"

"Major Lionside also discovered Nitin's plan and worked to thwart it. Due to circumstances, he was forced to flee the planet in order to effect the capture of the miscreants." I missed the Governor at times like this—I was running out of official pompous wording. I also wasn't sure what Lionside actually wanted me to say. "So, to be clear, your cousin isn't a traitor in any way, shape or form."

"Why do you assume he's my cousin?" Crissell was trying to keep a straight face.

"I recognize the sense of humor."

"Geoffrey, stop being coy." Lionside said over the com, sounding amused but annoyed.

Crissell grinned. "Just wanted to hear his story. I'm shocked it matches yours, Bryant."

"I told you, he's a spy for the Royal Family. They identified the threat and sent in a team to help us."

"A team of pirates," Crissell said with a laugh.

"You set a thief to catch a thief, Geoffrey." Lionside sighed. "Standard procedure does dictate that Captain Outland be detained for questioning."

"True." Crissell didn't bark orders, but I was being eyed by whatever military weren't dealing with Nitin.

Charmaine leaned closer. "Now what?" she asked under her breath.

"Good behavior should get you out in about ten years."

"No, seriously. How are we all getting out of this?" Was she kidding?

I looked at her. Nope, she really was serious. "Um, Charmaine?"

"Yes?"

"There is no 'we' that is 'us'. There is you and your family of wannabes, and there is me and my stellar crew of space pirates. The two don't really mix."

She gaped at me. "This is your plan? You're double-crossing me?"

"I'd have had to have been on your side to begin with to be double-crossing you."

She lunged at me. However, I'd already seen Nitin do it and was prepared. I grabbed her wrists before she could get me. "You're a worse weasel than my brother!"

"I prefer to think of myself as a sly alley cat who manages to land on his feet. You're a cute girl, doll, but I'm more interested in a girl who isn't all hung up on her family genealogy. You're a little too 'the blood of my forefathers' for me."

"I'll get out and hunt you down and kill you. We all will."

"See, that's the thing, babe. Some can get out of Herion HQ without issue. And some can't. I'm just betting you and your massive clan are going to fall into the can't column. But, you know, if you do get out before we're ancient old people, feel free to come after me. It'll keep things interesting."

"Catch me if you can sort of thing?" Nitin snarled.

"More like try to catch me if you can and then look all stunned when I blow your head off sort of thing, Nitin."

"You're being taken in for questioning, too," Charmaine said. "Was that part of your plan?"

"Nope." On cue the ship rocked and alarms went off. "This is."

CHAPTER 89

"**E**xplosion in the docking bay!" This wasn't Crissell shouting, but someone else, presumably someone closer to the action. "All personnel, immediate evacuation!"

I shoved Charmaine at the nearest Herion goons, who grabbed her and were thusly occupied.

I'd already judged the drop as a long one, but I'd jumped worse before. You don't sleep with half the women in the galaxy and not learn how to safely jump out of a high window, after all. And I had all my clothes on, which made it easier.

Leaped the railing and did a rolling dive. Happily, several Herion military were kind enough to break my fall. Rolled off them and ran for the escape pods. Dodged the laser fire—there was too much chaos to have to worry too much about being hit.

Fired the escape pods, all but one. It took a little time, but not too much. I'd kept one of the Plastiques with me. As some of the goons advanced on me I tossed it up. "Plastique in the hold!"

Everyone froze.

I stepped into the last escape pod and gave everyone a salute. "To all of the fine military personnel of the fine planet of Herion, and to the entire cast of the De Chance Family Players, let me say just one thing. Goodbye and good luck."

Slammed the door of the pod as the laser fire came towards me. The pod blasted free. I breathed a sigh of relief. There had always been the possibility that the gods of irony would have ensured that it malfunctioned.

As I sailed away, I watched the *Endeavor*. The Governor had set up the damage well. I took it as a given that he'd rigged the two French Tickler ships to blow. But it appeared he'd also set up some other explosions in the lower levels. The old coot could move when he had to. I knew he'd used the matter-shifter to escape before the explosions went off—the Governor truly planned to live forever.

Counted escape ships. No fighters made it, which was good. I didn't want any of them coming after me, since escape pods weren't set up for much, and evasive maneuvers were well beyond their capacity. If I'd marked them correctly coming in, the last evacuation ship left the *Endeavor* just before she broke apart. The Governor had really done his job well. Had to admit he probably hadn't lied about his ability to infiltrate the original Lucky Pierre's operation—the old man was, point of fact, the gold standard. I just never planned to tell him that.

Noted something mildly disturbing. My escape pod wasn't heading towards Trennile 7. It made sense—we'd been much closer to Trennile Main when we'd been "captured." Hadn't given it any thought until now. But if the atmosphere around Trennile Main was rigged unless you were allowed in, the chances of them allowing me in were slim to none. If they weren't monitoring, I was an unknown piece of space debris, and if they were monitoring, well, the chances of one or all of them in Trennile Mission Control being de Chance relatives or sympathizers were astronomical.

Found myself wishing I'd kept the matter-shifter. Or agreed to a comlink. Or had taken a fighter instead of an escape pod. Not only did I not want to die, but I didn't want to die this way, and I really didn't want to die before ever doing the space mambo with Slinkie. Sure, after, maybe I could die a happy man. But not before.

The air shimmered and I was no longer alone in the escape pod. "Nap, you're a worse birdbrain than I thought. Hold onto me."

"Never a problem. Great to see you, Slink. What kept you?"

She rolled her eyes, put the matter-shifter against her forehead and we moved. Far less nauseating to shift while holding Slinkie. Perhaps she did it better. Or having her breasts shoved up against me created enough distraction. Certainly was more distracting than holding the Governor had been.

Exited in the cockpit of the *Sixty-Nine*. Audrey was in the co-pilot's seat, and I could hear the others on the com, discussing things like what we were having for dinner and should we try to fill the order for magma or not. Nice to see my crew focused on the mundane when their leader was at risk of instant death.

Noticed something else. We were spaceborne. "Um, aren't we sort of out of hiding? As in, able to be followed out of hiding?"

"No, Captain," Audrey said cheerfully, presumably because she wanted to. "The Governor downloaded the schematics and programs from the pirate armada. Hulky and I spent some of the time waiting for you to enact your plan upgrading our systems. We now have the same cloaking technology as the de Chance armada did."

"But anyone with an Ultrasight can see us."

"Actually, the Hulkinator model had a jamming capability. Faulty and inconsistent, but that was when it was being powered by a lesser power source." The Governor wandered in. "However, since it's now running on the *Sixty-Nine*'s power, it can perform at the levels originally conceived and designed."

"You never told me your lifelong ambition was to be an autofloater designer or marry a tank. Talk to Randolph, I think he can fix you up."

He gave me a dirty look. "You might want to let go of Miss Slinkie and start flying, Alexander."

"And then again I might not."

"Nap, just get us the egg out of here." Slinkie gave me the hairy eyeball. "Just what were you doing with an Aviatus secret service card?"

"Borrowed it from a friend."

"Can I have it back?" Tanner asked as he shoved into the cockpit.

Decided I'd better sit. Pulled Slinkie into my lap. Then gave Tanner his card back. "Thanks, that came in very handy."

"You're good at thinking on your feet. I figured you'd find a use for it, somewhere along the way." He grinned at me. "One of the many reasons I like working with you."

"You sticking around?" Tried not to sound like I wanted him to say yes.

"No one else can cook, and my target's here. Have to stick around and guard Princess Seraphime. So, yeah, I think I'll stay on. If you want." He was clearly trying not to sound like he desperately wanted me to say yes.

"Like to have my friends with me, Tanner, so, yeah."

The kid looked about ready to cry, but he pulled it together. "Thanks, Nap."

"You two are nauseating," Slinkie muttered. But neither one of us got a glare.

"What about me, Outland?" Lionside had joined us. Waited for Randolph to appear so that everyone would be crammed into the smallest space in the entire ship that didn't have a showerhead installed.

"Up to you, Lionside." Hated to admit it, but it was true. If he wanted to stay, I was happy to keep him around. Wondered what was wrong with me. Assumed it was the glow of still being alive. "By the way, thanks for assisting with your cousin. At least, I assume you were talking to him on a private channel."

He laughed. "Of course. He'll turn in my resignation papers for me. After all of this, I'm not sure I could go back to Herion Military and not want to knock a lot of heads together. Nitin never should have been allowed to get where he did."

"You're sure you don't want to go back and ensure it doesn't happen again? Blood of kings and all."

"Same blood's in Geoffrey. If things are dire, he'll find a way to reach me. Besides, you need someone who knows the military channels, Outland. Saying you're a spy doesn't work all the time."

"Usually I just blow the place up and run, but the Governor's slipping in his dotage."

"I'll show you slipping," the Governor muttered.

"I've seen you slip, Governor. Not a pretty sight."

"Nap, where do you want us to head?" Yep, Randolph had joined us. I wondered if the crowding bothered Audrey or if she'd already put the acceptance of it into her programming.

"Much as I hate to say it, we have to go to Aviatus."

Slinkie stiffened in my lap. "I am not going home!"

"Yes, you are, Miss Slinkie. Not to stay. But we need to confirm that your family is alive and well, stop Peter Chance, and ensure the robotic 'you' is defused." The Governor looked at me. "I found no trace of the robotic on the *Endeavor*."

"I scanned all ships, Captain," Audrey added. "No robotic signatures other than ship's computers. Hulky confirmed." She was sounding very warm and fuzzy when talking about Hulky.

I checked Randolph's expression. He was glowering. Well, it could have been worse—Audrey could have formed a crush on Tanner or Lionside or, all gods forbid, the Governor. Put Hulky and Randolph together and maybe you had Audrey's perfect man. I ripped my mind away from this train of thought—Audrey or Randolph actually managing to effect this combination was too close to the realm of possibility for comfort.

"But," I said before Slinkie could start arguing, "we're not going to Aviatus right now. Right now we're going to go get some much needed and well earned rest and relaxation."

"Where're we going?" Tanner asked. "We shouldn't wait too long to go to Aviatus. I want to advise the king that Slinkie's alive and well, but I think we need to confirm all's well there first, and soon."

"We have a legitimate order of magma to fill, too," the Governor said. "Just because young Tanner initiated the order, that doesn't mean we can go back on the Butcher. Besides, we'll be paid by the Ipsita company, and may I remind you we can use the money?"

"Herion Military will be coming after us," Lionside added. "The sooner we can get the agreement from Aviatus that you were working in their interests the better. I can only hold Geoffrey off so long."

"And we need to recharge the ship," Randolph said. "Adding on all the new upgrades used a lot of power and most of my parts and supplies."

"Where do you want us to set course for, Captain?" Audrey asked. At least she was still listening to me.

"Libsuno."

There was silence in the cockpit.

"Oh, great choice, Nap. Plenty of good supply shops there." Randolph trotted out.

"Never been, but I've heard it's a nice planet." Lionside sounded like he'd heard all about it and couldn't wait to see if the rumors were true. Apparently the steroids were wearing off. He went off after Randolph.

"You sure, Nap?" Tanner sounded nervous.

"Kid, you had five girls at one time as your initiation into manhood. Libsuno will seem tame. Besides, the best chefs in the galaxy have restaurants there."

He brightened up. "Oh, great. I'll get dinner going, then. Just something light, since we'll be eating on-planet."

"I want a mineral bath," the Governor said, voice on full quaver.

"I'll make the reservation the moment we land." Slinkie said, annoyance in full force.

"Good. I'm an old man and I've been battered about for the past few days."

"Yes, yes, got it. Tanner, help the Governor back to his cabin, will you?"

"Sure, Nap." They left, the Governor still complaining about his aches and pains. Near as I could tell, no one had asked how he'd managed to rig an entire battle cruiser by himself. I hoped they never did. The Governor liked all the young folks. Janz the Butcher saw most of them as, at best, necessary evils. And he'd just proved we didn't really need more than him and me to be successful.

But, that was a worry for another time. I kept a firm hold on Slinkie while I set the coordinates for the jump. "You sure we have to go to Aviatus?" She sounded much quieter and a lot more scared now that it was just us and Audrey.

"Yeah, but I promise to make you forget all about it for the next few days."

"You could have had all the women of the French Tickler Armada, you know."

I sighed. "Slink, I keep on saying it, and you don't want to believe. If I've got the best girl in the galaxy, why would I want any of the others, or even all of them?"

Checked to make sure everyone was strapped in, per the grid. Seemed like it. Pulled Slinkie to me and planted the big one on her right as I hit the hyper-jump button.

Nine minutes straight of kissing. Not my record, but still, well worthwhile. Never let it be said that the Outland couldn't plan things down to the smallest details.

CHAPTER 90

Libsuno, like the Outland, always lived up to its hype. Nothing like vacationing on a planet that didn't allow extradition to make you feel a lot more relaxed. And if you wanted it, Libsuno found a way to ensure you had it.

Ran some fast errands, then took the whole crew to dinner at a restaurant Tanner insisted was run by the best chef in the galaxy. The food was good, but it wasn't what I was hungry for.

I booked us all into rooms at a nice hotel—not the top of the line, but one of the better ones—then shooed everyone off. Had Tanner and Lionside take the Governor to his mineral bath—Slinkie and I needed some alone time.

"How can we afford Libsuno?" Slinkie asked as I scanned for bugs and explosives. "I don't know how we could afford that dinner, let alone staying at this hotel for a week."

"Nitin had a small fortune on him. And I withdrew against his credit lines the moment we disembarked. Not sure if I managed it, but I'm hoping I drained the de Chance family coffers."

Another beautiful fact about Libsuno was that it didn't report financials to any other government. Money in a Libsuno account was money no one was ever going to trace. The Governor and I had drained every credit line Nitin had had a card for—the access information for his accounts were listed in the coded documents I'd lifted.

We'd run the money through several of Janz the Butchers' business accounts and it was now resting safely in Libsuno National. Everyone had a cut, though they didn't know it. Sure, the Governor and I had the biggest cuts, but those were the prerogatives of leadership and being the ones who were able to do all the fun things with credit lines and bombs and such.

Still hadn't found what the two Dragon keys and the one little key Nitin had kept in his wallet went to. Figured we'd find out sooner, later, or not at all. Until then, they were kept in my inner jacket pocket.

Room cleared of any dangerous explosives and all monitoring devices rendered null and void, I locked the door, dragged her into the bedroom, and locked that door, too. Put the intercom and phone on do not disturb. Slinkie laughed. "Nap, what're you doing, you featherbrain?"

"Making sure that, this time, nothing disturbs us. Hopefully the building won't catch on fire or fall down or something."

She shook her hair out. "You're sort of building this up to impossible heights, you know. I mean, I know your reputation. Maybe I'm not going to live up to your expectations."

"I'll risk it."

Pulled her into my arms and got us out of our clothes in record time. I'd fool around with the sexy undressing another time. Right now, I was still waiting for something, anything, to come and try to interrupt us.

Stopped worrying about that by the time I got her into the bed. Something about being up close and extremely personal with Slinkie's naked body made my mind focus on one thing only.

Making love to Slinkie was a revelation in a lot of ways. Probably the most shocking one was that, as everyone had said and this confirmed, I really was in love with her. It was the best, for me, ever. But, there was still the niggle of worry—what if it wasn't all Slinkie had heard it would be? Oh sure, she'd sounded like the planet had moved for her, but she'd also insinuated she knew how to fake a scream.

She rolled on top of me, and I got the dove-look, combined with something I'd never seen before. She looked ready to go and keep on going. Her body moved against mine in a way that confirmed this look. She really was my perfect girl.

"Oooh, Nap. You know... you really *are* da tomcat."

"You're quite the little tigress yourself."

Slinkie purred at me. "You have no idea. Now, take me Around the Galaxy again."

"Is that an order?"

"Royal decree. Make it so."

"You're my kind of princess, babe."

"You're my kind of pirate." She gave me a searching look. "You really willing to give up all the other women in the galaxy for me?"

Pulled her to me and kissed her. Not for nine minutes, but for a good, long time, emphasis on good. "What other women?"

She heaved a happy sigh. "It's official. I have to admit it—I do love the Outland."

"And just think—you haven't seen anything yet."

As I gave Slinkie her first patented Outland Horsey Ride, I realized it was official for me, too—I could, point of fact, now die a happy man.

As my Great-Aunt Clara always said, dying happy's great, but living happy's preferred by nine out of ten, and the tenth man's leaning towards it, too. My addendum to this adage? If you can keep the happy in bed with you for a week straight, that's good. But two weeks straight is even better.

ACKNOWLEDGMENTS

So many to thank, so little time. But I'll give it a shot.

First off, must thank the coolest, best agent out there, Cherry Weiner, for always believing in me, in this book, and these characters. And I do mean always. And forever. It's hard to find an agent so invested in her clients, especially on the first go, but, just like Nap, I got lucky.

Next up, the copy you're holding is a re-release that wouldn't have been possible without the good folks who took over Night Shade Books—the gang at Skyhorse Publishing, particularly Cory Allyn. Thanks for keeping the home fires burning and making me excited about the future of this series again.

To my crit partner, Lisa Dovichi, and all my beta readers, especially Mary Fiore and Veronica Cook, for lots of time spent. And for always laughing at the jokes. Even the tenth time around.

To all the friends who said "this book is great, of course it'll get published" I send a big "wow, you were right!" along with my thanks for their constant belief. Special shout outs to Adrian Payne, Matt Payne, Kay Moran, and Willie Everhart for going those extra special cheerleading miles.

Special thanks to author Seanan McGuire for guidance and support, even during deadlines.

Extra-special thanks to all those who bought the trade paperback version of this book, loved it, and constantly asked me when more in the series would be coming. Your love of Nap and his crew, and your devotion to getting "all the stories" and more if you could, kept us all focused on the prize, of which this version is, hopefully, the start.

Last but in no way least, love to my spousal unit and the fruit of our loins for all their love, support, and seeming willingness to put up with having to live with an author. It's a tough job, but you do it better than anyone and I love you for it more than you probably realize.

ABOUT THE AUTHOR

Gini Koch writes the fast, fresh, and funny Alien/Katherine "Kitty" Katt series for DAW Books, the Necropolis Enforcement Files series, and the Martian Alliance Chronicles series. *Touched by an Alien*, Book 1 in the Alien series, was named by *Booklist* as one of the Top Ten Adult SF/F novels of 2010. *Alien in the House*, Book 7 in her long-running Alien series, won the *RT Book Reviews* Reviewer's Choice Award as the Best Futuristic Romance of 2013. *Alien Nation*, released in December 2016, won the Preditors and Editors Readers' Poll for Best SF/F Novel of 2016. Book 15, *Alien Education*, will release in May 2017, with Book 16, *Aliens Abroad*, coming December 2017.

As G.J. Koch she writes the Alexander Outland series and other forms of space opera and science fiction. And she's made the most of multiple personality disorder by writing under a variety of other pen names as well, including Anita Ensal, Jemma Chase, A.E. Stanton, and J.C. Koch.

Gini also has stories featured in a variety of excellent anthologies, available now and upcoming, writing as Gini Koch, Anita Ensal, Jemma Chase, and J.C. Koch. Writing as A.E. Stanton, she will have an audio release, Natural Born Outlaws: The Legend of Belladonna Part 1, coming from Graphic Audio in 2017.

Gini is an in-demand speaker who panels regularly at San Diego Comic-Con, Phoenix Comicon, and the Tucson Festival of Books, among others. She's also been part of the faculty for the San Diego State University Writers Conference, Jambalaya Con, the Desert Dreams Writers Conference, and the James River Writers Conference, among others.

Prior to becoming a full time author, Gini spent over 25 years in marketing and advertising, first in small- to mid-sized direct marketing firms in Los Angeles, and then with IBM, and she was a social media maven before it was cool.

Reach her via: www.ginikoch.com